Kate Forster lives in Melbourne, Australia with her husband, two children and two dogs, and can be found nursing a laptop, surrounded by magazines and watching trash TV or French films.

Picture *Perfect*

KATE FORSTER

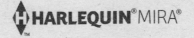

Published in Great Britain 2015
by Harlequin MIRA, an imprint of Harlequin (UK) Limited,
Eton House, 18-24 Paradise Road,
Richmond, Surrey, TW9 1SR

Formerly published as *Close Up* by Penguin Australia.

ISBN 978-1-848-45369-2

59-0415

Harlequin (UK) Limited's policy is to use papers that are natural, renewable and recyclable products and made from wood grown in sustainable forests. The logging and manufacturing processes conform to the legal environmental regulations of the country of origin.

Printed and bound by
CPI Group (UK) Ltd, Croydon, CR0 4YY

Picture

Perfect

'Half the people in Hollywood are dying to be discovered and the other half are afraid they will be.'

—*Lionel Barrymore*

Prologue

Los Angeles
11 May, 1996

The girl shivered and hugged her new baby closer to her chest. It had been a restless night in the hospital room, her friend shifting uncomfortably in the hard plastic chair, while the baby snuffled into her chest, trying to find the source of the scent of milk.

She felt sick, but she wanted it finished. Every second she was with the baby was another second that might change her mind.

Her friend sat watching her, her slim legs in skintight jeans, chewing gum and sipping from the can of Mountain Dew she'd bought from the vending machine down the hall. She was swinging one foot, a habit that her friend knew came from nerves, not restlessness.

'She's gonna have a real nice life,' her friend said for the millionth time.

'I know,' she answered numbly.

'Better than anything *we* ever had.'

The baby stirred and she shifted her up onto her shoulder, and she felt her breasts ache. She was bottle-feeding, as they had all agreed, but her body yearned for the feel of her baby on her skin.

Her milk was coming in, the nurses had told her this morning, as the baby rubbed her little face against the bare skin on her neck.

Skin hungry, she thought, her tired mind recalling what she'd read about babies trying to bond with their mothers.

Is this what love feels like? she wondered, and then she felt the let-down of her milk, soaking her one good T-shirt.

'Goddammit,' she said and stood up from the bed. 'Take her, I have to dry this,' and she handed over the warm bundle.

Her friend took the baby with the confidence of someone who had grown up around younger children.

'Hush now, little one,' she said to the babe, and started singing about Jesus.

All her friend's songs were about Jesus, thought the girl as she went into the bathroom and plugged in the hairdryer from the cupboard under the sink. This was a real nice hospital, with fancy toiletries and hairdryers in each room. Better than the apartment she shared with her friend. She waved the hot air over her milk-stained T-shirt. She saw the milk had left a shadow of two eyes on her front.

Proverbs 15:3, she thought. *The eyes of the LORD are everywhere, keeping watch on the wicked and the good.*

What was he thinking as he watched her now?

A knock at the door made her jump and drop the hairdryer.

'Give her to me,' she said, rushing out and snatching the baby back. *Time is precious, don't waste a moment,* she heard the preacher say in her head.

Her friend walked to the door and opened it. 'Hi there,' she said, like she was about to serve them at the Pick 'n' Mix candy store.

She heard the woman's breathless voice answering and she walked to the window and stared out unseeingly at the parking lot.

If the Lord was watching her, and he knew how she was feeling, then he would have found another way, wouldn't he?

'Sweetheart?'

Turning slowly, she saw the woman who was about to become her baby's new mother.

The first time she met the woman she had been a tired, scared teenager, heavy with this child. Everything had ached.

Now everything ached for a different reason.

This woman had everything she didn't and she had the one thing the woman couldn't have.

Too old to adopt, the agencies had said.

The woman didn't look at her, just at the beautiful baby in her arms.

'How is she doing today?' she asked, lines of worry and age on her face.

And here was she, too young to keep the baby without family support.

Who was anyone to say this woman shouldn't have a baby just because she was older? It was unfair, but then the girl had always known life was unfair.

The woman didn't dress like anyone she knew. No one in her life wore smart suits or scarves, not even in church.

The baby mewed. Though the girl's breasts still yearned for the sweet mouth of the baby, she held her out to the woman.

'Do you want to hold her?' she asked shyly.

The woman pounced on the baby and cooed and clucked her tongue at the child.

'She's perfect,' she said, looking up with tears in her eyes as she took her from the arms of the young mother.

'Nobody's perfect,' she said quietly. 'Not even a teeny, tiny baby.'

But the woman didn't seem to notice anything but the baby.

'You got the money?' asked her friend and the girl frowned at her bluntness, but then her friend had always been able to separate money and emotion. It was business, she had said to her when she balked at the amount her friend suggested for the baby.

The woman reached into her black leather handbag and handed a yellow envelope to the girl.

Her friend took a sip of Mountain Dew and opened the envelope. 'I need to count it.' She set to work, carefully counting the money.

'It's all there,' the woman assured her, tearing her eyes away from the baby for a moment. 'And the contract for you to sign.'

Her friend looked up from the money with cold eyes. 'She'll sign when I've counted the money,' she snapped.

The woman was rocking the baby. The girl looked, and saw the baby's feet poking out of the pink blanket.

'She'll get cold,' she said and she tucked the blanket more snugly around the baby.

The woman stared at her.

'You are going to sign the papers, aren't you?' she asked, her eyes searching the girl's face.

Her voice was filled with fear; something the girl knew well.

'I am,' she said in a low voice. She went to the drawers by the bed and pulled out an envelope, and held it out to the woman.

'This is for her, when she's old enough, just in case something happens...'

The woman tore her eyes from the baby and nodded, her expression kind, as she took the envelope from her.

'Can I read it?' she asked politely. The girl knew the woman would read it later, even if she had said no at this moment.

She nodded and the woman struggled to open the envelope with the baby in her arms. She thought about offering to hold her while she read it but she didn't trust herself to hand the child back.

She's not yours now, she reminded herself.

The woman started to read.

She knew the words by heart.

Dear Baby Girl,
I am your momma, and I love you, but I don't have anything a momma needs to look after a little baby.
I promise you I will come back for you when I can. Until then, be happy with this nice lady, who wants to be your momma for a while. She can take care of you and buy you a four-poster bed and good food and lots of clothes and lots of other things I can't.
One day, when I'm rich, I'll come and find you again and give you everything else you need.

*Until then, know that I will always love you, my
precious little girl.*
Your Momma
xoxoxo

The woman folded the letter and put it back into its envelope and she saw her eyes wet with tears, but still she refused to cry.

Crying never helped nobody do nothin', Grammy used to say.

The old woman had been right. Crying wouldn't make her rich, or magically give her everything she knew the baby needed. She didn't have enough money for her own food, let alone to raise a child. How would she clothe her? Educate her? Take care of her in a crisis? God knows she had had enough drama in her own short life to know things happened, terrible things that no child should ever go through.

And there was no way she was going to let her go into foster care, not after what she has been through. There was not a time she could remember when she had felt as though her life was turning out okay. Too many foster homes and too many of her grandmother's broken promises had shattered her trust that the world was a safe place for a young girl to raise a child alone.

There was no point in crying, no point in wishing. The best thing for the child was to be with someone who could make sure she would be safe, and that she would never go hungry. That she would have the opportunity to go to school, that she would have a packed lunch and shoes without holes and that no one would ever call her 'white trash' to her face.

Her friend nodded at her that the money was all there.

She picked up the pen and, with a shaking hand, she signed the papers on the table.

All those years of practising her signature for when she was able to make her own decisions instead of the welfare department, and this was the first time she got to use it for something grown-up.

With aching breasts and a breaking heart she pushed the papers over to the woman and nodded to her friend.

'She's yours now until I can come back,' she said dully.

'Would you like to hold her again?' asked the woman.

She shook her head.

She knew that if she held her baby again, she would never let her go.

'No, thank you, you're her momma for now,' she said, and the woman who at forty-five had nearly given up on being a mother, blinked and nodded.

'Please. You should hold her again,' said the woman as she walked over to the girl. 'It will help you say goodbye.'

But the girl shook her head and picked up the plastic bag that contained her few personal belongings.

'There's no goodbye,' she said. 'Just take care of her till I can. I'll be back for her, I promise, and I'll pay you back the money and take care of her myself.' She spoke with absolute certainty.

Without a backwards glance, she left the hospital room, her friend following, with a copy of the adoption documents, thirty thousand dollars and a desperate dream that one day she would have everything she ever wanted, including her baby girl.

Chapter 1

Zoe Greene checked her reflection in the mirror and carefully blotted her neutral-coloured lipstick. Her tawny hair was blow-dried straight, her make-up flawless but subtle. She never liked to take the attention away from her clients but she was a beautiful woman and men noticed her, although she rarely noticed them in return.

Dating an actor was out of the question, she had yet to meet an actor who wasn't self-obsessed, and the power-players in Hollywood didn't want a relationship with a woman who might negotiate them out of their last million.

She heard that familiar sniff in the stall behind her and rolled her eyes at the bathroom attendant. The only drug Zoe ever needed was making deals and the annual *Vanity Fair* Oscars party was the ultimate place to make the deal of a lifetime.

Picking up her Judith Leiber clutch, she left the bathroom, ignoring the attendant's offer of a spray of bespoke perfume.

She didn't need a spritz of perfume, she needed a stiff drink, but that would have to come later. First she had the meeting from hell to get through.

'He's ready,' she heard from one of his assistants, who seemed to come out of nowhere to murmur in her ear. Squaring her shoulders, Zoe followed him into the private VIP room, where the truly famous partied together, away from the merely famous.

Angie and Brad sat in corner, talking intently to Anderson Cooper; Maggie Hall, her best friend and truly famous movie star client, was discussing something at length with Charlize Theron, and Sandy Bullock was sitting on Clooney's knee, laughing like they were the funniest two people in the room.

Actually they *were* the funniest people in the room, Zoe thought as she walked towards Jeff Beerman's table, trying to act nonchalant, but knowing all eyes were on her.

She lifted her head out of pride, as though she were the one accepting the Oscar. This was her moment and she had damn well earned it, she told herself.

She thought of the years of grovelling to men who couldn't think without being told what to think about, men who dismissed her and asked her to get coffee when she walked into a meeting, men who tried to make deals with her while trying to get her into their bed.

Zoe had never had a formal meeting with Jeff Beerman; she had only met him at industry events and parties, where he would usually have a circle of hangers-on, and an extremely beautiful girl on his arm when he was in between wives.

Although the Oscars party wasn't really a formal meeting, she still knew it was going to be the biggest moment of her professional life and if she was going to take a gamble, she might as well go for broke.

Zoe's poker face was the best in the business but a rare smile crossed her lips as she thought of her trump card, or manuscript, as it were.

'What are you smiling at, Greene?' Jeff asked with a curt nod of his grey head.

He called everyone by their surnames, as though he was the captain of Hollywood and they were all his junior officers.

'Nothing, just enjoying myself,' she said, making sure her poker mask was firmly back in place.

'You should smile more, it suits you,' he said, as though this was a certain fact.

'Thank you, I think,' she answered, thankful she was wearing a simple yet elegant Calvin Klein black dress. This was not the time for big hair and low cleavage; she would leave that to the starlets. She was there for business and nothing more.

'Don't think, just smile,' he said and Zoe laughed.

'Isn't that the standard advice you hand out to all your girlfriends?' she half joked and then almost gasped at her lack of control.

She was always in control, especially in meetings, but Jeff had disarmed her with that whole smiling schtick. She knew his game and she wasn't about to play by his rules.

'Give us a moment,' he said to his assistant, not taking his eyes off Zoe. The man backed away quickly.

'Sit,' he ordered and she did.

'You wanted to see me?' she asked, as though she had

anywhere better to be than at a private table with studio head Jeff Beerman.

Jeff leaned forward. Maggie and Zoe had always agreed that he was handsome enough to be a movie star, except he loved the business of movies more than the films themselves.

Like Zoe, he loved the deals but unlike Zoe he was a very rich man and, at times, a very despised man.

'I hear you've just signed Hugh Cavell,' he said, his eyes running over her, and she squared her shoulders and sat up straight.

'I have,' she answered, trying to be casual but professional.

'I want the option to his book,' he barked. 'How much does he want for it?'

His presumption annoyed her and fuelled by the thought of Hugh being her royal flush, she smiled sweetly.

'You could try asking nicely, Jeff. Manners are free, you know.'

'Don't fuck me around, Greene. I want the rights to this book!'

'You and everyone else,' she answered, meeting his icy gaze.

They stared at each other, neither moving, and then Jeff broke.

'You're braver than you look,' he said, leaning back in his chair.

'You don't intimidate me,' Zoe lied, bestowing Jeff with another smile.

He narrowed his eyes at her for a moment. 'Good for you. Most people shit themselves when they meet me,' he said, almost proudly.

'Should I be impressed or concerned for them?' she asked. 'I'm sure there's an operation for that.'

Jeff's expression changed from steely to resigned, and he rewarded her with the flicker of a smile. What a shame he was such a bastard, thought Zoe, before his voice broke into her thoughts.

'Greene, listen to me, I have to have this book. I can make the movie a huge hit.'

'So can Harvey, Brian or David,' she said, listing the other studio heads who had all offered her meetings since word had spread that she had Hugh Cavell in her managerial stable.

'Yeah, but why would you work with those morons? My studio will make the best picture—you know it and I know it—so stop playing games. What does the guy want? Money? A shot at writing the script? Casting approval?'

Zoe sat back in the leather seat and crossed her legs. 'Yes, he wants all of those things, and the other studios have already offered them.'

'So, what the fuck else does he want then?' Jeff looked impatiently at his Breitling watch.

Zoe paused for effect. She might not be an actor, but she knew how to play the role.

'Actually, Hugh wants me as the lead EP on the film,' she said. 'He doesn't trust anyone to produce it, unless I'm involved.'

'*What?*' Jeff recoiled as if she had just announced she was pregnant with his child.

'You heard me,' she said calmly.

A passing waiter placed two flutes of champagne in front of them, but Jeff pushed his away.

'Scotch, neat,' he snarled at the waiter, who retreated as though stung.

Zoe, glad for the distraction, picked up her glass and took a sip, trying to not let her hand shake. *Show him nothing,* she reminded herself, *not how much you want it, and certainly not how much you care.*

Jeff looked Zoe up and down dismissively.

'Come on, Greene, get real. You're a fucking talent manager not an executive producer. '

'Yes, I am.' Zoe wasn't insulted. She represented some of the biggest stars in town and could pull a deal together faster than any of her peers. She knew her own worth. 'But that's about to change.'

'You've got no runs on the board,' he said. 'What else can you bring to this besides the author?'

'My expertise, my people skills, my industry knowledge. I'm good at what I do.'

Jeff rolled his eyes. 'You and everyone else in this room,' he scoffed.

Zoe sipped more champagne and felt the amber liquid roll down her throat, hoping it would be an elixir of courage. 'It's simple, Jeff. The book comes with me attached as EP, that's what Hugh and I have agreed, so don't even *think* about going over my head. We have a contract even you couldn't pull apart.'

Jeff was silent. Zoe pushed her chair back and stood up.

'Think about it and call my office tomorrow if you're interested, my assistant Paul will patch you through to my cell,' she said, and made to walk away from the table.

'Sit down and don't make a scene,' he snapped and again, she did as he asked.

Who needs who more? she wondered, as she felt the eyes

of passing guests on them and saw waitstaff nervously pacing nearby, ready for the snap of Jeff's temper.

There was silence, each one holding their cards close to
their chest.

'So you want to make movies, huh?' Jeff asked finally
with a sigh, as though she had just asked for the right to
vote. 'Not many women make it in this business. Do you
think you can handle it?'

'Don't patronize me because I'm a woman,' she said politely. 'I can do any job as well as a man.'

'I'm not. I don't care what's between your legs,' he
laughed. 'I want to know you can handle the bullshit and
the drama when your leading stars hate each other and I'm
screaming at you on the phone and the director's losing the
plot and you haven't slept in a week.'

Zoe smiled. 'My film wouldn't be like that,' she stated.

'Oh, really?' Jeff smiled now, and he stared at her for a
long time. 'Why's that?'

'Because I would make sure everything was sorted before we got to set,' she said, knowing she sounded naïve but
she believed in thinking ahead, her whole life she had had
to be one step ahead of everyone else.

Jeff pulled at the cuffs on his shirt, a glimpse of silver
cufflinks caught the light and Zoe's eye.

'You can't always be prepared for what happens while
making a movie,' said Jeff. 'Life throws curveballs at all
of us, even me.'

Zoe felt the room's eyes on her, the sound of gossip and
conjecture about why Zoe and Jeff were talking so intently.
She heard laughter and some music, and somewhere a glass
smashed but it was Jeff's eyes boring into hers that stead-
ied her.

'Why do you want to make this movie, Greene?' he asked.

'Because it's the most beautiful book I've ever read,' she answered truthfully.

Jeff squinted and frowned and then he rolled his eyes and Zoe laughed as she continued.

'*And* because it's box office gold: the man who learns about love only after his wife is declared terminally ill? I mean, what about that isn't perfect chick-flick fodder?'

'And the author, do you think he can write a decent script?'

'Yes, I think he can write a great script,' she replied, crossing her fingers under the table.

Jeff swilled the Scotch in his glass, drained the last of it, and then cleared his throat.

'This is the biggest hit in books since fuck knows what,' he said. 'I want it to be the best movie Palladium Pictures has ever produced, do you understand? This is the movie people will talk about when I die.'

Zoe nodded, secretly marvelling at Jeff's ego. Did he come to Hollywood with that intact or did he earn it?

'I understand,' she said and then she appealed to his ego. 'And this is why I'm coming to you,' she said. 'I want to learn from you.'

Jeff watched her as she sipped her drink, his eyes narrowed.

'How old are you?' he asked rudely, but Zoe didn't flinch.

'Thirty-six,' she said.

'You're too old for me.'

Zoe laughed. 'I don't want to date you; I want you to teach me. You're the perfect age to be my wise old teacher,' she said with a cheeky smile, and she saw a flash of displeasure cross his face.

'I thought you weren't into men?' He smirked, but she swallowed her temper.

'Oh, I am into men, just not old ones,' she said. 'I prefer to leave them to the piranhas with silicone breasts and gold-digging dreams.'

Jeff laughed. 'God knows there are plenty of those fish in the sea; I even married a few of them.' Then he looked up at her, his face unreadable. 'But not many like you, it seems.'

She sensed Jeff's respect that she could hold her own.

'Every agent, manager and motherfucker in LA was after this Brit. How the hell did you get him to sign with you, Greene?'

Zoe thought about her trip to London. She remembered the taxi ride to Hugh's little house and the desolate, drunken state in which she'd found him. She had been shocked. The guy was so self-destructive he made Hemingway seem like a lightweight, but for some reason he had trusted Zoe. She had cleaned him up, brought him back to LA in secret, and rented him a secluded, light-filled house in Malibu where he could write, and dry out. She hadn't even told Maggie that Hugh was in LA. 'He trusts me,' was all she said with a shrug.

Jeff nodded and shook his head. 'You know I'm gonna try to screw you on the backend deal,' he said.

'You can try, but I doubt you'll succeed,' she answered, and for a brief moment, she saw respect in his eyes.

'Come and see me tomorrow. I'll get my assistant to call yours,' he said.

'So we have a deal?' Zoe asked.

'No, we don't have a fucking deal! I asked for a meeting, not to fucking marry you.'

Zoe resisted the urge to punch him in his handsome but arrogant face.

Men like Jeff made her angry. Angry that they had more power than her and angry that she was just as deserving yet was still overlooked because she was a woman.

'Okay, then you won't mind if I go and meet with Harvey before you?' she asked, using one of her last cards.

But what she understood about men like Jeff Beerman was that he hated competition of any kind.

Jeff stared at her, making her feel like she was twelve years old again and under the eyes of the social worker. Judging, assessing, making plans for her that weren't in her best interest.

A small amount of bile rose in her throat but she swallowed it down with a sip of champagne.

'Jesus, you're a bitch, Greene,' he muttered under his breath.

'Why?' she challenged, the heat rising in her cheeks. She couldn't tell if it was him or the champagne that was making her flushed. 'Because I want what I want? You get to be ambitious but I'm a bitch? I'm disappointed in you, Jeff. I thought you were better than that.'

Actually, this was a lie. Jeff could be a misogynistic prick, whose three ex-wives would all testify to the fact, but Zoe wanted to give him a chance to dig himself out of his gender-biased grave.

To his credit, Jeff took a moment and then looked Zoe in the eye. 'You're right, that was unfair. You're not a bitch; you're just a pain in the arse.'

Zoe laughed a little, despite herself. 'You have no idea how big a pain in the arse I can be.'

Jeff put his hand out over the table. 'You've got a deal,'

he said. 'Bring yourself to my office tomorrow to discuss the terms.'

Zoe took his hand in hers, feeling the smooth skin of a man who worked behind a desk all day.

'Thank you, Jeff, you won't regret it. This movie is going be a huge hit.'

'It fucking better be. If it's not, I'm gonna blame it all on you and you'll never eat lunch in this town again.'

Zoe smiled. 'That's okay, I don't eat lunch anyway,' she said, and without a backwards glance, she walked out of the room that everyone wanted to be inside.

Outside, in the crisp midnight air, she handed the valet parking attendant the ticket for her Jaguar and shivered, not from the cold, but from the feeling that there was something exciting in the air.

She laughed as she got into the car and she thought about Jeff saying she was too old for him. The last thing she wanted was to be the next Mrs Beerman. She wanted something bigger than that: she wanted to be the next Jeff Beerman.

After nearly twenty years in Hollywood, Zoe Greene had finally got the break she needed, and she wasn't going to let anything stand in her way.

Chapter 2

Maggie Hall was careful not to trip over the train of Penelope Cruz's enormous silver ball gown as she manoeuvred through the room to gain a better view of Zoe's conversation with Jeff Beerman.

The room was buzzing with celebrities catching up, waitstaff trying to keep up with the request for drinks and power brokers shaking hands and comparing egos.

The finest haute couture was being worn by the beautiful as if they deserved nothing less: clothes that hadn't been worn by anyone else in the world yet but would dictate fashion pages for the next year. Trends were being started, careers were being launched, and deals were being made in every corner of the room.

Arrangements about management, pacts around casting, transactions in marriages and compromises with lovers. It was a cacophony of perfume and ambitions, the perfect night, thought Maggie as she watched a starlet make a play for Brad Pitt and Angelina smile as though indulging one of her youngest children.

Maggie was a people watcher, which was part of what made her a brilliant actress, but she wasn't trying to play either Jeff or Zoe in a new role. She knew there was something going down, and—given Zoe was both her best friend and her manager—automatically assumed it had something to do with her.

But Zoe had already left the table by the time Maggie got a decent view and she was left talking to Gwyneth Paltrow about colon cleanses.

Damn you, Zoe, she thought, *at least tell me which project Jeff wants me for so I can prepare.*

Did she need to lose weight or gain it? Change her hair colour from blonde to brunette? Change her body shape with four-hour-a-day workouts?

Transforming herself came naturally to Maggie—she'd being doing it for nearly thirty-seven years. It was being herself she sometimes had trouble with, she thought wryly.

Gwyneth Paltrow had been joined by Willow Carruthers, and the two were now talking about London's best colonic clinics.

God help me, Maggie thought when she heard her name.

'Maggie?' She turned and found herself face-to-face with her ex, Australian actor, Will MacIntyre and his Spanish girlfriend, Stella. Stella glared at Maggie as though she were the worst person in the world, which, to Stella, she probably was.

'Thank you, I was about to have to make colonic conversation with Goop about her poop,' she mock whispered and smiled at him brightly. On paper they had been the perfect couple, but things had never been so easy behind closed doors.

'I like colonics,' said Stella. 'They help me lose pounds and pounds.'

Maggie thought about making a comment regarding what Stella was filled with, but left it alone. She didn't need a scene, not with her mind on Zoe and Jeff's meeting.

'You look beautiful,' Will said, his eyes scanning Maggie in her lilac strapless gown. Stella's face fell at Will's words, and for a moment Maggie felt bad for her. Stella would be in the colon clinic tomorrow, trying to rid herself of the 'pound and pounds', when in stead she'd be better off just dumping Will, who really was a big shit.

Stella was sexy, a tumble of dark hair, breasts and curves, but Maggie was tall and willowy, and often described as a classic beauty. Tonight her blond hair was drawn into a sleek chignon, accentuating her high cheekbones and piercing blue eyes. And though her Nordic looks afforded her an enviable elegance, Maggie knew it was her trademark smile, the one that warmed her face and lit up a room, that earned her at least fifteen million dollars a movie, plus a cut of the backend. Zoe once famously said that when Maggie Hall smiled, a person would buy whatever she was selling, rob a bank or commit a murder just to keep the light in the room.

Maggie ignored Will's compliment, not because it wasn't pleasant but because she knew he'd only said it to annoy Stella, who was now glaring at Maggie as though she was putting a curse on her.

'How's Elliot?' She asked after Will's son. 'He hasn't returned any of my calls.'

Will shrugged. 'Still in his room, playing video games.'

'He's too old for games,' said Stella impatiently as though

Maggie had addressed her. 'He's twenty-three, he needs to be out in ze world.'

Maggie shot her a look that made Stella toss her head but turn away from Maggie's dislike.

Yes, Elliot needed to get back out into the world but the kid did have a reason to stay inside for a while, she thought tenderly. She may not have birthed Elliot but she loved him like her own child.

'It's been six months since the transplant. Haven't the doctors said he can go back to college?' she asked.

'He doesn't want to,' said Will, looking exhausted just talking about it. 'He doesn't want to do anything.'

She and Will had only been divorced for eighteen months, and while Maggie was still single, Will had wasted no time in finding a replacement. Someone younger, someone who would no doubt give him the child they had fought about throughout their eight-year marriage.

'We have Elliot,' she had argued at the time. 'He needs us, and we can't bring a child into this home when he's so sick.'

Her argument had contained a thread of truth, but what she had never said was that she just didn't feel ready to have a child with Will. She thought her body would tell her that the time was right to be pregnant but it never did and when Elliot's congenital heart condition had worsened, the idea was parked permanently.

But she couldn't stay in a loveless marriage, not even for Elliot. Eventually she realized she didn't love Will, and Elliot wasn't enough of a reason to stay.

She had tried to stay in Elliot's life—she was the closest thing to a mother that he had and she knew he wanted to see her—but Will's anger at her leaving him made it difficult.

'Do you want me to talk to him about it?' she asked now.

'He won't return my calls but I can come over and I can stage a care-frontation.'

Stella rolled her eyes, and Maggie only just resisted the urge to slap her.

'I see Zoe's been doing the deal with Jeff,' said Will, obviously trying to change the subject and taking a large sip of his wine.

The *Vanity Fair* photographers were circling, looking for a good candid photo of the past couple and the new girlfriend. Maggie took care to smile, radiantly, as she asked casually, 'What deal is that?'

But before Will could answer, Arden Walker swept into the circle.

'Hello, darlings,' she said, but Maggie noticed she only kissed Will, touching his face in a way Maggie knew made him uncomfortable—she could see it in the way his eyes blinked too many times and his jaw tensed.

Poor Will, she thought, Arden Walker would never take no for an answer; she had ambition and charisma in spades, something that poor Stella didn't have.

Arden worked her charisma the way Stella worked her body, and right now she was clinging to Will's side like a lemur.

Will and Arden had made a film together, a big-budget action movie, two years earlier, when Arden was a mere twenty years old. Will had played her father. The film had done well at the box office, although Elliot and Maggie had watched it at her house and laughed at Arden trying to make a mediocre script sound like Chekov.

Maggie glanced at Arden's ensemble for the evening: a mess of black leather and tulle, with a black lipstick that only accentuated her thin lips. It wasn't that Arden was unattractive—she had a certain Euro-chicness about her with her blue-black hair—it was just that she looked mean. She looked like she would throw a sack of kitten in a lake and not turn back, Elliot had once said, and Maggie knew just what he meant. Elliot knew people, it was a shame his father didn't have the same sixth sense.

Arden pushed in between Stella and Will. 'Is it true you're going to be my new leading man?' she purred. 'We could be the next Julia and Richard.'

Maggie rolled her eyes. She knew Arden was hoping to topple her from her pedestal and had gone from playing edgy, asexual roles to a recent part in a romantic tragedy.

'Arden, what are you talking about?' Will asked impatiently, draining his wine and waving the empty glass at a waiter for a new one.

'I had lunch with Zoe's old assistant Josh,' she said knowingly. 'He told me all about the film.'

Maggie, Will and Arden all shared a manager but Zoe was, and would always be, Maggie's closest friend and confidante.

'According to Josh, Zoe wants to know if I'm interested in the role. I knew she was seeing the big four studios, but I kind of guessed she'd go with Jeff, he's a class act, despite what people say about him as a person.' She looked at Maggie pointedly. 'I always think it's important to judge people on their talent, not their reputation.'

Maggie smiled. 'I always think it's important not to judge people,' she said politely.

Arden looked like she knew she had lost that round and she turned back to Will, touching his chest with one black-leather-gloved hand.

'Let me know if you're going to be my leading man, Will;

I certainly hope so,' she said in a feverish voice, which made Maggie glance at Stella and make a face. It wasn't easy being with Will. Women loved him, and girls like Arden would always be using him for the next career move.

But what was the role Arden was talking about? Her brain was screaming. Will was a superb actor, at the top of his game right now. If there was a film he was being considered for, Maggie wanted to know. The only part of their marriage that worked was when they talked about work and although Zoe managed both of them, Maggie still felt proprietary towards Will and his career moves.

The movie he made with Arden had been something Maggie and Zoe had thought was a bad idea, which proved to be true at the box office. She didn't want Will to make any more stupid choices—God knows he had made enough of them over the years.

Arden swanned off towards Bradley Cooper, and Maggie turned to Will.

'What role is she talking about? She seems thrilled to have the chance to work with you.' Maggie imitated Arden's breathy delivery.

Will scoffed and took a large slug of wine. 'As I said to Zoe, if you think I'm interested in the book that was responsible for ending my marriage, then you're kidding yourself.'

Maggie gasped. 'Zoe's casting *The Art of Love*?'

'Casting?' exclaimed Will. 'She's trying to produce it as well, which is why I guess she was sitting with Jeff. I heard she signed that sad sack writer you love so much.'

Maggie clutched the stem of her glass and nodded. 'Excuse me,' she said and rushed to the bathroom.

Pushing open the door, she was grateful to see the plush bathroom was unoccupied except for the bathroom attendant.

Zoe had signed Hugh Cavell? She wanted to produce *The Art of Love* and hadn't told her? Why hadn't she asked her to be involved? They did everything together.

This was how they had rolled for twenty years and now Zoe was keeping secrets.

Christ, she was the one who had introduced Zoe to the goddamned book.

It was the most profound and beautiful book about love that Maggie had ever read, not that she had read many books. Hell, she had cried over this book, bought copies for everyone she knew and then walked out of her marriage.

She wanted what the author and his wife had had in *The Art of Love*, and nothing less.

The author had nursed his wife through cancer, had seen her through her best and worst, and he spoke of his wife in a way that Maggie doubted any man had ever spoken of her. It was her greatest desire to meet Hugh Cavell and learn from him everything she needed to know about love, and how to have a decent relationship.

She had even told Zoe all this. It was only now that Zoe's reaction at the time made sense.

'Maybe he doesn't want to be some sort of relationship guru,' she had said. 'He's just a journalist who wrote a memoir, I don't think he's really able to offer anything else beyond this.'

Zoe must have already met him by this stage.

The treachery of Zoe excluding Maggie from this deal made her both confused and angry as she faced her reflection in the mirror.

She was still beautiful, she was still slim and elegant, but there were subtle changes around her eyes, tiny highways of lines. All roads lead to Hollywood, she thought as she pulled at one to see if she should consider a facelift, but she couldn't concentrate on her own reflection, so she knew she was upset.

Zoe knew she wanted to play Simone, she had told Zoe this when she'd given her the book. Even though Maggie was the wrong side of thirty-five and Simone was only thirty when she died, Maggie could still play younger—

The bathroom door opening interrupted her thoughts as another attendant came in to relieve the first one. Maggie watched the new girl in the mirror as she straightened the perfume bottles and made sure the hand towels were perfectly lined up.

She was beautiful, Maggie thought with envy, as she looked back at the mirror, aware of the slight crêping of the skin on her décolletage in the light. She stood taller and pulled her shoulders back.

Maybe Zoe had decided that she, Maggie Hall, was too old to play Simone? The thought hit her like a slap to the face.

'Are you an actress?' she asked the girl. Girls like this worked industry parties for any opportunity, each girl seemingly more lithe, beautiful and willing than the one before.

This girl would have more luck in the men's bathroom, thought Maggie wryly.

'No,' said the girl, in a voice that was husky and low, the voice many voice-over artists wished they had. The girl was a complete package.

'Really?' she asked, surprised.

The girl shook her blond head and shrugged. She could have been a model, thought Maggie, taking in the long slender frame and startling green eyes.

'So what do you do?' asked Maggie, intrigued.

She must be the only beautiful girl in LA who doesn't want to be an actress, she thought, almost laughing aloud at the irony. The girl reminded her of someone, but she couldn't quite place her.

The girl paused. 'I'm working on a research project,' she said vaguely.

'Oh, you're at college?'

'Kind of. I'm working on a thesis of sorts.'

Beautiful *and* smart, thought Maggie, as she turned back to the mirror. Beautiful and dumb had far more currency in LA, but still.

'I never went to college, but I would have liked to,' said Maggie.

'You seem to have done okay without it,' the girl said with a little laugh.

'I guess I have,' said Maggie, smiling along with her. 'Do you work this kind of event often?' she asked, wondering why she cared.

'If I can,' the girl said. 'I also do waitressing and valet parking, anything really.'

'Good for you,' said Maggie, aware that it might sound patronizing, but she truly did respect hard work.

Maggie sat on the round love seat in the centre of the room, and pulled off one purple Givenchy shoe.

'Wearing these shoes is what I imagine Chinese footbinding was like,' she said as she rubbed her feet. 'I said I'm an eight but I think I should have taken the eight and a half.'

'Yeah,' said the girl. 'I'm an eight in some shoes and an eight and a half in others.' There was a pause and then the girl spoke again. 'Your dress is amazing.'

Maggie looked down at her figure-hugging lilac Lanvin dress and sighed. 'It's okay, I guess. Took me and my stylists over half a year to organize this outfit and I wasn't even presenting. Sometimes it's exhausting being perfect,' she said dramatically and laughed.

The girl smiled shyly and Maggie shook her head. 'Are you *sure* you're not an actress? Have you ever tried it? Even modelling, perhaps? The camera would absolutely love you, you're incredibly beautiful.'

'I never really thought about it,' said the girl, blinking a few times and frowning. 'My parents think being an actor is a waste of time and education, unless of course you're on Broadway in some obscure Russian play.' She laughed.

'Maybe,' said Maggie defensively. 'But my house in Malibu is evidence that they're wrong.'

The girl laughed politely. 'I guess I've never even thought about acting.'

Maggie narrowed her eyes at her. Was she being disingenuous or was she serious? False modesty was something Maggie couldn't stand, along with liars and cheaters, which often made her wonder why she was still living in LA.

'What do you want to do?' she asked.

'My mom would like me to do law, but I can't see myself doing all that arguing every day,' she said. 'If I get to choose, I guess I'd like to be a social worker or something.'

Maggie's head snapped up.

'What for?' she said. 'Social workers are assholes. They say one thing, but do another.'

'Really?' The girl frowned. 'I just like helping people.'

'Then I suggest you find another way,' said Maggie roughly as she stood up, shoes in hand.

'Okay,' said the girl, looking intimidated.

Sometimes, Maggie knew, she could be almost too candid, too raw. But this was also what made her such a powerful presence on screen. She wasn't afraid to show her character's pain on her face or in the way she moved.

Softening, she smiled at the girl.

'I haven't introduced myself, I'm Maggie Hall,' she said, extending her hand. She hated it when big stars just assumed everyone knew who they were. Manners are free, as Zoe always reminded her clients.

'I know who you are,' said the girl shyly, taking Maggie's hand. 'I'm Dylan Mercer.'

'And now I know who you are,' said Maggie warmly. 'Great name; you really could be an actress,' she said again, laughing.

'And you could be an agent the way you hustle,' Dylan laughed back. 'I've been watching all the business going on here tonight, it's crazy.'

'I know.' Maggie shrugged. 'I could have been, but I like the free clothes too much.' She winked at Dylan, looked a little closer at her and shook her head. 'God, you remind me of someone,' she said. 'Hey, can I have your number? I mean, I know you don't want to be an actor, but sometimes my assistant needs a little help. And you did say you like helping people. Maybe, if you're interested, you could do a few errands for me here and there?'

Dylan nodded excitedly, pulled a pen from her pocket, and wrote her details on the back of a card from the events company.

Maggie took the card and handed her shoes to Dylan.

'Hold these, would you?' she said as she put the card into her clutch purse and smiled. 'Thank you, Dylan, I'll be sure to keep you in mind.'

Turning, she walked towards the door.

'Your shoes,' said Dylan, holding out the strappy Givenchy's.

'Keep them,' said Maggie with a toss of her shining blond head. 'I don't need them. You might make something on eBay with them—Maggie Hall's shoes from Oscars night—or keep 'em and they might make a great story one day. Either way, you win.'

Chapter 3

Dylan stared at Maggie Hall's discarded shoes in disbelief, turning them over and studying each detail.

She had never owned anything as gorgeous and frivolous as these, she thought, quelling the desire to slip off her plain black flats from the Gap, and try on the Givenchy's. Her mother believed in buying the best you could afford, but 'functional is always better than fancy,' she would tell Dylan whenever she lusted after something pretty and useless.

She shoved the shoes in an empty gift bag left by a guest and placed them under the bench, then looked at herself in the mirror. Was she really as beautiful as Maggie Hall said?

She was okay-looking, she thought, but growing up with intellectual parents meant you were much more focused on your brain than your looks.

Dinner time in the Mercers' brownstone was spent discussing her mother's ethical legal riddles from her university tenure and her father's more bizarre psychiatric cases, while Dylan tried to keep up with the conversation.

She was bright, but she had to work hard for her marks and staying on the honor roll wasn't easy but she did it because her parents expected nothing less of her.

Sometimes Dylan longed to remind them that she didn't have their genetic code so it was unreasonable to expect her to be as brilliant as them, but a part of her was grateful that they treated her as though she was an extension of them.

That was until she found the letter they had never shown her.

'Excuse me.' She heard a voice and turned to see another famous face, a starlet who had recently been named as the sexiest woman in film. 'Do you have a Band-Aid? My shoes are killing me.'

Dylan opened the first-aid kit, took out a Band-Aid and handed it to the girl. Now *she* was beautiful, Dylan thought, after the girl had left the bathroom.

She glanced at her face in the mirror again. It was too wide; the sort of face that didn't look right in everyday life, but it did kind of work in photos. She might have sought out modelling work, if she'd even known where to start, but it never seemed like the right time to say that to her law professor mother, with tenure at Columbia, or her ailing psychiatrist father, who had recently been diagnosed with Parkinson's disease.

As more women came into the bathroom, there were several faces Dylan recognized, but she wasn't as star-struck any more. Hell, she had Maggie Hall's Givenchy shoes! She couldn't wait to get home and tell her best friend back in New York.

That was the sort of thing Addie loved to hear. During their almost daily Skype sessions, Addie always wanted to know what celebrities Dylan had seen in LA.

But in the two months she'd been in LA, Dylan hadn't seen many, until tonight. She thought she'd glimpsed Kevin Bacon in a frozen yogurt store, but couldn't be sure. A Kevin Bacon sighting probably wouldn't impress Addie anyway, but Maggie Hall was different.

Her supervisor walked into the bathroom with a sour face. 'You can go now. Make sure you sign your hours sheet before you leave.'

'Okay,' said Dylan politely. The woman had been a total bitch all night, but Dylan refused to let it bother her. This job had been way better than working nights at the greasy chicken shop downtown, trying to avoid the slick on the floor and the even more oily owner.

Dylan picked up her bag and put the gift bag with the Givenchy shoes in it over her shoulder. 'Thanks, it was fun.'

The woman looked at her and made a face. 'Being stuck in a bathroom with needy celebrities bitching about each other and fighting over the mirror was fun? You're nuts.'

Dylan smiled as she stepped into the elevator, feeling the slight weight of the shoes in the bag slung over her shoulder. Tonight had been a rare good night.

'How you doing?' she heard as the elevator doors opened and she saw a handsome man leaning against the opposite wall, one hand in the pocket of his tuxedo pants as though he was posing for a cologne advertisement.

It was both cheesy and funny, and she started to laugh.

'What?' he asked, looking behind him.

As he turned, she pressed the button and the doors of the elevator closed again, leaving her laughing out loud.

Was he serious? He probably worked that move in the mirror over and over before trying it on countless girls.

Maybe some fell for it, but not Dylan. She liked boys who were less handsome and less presumptuous, guys who made her laugh and didn't act like they were in a perfume ad.

So far she hadn't met anyone close to decent in LA. Every guy wanted to be an actor, and assumed Dylan wanted the same thing. They all asked her who her manager was, who was her agent? Would she do nudity?

Checking her phone, she saw it was after two in the morning and she sighed as she walked towards the cab rank. Even though the cab was expensive, at least she'd get home to her studio apartment in Koreatown in time for a few hours' sleep before her next shift.

She had to be at work again in five hours' time, waitressing at a breakfast in a private home in the Hollywood Hills. She had begged for the shift as it was extra money and she could then afford to take two days off for her research.

Her furnished apartment was cheap because the owners were planning on pulling it down and rebuilding on the site, but according to her new neighbour they'd been saying that for ten years and there was still no sign of any development.

At seven hundred and twenty dollars a month, the apartment was manageable, just. There was no way Dylan would ask her parents for help. Not after what she knew now.

Inside her one room, she pulled her laptop out from under the mattress—it was the only thing in her room of any value—and opened it to check her emails.

An overflowing laundry basket sat in one corner, and a bowl half-eaten ramen noodles sat on the linoleum floor.

Her mom would freak if she saw how messy her room was, she thought, making a mental notes to clean it after tomorrow's shift.

Nothing of any importance, she thought crossly as she slammed the laptop shut and went and lay back on the uncomfortable single bed that had come with the apartment, along with a dripping sink and some oversized cockroaches. They probably had fillers also, she thought, thinking of some of the faces she had seen at the party that night.

Why did people think they had to do that to their faces? she wondered as she rolled over on the lumpy mattress, her eye caught by the gift bag on the floor.

Clambering out of bed, she put on the strappy shoes and stood up. Maggie Hall was right, they hurt like hell, but they looked amazing. Taking her phone, she sent a picture of them to Addie with the text: *Maggie Hall let me walk in her shoes. They are now mine.*

It was six in the morning in New York, no chance Addie would be awake, but she knew her friend would be thrilled.

Tottering back to the bed, Dylan lay down again and lifted one leg to admire the shoe. What did shoes like this even cost? she wondered idly, as her phone started ringing.

'Why the hell are you awake?' Dylan said, as soon as she saw Addie's number.

'I wasn't really, but I heard the message come through and saw it was from you. How the hell do you have Maggie Hall's shoes on?'

Addie's voice was groggy but excited, and Dylan laughed.

'You didn't need to call me *now*, Ads,' she said. 'I meant it to be a surprise for when you woke up.'

'I always keep my phone on,' said Addie. 'Now spill.'

Dylan told her all about her night and her encounter with Maggie in the bathroom. Addie, as she'd expected, was duly impressed.

'God, I wish I had your life! Instead I'm stuck here, it's

snowing, it's boring, and I have no idea why I'm studying when my degree is just a ticket to working at Starbucks for the rest of my life.'

'You don't have to do that course,' Dylan said for the one hundredth time.

Like most of Dylan's friends from her prestigious private school, she and Addie had been spoiled for choice when it came to deciding which college to attend. Addie had ending up enrolling in a comparative literature degree because she didn't know what else to do.

'Show me the shoes again, without your ugly feet in them,' Addie demanded, sounding more awake by the second.

Dylan obediently took off the shoes and sent the new photo. 'She asked for my number,' she said, when she put the phone back to her ear.

'For what? Like in a date? Is she a closet lesbian?' Addie squealed.

'No, you tawdry hoe, I told her I'm looking for work and she said sometimes her assistant needs an assistant.'

'Jesus,' said Addie, 'what a world.'

'I know, right?'

'How's the search? Any more leads?'

Dylan was a smart girl, with a four-point average and acceptance letters to both Brown and Wellesley, so why was her task proving so hard?

'None. I feel like I'm going about it in completely the wrong way. I can't find anything. I've contacted the agencies, but no one will give me any information unless I have both parents' signatures because I'm under twenty-one.'

Addie paused. 'You know, babe, you *could* just ask your

mom and dad who your birth mother was and save yourself all this trouble?'

'I can't,' said Dylan. 'It would kill Dad.' She put on the
heels again and flopped back on the bed. 'Besides, I don't
think I could stand to hear any more of their lies right now.'

'I get it,' said Addie softly.

Dylan nodded, forgetting for a moment that Addie
couldn't see her. This was why she and Addie were so close.
Addie really did get it, she got everything about Dylan,
even her hare-brained scheme to head to LA and find her
birth mother.

'Hey, I have to crash. Gotta be at another job in a few
hours,' said Dylan, yawning.

'Okay, sleep well, I love ya, you crazy bitch.'

'Love you too, loser,' said Dylan, and she went to sleep,
still wearing Maggie's shoes.

West Virginia
September 1995

Shay Harman looked at the pregnancy test and shook it
vigorously.

'It's not a Magic 8 Ball,' her friend Krista said, as she
swung her skinny legs from her perch on the bench in the
mall's public toilet.

'I wish it was,' said Shay.

Someone had once left a cigarette on the bench, burning the lino into a perfect groove, which Krista now lay
her finger in.

'What are you going to do?' Krista asked.

'Go back and finish my shift,' said Shay. 'I'll think about
it later.' Denial was always a good choice in the face of
chaos, she thought.

* * *

Back at the Great American Cookies stand, the smell of the dough made Shay feel ill. She fought down the nausea, staring out at the crowd in the mall.

She didn't feel like she belonged there, but soon she would become one of the throng, pushing a second-hand pram and living on welfare.

'You okay, honey?' asked her coworker Jackie.

Shay had no idea how old Jackie was. But as far as she could tell, after four babies in six years, Jackie wasn't living, just existing, sleepwalking through her shifts at the cookie stand.

Jackie said she was lucky—she and her husband both had jobs and her kids went to school—but Shay couldn't work out what was so lucky about that. Wasn't that something everyone should have?

This attitude had gotten her into trouble with her foster families.

'You need to be more grateful for what you get,' said the social worker.

Eventually the social worker convinced Shay's grandmother to take her in. At least Shay didn't have to pretend to be grateful then. She knew her grammy only agreed so she'd get the extra welfare cheque for her dead son's only child.

Shay served a teenage girl whose swelling stomach couldn't be hidden by the oversized Disneyland sweatshirt. Was everyone pregnant all of a sudden?

Was she really any different to this girl? Shay wondered. Was her future now to raise a baby when she could hardly raise herself? And what would Grammy say when she went home to the trailer and told her she was pregnant to the first guy she'd slept with?

Bud Harris wasn't her boyfriend. She'd only had sex with him because she'd yearned for someone's loving touch. She knew damn well he wouldn't want this baby; he was already working down the mines, never calling Shay again after he had left school.

Finally the shift ended and she was relieved to find Krista waiting for her.

'Let's get out of here,' said Shay as she walked up to her best friend.

'Sure,' said Krista, tossing her bleached hair over her shoulder, 'but I don't want to go to my place, they're all down on their knees praying for something that doesn't include me.'

Shay laughed wryly. Some foster homes were better than others, but each had its own special way of reminding you that you didn't quite fit in. It might be special food that wasn't for the welfare kids, or second-hand clothing that was the wrong size. In Krista's current 'home', it was prayer.

Shay looked around. 'I don't know where we *can* go,' she said, and then she started to cry.

'Hush now,' Krista said, in that voice that always calmed Shay. 'I'll think of something.'

And Shay nodded, knowing that Krista would. She had never once let her down.

Krista's eyes lit up and she smiled the magnificent smile that made social workers believe she really had changed this time.

Soon, Shay and Krista were sitting up the back in the only movie theatre in town, let in for free by the pimple-faced projectionist who had a thing for Krista.

'What's the film?' whispered Shay.

'Matilda,' whispered Krista. 'It's about a little girl who

uses her magic to get her revenge on her shitty family and school, and finds a new mom to adopt her. I've seen it twice already, it's my favourite film ever.'

Shay smiled and took Krista's hand and squeezed it tight.

'Thank you,' she said and Krista smiled in the darkness as the screen flickered to life.

Chapter 4

Zoe was driving out to Malibu in her new Jaguar sports car, the top was down and Bruno Mars was blaring out of the stereo. The overcast day couldn't dull Zoe's mood. Even when it was turning to winter, it wasn't cold. She hated being cold almost as much as she hated being overlooked just because she was a woman. People assumed she was the mother hen of her clients, and to some extent she was, but this new deal with Jeff Beerman meant she was now a power-player. She couldn't wait to tell Hugh the news about the deal and how well she had played her hand at the party, when her phone rang.

Christ it wasn't even eight a.m. and people were hassling her already? The morning after the Oscars should be a public holiday in Hollywood, she thought crossly as she pressed the answer button on her steering wheel.

'Zoe Greene.'

'Zoe, it's Rachel Fein, from *Hollywood Reporter*,' came the nasal tones of the woman who could make or break a film with a single article.

'Rachel, sorry I didn't see you last night. How are you?' said Zoe silkily.

'You may not have seen me, but everyone saw you,' laughed Rachel. 'So what's the dealio with you and Jeff Beerman? Is it business or pleasure?'

The dealio? Zoe rolled her eyes as she turned the corner and took the highway towards Malibu.

'Rachel, we both know I'm too old and too smart to be anything other than business in Jeff's life,' she said.

Jeff's three ex-wives would all attest to his penchant for young starlets, which was well known in the industry. Rumour had it that his last marriage had cost him twenty-seven million dollars.

'So it's true you're executive producing *The Art of Love* with Jeff and Palladium Pictures?' Rachel asked.

Zoe gripped the steering wheel a little tighter, imagining it was Rachel's neck.

'I can't comment on any deals right now. But when I have an announcement to make, you'll be the first to know,' she answered. *Just as soon as I've signed the papers*, she thought.

'I see. Well, is it true that Palladium Pictures is in financial trouble, and that Jeff Beerman has put up his own money to get this project off the ground?'

Zoe glanced in the rear-view mirror and pulled over sharply to the side of the highway.

'Rachel, I have no idea what you're talking about,' she said evenly. *Stay calm, girl*, she reminded herself. *You've got this.*

'Then I suggest you find out before you sign anything because you might find you just sold yourself, your writer and the book of a lifetime to a man who a few people are saying is on the downhill slide.'

'What people? What are they saying?' Zoe tried to keep her voice calm, as the cars went whizzing by her. Everyone was going in the right direction and here was Rachel telling her she wasn't and if anyone knew what the state of affairs were with Jeff, Rachel knew.

'Zoe, not everyone can stay on top for ever, not even Jeff Beerman. I've just heard a few money men saying Jeff needs a hit and soon. I'm just warning you. Anyway, you've given me a few leads over the years; I'm giving you one now.'

The line went dead and Zoe sat in the car staring at the road ahead.

This isn't how it's meant to play out, she thought, dialling Jeff's number, knowing he would be in his office. People may question his morals but they could never question his work ethic.

'Jeff Beerman's office,' an assistant answered.

'Zoe Greene for Jeff,' she said, tapping on the steering wheel with her fingernail.

'Greene, how's the head this morning?' he asked, his voice filled with cheer.

'Listen to me, I have to ask: are you in financial trouble? Because if you are, obviously I have to go elsewhere with this project.'

'Good morning to you too, Greene,' he said calmly.

'Well?' she demanded.

'Say good morning and I'll answer you,' he said calmly. 'Manners are free, remember?'

Zoe shook her head in frustration and gritted her teeth. The man was the worst game player she had ever met.

'Okay, okay. Good morning, Jeff. Now, stop fucking me about. Are you in financial trouble?'

'Me? Personally? Not at all.'

'What about the studio?' She asked. It was always best to be straight up with people, she had realized over the years, even if they found it confrontational.

Jeff took a moment to answer, and during those seconds Zoe felt herself fly backwards in time and space and she was outside, hearing the chickens roosting for the night, cold, alone and hungry. The emotional memory of her body always betrayed her, she thought, as she tried to remain present.

'Greene?' Jeff's voice jerked her out of the chicken coop and back onto the side of the highway. 'Did you hear what I said?'

Zoe blinked and breathed away the anxiety in her chest.

'No, I didn't, can you repeat it please?' she asked, trying to keep the edge out of her voice.

'I said, there isn't a problem, as long as we keep costs down,' he said. 'Why don't you come in now and we can go through them together? I have your contracts here too.'

'Really? That was quick, even for you,' she said, thinking aloud.

'I know a good thing when it's offered to me,' said Jeff, sounding as though he didn't have a care in the world. 'I had my lawyers draw them up last night.'

They must have loved that, thought Zoe. The night of the Oscars and they had to work? By all accounts, Jeff was a punishing man to work for, exacting and relentless, but there was no doubt he was brilliant and to learn from him was a once-in-a-lifetime chance.

And she didn't know if one of the larger studios would

give her a producer title if she asked. Time was running out. If they didn't move now, then the momentum of the book would be lost.

'I'm on my way,' she said.

Before she pulled out into the morning traffic again and headed back to Hollywood, Zoe dialled another number.

'Zo.' Maggie's voice was groggy. 'What's up?'

'I need your help,' said Zoe as she did a U-turn. 'But it's a secret so you have to promise me you won't tell anyone.'

There was a silence on the end of the phone and then Maggie's voice came through clearer this time.

'When have I *ever* let a secret of yours out into the world?'

Maggie's voice was terse, but this deal meant everything to Zoe at this moment. She needed someone she could trust and who was nearby in Malibu.

'I know, but listen this is a big one,' she said.

'Has it got something to do with casting *The Art of Love*?' said Maggie.

Zoe gasped. 'How the hell did you know that?'

'Will told me,' Maggie answered crossly.

Damn you, Will, thought Zoe. He used any chance he got to needle his ex-wife, even privileged information like the initial casting discussions for *The Art of Love*.

'He really shouldn't have done that.'

'It was actually Arden Walker who spilled first. She claims she'll be playing Simone opposite Will,' Maggie said in a tight voice.

'What? She isn't Simone. The movie hasn't been cast yet. Hell, we don't even have a studio on board!' said Zoe, exasperated.

'But the unofficial casting has begun?' Maggie demanded.

Zoe made a face at the road ahead. The book was her baby and she wanted to bring it to life, the last thing she needed was Maggie and Arden fighting over a role, and causing drama.

'No. I only asked Will because Hugh mentioned he liked him as an actor, but nothing more than that. Arden's kidding herself if she thinks she's right for this role.'

'Arden thinks she's right for every role,' said Maggie wryly and Zoe laughed.

'This isn't funny, Zoe. I'm really hurt you didn't tell me. You hadn't even heard of that book before *I* gave it to you!'

Zoe sighed. 'I didn't tell anyone, I promise. It wasn't personal, it was business.'

'But you told Will,' Maggie argued.

'Yes, I admit that, but I had to see if he was interested before I went to the studios, so I could take a big name with me. I was going to talk to you about it, but I had to do the deal first,' Zoe tried to defend herself.

'I'm a big name,' said Maggie, her voice sounding small. 'You could have taken me.'

Zoe could have used Maggie as bait for the studios, but Will was an even bigger star at the box office, and she knew Maggie was too old to play Simone even if Maggie didn't realize it yet.

They needed someone new, younger and without any expectations from the public. Someone audiences could easily fall in love with and identify as Simone. They needed to create a star.

'Mags, I know you hate me right now, but I need your help, I'm going to tell you something no one knows, not my assistant, not even Jeff. Can you help me or not?'

Maggie was silent while she weighed it up. She loved to

be included in anything, a legacy of having so often been left out and overlooked as a child, she would regularly remind Zoe.

'Okay, I guess I'll help,' she said eventually. 'But believe me, I'm still pissed at you.'

'I know, hate me later, but help me now. I promise I'll make it up to you,' Zoe pleaded.

'Go on then.'

'Okay, so the thing is, Hugh Cavell is in LA,' said Zoe. 'He's been here for about six months.' Zoe paused. 'He's, ah…he's been drying out.'

Maggie didn't say anything, so Zoe continued.

'He just did four months in Promises and he's trying to stay on track. But he's pretty self-destructive, Mags. I don't like to leave him alone for long periods of time.'

'Jesus,' breathed Maggie, 'that's awful. I had no idea he was such a mess.'

'If your wife died of brain cancer and you became a millionaire from the story of your grief, wouldn't you feel kind of bad?'

'I guess,' said Maggie quietly.

'You guess?' Zoe started to laugh and Maggie joined in.

'I don't know, I suppose so,' said Maggie. 'What do you need me to do? Author-sit for you? Just so you know, I'm expensive.'

'I do know, I write your contracts, remember?'

Zoe had checked in on Hugh every day via phone or email, and usually Hugh was fine, but he had sounded odd yesterday when she'd called. She didn't want him to fall off the wagon when they were so close to what she wanted.

'Where is he and what does he need?' Maggie sighed.

Zoe gave Maggie the address in Malibu. 'But don't talk to him about the book,' she warned.

'What? How can I not? You know I love that book,' cried Maggie.

'I know, but he doesn't.'

Hugh would roll his eyes whenever the book was mentioned. He said he felt uncomfortable about the hype around his wife's death, that his readers were the ravens on the carcass of his marriage. He said he wished he had never written the book but then he took the film deal, which Zoe never quite understood. She had tried to understand it at first, but eventually she gave up trying to prise open Hugh's armour.

She saw it was a façade of self-protection covering enormous grief. She understood grief, she had wanted to tell him, but she didn't. She never told anyone about her own loss. Managing other people's lives had suited her to a point, that way she didn't have to focus on her own life, until now. It was now or never with the film and if it worked, then she really would be able to say she had made something of herself in Hollywood.

Maggie's voice broke through her thoughts. 'Okay, so what do I do? Sit and read him stories until you return?'

'Whatever it takes, babe,' said Zoe as she drove through Hollywood.

It was a rare grey day in LA and everything looked tired, even the palm trees, or was she just her projecting her own sudden weariness.

'You know I want to play Simone,' Maggie said.

Zoe paused. 'I understand that. But you should know that Hugh has final casting approval, along with Jeff,' she said carefully.

'But you can help me make it happen, right? I want this, even if I have to play opposite Will,' said Maggie firmly.

'I'll call you when I've finished with Jeff and see how things are going with Hugh,' said Zoe, avoiding the topic.

One problem at a time, she thought, as she pulled up in front of Palladium Pictures. First Jeff, then Hugh and then Maggie.

She could handle it all, she thought as she locked her car. She had been solving other people's problems for years, why couldn't she handle a few of her own?

Chapter 5

Maggie hung up from Zoe and rolled over in her king-sized bed, groaning. It was too early to be up, she thought crossly, especially the day after the Oscars.

Her feet ached and so did her head, but her best friend had just asked her for help and Maggie had never let Zoe down.

She got up and padded to the window, opening the blinds to look out over the beach. A grey sky, to match her grey mood, she thought as went into the bathroom and stood under the fifteen jets of water in her polished stone shower.

Maggie's modernist home had been showcased in *Architectural Digest* and was revered for its classic beauty and clean lines. These were also qualities Maggie was known for, and when she'd commissioned the house, they were what she had specified in the brief.

She bought everything that was expected of a woman of her taste and money. She had the right artists, the right clothes, she was on *Vanity Fair*'s best-dressed list six years in a row, and when she'd married Will her wedding dress had been considered a classic, along with the lace modesty of Grace Kelly's gown and Carolyn Bessette-Kennedy's A-line shift.

She did whatever it took to rid herself of the stains from her past, wrapping herself in a bright, white, perfect world. She never missed a hair appointment or a session with her trainer, and her nails were always done. She was impeccable on the outside, but always felt she could improve on the inside, if only she knew what her heart and mind truly wanted.

A lifetime of being valued for her looks above all else ate away at her, particularly now she was getting older. She found herself wondering what more she had to offer.

And right now she was faced with the pressure of what to wear to meet the man who had shown her what true love really was. Just about everything she had learned about love was from movies, but Hugh Cavell's book had taught her more than any script.

Meeting the author of the book that had changed her life and helped her leave her marriage was something she had wished for. Though she hadn't factored in that the author was a drunk and didn't want to discuss his own marriage, let alone Maggie's failed union.

It wasn't warm outside, she gathered from the empty beach and the choppy waves. A lone, scrappy-looking dog ran along the water's edge, as though waiting for its ship to come. Hell, who wasn't waiting for something somewhere? she thought as she pulled together an outfit. Stella McCartney white jeans, a white silk tank top, an oversized pale-pink Rag & Bone light cashmere knit that hung off one shoulder, and white ballet flats by Chloé, she decided. Elegant and refined, but relaxed. Without false modesty, she knew she looked good in white, and perhaps it would help to lift her grey mood.

Choosing outfits was Maggie's second favourite thing to do. Her first was doing her own make-up.

After years of sitting in the make-up chair being worked on by professionals, Maggie could do her make-up almost as well as the best in the business. Working through her beauty routine, she carefully applied her products. When she was finished, she spritzed herself with Eau des Merveilles by Hermès, picked up her bag and a bottle of water, and headed out to her Mercedes SUV.

The address Zoe had given her was nearby, but Maggie would never dream of walking anywhere, unless it was on the beach and even then it was under duress.

Some people loved the beach, but Maggie had chosen to live in Malibu because it was expensive and elegant. She also liked the village feel of the shops there and the comparative lack of tourists. Privacy was something she valued above all else.

Growing up in the homes of strangers will do that to you.

A short drive later she found herself at a large nondescript house, with a white wall and green security gate. She pressed the button, and waited, but no one answered.

She tried again. Still no answer. When she tried the handle, the gate swung open.

He was certainly no native, she thought as she closed the gate behind her. No one in Los Angeles left a gate—or anything else, for that matter—open.

She knocked on the front door and a male voice with a British accent called out, 'It's open, Zoe.'

'It's not Zoe,' she said as she walked down the hallway and into a large open living space.

Standing unsteadily near the big windows overlooking the water was the author she had been so desperate to meet. He was wearing grey boxers and nothing else and was holding what looked to be a whiskey bottle. He was thin, too thin, she thought, which was saying something in Los Angeles. He had the pallor of a man who spent too long indoors, with the curtains closed, wallowing in his own grief and swill.

'You're drunk,' she stated aloud, the words sounding more accusatory than she'd intended. 'I thought you would be more together than this.'

'And you're Maggie Hall,' he answered, peering at her. 'You look older than I thought you would.'

Maggie flinched and felt her jaw drop open. 'And you look more pathetic than Zoe said you would,' she snapped.

'I'm a sad widower, didn't you hear?' he countered, dropping on to an oversized sofa and placing the bottle on the glass table in front of him.

She picked up the bottle and went into the open-plan kitchen, pouring the whiskey down the sink.

'Hey, that's mine,' he said in his cut-glass accent, which reminded her of a television detective one of her foster mothers had loved.

'Not any more,' said Maggie. She handed him the bottle of water she had brought with her. 'Drink this,' she said impatiently.

'It stinks in here,' she said, turning up her nose. 'Open a goddammed window, you're not a teenager.'

She moved to the glass doors and opened them up, letting in the fresh sea air.

'You seem upset with me, Maggie Hall,' he said, looking at her sadly.

She saw his face was covered in grey stubble that matched the day. 'I don't know you, so how can I be upset with you?' she said, crossing her arms.

'You don't like people who drink, do you?'

There were grey hairs in his chest hair and his skin had the tired look of someone who didn't eat properly or do any exercise. He wasn't fat, he was just, well, she tried to think of the word. Unremarkable, that was it. What a let-down Hugh Cavell was turning out to be, she thought, not hiding her disapproval.

'I don't have an opinion about your drinking,' she lied.

She sat, crossed her legs and smoothed out the white fabric of her pants.

'You look like a wedding cake,' he said. 'All white, pink and hopeful.'

'An *old* wedding cake, remember?'

Then Hugh laughed. It was clear as a bell and Maggie felt the hairs on her arms stand up in response.

'Shall we start again?' he asked, seeming less drunk now, or was she just getting used to it?

'I'm Hugh Cavell: author, alcoholic, widower and general emotional recluse.'

Maggie stared at him unsmiling. 'Maggie Hall: actor, divorcee, and part-time babysitter for alcoholic novelists.'

Hugh laughed again and this time her body tingled a little as their eyes met.

'Where's Zoe?' he asked, squinting at her. 'And why did she send you?'

'Because she said you weren't to be trusted on your own, and it seems she was right.'

Hugh stood up and swayed a little. 'She's a smart one that Zoe Greene.'

'She certainly is. Why don't you go take a shower and then we'll get something to eat. You need some food,' she said sternly.

Hugh looked her up and down and nodded.

'So do you,' he said as he wandered off.

Maggie stayed where she was until she heard the sound of running water coming from a distant room and then she started snooping.

On the glass table sat a laptop, a copy of *Scriptwriting for Dummies*, a selection of notebooks and pens and a pile of magazines and mail, still in plastic wrappers, forwarded from an address in London.

Besides these few personal items, the room was actually very neat.

Moving into the kitchen, she checked the fridge and the cupboards. There was no food in either, but the rubbish bin was overflowing with takeaway food containers, cigarette packets and crumpled, handwritten letters.

She pulled out one of the letters with the fewest questionable stains and smoothed it out on the kitchen bench.

Dear Hugh,

Thank you for writing your book about your wife Simone's battle with brain cancer. You had a beautiful marriage and I know she will always be in your heart. A love like that never dies.

My own husband died four years ago in a car accident. I will never get over him, just as you will never replace Simone.

I hope you remember all the love and the happiness

*and know that one day you will be together again in
the house of God.
Sincerely,
Jenny Wallins*

Maggie grimaced as she turned the letter over and saw
the sign of the cross in one corner.

'Reading my fan mail, are you?' she heard and looked up
to see Hugh in a towel, his hair wet, and wearing a freshly
shaven scowl.

Maggie shrugged. 'It's better than some of the fan mail I
get. The last time I dared to look, I was offered the chance
to be impregnated, raped or murdered, I can't remember
which. Maybe all three.'

Hugh walked over and looked at the letter.

'Ah yes, Mrs Wallins of Miseryville,' he said and then
scrunched it up again and threw it back in the bin.

'Why be so mean?' Maggie asked. 'And why read the fan
mail and not your other letters?'

'None of your business,' he said and then walked out
of the room. Maggie pulled out her phone and texted Zoe.

I hate it when I meet someone I've admired and then find
out they're an egotistical idiot.

Within minutes Zoe texted back.

Ha. Now you know how your fans feel after they've met
you. PS: I'm really grateful, is he okay?

Maggie looked at the overflowing bin and sighed.

Fine. He's just a bit of a disappointment. I thought he would be nicer. TTYL

Zoe's text came flying back.

WDYM? He's TOO nice, that's his problem.

Maggie heard Hugh's footsteps and slipped her phone into her pocket.

'I'm somewhat more sober and now desperate for a fry-up,' he said as he walked into the room, in jeans, sneakers and a surprisingly nice white shirt.

It was the sort of shirt that a woman would buy a man, well cut, in beautiful cotton that would only look better with age.

Had Simone bought him that shirt? Maggie found herself wondering as she followed him out of the house. She almost felt like she knew the woman as a sort of friend, except she was dead and everything Maggie knew about her she had learned from a book.

'You'll have to drive because I can't get the hang of driving on the other side of the road here,' he said, as he stood next to her car.

'And because you shouldn't drive drunk,' said Maggie as she opened the car.

'Just for the record, I would never drink and drive,' Hugh said. 'I may want to kill myself, but I have no plans to kill anyone else.'

'That's good to know,' she said sarcastically. 'I'm sure your legion of fans will be thrilled to know their lives are safe.'

Hugh was staring out the window and the car filled with an uncomfortable silence.

How could the man who wrote the most beautiful book in the world be such an angry, ungrateful person? Where was the man who nursed his beloved wife for two years until she died in his arms?

Maggie had thought Hugh Cavell was perfect and now the realization that he was broken and bitter felt like a punch to the stomach.

Hugh cleared his throat and then he spoke. 'I read my fan mail, all of it, and most of it's very nice, very thoughtful. But I don't keep it, like I didn't keep the condolence notes after Simone died, they're not something you want to read over and over again.'

Maggie stayed silent, feeling like he hadn't finished.

'But it's more than that. I'm waiting for someone to recognize the truth about what I wrote, to see what lies beneath the words, but no one does, everyone takes it at face value and you, Maggie Hall, know more than anyone that it's dangerous to think anything is perfect, especially people.'

She drove, grasping the steering wheel tightly. She did know what he was referring to; she had lived it every single day.

Maybe he wasn't so terrible after all, she thought, and she glanced at him smiling, only to see he had fallen asleep, with his mouth wide open like he was a small child.

Chapter 6

Elliot was still lying in bed when he heard his father calling his name from upstairs.

'Maggie's here to see you,' his father yelled and Elliot groaned.

The last thing he felt like was a lecture from Maggie about his lifestyle.

Maggie had a way of getting to the heart of the matter. Elliot almost smiled at his own pun, but decided that would take too much effort.

'Get up, you lazy ol' porch dog,' said Maggie in the thick southern accent that always made Elliot laugh.

'Go away,' he said, burrowing deeper under the covers.

Light flooded in as Maggie flung open the blinds and pulled back the duvet.

'Jesus, Maggie,' Elliot said, sitting up abruptly and blinking at the day's brightness.

'Your scar looks intense,' she said. 'Very *Sons of Anarchy*.'

Elliot looked down at the angry red scar running down the centre of his chest.

'Did someone on *Sons of Anarchy* have a heart transplant? I must have missed that episode,' he said as he stalked into the bathroom and turned on the shower.

'I'll still be here when you get out, so be modest,' she called as he closed the door.

Maggie made the bed and opened a window to let out the smell of stale air. Why did men never open windows? She wondered, thinking of Hugh briefly.

Glancing down at the desk, she saw a photograph of an Indian man, surrounded by genuflecting people, all in pink and red robes. She turned it over and read a note from Elliot's mother, Linda.

Guru Sam says you're healed now, that he spoke to the Universe and it happened. BE grateful to him, we are fortunate to have him in our lives. Namaste Linda.

Maggie rolled her eyes at the note. It wasn't Guru Sam that saved Elliot's life, it was the donor and the doctors, she thought angrily.

Linda had been missing in action for ten years and now she thought she had the right to send Elliot a note telling him to be grateful?

If Maggie was still Elliot's stepmother, she would tell Will to intercept any communication at all from his first wife, but that wasn't her role any more.

She moved about the room, picking up dirty clothes. Clearly Elliot wasn't letting the housekeeper down here to do her job, she thought, as she made neat piles of the books he had been reading. She turned one over in her hand, *Scriptwriting for Dummies*, the same book as Hugh, she thought briefly and she put it on top of a book on writing your life story. Frowning, she checked the other books, all of them to do with writing of some sort.

Unopened letters from Berkeley sat on the table and Maggie resisted the urge to open them, as she heard the shower turn off.

Grabbing a film magazine from the bedside table, she sat on his made bed and leafed through it casually.

'Apparently your dad and I were the greatest couple since Liz and Dick,' she said, holding up the magazine for him to see the shot of her and Will attending the Oscars years before.

'Yeah, but they didn't have to listen to the fighting.' Elliot had pulled on what she hoped was a clean T-shirt and boxer shorts.

'True,' said Maggie with a wry smile and she reached down to her handbag. 'Here,' she said, and threw a disc at him.

'What is it?' he turned it over in his hand.

'The first cut of the next James Bond. Don't tell anyone, and don't share it,' she said firmly.

Elliot smiled. 'You don't always have to bring me presents when you see me, Maggie,' he said. 'You brought me so many thing when I was in hospital, I think you brought me thirty presents in all.'

'A present for every day I saw you,' she said, trying not to think of that month in Elliot's life where they didn't know whether his body would accept the new heart.

Elliot placed the disc down on the desk and she saw him glance at the neat piles of books.

'Come on then, give me the lecture about how some poor bastard died and gave me his precious heart and how I only have one life to live and that I'm wasting it. And I'll listen to you and nod, and change for twenty-four hours, and then we can all pretend the lecture worked.'

Maggie stared at him and then frowned. 'Damn you, no spoilers please. If you knew how this was going to play out, you should have saved me the trip over.'

Elliot shrugged. 'It's the same shit I hear from Dad every other day, Mags. Lather, rinse, repeat.'

Maggie said nothing, she just watched him until he held his hands up at her.

'What do you want me to say? I still feel like shit and I have no idea why I survived and some poor person died.'

'Have you told the doctors?' she asked.

'No, it's not the heart, the heart is fine, it's in here,' he said, tapping his head. 'I don't feel myself any more, but I don't want to anyway, you know? I didn't much like who I used to be. But I feel different and no one understands. I can't go back to college; it feels like a waste of time, even though Dad's freaking out.'

'How can it be a waste of time when all you do is stay down here every day wasting time?' she asked.

'I knew you wouldn't get it,' he said and he slumped in the desk chair.

Maggie nodded. 'I'm sorry, I do get it. I don't understand what having a new heart feels like, but I get the whole bit about trying to be something or go somewhere without directions or a destination.'

Elliot said nothing, just stared at the floor.

'Why don't you leave the house at least? Go and *do* stuff, whatever it is young people are doing these days.' Maggie smiled. 'I mean, I know this place is like living in the Hotel California, with everything you need at your fingertips, but you really need to get out of here. Go see your friends, get drunk, have sex.'

'Most of my old friends are away at college. And those that are here just want to party, and I can't party like that,' he said, looking down at his chest.

'So you're friendless, depressed and aimless,' she said. 'That sounds normal for Hollywood.'

Elliot tried to raise a smile, but couldn't. Just the idea of heading out into the world made him anxious.

He felt Maggie staring at him as he ran his fingers through his dark hair.

'Are you *sure* you don't want to be an actor? Zoe would rep you in a heartbeat.'

Elliot gave her a look.

'Okay, a poor choice of words, I admit, but you know you're good-looking enough.'

'Good looks don't translate into being a decent actor, Maggie, you know this,' he said wryly.

'Are you saying I'm an average actor because I'm so beautiful?' she asked, in mock horror.

'No, you know you're both, but how many kids my age want to be actors just because they're good-looking? It's insane. Half the girls in my final year at school were making sex tapes and the guys were taking steroids so they could all be famous and hot.'

'And this is why I weep for the future generation.' She sighed.

They were silent for a moment and then Elliot found himself saying out loud what he had only admitted to himself.

'I feel like I've been sick for so long, in and out of hospital and stuff, I don't even *know* how to live normally.' He shot her a look. 'I mean, I'm twenty-three and I'm still a freaking virgin, Maggie. I'm a joke!'

'Oh, El, you're so not. Having sex doesn't make you a grown-up, trust me.'

The room filled with an awkward silence and Maggie took a new tack.

'If you don't want to go to college, then what do you want to do?' She glanced at the books. 'Writing?'

Elliot laughed meanly. 'As if Dad will say yes to that. You know what a prick he can be.'

Maggie nodded. 'I was married to him, remember? But in a perfect world, if you could write, what would it be about?'

Elliot took his eyes off the floor and met hers. 'I'd like to write a book about what I've been through,' he said slowly. 'Is that self-indulgent?'

Maggie smiled. Her voice was gentle. 'Nothing about you is self-indulgent. You're amazing.'

Elliot laughed. 'No, I'm not, I just have a few ideas I wouldn't mind trying to put down. Except I don't really know how to start.'

Maggie leaned forward. 'I know an amazing writer,' she said. 'He's a bit of a mess right now, but I think you two need to meet.'

'Maybe,' said Elliot. 'I don't really want to share my sad story with strangers.'

'Isn't that what writing a book is, though?' asked Maggie with a smile.

'I guess,' said Elliot, looking down at his clasped hands. He was such a lovely kid, thought Maggie, wishing life had been different for him, and then she thought about herself at that age.

At twenty-three she was just coming up through the ranks

of Hollywood, and while she may not have had a heart transplant, she did have an emotional, geographical transplant.

'El, here's the thing,' she said slowly, formulating the tack to take to not put him offside.

'What happened to you is awful and the fact you have a dead person's heart in you is weird and unsettling,' she said.

Elliot looked up at her, surprised by her candour.

'But I think things happen for a reason. And while you can't change the past, you can change your future, because you have one now. Write your story and see what happens afterwards, get the thoughts out of your head so you can start to think clearly.'

Elliot was nodding profusely. 'Yes, that's it, my head is filled with thoughts, I need to get it all out. I will write, I don't care what Dad thinks, I have things to say.'

His eyes were wide and his voice passionate and Maggie bit her lip to stop herself from crying out in joy at finally seeing some excitement in him.

'And if you're writing a book, you'll need an assistant,' said Maggie, her eyes shining.

He laughed. 'What the hell for? Sharpening my pencils?'

'To help you write, research, do writer jobs,' she said emphatically. 'And maybe they could become your friend also.'

'Jesus, Maggie, I'm not that desperate. You can't *hire* me a friend, that's stupid.'

But Maggie wasn't listening.

'Baby, this is Hollywood, I can hire you anything you want. I'm going to set up a meeting with my writer contact and then I'm going to find you an assistant.'

Elliot shook his head. 'Dad won't let you do it. He's going to throw a fit if I don't go to college. It's his whole thing. *My son, who will be attending Berkeley.*'

Maggie scoffed. 'When has your dad ever been able to say no to me? Anyway, he understands the need for assistants better than anyone.'

'Assisting in what?' asked Elliot, putting up his hands in confusion.

'Life, kiddo.' She clapped her hands and stood up. 'Life.'

West Virginia
September 1995

Krista Calkins walked home the long way, through the back streets and the small wooded area where no one ever went after dark.

Some trouble only came out at night, but Krista had enough trouble during the daylight hours.

As she walked along the path, something glinted on the ground and she bent over to pick it up.

A penny, head side up. Everyone knew head side up was a good omen. Good luck was on its way, she thought happily, and put the penny in her pocket.

Back at the foster home, her foster family had stopped praying, and were now drinking. Her foster mother's show poodles were barking wildly from the large spare bedroom that was used as their area.

Sliding the screen door across as quietly as she could, Krista hid her purse down the front of her blue-wash jeans, stolen from JC Penney, and hurried to the tiny boxroom where she slept. Everything nice she owned was shoplifted; even the slippers she had given her God-fearing foster mother for Mother's Day had been stolen.

It made Krista happy to think her foster mother was wearing something stolen, when all she did was spout the Ten

Commandments at anyone unlucky enough to be passing her way.

Krista had a job babysitting for Preacher Garrett over at the Haven of Jesus Pentecostal Church. His wife paid her in crumpled five-dollar notes from the offering bowl and Preacher Garrett made up for it with ten-dollar notes for the hand jobs Krista gave him in the back of the church.

After she saw the double lines on Shay's pregnancy test, Krista knew she was right to convince the preacher that a hand job wasn't real sex and that she was happy to keep doing it as long as he kept handing over the greenbacks.

The poor man was so desperate for any touch he probably would have let one of the rattlesnakes he kept in a glass tank bite him on the penis just to relieve the tension, she thought.

Krista hid her purse under the floorboard she had prised loose last year. If her foster mother saw any money she would take it, telling Krista she had to pay Jesus for bringing her to such a loving Christian home.

So many times Krista bit back the retort that Jesus didn't get the money anyway seeing as how her foster mother spent it on cigarettes and whiskey, but she knew it wasn't worth her breath.

She was sixteen and in two years' time, she could leave and go to California, where she wanted to be Cinderella at Disneyland.

She was pretty enough, even she knew that. With the money she was saving she would have enough for a bus trip and to rent a costume for her audition.

But she couldn't leave Shay here in Butthole, West Virginia, as they called it, she would die a slow death, like every other woman in this place.

Krista lay on her small, lumpy bed and stared at the ceiling, calculating how much money she had in her hidden stash. Maybe she could pay for an abortion for Shay?

So far she had saved two hundred and eighty-three dollars, but even she knew that wasn't enough.

Closing her eyes, she thought about Shay and her predicament and then knew what she had to do.

She would tell the serpent-handling preacher she would sleep with him for two hundred dollars, and get Shay her abortion. Then the two of them would get the hell out of Butthole and move to California where everyone was rich, the sun was always shining and they would both live happily ever after.

Chapter 7

'I don't think I can last here much longer.' Dylan was Skyping Addie from a corner of the UCLA library. 'I'm down to my last packet of ramen noodles.'

Addie was lying on the bed in her dorm room at Columbia, a huge poster of movie star Will MacIntyre, looking moody in a dinner suit, behind her on the wall. The computer on her lap was reflecting blue light onto her face, making her look as though she was in a spaceship. 'Why? What's going on?'

'I lost my job with the catering company, I'm being evicted and I'm still no further forward on my research.'

'Where are you now?' Addie leaned forward as though trying to see over Dylan's shoulder.

'The UCLA library. It's peaceful here, and I can use their Wi-Fi,' said Dylan, holding up her mother's library pass, which was good for all universities across the country. 'I might end up moving in here if I don't get a break soon.'

'You could sell Maggie Hall's shoes on eBay,' Addie suggested.

'What? No way.' In truth, Dylan had already thought about it, and decided it would be a last resort.

'Well, you could ask your mom for some more money.'

Dylan shook her head. 'I can't ask my mother to fund what she sees as a betrayal. She hates that I'm here, she thinks I'm lowering my intelligence.'

'Hey, speaking of which, I got you a present,' Addie cried out. 'Wait a sec.'

Addie disappeared from camera and Dylan looked at the pile of books on the table from the previous occupants.

Three books on business management, one book about walnut tree growing and two novels. Picking up the first, she glanced at the back, something about a soldier, and another with an ornate painted heart, cracked down the middle.

Her mother would be appalled if she knew Dylan was entranced by the cover of a book, and she heard her voice in her head: *Never judge a book by its cover, Dylan, some of the best books in the world don't have pretty pictures on the front.* She turned it over and read the blurb anyway.

'I'm back,' said Addie and Dylan looked up at the screen.

Addie was wearing a T-shirt with black writing on the front.

Dylan leaned forward to read it.

'"Too stupid for New York, too ugly for LA,"' she said and then cracked up.

'And I got me one as well.' Addie peeled off the T-shirt to reveal another one underneath, and read out, '"Too smart for LA, too ugly for New York."'

Dylan started laughing so loudly that the other occupants of the library turned to glare at her.

'God, that's funny, can you send one to my mom?' she said, wiping her eyes and leaning on the book on the table.

She picked it up and held it up to the screen. 'Do you know this book?'

Addie nodded. 'Yeah, why?'

'I don't know, I just saw it here and I was wondering what it's like,' said Dylan, turning it over in her hands.

Addie leaned in close as though she was telling a secret. 'Don't tell anyone in my lit class but I loved that book. I bawled my eyes out at the end.'

'Why can't you tell your lit class?' asked Dylan. 'Surely they're not that snobbish?'

'Are you kidding? One critic said the book was *Marley & Me* but with a wife, not a dog,' said Addie. 'But he writes really well; it's worth reading. And your mom would hate it,' she added.

'Then I'm gonna read it,' said Dylan in a wicked voice and Addie giggled.

The sound of her phone ringing broke through the library's hush again. 'Hey, I've gotta go, this might be the catering company with an emergency reprieve.'

'Call me tomorrow,' said Addie before Dylan finished the session, and picked up her phone.

'Dylan Mercer speaking,' she said in her most professional tone.

'Dylan, it's Maggie Hall. Have you still got those shoes of mine?'

Dylan froze then looked around, waiting for Ashton Kutcher to come out and say, 'Punked.' Thank God she hadn't sold them, she thought.

'Yes, I do, would you like them back?'

Maggie laughed. 'No, sweetheart, but I was wondering if you were busy right now?'

'No, I'm at the library,' said Dylan.

'The library? Good for you,' said Maggie, sounding sort of pleased or proud of her, which was totally weird but Dylan wanted to hear more.

'Yeah, I've been working all morning,' she lied.

'Isn't that great? Now listen, Dylan, do you have an hour to meet with me? I'd like to discuss a job I think might be good for you.'

Dylan did a triumphant fist pump in the air and then realized she looked like a complete idiot.

'Yes, of course,' she said casually, but with a hint of deference.

'Great, meet me tomorrow at Culina at seven,' said Maggie and before Dylan could answer Maggie had hung up.

Dylan typed Culina into the search engine and saw it was a bar at the Four Seasons Hotel. Jesus, she thought, she had nothing to wear that was close to good enough for either the venue or Maggie Hall.

Perhaps she should call Addie back and get her to FedEx the T-shirt, she thought as she quickly packed up her things and left. But at the door she stopped, rushed back to the table to pick up the book and checked it out using her mom's library card.

The following evening, at exactly seven o'clock, Dylan was sitting at the bar in the simple black dress she had worn to graduation, paired with Maggie's shoes, when she felt the energy in the room grow charged.

Turning, she saw Maggie approaching the bar. She was wearing a white jumpsuit split to the naval and silver heels. With her blond hair slicked back showing off her cheekbones and silver dangly earrings showing off her long neck, she looked like she was off to Studio 54 to chill with Jerry Hall.

Maggie kissed Dylan on the cheek and nodded at the barman, who immediately walked them to a private booth.

'Dylan, how are you?' said Maggie as she slid into the booth.

Dylan felt the eyes of all the other bar patrons on them, and wondered if Maggie even noticed the attention any more.

'I'm fine, thank you.' She wiped her sweating hands on her dress.

Maggie smiled at her and Dylan tried to relax, clenching and unclenching her toes as her father had taught her, but all it did was make her feet hurt even more in Maggie's shoes.

'Is your thesis going well?'

Dylan frowned and then remembered her lie in the bathroom at the Oscars party.

'Well, it's mostly research at the moment, I haven't got onto the writing part yet,' she said.

'Ah, good, so you write as well?' Maggie leaned forward and Dylan saw the edge of some tape that was making sure the jumpsuit didn't gape open.

Dylan nodded. 'A little,' she said.

Maggie looked up at the waiter who had appeared at the table.

'A soda water with lime, thanks. Dylan?'

'Same, thanks,' said Dylan, trying to emulate Maggie's casual body language.

'Are you twenty-one yet?'

'Nearly nineteen,' said Dylan, hoping this wasn't a problem. 'I finished school last July and took some time off, before I came out here.'

Maggie nodded, but didn't seem especially interested in Dylan's past activities.

'Well, as I said, I have a job I need to talk to you about. It's not a long-term thing, it may be just for a few months, but I thought it could work with your college schedule.'

Dylan paused, wondering whether to spill the beans about college. Then she remembered the lone packet of noodles sitting in her soon-to-be-vacated apartment. She *needed* this job. Beside, she justified to herself, she *was* going to college next year...

'And if I were to get the job, what would I be assisting you with?' she asked politely, as though she was offered jobs by movies stars all the time.

'Ah, well, you see, you wouldn't actually be working for me,' Maggie said, and Dylan felt disappointment wrap around her like a shawl. If Maggie noticed, she didn't say. 'It's for a dear friend of mine, who wants to write a book,' she went on.

'Oh,' said Dylan. She didn't know how to write a book, and if she lied, she would be found out in a heartbeat.

'My friend has been sick, and he's kind of an introvert,' Maggie added.

Dylan watched Maggie as she spoke. Dylan had grown up watching that beautiful face on the screen. Maggie had starred in so many movies, mostly ones about love, and she was still adored. She was the woman every girl wanted to be best friends with, and the woman every man wanted to marry. Dylan didn't want to let her down, but she knew she had to tell the truth.

'I'm sorry, but I don't see how I can help your friend. I'm not a writer,' she said apologetically.

Maggie laughed. 'Oh no, Dylan, I don't want you to help him write it. I want you to help get him out of the house!'

Dylan frowned. 'I don't understand.'

Maggie paused. 'He had a heart transplant and it's kind of knocked him around. He was sick for a long time before the new heart and we all thought the heart would make him excited to live again, but he's depressed.'

'Why doesn't he try therapy?' Dylan asked, thinking of her father.

'He doesn't need therapy,' Maggie snapped. 'Taking about his feelings isn't going to help anything; he needs someone his own age to help him engage with life again. You know, to take him out to see friends, concerts, movies, go shopping, just to do stuff with him.'

She threw her hands up as she spoke, as though tossing confetti into the air.

Dylan was worried. 'I don't know if I can look after someone who's had a heart transplant.'

'You don't need to nurse him,' laughed Maggie, 'you need to show him fun things to do.'

'I don't know LA that well yet,' Dylan explained. 'I've only been here eight weeks and I have to find a new apartment and I have no idea where to even start looking.'

Disappointment flooded through her that this wasn't the opportunity she had hoped it would be. Everything about this person that Maggie wanted her to help sounded difficult. An introvert heart transplant patient who wanted to be a writer? Hell no.

'Did I mention it's a live-in position,' said Maggie, 'with full use of a car? The salary is a thousand dollars a week.' She paused for effect, then said, 'Cash.'

Dylan only just succeeded in not spitting her soda water across the table.

'Will you at least come and meet him?' asked Maggie, smiling radiantly. 'I can't say any more until you've signed a confidentiality agreement, but I really think you'll like him. He's gorgeous, *such* a sweet guy.'

Dylan did a backflip on her thinking. How hard could it be? He was probably some old guy who'd been in love with Maggie, and all she'd have to do was take him to concerts at the Hollywood Bowl and drive him around to medical appointments.

She remembered her mother's words: *You can do anything you put your mind to, Dylan.*

'Sure,' she said with a smile that she hoped covered her nerves, 'I'd love to meet him.'

After all, who could say no to Maggie Hall?

Chapter 8

Zoe woke in the middle of the night and sat bolt upright.

There were two things that caused her to wake up fretting at night. One was money—even though she had plenty, it never felt like she had quite enough.

The other was the fear that a stranger was in the house—even though she had a serious security system and nothing like that had ever happened the whole time she'd lived in LA.

But old habits die hard and she was sure she could hear the creak of footsteps in the hallway.

Turning on the bedside light she listened to the silence, trying to calm her racing heart and telling the panicked voices in her head she was safe in her own home. There was no leering foster brother with rough hands about to creep in to her room. Hand jobs had kept him at bay, but she'd always wondered how long that would last.

And still, after all these years, Zoe worried that she would never be safe again.

Just to be sure, she got out of bed and walked into her dressing room.

Her house was modest by Hollywood standards, but her dressing room, the size of a small bedsit, was a tribute to her success.

It was her sanctuary, custom built to her design.

There were shelves for all her bags, racks for her shoes, a centrepiece for her belts and accessories, and all climate controlled by the same people who did the system for the Museum of Contemporary Art.

All of Zoe's work clothes were elegant, in muted tones and blacks. She preferred to blend into the background at work events, leaving the colour to her clients. However, they were all the best quality: Calvin Klein tunics, Armani suits, Roland Mouret cocktail dresses and white shirts from James Perse.

Her off-duty clothes consisted of jeans, yoga pants and anything that was comfortable and soft. Cashmere cardigans and T-shirts worn till they were as soft as a baby's wrap. At work she was Zoe Greene, but at home she was herself with a love for beautiful things.

Sometimes, to calm herself, she would clean her leather handbags with a special cream. Other times she would check the soles on all her shoes to see which ones might need repairing. Zoe believed in repairing things. When you had worked so hard to get things, you had to look after them.

She did whatever it took to calm the thoughts and her racing heart.

But when she wasn't at home, and the fears took over her mind, the only place in the world that could calm her was a department store.

Walking through Barneys, she would feel the weight of her troubles slide off her shoulders.

Now Zoe sat on the padded chair in her dressing room and contemplated her success, but still she felt troubled.

The rumours that Jeff's studio was in financial trouble had to be true, she thought, and explained his demand that Zoe find a new star for the role of Simone. Clearly he didn't have the money to pay for an A-list actress.

Jeff had also demanded a lower cost director, maybe someone from Europe, he had said. During the meeting in Jeff's plush office, staring at the Kandinsky on his wall, Zoe had wondered if it was too late to get out of the deal. But she had signed the papers and was an official executive producer on *The Art of Love*.

She picked up a pair of Sergio Rossi boots and ran her hand over the smooth, handcrafted leather but she didn't feel the calm that usually came when she spent time with her possessions. An unfamiliar restlessness surged through her and she wondered what Jeff was doing. Probably taking some young actress to bed with promises of stardom.

Tonight her wardrobe couldn't fix what she needed, she thought. The only remedy was Barneys and a serious shopping spree.

The next morning she nursed a coffee and ninety-nine problems, as she entered Barneys.

The store felt like retail valium, she thought, as she took in the marble, silver and soft music.

Sleep had finally arrived at her house at four a.m. and now at eleven in the morning, she was feeling slightly hungover when she heard her name.

Turning, she saw Stella Valancia coming towards her in a cloud of leopard print and musk scent.

'Stella, how are you?' she asked politely.

'I am fine,' said Stella, over-pronouncing the 'fine', so it sounded like the word was never going to end.

She really was gorgeous, thought Zoe, it was just a shame she couldn't act. But with a spectacular body and more ambition than talent, Stella hadn't looked back since moving to Los Angeles.

Will had asked Zoe to manage Stella, but she had refused on the grounds she didn't have any more room in her talent stable.

'I want to audition for *The Art of Love*,' Stella said abruptly.

Zoe felt her jaw drop. She could not be serious, could she?

Simone and Stella were as similar as Meryl Streep and Marilyn Monroe. Zoe was familiar enough with Stella's work to know she couldn't possibly bring the gravitas to the role of Simone that was required.

Zoe paused, trying to find the right words. 'I will put your name forward to Jeff and the author, Stella, but they have ultimate sign-off on auditions. I'm sure you understand this is going to be a highly sought-after role.'

Stella shrugged. 'Of course, but I want to try.' She paused. 'I also think, if I do the role, she shouldn't die in the end.'

Zoe wondered for a moment if she was dreaming.

'But she does die in the end?' she said slowly, making sure Stella understood. 'Simone did actually die, in real life.'

Stella shrugged. 'Yes, but it would be nicer for ze audience if she didn't die, no?'

'Okay,' said Zoe, shaking her head, now wishing she were at home in her wardrobe again.

Stella picked up the Marni shoe on the stand next to Zoe. 'Why does Maggie come to Will's house so often?' she asked.

'I don't know, why don't you ask her?' Zoe said, looking Stella in the eye.

'Is she still in love with him?'

Was she ever in love with Will? Zoe wanted to say. Perhaps for a time Maggie had convinced herself that she was, but Elliot was the reason she had stayed in the marriage, Zoe knew, and why she couldn't keep away now.

'Maggie's just very close to Elliot, that's all,' Zoe said, trying to edge away from Stella.

Stella rolled her eyes and Zoe felt dislike welling in her.

'I don't understand why he is still at home. When I was twenty, I was already out in the world trying to become an actress,' Stella said.

'He's been sick for the past ten years. For God's sake, the kid's just had a heart transplant,' Zoe snapped, and then she shook her head, desperate to get away from Stella the Insensitive.

'Have a good day, Stella,' she said and quickly walked away.

What a cold-hearted bitch, Zoe thought furiously. She had no empathy for Elliot at all. There was no way she would be presenting her name as a potential Simone, she decided, as she headed out of the store.

The self-obsession of actors like Stella made her angry, arrogant men like Jeff made her angry, the self-destruction of talents like Hugh Cavell made her angry, the unfairness of kids like Elliot nearly dying made her angry.

Picking up her phone, she dialled the only person who would understand.

'Mags, I hate everyone today,' she said as soon as Maggie answered.

'Oh, babe, I hate everyone most days,' Maggie answered with a laugh. 'Where the hell have you been? I've been trying to call for the last two days. That Hugh is one messed-up writer and that's saying something in this town.'

'I know,' said Zoe. 'Was he drinking?'

Maggie paused. 'No.'

'Thanks, Mags. I am so grateful you could help out,' said Zoe as she got into her car. 'What are you doing now?'

'I'm on my way to see Elliot and Will,' Maggie said.

'Oh, I just saw Stella. She thinks you're still in love with Will.'

Maggie started laughing. 'She's an idiot,' she said. 'Besides her body, I don't know what Will sees in her.'

Zoe debated whether to tell Maggie about Stella hoping to audition for the role of Simone, but something told her to stay quiet.

Zoe's call waiting sounded and Jeff's name flashed on her screen. 'Mags, I've gotta go. I have Satan on the other line.'

'Say hi to Jeff from me,' Maggie laughed as she finished the call.

'Hi, Jeff,' Zoe said as she pulled into the driveway of her home. Banana palms and white bougainvillea screened the low, mid-century house, giving Zoe privacy and also the sense she was in the wild from the inside of the house. It certainly wasn't anything Jeff would like, she thought as she stopped the car.

'What the fuck is going on, Greene? I just had Stella Valancia's manager on the phone, saying you offered her the role of Simone. I thought you had better taste than that. Tits and teeth ain't gonna cut it for this role.'

At least we agree on something, she thought.

Three days ago she had signed the papers in his office, and since then he had rung her at every given opportunity to throw names at her, names that she knew were too expensive and to ask her how her hunt was going.

She still had a business to run, she wanted to remind him, but part of her wanted him to think she could do it all, and then some.

But God, he was a demanding asshole. Zoe gently banged her forehead on the steering wheel a few times. Was it worth it? she wondered, as Jeff's voice lectured her.

'She's trash and why the hell she's with Will MacIntyre I don't know, not when he had Maggie Hall in his bed. I've a mind to call him and tell him he doesn't know a decent woman when he has one.'

Zoe secretly agreed but she felt bad for Stella, despite her misgivings about her earlier.

'Can you not talk about Stella or any other woman like that, please?'

'Oh, Christ, don't tell me I've just hired a lesbian feminist!'

'It's none of your business what I am,' said Zoe calmly. 'Just don't speak of women like that to me. You've got a daughter, haven't you? I'm sure you wouldn't like it if you heard someone talking about her like that.'

There was a silence.

'Just tell Stella she's not right for the role,' Jeff barked, and slammed down the phone.

Zoe sat in the car, her head still on the steering wheel,

and wondered why the hell she'd ever thought working with Jeff Beerman was a good idea.

She wanted to be powerful, but would that mean she had to turn into a tyrant like him?

Chapter 9

'He doesn't need a bloody assistant!'

Will was yelling at Maggie, who sat at the far end of the enormous seventeenth-century oak dining table, bought when they were still married.

'You said I could do whatever it takes to get him out of the house, so this is what it's gonna take, Will,' she yelled back.

'I am not paying her wage,' he said firmly.

'I will,' she stated.

'And she can't live here,' he said.

'She needs to live here in case Elliot has writer tasks that need to be done,' she said vaguely, unsure what they were exactly and hoping to God Will didn't ask her to elaborate.

They stared at each other at a stalemate, just like when they were married.

Maggie tried a different tack. 'He wants to write a book, he needs help and he needs a friend, what's the harm in that?'

'He needs to go back to college.'

Maggie bit her lip and then spoke calmly.

'He hates college,' she said.

'Too bad,' Will snapped.

Maggie stood up. 'Will, you nearly lost him once; don't make him leave you this time. You may not get him back again.'

Will looked up at her. 'Do you really think this is the right thing to do?'

Maggie nodded. 'He wants to meet Dylan, the person I think is right for the role, and how can that be a bad thing? I mean, at least he wants to do something. It's all part of the process, isn't it? Trying stuff?'

Will sat in silence. Maggie glanced around the large airy dining room. This was where she and Will had planned to entertain their friends when they first bought the house. But their busy schedules hadn't made it easy to create those Martha Stewart at-home moments Maggie had dreamed of when she was younger and living in a boxroom with another hypocritical foster family.

He frowned at her, but his tone was softer now. 'You do know you're nuts, don't you?'

'I know. Completely.'

Their eyes met for a moment and then Maggie looked away. She could read the pain on Will's face and the guilt of leaving him was still too much to carry.

The sound of a knock broke the moment and Elliot stood in the doorway, clasping and unclasping his hands.

Maggie smiled at him. His hair was still damp from the shower and despite the swelling in his face from the anti-rejection drugs, he looked like any other young guy about to go to a job interview in his navy blue linen shirt over pressed chinos and decent sneakers.

'You ready?' he asked.

'Yes, I'm ready.' She walked over to Will's chair and hugged him. 'Just because you hate me, don't take it out on El,' she whispered in his ear.

'I don't hate you, Maggie,' Will said in a low voice and he looked up at her, 'not even a bit.'

'Where are we going?' asked Elliot, as she pulled out of the driveway and drove past the manicured lawns and the perfect houses of the rich and famous.

Maggie had hated living in Beverly Hills when she was married to Will. All the bullshit homes and the lack of community made her feel isolated. Everything was always the same, without any personality. At least when she looked out at her view each morning, it changed with the tides.

'I'm taking you to meet Hugh Cavell,' Maggie said, as she turned off onto the Pacific Highway and passed a sign reading Malibu.

'Who? I thought I was meeting the assistant today,' Elliot looked unimpressed by the name.

Maggie rolled her eyes. 'You will, but first you need to meet Hugh. He's only the best author I ever read. He wrote an amazing book about his wife and her death, you must have heard of it? It's called *The Art of Love*.'

Elliot shrugged and shook his head and Maggie sighed.

Elliot fiddled with the car stereo, flicking through stations until Maggie snapped, 'Just choose something, for Christ's sake.'

Elliot laughed and sat back in the seat as the sounds of an English rapper came through the speakers.

They drove in comfortable silence, the music adding to the backdrop of the beauty of the coast. This would make a great scene in a film, thought Maggie. She often thought like that, seeing scenes and directing in her head. It was a shame the other actors in her life didn't follow her internal script, though, she thought with an inner laugh.

'What did you say to this dude about me?' Elliot asked.

Maggie tapped the steering wheel in time to the music. 'I didn't say too much,' she said carefully as the Pacific Ocean came into view.

The water was calm and glittered invitingly. Maggie never tired of the view of the ocean, as the seagulls flew over them and down towards the water.

Elliot lowered his window and put his head outside, like a dog sniffing the possibilities of the day.

Maggie glanced at him and she smiled. Then she turned up the music and drove a little slower. Some days were worth slowing down for, she thought, as Elliot turned to her, his face flushed from the wind.

'It's good to be out,' he cried over the music.

Maggie beamed back at him, relieved. Stage one of her plan was working out, she thought as she turned into Hugh's street.

Pulling up, she turned to Elliot. 'Now, don't freak out if he seems a bit angry.'

'Why would he be angry?' Elliot looked concerned.

Maggie looked at the closed gate. 'He doesn't actually know we're coming,' she admitted.

'*What?* Jesus, Maggie, you can't just turn up and say, "Hello, this is my ex-stepson, can you teach him how to write a book?" Does he even know you?'

'He knows me,' she said firmly. 'And he owes me a favour. Now come on, get out of the car.'

Maggie pressed the intercom, feeling nervous. People

didn't usually say no to her, but then Hugh Cavell wasn't most people, she thought, remembering their brunch.

Hugh had swung wildly between charming, morose and fascinating and never once did he hit on her. Instead, he regaled her with stories about his childhood, his family. He never mentioned Simone.

She had glossed over her own life, like she did in all her interviews. No one knew the truth about where she had come from, only Zoe.

She had the patter down straight: grew up in the south, raised by an aunt, parents died in a car accident, and met Zoe at church, which was the only true part of the story.

'Hugh, it's Maggie Hall.' She announced herself as though she was expected. 'I'm here as we discussed.'

There was a pause. 'Oh, hi.' The voice was uncertain. Perfect, she thought.

The gate clicked and she pushed it open.

'Let's go,' she said and Elliot followed her down the path to the house.

Hugh was waiting at the door, in jeans, a T-shirt and bare feet.

'This is a surprise,' he said, titling his head to the side.

'Not really, we discussed it when we had brunch,' she said with a smile and breezed past him into the house.

'I hate the word brunch,' he muttered as he turned to Elliot. 'Why can't people in LA just choose a meal? It's either breakfast or lunch, it's ridiculous.'

'This is my stepson, Elliot,' she said, ignoring Hugh's mutterings. 'He's here for his writing lesson.'

'Writing lesson?' Hugh baulked. 'I didn't say I'd give him a writing lesson.'

'Maggie,' Elliot implored, but she ignored him and walked back to Hugh.

'When I arrived last week, before we went to breakfast, you agreed to meet Elliot and help him with his story.' She looked into Hugh's faintly bloodshot eyes.

'Did I?' Hugh looked confused. 'Ah, can I speak to you for minute, please? Alone?'

'You wait inside,' she said to an uncomfortable-looking Elliot.

Maggie followed Hugh outside.

'I don't know what the hell I promised, but I say a lot of crap when I'm pissed and most of it should be ignored.'

She shrugged. 'That's not my problem. All I know is, you promised me, and I'm taking you up on the offer.'

Hugh shook his head. 'You don't understand. I never give writing advice. Anyway, I'm sure I can't help your stepson. I wrote a memoir. He probably wants to write a sci-fi porno with Megan Fox as the lead.'

'He wants to write a memoir too,' Maggie said.

Hugh laughed. 'On what? My life as an entitled Hollywood teenager?'

Maggie felt rage welling up.

'No, actually. He wants to write about how he lost half his life to heart disease and nearly died. How he had a heart transplant last year and how he's trying to learn to live again with someone else's heart beating in his chest.'

Hugh stood still and Maggie wished she felt some sort of victory at his silence. Instead, she felt her eyes smarting with unshed tears. Why did she feel like she was the only one who ever gave a crap about Elliot?

Probably because she was, she thought as she crossed her arms and lifted her chin in defiance at Hugh. He was fast becoming a major disappointment to her, just like every other man she had met in LA.

He put his hand on her shoulder and his touch was vaguely comforting, even though he was the reason for her aggravation.

'I'm sorry. But I honestly don't think I can help him,' he said softly. 'I can barely help myself.'

Maggie leaned forward so their faces were almost touching.

'If I tell Zoe you've been drinking,' she hissed, 'then she will have to tell the insurance company, and they won't sign you off to work on the film in any capacity. *Capisce?*'

'*Capisce?*' Hugh laughed. 'Who do you think you are? Don Corleone?'

But Maggie stood her ground.

Hugh's eyes widened and he turned and walked back inside the house to where Elliot was standing, his hands awkwardly by his sides.

Hugh stuck out his hand. 'Elliot, I'm Hugh Cavell; it's good to meet you. Let's sit down and have a chat.'

'I'm going shopping, El. I'll be back in an hour, just text me if you need longer,' Maggie called out as she closed the front door behind her.

But Maggie didn't feel like shopping, she needed time to think.

Heading out onto the road, she drove to the nearest lookout and stopped the car. Opening her door, she put her seat back and put her feet on the dashboard, and thought about Elliot.

She may not be his actual mother but she would do anything for him, even if that meant crossing Will.

Everyone needed someone in their corner and for a brief

moment, she thought about Hugh. Who did he have in his corner? she wondered. Why had Zoe been the one to rescue him from London? Where were his friends and family?

Maybe he only had Simone, she thought.

She had Zoe, and Elliot had her, but what happened when the person in your corner died?

Poor Hugh, she thought. No wonder he was a drunk and bitter as all hell, and she resolved to be kinder to Hugh.

After all, everyone needs a little kindness, even angry writers.

West Virginia
October 1995

'Come in, Shay,' said the woman in the white coat with a smile.

Krista nodded encouragingly, and Shay handed her the small leather bag Krista had given her on her last birthday. Shay knew the bag was stolen, but she didn't mind. She loved that Krista had been prepared to risk getting caught just to give her something she had admired in Target.

Shay followed the woman into her office.

'Are you the doctor?' she asked.

Shay had found the number in the Yellow Pages.

The woman didn't answer, instead reading the notes on her desk.

'You say here you're nine weeks pregnant?'

Shay nodded.

'Did you know your baby has little teeth forming?'

Shay frowned. 'No, I didn't know that,' she said. Teeth? Why was this doctor talking about teeth?

'And that your baby's organs are fully formed now? It's little heart is beating away.'

Shay drew in a sharp breath. 'I'm here to get an abortion.'

'But what if your baby wants to live?' asked the woman, the smile now gone. 'Did you know that women who have abortions are more likely to die than if they give birth?'

'That's not true,' cried Shay, feeling herself start to shake.

'And that your risk of breast cancer doubles,' said the woman, leaning forward on the desk. 'God wants you to have this baby, Shay. Otherwise he wouldn't have made you pregnant.'

And then Shay realized she had walked into a trap.

She stood and rushed from the room.

'They're Christian,' she cried to Krista. 'It's a fake clinic.'

'I read about that in the church newsletter,' Krista said, her face red with fury.

'Shay, please come back so we can talk.' The woman in the white coat was standing behind them now. 'Let's pray together. We're here to help.'

'Fuck you!' yelled Krista. 'You say you want to help? Are *you* gonna look after the baby so she can finish school? Give her money and help her feed it and buy it clothes? Can she come to you when she wants a break from being a momma at seventeen? With no man to help her and no family who cares about her neither? You think *praying* is gonna help this situation? Then you're a fucking idiot!'

Krista was screaming, but Shay put her hand on her friend's arm.

'Let's go,' she said softly.

Krista kicked the coffee table and a stack of magazines went flying and then she and Shay went out into the street.

Winter was coming and Shay dreaded winter in the trailer. It didn't matter how many clothes she wore, she couldn't get warm, so mostly she worked extra shifts to stay near the cookie ovens.

'I'm gonna burn this place down,' said Krista, and Shay didn't doubt it for a minute.

'And then they'll open a new place and I'll have drive all the way to Point Pleasant to visit you in Lakin,' she said, shuddering at the thought of the notorious women's prison nearby.

Krista walked away and Shay followed her.

'At least I didn't spend your money,' she offered.

Krista had given her the four hundred dollars for the abortion. She said she'd saved it from babysitting. Shay thought that maybe she had stolen some of it, but she didn't ask.

'I'm gonna keep the baby,' she said now.

'What are you talking about?' Krista turned to her, shock on her face. 'You can't look after a teeny baby.'

Shay lifted up her chin and stared at Krista. 'I can do anything I want and I want this baby. It's got teeth.'

'You just got fed a whole pile of crap from that stupid bitch and now you're scared.'

'Don't tell me what I am,' said Shay. 'You don't know what I am at all.'

Krista narrowed her eyes and stuck her hands in the pockets of her blue jeans and kicked the ground with her stolen Reeboks.

'I know you're throwing your life away if you stay here and have a baby.'

Shay shrugged. 'Maybe I am, but it's my life to throw away.'

She walked away from Krista.

'And your baby's life,' Krista called after her. 'You gonna

raise a baby in a trailer, like you and your momma and your gram? Come on, girl. You *know* you don't want that life.'

Shay blocked out Krista's truths. Her baby had a teeny-tiny beating heart. Who was she to decide if it deserved to live or not?

As she approached the trailer, she steeled herself for her grandmother.

She was a hard woman with no discernable maternal skills and Shay wondered how she would feel about having a baby in the trailer.

Her question was answered as she walked inside.

'Where the hell have you been?' her grandmother screamed. 'I have to go to town and you have my money.'

'I don't,' said Shay.

'Yeah, you do. Hand it over, I know you got your wages,' she hissed, her pink lipstick on her teeth.

Shay swallowed nervously as she opened her leather bag and pulled out a wad of twenties. Her grandmother snatched them from her.

'Don't ever think you can hide anything from me, girl,' she said. 'Now clean up this pigsty. I'm going to town.'

Shay watched her leave, her resolve to keep the baby ebbing away. Krista was right. There was no way she could raise a child in this trailer, let alone this town.

But where the hell could she go?

Chapter 10

Elliot looked at the man who Maggie said was the best writer in the world and wondered if she was drunk at the time she made her assessment. The man had a slight scent of alcohol and abandonment about him, his face lined and skin grey.

'You know Maggie has hoodwinked us both?' Hugh asked as he walked through the house towards the kitchen.

Elliot followed, glancing at the state of the house. Unopened mail, several gift baskets, some opened, the wine missing from them, a packet of scorched almonds had spilled onto the floor, creating a little trail of salt from where Hugh had obviously walked through the mess, not bothering to clean it up.

'So you want to be a writer?' asked Hugh, as he took a coffee cup and pour neat vodka into it, then waving it at Elliot. 'Can I get you one?'

'No thanks,' Elliot answered, wishing Maggie would come back and take him home.

He hated to side with his father but sometimes Maggie really didn't think things through, he thought glumly.

'Please sit,' said Hugh, leading Elliot into the living room, which had an incredible view of the water and an incredible mess of papers and clothes and stuff on the sofa.

Hugh swept the lot onto the floor and gestured for Elliot to sit down.

'Tell me about your new heart,' he said as he crossed his legs and sipped from his coffee cup.

'I had cardiomyopathy; it's a disorder that came from a bad infection I had as a kid. My heart became weaker and couldn't pump the blood properly, so I went on the list for a new heart and then I lucked out, I guess, and one came my way.'

'That's an interesting turn of phrase, "you lucked out",' said Hugh. 'What makes someone lucky? Some people would say they've been blessed with a new heart, but you say it's luck.'

Elliot thought for a moment, and looked out over the water, where a dog was running alone along the sand.

'I guess I think I'm lucky because to say I'm blessed means that God, if there is such a thing or being, thinks that I am more worthy of receiving a new heart than someone else. If that's true, then that's too much pressure to live with.'

'Why?' asked Hugh.

'Why would God kill someone else to give me a new heart? Why is my life any more worthy than the person who died?'

Hugh stared out the window and they sat in silence for a while, and then he spoke.

'Writing isn't easy, especially when you write about your

own life. The best writers tell the truth and don't shy away from the warts and bumps.'

'Maggie said that you're the best writer she's ever read,' Elliot said.

'Maggie's a pretty fool,' said Hugh. 'I am the worst kind of writer.'

Elliot realized Hugh was close to drunk.

'Maybe I should make some coffee,' he said, hoping Hugh had something that might be coffee in his bare kitchen.

'You're like Maggie,' Hugh laughed, 'trying to sober me up.'

Elliot wasn't sure if that was a yes or a no but he took the opportunity to go into the kitchen and peer into the cupboards, looking for something non-alcoholic to drink.

Coming up empty in the cupboards, he rifled through the gift baskets and found some vanilla and orange herbal tea bags, and quickly dumped them into coffee cups and boiled the kettle.

'Have you got a girlfriend?' asked Hugh, who was now lying on the sofa, the coffee cup balanced on his chest.

'No,' said Elliot.

'Why not?'

'It's hard to meet people when you're sick, unless you want to date a nurse.' He laughed.

'Did you want to date a nurse?' asked Hugh.

'Not really.'

'What about your friends from school?'

'They kind of drifted,' Elliot answered. Or had he drifted away from them? Either way it was hard enough to be a movie star's kid without adding a chronic illness on top. People assumed he had lots of friends, because his life looked so rich and full. But it wasn't like he had the sort of house that people could call into or tap on the window to see if he was home.

'What about university? Don't you want to go there?'

Elliot poured the hot water over the tea bags.

'Maybe, but not yet,' he said.

Hugh sat up when Elliot bought the tea to the table, and he leaned down and sniffed it.

'Why are you serving me hot toilet cleaner?'

Elliot started to laugh and he took a sip of his own.

'Yeah, it tastes pretty gross.'

'Tea should be served properly,' said Hugh, his words slurring a little.

'Like your vodka? In a coffee mug?' asked Elliot, wondering if he would be kicked out of Hugh's house.

Instead, Hugh laughed loudly.

'I like wit, or are you being just smart? I'm too hungover to tell.'

Elliot felt himself redden with pride at being told he was witty, or smart. He didn't mind which it was, instead it felt good to be told he was something other than unwell.

'Tell me about Maggie,' said Hugh, crossing his feet on the coffee table.

'What about her?' Elliot felt his defences rise. Having one of the world's most beautiful women as your stepmother was a curse, with people wanting information from him about her, or some idiots making smart comments about Elliot having a crush on his sexy stepmother.

'She's a pain in the neck,' Hugh said. 'She's relentless. I don't think anyone ever says no to her, spoiled Hollywood princess.'

'I don't think you know her well enough to say that,' said Elliot carefully.

When it came to Maggie, he refused to let anyone, including his father, make comment on her behaviour.

'She might come across like that but she's actually the kindest person I know,' he said, noticing his voice was strained.

'Why? Because she gives you things?' said Hugh somewhat nastily.

'No, because she gives me time,' he answered. 'She gave me time and conversation, and she treated me like I wasn't dying. She lets me be a kid and she listens. She is an amazing listener, and gives seriously good advice.'

'Harrumph,' came from Hugh. 'I will admit they're good qualities to have.'

'And she's amazing with secrets,' said Elliot. 'She's a vault.'

Hugh picked up a coffee cup and drank.

'Jesus, this isn't vodka,' he said, as he spluttered it across the table.

'No, it's toilet cleaner,' said Elliot and Hugh nodded.

'It bloody is, you know.'

Sitting back on the sofa, Hugh looked at Elliot until Elliot felt uncomfortable and looked out the window and watched the lone dog run the other way along the sand.

'All right then, you seem to have a grasp on human nature, and you're perceptive, so I guess we should talk about writing.'

'Wow, that's great,' said Elliot, feeling genuinely pleased.

'And also I am deeply afraid of saying no to your crazy stepmother.'

'Does she have something on you?' laughed Elliot.

'What do you mean?'

'Maggie, does she know a secret about you? Is that why you can't say no to her?'

Hugh closed his eyes and put his head back on the sofa.

'She does,' he said with a laugh.

'Is it a big one?' asked Elliot, curious about this shell of a man who looked like someone who once had something very important but had misplaced it and now had given up looking for it.

'Big enough,' said Hugh. 'But not the biggest I own. Now, shall we begin?'

Chapter 11

The cab dropped Dylan in front of a set of iron gates that, to her eyes, rivalled those of Buckingham Palace. Ivy grew along the high walls and a sweeping driveway had boxes of meticulously manicured green grass running down its centre, like an emerald road.

The house was obscured by a thicket of palms and huge birds of paradise, sprinklers were watering the perfect lawn, adding rainbows across the scene.

You ain't in Kansas any more, she said silently as she pressed the intercom and waited.

'Yes?' asked a voice in a Spanish accent.

'It's Dylan Mercer for Elliot. Maggie Hall sent me,' she said, marvelling at being able to use Maggie Hall's name in such a familiar way.

Dylan was wearing her skinny-legged black jeans, black flats and the black short-sleeve knit her mother had bought her back in New York. She had pulled her hair back in a neat ponytail and was wearing her black-framed reading glasses. She hoped she looked like the New York intellectual who could encourage Elliot with his book and to move back into life, while she could stay longer and find what she was looking for.

The gates swung open and Dylan started the long walk up the driveway, her satchel containing her laptop and a fresh notebook and pen swinging against her hip.

Maggie had only told her the basics about Elliot. Dylan knew that he was twenty-three years old, that he'd been very sick and had a heart transplant, and that his father was the famous Australian actor, Will MacIntyre.

She had Googled Elliot and Will for three days straight since her meeting with Maggie, but other than the information about their marriage and some small references to Elliot, there was nothing else, especially about Elliot's heart transplant.

Somehow they had managed to keep it out of the media, which explained the intense confidentiality documents sent by Will's lawyers, which she had to sign that morning.

Elliot was lucky he had Maggie, she thought, as the front door was opened by what she supposed was a housekeeper in a blue uniform, like a maid.

'Come in,' she said politely.

'Hello? Are you ze assistant?' she heard a voice and looked up to see the actress Stella Valancia in the foyer. She remembered reading an article in *People* about her when she was Googling Will and Elliot.

God, she's beautiful, Dylan thought, until Stella looked Dylan up and down in a way that Dylan had only experienced since moving to Los Angeles. In New York, she didn't think much about the way she looked, but here it seemed that was all she was judged on.

'Yes, I'm the assistant,' said Dylan, trying not to stare at Stella's huge breasts, which looked like two space hoppers coming out of a red bandage dress. Were they real?

This was a question she asked herself most days in LA, she thought. The people, the tans, the careers and even the weather seemed unreal at times.

She looked around the foyer, trying to find something to distract her from Stella, and took in the ornate circular staircase and huge chandelier. By New Yorker standards, the foyer alone was the size of a studio apartment and Dylan couldn't help wondering about the size of the guesthouse. She had a week to get out of her apartment in Koreatown and if she didn't find somewhere to live soon she would be on a plane back to New York.

'I will send Elliot up for you,' Stella said and turned to the housekeeper who was lurking in the background. 'Tell Elliot that Dylan Murker is here,' she said grandly and then left Dylan feeling awkward and alone in the foyer, without another word.

Dylan moved to the table and looked at the photos of a younger Elliot and Will in silver frames. None of Elliot with any women who might be his mother, she noted, and none of Maggie either.

'Dylan?' She heard her name and glanced up and saw a tall guy walking towards her wearing jeans, a simple white T-shirt and bare feet. He was exactly how Maggie had described him: cute, but manageable cute, because she was sure he had no idea that he was good-looking. He was tall and slightly stocky, with a round face, dark hair and piercing blue eyes and with no swagger at all.

'Hey,' she said with a smile, suddenly regretting her decision not to wear any make-up.

He beamed back at her. 'Hey yourself.'

God, he was so *cute*. Her stomach filled with butterflies.

'Come on through,' he said, gesturing for her to follow him down a staircase to what looked to be his own floor.

It was a combination of what adults thought teenagers liked: a few scattered beanbags and then more adult furniture consisting of a large leather sofa and a white coffee table in the shape of a surfboard.

'Do you surf?' she asked casually.

'No,' said Elliot as he glanced at the surfboard. 'It's a stupid thing the interior decorator did when I was sixteen.' He laughed. 'Not much has changed in here since then.'

Dylan smiled politely and wondered if she sat in a beanbag, would she ever be able to get up again, so opted for the sofa instead.

'You look like a born and bred New Yorker,' he said and sat on the opposite side of the sofa.

She looked down at herself. Maybe she had tried too hard in her attempt to look intellectual?

'I guess I am—bred, that is. I was actually born in Cali.'

'Oh, yeah? That's cool.' His Californian drawl carried a slight Australian accent, from his father, and when he smiled, she almost had to look away he was so good-looking.

Elliot leaned forward and picked up a piece of paper from the surfboard table.

'I'm sorry to ask this and I'm sure you're trustworthy, but I have to get you to sign this before we can talk,' he said, looking uncomfortable. 'It's a confidentiality agreement. Maggie's a total freak about privacy.'

'Absolutely,' said Dylan, nodding her head. She quickly scrawled her signature where he pointed.

He smiled. 'You didn't read it?'

'I don't need to,' said Dylan with a shrug. 'I never tell secrets, I'm like a vault.'

Elliot blinked a few times. 'Well, that's good to know.'

Dylan opened her satchel and took out her notebook.

'So Maggie says you need an assistant,' she said in her best professional tone, crossing her legs and then uncrossing them again. She didn't want to seem too casual. God, he was cute, she thought again, and crossed them back again.

Elliot laughed. 'Nooo,' he said, drawing out the word with laughter. 'Maggie thinks I need friends, and that's why you're here. I don't need an assistant yet, I haven't even started writing.'

Dylan felt disappointment flooding her. He was only seeing her as a favour to Maggie. 'Oh, okay,' she said, placing her notebook down on the table.

'What did Maggie tell you about me?' he asked, his face unreadable.

'She said you'd been unwell and now you wanted to write about it,' she said carefully.

'And what else?' he asked, leaning back and crossing his arms. He had nice arms, she thought, like he played tennis or guitar.

'And that you were in a bit of a rut and needed someone to help get you on schedule.' Dylan smiled diplomatically.

Elliot shook his head. 'What she *meant* was that I have no friends, no hobbies and that I'm shit scared to get out of bed every day.'

Dylan frowned. 'Do you see a therapist? Are you depressed?'

'No, Miss New York, I don't,' he said, but he was smiling.

'You should, therapy is great! I've been seeing someone since I was seven.'

Elliot burst out laughing.

'What?' she asked.

'You're like a character from a Woody Allen film. You know, the beautiful girl who's uneasy with her looks and tries to dull them with reading glasses, wearing all black and talking about your therapist... It's funny, that's all.'

Dylan was about to be offended until she realized he'd just said she was beautiful and she blushed instead.

Their eyes met and Elliot's face became serious. 'Why do you want this job, Dylan? I don't get it. I mean, it's not exactly normal to babysit a twenty-three-year-old guy, is it?'

Dylan shrugged. 'What's normal? If I wanted normal, I'd be at college studying something completely useless and racking up debt.'

'Aren't you at college here? Maggie said you're writing a thesis or something?'

He ran his hands through his hair in an unconsciously sexy way and Dylan had to work hard to focus. It was important not to lie now. She felt strongly that the lifeline she needed to allow her to stay in LA would only come if she told the truth.

'I'm here to find my birth mother,' she said. 'It's complicated to explain, but my adoption didn't go through the normal channels and I'm looking for the lawyer who did the contract. Hopefully he'll lead me to my mother. But please don't tell Maggie or anyone else. It's private and I want it to stay that way.'

Elliot nodded and his eyes were very serious as he looked at her.

'Sure, of course, but I don't think Maggie would care, you know? She's very cool about stuff, more than people think.'

There was silence for a moment and then Elliot frowned. 'This might sound a bit weird,' he said, 'but what if... I mean, have you thought about what happens if your birth mother doesn't want to be found?'

'She *does* want to see me, that's the thing, she wrote me a letter saying she'd come back for me and yet she never did, so that's what I have to find out. Why didn't she come for me? Did my parents hide me from her? I have to know.'

She paused for breath and realized she was babbling. 'God, sorry, this isn't supposed to be about me! I don't even know why I'm saying all of this. I just need to know, I feel like I'm on hold until I know who she is, if that makes sense?'

He stared at her for what felt like the longest time.

'Perfect sense,' he said. He placed his hand over his chest and leaned forward and his voice lowered as he spoke, 'I want to know whose heart I have. It's all I think about. It feels like *not* knowing is holding me back from living.'

'I get it,' she said, and Dylan felt the room was filled with camaraderie and something else she couldn't quite name, and then she clapped her hands together and laughed.

'Hey, I know, I could help you find the donor. My research skills are quite good now, if I say so myself.' She smiled proudly at her own idea.

But Elliot looked sceptical. 'Do you think we could? I mean, the hospitals are pretty strict about it all.'

'Well, we could at least *try*,' said Dylan. 'There's no harm in trying, is there? And then maybe you'll have somewhere to start from in your book?'

Elliot sighed. 'I met with a writer yesterday, actually. He

said he'd help me, but I think I lose focus and get easily distracted. I think about stuff too much.'

'Oh, don't worry about that, I'm exceptional at keeping people on task. I have a psychiatrist father and a lawyer mother—they taught me so many ways to make sure of getting things finished.'

'Well, that explains the therapy since age seven,' he said with one raised eyebrow.

'I know, right?' Dylan said, laughing again. Maggie hadn't mentioned that Elliot was funny. This was a definite bonus to the job.

'Just so you know, my dad isn't a big fan of me having an assistant or writing a book,' Elliot said, watching her face, but Dylan just shrugged.

'Well then, your dad shouldn't have an assistant or write a book,' she said. 'This is about you, not him.'

Elliot looked as though he'd unwrapped a present and found something he liked very much inside.

'So, when can you move in?' he asked with a shy smile.

Dylan felt herself beaming back at him. 'Is tomorrow too soon?'

Chapter 12

Another red carpet was just another night of hustling to Zoe, expect tonight's premiere was a Palladium Pictures production, and if what Rachel Fein said was true, Jeff Beerman needed a hit.

Adjusting the tie on her peacock-print, silk Diane von Fürstenberg wrap dress, she walked up the red carpet in her new spiked Prada heels. The cameras were conspicuously silent as she passed. No one behind the barricades knew who she was and if they did, they didn't care.

She was merely the talent wrangler, the monkey trainer, as Maggie once called her, not that she would ever say that to her clients.

Usually Zoe avoided premieres but when Jeff's invitation came via one of his many personal assistants, Zoe knew it was more of a summons than a request.

No one said no to Jeff; not even Zoe, it seemed.

Part of her wished she could have messaged back to Jeff saying, 'Thanks, but I have other plans.' But she had no plans, and no guts, she thought, slightly cross with herself for not being true to herself.

'Zoe, you're here!' exclaimed Deliah Ryan and enveloped Zoe into a hug, the cameras flashing madly at the sight of the movie star.

Deliah was a rare breed in Hollywood—an actress over sixty who was still in constant demand. She defied the odds with an enviable figure, a marriage of over twenty years, kids, a grandchild, and was considered by a sexist college humour site as the ultimate GILF.

Zoe leaned forward and kissed Deliah on her smooth cheek, only a few laughter lines around her eyes showing her vintage.

If she'd had work, it was minor and subtle, Zoe often said to Maggie, as a hint when Maggie's first and only Botox experiment went awry and Zoe had to release a statement saying that Maggie was suffering from Bell's palsy.

Maggie was then made honorary spokesperson for a Bell's palsy charity and for a year she had to talk about her dribbling, a slightly maniacal expression on one side of her face.

'Yes, I thought I should come out and see what my favourite client was up to,' said Zoe warmly.

'Ha, you're a smooth talker. We know Maggie is your main girl,' said Deliah with good humour.

'I have two main girls,' said Zoe as they walked a few steps and then stopped to allow the next lot of cameras to flash in their faces.

Questions were being fired at Deliah, and Zoe stepped back out of the way, then she heard a loud, 'Fuck.'

Turning, she saw Jeff behind her, a scowl on his face and murder in his eyes.

'Have a look, will you?' he snapped at Zoe.

'God, I'm so sorry, really I am. Jesus, are you okay?'

She looked down at his feet, clad in suede loafers. There was a mark in the nap of the suede, indicating where her heel had gouged into the top of his foot.

Jeff frowned but nodded and brusquely walked past her and along the carpet.

'He's a prick, isn't he?' Zoe heard Deliah's voice in her ear.

'Really,' said Zoe without thinking. Usually she was more neutral with her opinions but Deliah was right. He was a prick.

'I hear he's screwing Arden Walker,' Deliah went on.

'Arden? Are you sure?' Zoe didn't know who to be more disappointed in, Jeff or Arden.

'She said she's in love with someone older, powerful and the biggest in the biz, and someone saw him and Will Mac-Intyre having a heated argument at the Ivy, with Arden crying in a car.'

Zoe nodded but she didn't say any more.

It wasn't Jeff and Arden that was the problem, she thought, as Deliah was called away by a studio official for interviews.

Jeff appeared in front of her. 'Greene, your shoes are too high.'

Zoe looked down at her feet. 'No, my shoes aren't too high, you were in the way.'

'You didn't look where you were going,' he said, a slight look of amusement on his face.

'You didn't look where you were going either,' she said, matching his attitude.

'Hmmm,' said Jeff.

'And I did apologize,' said Zoe with a smile. 'So you can accept the apology or hang onto a grudge about an accident where neither of us looked and merely we collided.'

Jeff's face frowned for what felt like an eternity and then finally relaxed. 'You're good at calming people down.'

'I am,' said Zoe. 'It's my job.'

'You busy this weekend?' he half barked at her.

'This weekend?' Zoe wasn't sure what he was asking.

'Yeah, this weekend, you busy?'

'Um, I'm not sure.' Zoe didn't know what was happening or why he was asking her what her plans were.

Most likely they would be binge-watching Netflix and making sure Hugh was writing his script, but she would never tell a man like Jeff how lonely her weekends were. Sometimes the weekends were drawn out like a long punishment. No phone calls or meetings to distract her from her thoughts.

'Come to Maui,' he said. Again it was a statement not an invitation.

'Maui? Why?'

Did Jeff think she would sleep with him? That he could get control of her that way? The sheer presumption was insulting to every part of her mind and body.

Just as she was about to let fly her opinions of him and Maui, a young starlet in a silver body-con dress sidled up to him.

'You left me all alone,' she purred, as her hand sneaked around his neck and she pressed her body against him.

'You can't handle being alone?' he asked, as he rolled his eyes at Zoe. 'What sort of person doesn't like being alone?' he asked her and shook his head. 'If you can't stand being alone with yourself, then why the hell would other people want to be alone with you?'

Zoe laughed half-heartedly. She needed to work on being alone and liking it, she thought when Jeff's voice broke into her thoughts.

'So? Maui?' It was more of a question this time and Zoe shrugged.

'Why?' she asked him straight up, as honestly as possible. No games, just a question. He didn't need her for sex, he had the mono-phobic starlet for that, and the contract papers were signed.

The starlet was wandering in the direction of the cameras now, hoping for some good shots to land in the gossip pages.

'Who wants to spend the weekend alone?' He laughed.

'You said you liked being alone,' Zoe asked, confused now.

'I said I could stand my own company but there are others that I like more, and you, Greene, even with your stupid shoes and sass, are someone whose company I think I could get used to.'

Zoe didn't know what to think but a montage of her weekend flashed before her and she sighed.

'Will your girlfriend be there?' She glanced at the starlet now posing harder than a Victoria's Secret model.

'Why?' asked Jeff, his eyes widening in mock exaggeration. 'Do I sense some rivalry?'

Zoe burst out laughing. 'Are you serious? That's the funniest thing I've heard in a long time.'

Jeff frowned. 'Why is it so funny?'

Zoe was laughing as she spoke. 'I don't know what's more amusing, the idea that you think I want anything from you other than business, or the thought that she would be competition for me.'

'She's very beautiful and young,' said Jeff, his eyes flickering over the girl's perfectly shaped behind.

'Sure, we all were once,' said Zoe as she leaned towards Jeff, her mouth nearly touching his ear. 'You said I am too old for you and in return, I say that you are too old for me. And as for her being competition for me? I may not have her beauty or her youth but I am, without a doubt, the smartest, bravest, gutsiest person on this red carpet right now and a tight butt cannot compete with that, not even hers.'

As she pulled away, she felt Jeff's eyes boring into hers.

'Hollywood's really made you a tough bitch,' he said.

'Hollywood? Hollywood's easy,' Zoe laughed, failing to keep the bitterness out of her voice. 'It's the backstory that makes us who we are.'

'So what's your backstory?' he asked, his voice serious now.

'Nothing you'll ever need to know,' she said as the starlet oozed up to him again.

'Goodnight, Jeff, I hope the film is a huge hit,' she said and going against the crowd, she walked off the red carpet and into the night.

West Virginia
November 1995

Krista walked into the preacher's home to find his wife, Melinda, feeding the smallest of their nine children.

Why did they have to have so many children? Krista asked herself. Didn't they understand that babies needed more than prayer and stewed apples?

God, she could write a book on what babies needed, she'd

looked after the small ones in every foster home and group home she had been in, but as if anyone would listen to her.

Sitting down on the nearest chair, she could feel her sock was wet inside her left sneaker from the hole in her Reebok. She hadn't had the time to steal a new pair from Foot Locker. It was a big job, requiring a pair of pliers to undo the security tag and the wile to get to the back of the store to find the right size.

Lately, she couldn't be bothered doing much of anything. Without Shay, nothing seemed fun. To make matters worse, the preacher wanted more sex, and now he was refusing to pay.

'I'll tell your momma you came onto me, that you had the devil in your eye,' he threatened.

'She's not my momma,' Krista had said, but she feared being cast out into the cold winter. So she let him lie on her again, gritting her teeth in disgust.

She hated his fast thrusts, like a jackrabbit, and the sound of his grunts in her ear as they lay on the floor in his office, the only light in the room emanating from the snake cabinet.

'The preacher's out doing his ministry,' Melinda said to Krista now in a dull voice. Krista looked at the overweight, grey-haired woman wearing odd shoes and felt sorry for her. *Too many children will make a woman old before her time*, thought Krista.

She thought of Shay and wondered how she was. She hadn't come to school for a few days and nor had she been at work whenever Krista had gone past the mall.

'I have to go up to the store,' said Melinda, standing up and handing the baby to Krista. 'Then I'll be seeing to a sick lady who needs some help.'

Krista gently wiped snot and apple sauce off the baby's face and sniffed it and made a face behind Melinda's back.

She doubted the child had been bathed in the last few days; in fact, she doubted even Melinda had been washed.

The older children sat in a row in the worn sofa and stared at Krista after their mother had gone.

'You can watch some TV, kids. I'm gonna give Caleb a bath,' she said.

Preacher Garrett was always yelling about the devil inside the TV, yet he had one and a video machine, she noticed, probably to watch those movies she'd seen in the bottom drawer of the desk in his office.

She bathed little Caleb in the tub, gently sponging the ingrained dirt off his neck and ignoring his cries as she shampooed his hair twice.

Finally, when he was dried, dressed in pyjamas that were too small, but at least clean, she gave him a bottle and put him down to sleep. The other children were happily watching *Sabrina, the Teenage Witch* on the forbidden box.

Krista chuckled at them watching a show about black magic as she snuck off to check out Garrett's office. Maybe she would find a few dollars lying around in there.

The two rattlesnakes were asleep under the light in their glass cabinet and she poked her tongue out at them as she walked past to the desk.

Rifling through the drawers she found a few quarters, but nothing else worthwhile.

She sat back in the chair and wondered what it would be like to have a desk and a job like this. Though she could think of many other things she'd rather be than a preacher, she did like the idea of people coming to her for help and guidance. She was smart, even if the social workers said she had a learning difficulty. She knew that wasn't true, she just didn't have enough practice when she was learning to read.

If she practised, she would be better, she could do anything she wanted, she thought defiantly, her eyes drawn by the slight movement of one of the snakes in their cabinet. And that was when she saw the treasure chest.

Proverbs 2:4–5, she thought, remembering what the preacher always said: *If you seek it like silver and search for it as for hidden treasures, then you will understand the fear of the Lord and find the knowledge of God.*

So *this* was where Garrett kept the Sunday collection money. After all, no one would dare to reach in amongst the rattlesnakes for the money, would they?

Then again, no one else was Krista.

Chapter 13

Zoe pressed the button to lower the window of the rental car as she pulled out of the airport and started the drive to Jeff's estate in Maui.

She wished she had rethought her outfit for the trip. In black pants and closed-toes shoes and a stiff white shirt, she felt overdressed and uncomfortable in the humidity, but she didn't want to give Jeff the impression she was there for anything more than business.

Zoe had been to Maui a few times with clients and Maggie, and she had always loved the mountains and beaches. Maui had a deep sense of culture and spirituality that Los Angeles lacked, in spite of the yoga centres on every LA street corner, she thought wryly.

It had just been raining, she noticed as she glanced out over Kahului Bay, and a rainbow hung like a mobile over the ocean.

She hoped it was a good omen for her meeting with Jeff. Her mind wandered to Hugh, who she had left in Maggie's care. She wasn't sure this was a great idea and Hugh hadn't been too enthusiastic about it either.

'Maggie looks delicious, but she's cold, like an ice cream cake,' he'd said.

Zoe had rolled her eyes at him. 'She claimed you said she was like a wedding cake.'

Hugh had laughed. 'Yes, that's right. But ice cream is a better way to describe her.'

'She's not what you think,' Zoe had said loyally. 'She's kind and smart, way smarter than people give her credit for.'

'Then why does she try to hide it?' Hugh had asked. 'She's pushy and a snoop.'

Zoe had just laughed. Yes, Maggie was a snoop; it was part nature and nurture. It had been impossible to have privacy when she was shunted from foster home to foster home and then into a group home and just as hard now that she was a movie star.

Zoe drove past the lush greenery of Maui, wondering what it would be like to be able to head to your own estate in Hawaii whenever you liked. She was happy with her home in Hollywood and her amazing walk-in wardrobe but this level of wealth was something even she found hard to digest. There was rich and there was wealthy and then there was Jeff Beerman, who lived down the road from Oprah and Clint Eastwood.

As the clear, clean scents of Hawaii came through her car window, she almost enjoyed herself, except for the nagging worry about her meeting with Jeff.

He had been so unforthcoming about the state of the studio that her lawyers had strongly advised her to not sign with him and find another deal. But she wanted to learn from Jeff, who was arguably the smartest man in Hollywood right now. Sure he'd had a few misses, but when you took his box office earning as a total of the films he had produced, then Jeff was still the king and so she had signed the papers.

She knew he'd given her the deal because of two things. One because she owned Hugh and the other because she knew he believed he could control her. But Zoe had never been easily controlled—just ask the social workers, she thought, as she pulled up to the gate and announced her arrival on the intercom.

The gates swung open and she drove down the gravel driveway and parked at the front of what could only be described as a plantation mansion.

Jeff, dressed in white linen, was waiting for her at the top of the stairs.

'Hey there, Rhett, how're those damn Yankees doing?' she said in her best hick accent as she got out of the car, her neck craning to take in the white home with surround porches and shutters on every window.

Palms swayed by the side of the house, as though celebrating the beauty around them, while the green lawns lay around the house like a royal carpet.

'Morning, Miss Zoe,' he said in a decent southern accent.

'This is quite a place you have here,' she said as she walked up the stairs to meet him.

'When *The Art of Love* becomes the mega hit you know I will make it, you can have one too.' Jeff leaned forward and kissed her cheek.

The gesture confused her. Why did he kiss her cheek? What did he expect from this weekend? He had never even offered to shake her hand before.

'Come in,' he said, opening the heavy, intricately carved door. Then he turned and looked at her outfit.

'Will you be serving cocktails while you're here?' he asked with a smile.

'What do you mean?' Zoe looked down at her Prada ensemble.

'You look like a waitress,' he said. 'Go up stairs and change into something more island appropriate and meet me on the balcony. Marvin will show you the way.'

Zoe was about to unleash a torrent of abuse at him for commenting on her appearance but Jeff had already left the entrance and a smiling man in smart shorts and shirt stepped forward.

'Come with me, Miss Greene,' he said, and Zoe soon followed him up the staircase. The inside of the house was more Bahamas than Hawaii, all tasteful whites with blue accents, and honey-coloured polished floorboards. All chosen by a decorator who had, no doubt, joyfully spent Jeff's money.

Marvin opened a door and Zoe stepped into the room and tried not to cry out in joy.

An enormous white bed stood against one wall, and two glass doors opened onto the balcony that encircled the house.

The sound of the waves hit Zoe's sense first and then the salty smell and finally, as her eyes adjusted to the light, she saw the ocean spread out before them like a gift and she gasped.

'Jesus, it's incredible,' she said, forgetting herself for a moment and rushing to the white railing, trying to take everything in.

Volcanic rocks dotted the yellow sand like stepping-stones, and seemed to beckon her on as the cobalt-blue sea lapped the shore, like a siren song.

'Would you like me to unpack your case, Miss Greene?' asked Marvin.

Zoe tore herself away from the view and shook her head. 'No, that's fine,' she said and went back to inhaling the perfect view.

The room was the epitome of island luxury, part hotel, with a touch of home with scented candles and a collection of seashells on the nightstand.

Zoe opened her case and pulled out the only vaguely 'island appropriate' item she had brought with her: a raspberry Calypso strapless dress, really meant for going over her bikini, but it would have to do, she thought, and she pulled off her constricting LA clothes and pulled on the linen dress.

She looked in the mirror in the enormous bathroom and took a hairband from her bag and pulled her hair up into a ponytail and rubbed a little gloss onto her lips.

There was no point wearing make-up in this humidity, she thought, as she slipped her feet into her plain white Zanotti sandals and walked back the way Marvin had shown her.

Eventually, she found Jeff on the balcony, sitting in a large cane chair, looking every bit like a plantation owner, overseeing his land.

'Seriously? You could be looking at this every day and you choose to live in LA? You're crazy,' she exclaimed.

Jeff turned to her and she saw his eyes glance over her dress and her bare shoulders.

'Feel better?' he asked, and Zoe felt almost naked under his gaze.

She understood why younger, less smart women fell for his charms.

'Yes, thank you,' she said primly and sat down on a chair.

'It's an amazing view,' she repeated, wondering why she cared what he thought when he glanced over her. Why did his opinion on her looks matter to her all of a sudden? She was a beautiful woman, maybe not in the Maggie Hall way but she still turned heads, not that she cared until that moment. *Damn you, Jeff*, she thought.

He was staring into the distance. 'I guess it's an okay view, I'm kind of used to it,' he said.

She laughed and shook her head at him. 'You're unbelievable.'

'What's so funny?'

'It's just that you're so entitled, you think it's your right to ignore such beauty, as though it was made for you. If I lived here I'd bow before this view every single day.'

Jeff looked at her in a way she couldn't read. She was unsure whether he thought she was being rude or funny, but she didn't care. There was no way she was going to let Jeff think he was better than her because he had more money, more power and a set of balls.

His eyes narrowed as he stared at her. 'You've got a smart mouth, Greene.'

'Takes one to know one,' she said unapologetically.

Jeff sighed. 'You also happen to be right. I do take it for granted. According to my last wife, I take everything for granted.'

'Rich men usually do,' she said with a half smile.

'And what about rich women?'

'I don't know, I'm not rich.'

'But you're comfortable?'

'Moderately.'

Jeff scoffed. 'I'd say that owning your own home in Brentwood, not to mention owning a company that took in eighteen million dollars last year and no family to support means you're rich,' he said. 'Now who's taking what they have for granted?'

Zoe felt her mouth drop open. 'You've been doing your homework.'

'I always do before I get into bed with someone,' he said and his eyes twinkled as they met hers.

She uncrossed her legs and leaned forward. 'Don't bother, Jeff. I'm not one of the actresses who sleep with you for the next big role or a wife out to shaft you after five years of marriage. I'm not after anything from you except respect and honesty and to learn. Now tell me, how bad are things at Palladium?'

He paused as a staff member brought out a tray of iced tea and fresh fruit and laid it out in front of them.

Zoe waited impatiently while Jeff seemed to be using the break to gather his thoughts. Finally they were alone again, and he cleared his throat.

'Okay, here's the truth. I took a big hit on that piece of shit gladiator film, it nearly fucking killed me, physically and financially,' he said.

His face was drawn and grey and Zoe felt her stomach churn anxiously.

'For a while the takeover vultures were circling but I managed to stave them off. I know what people are saying, I hear it all. I should've listened to my gut when that project was pitched; the director was an idiot, who wasted up my money every single day of the shoot.'

Zoe was silent. The film had been a disaster, everyone

talked about how terrible it was, there was even a sketch about it on SNL, which garnered more hits on YouTube than tickets sold at the movies.

'Then I had a small heart attack,' Jeff went on with a shrug, as though he was telling her he'd had a splinter removed. 'No one knows except my doc. Afterwards, I decided I needed to focus on smaller films that smart people might enjoy. I mean, I don't mind a car chase but some clever dialogue doesn't go astray either.' He laughed as he spoke and Zoe watched him.

This was a Jeff she had never seen before, and it wasn't just the white linen pants, she thought with a smile, but the candid disclosure of his failings. She found she liked him more than the other Jeff.

'So how does the studio's financial state impact on the making of the film?' she asked. 'What do I need to know?'

Jeff thought for a moment. 'We can't afford a major star, we need a low-cost director and we need the script to be brilliant. Think *The King's Speech*—a budget of twelve million and that picture has made over three hundred and forty million dollars.'

'But that had Colin Firth in it! It was always going to make money.'

'Okay, maybe we can afford a major star. But they'd have to take a cut of the backend. I can't give away half the budget on salary.'

Zoe nodded. 'I agree. What about Maggie Hall? She said she'd do it for a cut price,' she added, thinking aloud.

'Too old,' said Jeff dismissively.

'She's thirty-six, same as me,' said Zoe, making a face at him.

'Like I said, too old.'

Any thoughts she'd had that Jeff might be a decent human being vanished, and he was right back where she had originally placed him in her mind; with all the other people in her life who had made her feel like crap.

'Who else do you have?' he asked.

Zoe spat out a list of names but Jeff threw them all back at her with a barbed comment about each one.

'Why are you so rude about people?' she asked, tired of his negativity.

'I'm not, I'm a realist. Everyone wants something from me, so I have to make sure I see through the bullshit. It's my job,' he said.

To be an asshole? she thought.

'Jeff, I repeat, I don't want anything from you but the resources from the studio to get this film made. Do you understand me? I just want to make a great film, and so do you, so cut the crap.'

Jeff narrowed his eyes at her and then snorted. 'Everyone wants something from me, especially women. And it usually turns out to be money.'

Zoe shook her head. 'I've been looking after myself since I can remember. I learned a long time ago not to ask for help, least of all from a man. If I want something I do it myself, always have.'

Jeff sipped his tea. 'Well, aren't you little Miss Independence?' he mocked.

'Better than being little Mister Misogynist.' She ate a piece of not quite ripe pineapple, and wasn't sure if it was the fruit or Jeff that left the most bitter taste in her mouth.

Chapter 14

Hugh ran his hands through his dirty hair as he watched a dog run along the beach, as though he was tracing a scent that finished at the water's edge.

Most days he saw the same dog running for its life along the sand, avoiding people, ignoring other dogs. Sometimes he observed it just sitting watching the waves, as though waiting, like a widow looking out for her sailor husband lost at sea.

Fighting the desire to open the bottle of vodka that lurked in his freezer, Hugh stared at the dog some more.

The vodka was only to be opened in case of emergency, but wasn't writer's block an emergency?

A knock at the front door broke through his internal argument for alcohol.

When he opened it, Maggie Hall was standing there.

'You really need to lock your gate,' she told him sternly, as if she hadn't just marched in unannounced. 'Any crazy person could come onto your property.'

'Too late, it seems,' said Hugh with a sigh and he turned and walked back down the stairs.

Maggie was a cyclone of ideas, judgement and perfume, everything he was trying to avoid. And she was relentless, he was beginning to realize.

'You didn't bring Elliot with you this time?' he asked as he turned on the kettle.

Maggie put her handbag and sunglasses down on the kitchen bench. 'No, but he loved talking with you last week.'

'I don't know why, I'm not really very good company,' said Hugh as he dumped a tea bag into a mug.

'True' she said. 'I'll have mine black.'

Hugh looked up. 'Black what?'

'Tea, of course. Isn't that what you're making?'

He couldn't let it pass. 'Black tea what?'

Maggie was staring at him with what could have been either dislike or admiration, he wasn't sure which. Then she laughed and walked over to his side of the bench, took another mug from the cupboard and dropped a tea bag in it.

'Don't treat me like a child, Hugh.'

She was standing very close to him and Hugh stopped thinking about vodka and instead looked at her mouth.

'Then don't act like an entitled princess.'

There was an uncomfortable silence between them as she fixed her eyes on him and glared.

'Why are you here, anyway?' he demanded as he put an open packet of digestive biscuits on the counter.

Maggie didn't flinch under his gaze, the look that Simone once told him could wither a Hackney pimp.

Instead, she smiled sweetly. 'Zoe told me you'd be fine on your own for the weekend, but I know better.' She held his gaze. 'How's the battle of the bottle going today? Are you winning?'

Hugh felt himself turn red and he turned to make the tea.

'I don't need to be checked up on, thanks very much. Don't treat me like a child,' he mimicked.

Maggie took her mug over to the sofa, ignoring his tone. 'How's the script going then?'

Hugh sat down opposite her.

'Oh, splendid thanks, it's coming on a treat,' he lied. The truth was that writing the script was even more difficult than writing the book had been. Having to relive the best and worst moments of his old life was sending him mad.

Why had he said yes to coming out here and writing the script?

Because back in London he'd seen Simone's face reflected in every shop window. He saw her amongst the crowds on the street, posting letters or stopping to smell new jonquils at the flower stand on the corner...most of all, he saw her whenever he went back to their small flat.

When he drank he couldn't remember the past and when he was sober, he couldn't stop remembering. If he could have hooked himself up to a mobile vodka infusion, then perhaps he might get through the rest of his life.

Maggie sipped her tea and smiled at him. 'I call bullshit. You haven't written jack, have you?'

Hugh had a burning desire to tell her to piss off. Why couldn't she just go back to her celebrity life and stop hounding him? But he was too tired to argue with her obstinately beautiful face.

'You look better in black,' he said aloud and was as surprised as she at his observation.

'Um, thank you,' she said, knowing she was blushing

and hating herself for the betrayal. 'Does it make me look less like a wedding cake?' She raised her eyebrows at him but he didn't show any shame in his insult from the first time they met.

'Funereal is so hot right now,' he quipped.

'Just the look I was going for,' said Maggie archly.

'I'm your man then, I know all about funerals,' he said half jokingly but Maggie didn't respond to his gallows humour. Most people were uncomfortable with the talk of death, especially his loss, and Hugh threw in the odd joke to see if people could stomach his pain.

If he couldn't handle it himself, then how on earth could anyone else?

Maggie gave him a half smile and raised her eyebrows at him, as though she saw what was inside his heart. She really was exceptionally pretty, he thought as he glanced at her. And for some reason the way she was curled up so casually on the sofa, as though she sat there every day, made his heart beat faster.

Was forty-five too old to have a crush on someone? There had been no one else since Simone crushed his heart, but then Maggie was a safe crush, like a girl on a poster for a fashion label.

Did she have a crush on him also? Was that why she was here? He wondered for a moment and then he remembered who Maggie actually was and who her ex-husband was. There was no way in hell Maggie Hall was interested in him. He almost laughed aloud at his own self-delusion.

It wasn't like women had avoided him since Simone's death. To be honest, he'd found being a widower had made him like catnip for some women. And there were the ones who wrote to tell him how happy they would make him, if only he would let them soothe his broken heart. Grief porn, he called it.

Why on earth would a woman like Maggie Hall like a drunk faker like himself? She didn't want him, she wanted something from him.

'Why don't you tell me what you're really doing here, Maggie? I don't think it's just to make sure I'm not soaked in alcohol, is it?'

She put down her mug and clasped her hands in her lap.

'I need you to write that script, Hugh.' She smiled as she spoke. 'And I need to make sure it's not a piece of crap.'

Hugh laughed. 'If this is coming from Zoe, then you two need to do some work on your double act. It's not really creatively inspiring to be bossed around.'

Maggie didn't say anything. She just stared at him until he felt awkward under her unrelenting gaze and he stood up and walked to the kitchen counter wondering if he should start on the vodka now or later.

'Anyway, you're not even in the film, so why should you care?' He couldn't help himself. Maggie Hall was infuriating.

Maggie lost her smile and her eyes hardened. 'But I want to be. I need to play Simone.'

'So you're here because you want to play Simone?'

'Not want, *need* to,' she corrected.

'Wow.' He felt his crush crumbling into pieces around him. 'Aren't you supposed to offer to sleep with me, then? Isn't that the way things work in this place?'

Simone said that lashing out at people who'd hurt him was one of the things Hugh did best, perhaps even better than writing. It hurt then and it hurt to remember it now.

But Maggie just laughed, as though he were the funniest person in the world. 'You've seen too many movies,' she said.

Maggie stood up and walked towards him. 'I need this role,' she repeated. 'I loved the book. I am Simone.'

'God, I hope not,' he muttered.

Maggie was now standing next to him, her blue eyes imploring him. Was she going to kiss him? he wondered, half scared to death and half hopeful, but instead she leaned over and took a biscuit from the packet.

It was a deliberate move to make him feel vulnerable, he thought, like she was the huntress and he her prey.

It pissed him off no end and he turned and snapped at her.

'Why do you need this role anyway? Isn't there some zany romantic comedy you should be filming in the Hamptons somewhere?'

But Maggie just laughed again. 'Probably but I would much rather be trading jibes with you,' she said almost flirtatiously.

Hugh felt himself both turned on and filled with dislike for her for making him betray his memory of Simone.

'Tell me why you want to play my dead wife. Give me your—oh, what do they call it?' He thought for a moment. 'That's it. Give me your elevator pitch.'

He waited for the standard speech about how Simone was an angel, the most enchanting woman in literature since Elizabeth Bennet, and how she deserved to be represented on screen in a way that embraced and celebrated the woman.

'Because she wasn't perfect. I saw that in your book. I know you tried to hide it, but I feel like there was so much more to her than you put in the book. It's almost like you promised her memory you'd only show the good, and none of the bad. But people need to see her complexity, see this woman with her wit and brilliance *and* her imperfections—because they're the very things we can relate to, which will bring her alive for the rest of us.'

Hugh stood very still.

'She's not the sacrificial martyr so many readers have made her out to be. I mean, I didn't know her, but I think Simone was angry as fuck to die. I think there must've been times when she hated you for being well, and that's a terrible thing to have weighing you down. You live every day with that guilt, don't you, Hugh? You can't swim, you can barely tread water, and now you're just waiting for that last big wave to come and wash you away.'

He didn't know he had tears running down his cheeks until Maggie reached over and wiped his face with her fingertips, in a gesture both familiar and intimate. He realized this was the moment he had been waiting for ever since the book had been published, so of course, in his usual self-destructive style, he ruined it.

'Get out,' he said in a low voice.

'What?'

'Get out. How dare you think you can speak to me about Simone and what she was like? You have no idea about her or me or anything,' he said.

Maggie swallowed and lifted her head. Then, picking up her bag, she walked out of his house.

Hugh stood in the kitchen for what felt like an age, trying to gather his thoughts and compose himself.

Every time he opened a fan letter or signed a copy of his book for a willing reader, he'd been waiting without even knowing it, for someone to recognize Simone as a human being rather than a saint.

And that someone had turned out to be a woman he'd

judged to be plastic, pushy and shallow. Simone lived more in what wasn't said, than what was written, and Maggie Hall had just seen right through him.

He just wasn't sure he was ready to lift the veil of St Simone to the world so instead he opened the freezer and took out the vodka.

Bugger off, Maggie and Simone, he thought and took the bottle to bed, hoping to God that he would forget everything expect Maggie Hall's smile.

Chapter 15

Dylan could hardly believe it. The guesthouse was nearly as large as her parents' whole apartment back in New York and they had what was considered spacious for the city.

Her luggage had already been unpacked by one of the smiling but silent maids, who just nodded every time Dylan spoke to them.

'Everything all right?'

She heard Elliot's voice and turned to see him in the doorway.

Yep, still cute, she thought, turning away before he saw her blush.

She had already called her parents and told them about her good luck. Her father thought the job sounded ideal, but her mother was suspicious. She knew Dylan was up to something in LA other than pursuing an acting career, which was what Dylan had told them, she just didn't know what.

Finding the letter in her mother's private files had been a total shock for Dylan. She'd always known she was adopted, her parents had told her the truth about that. What they *hadn't* told her was that her birth mother had written her a letter promising to come back for her before too long.

So why hadn't she? The question plagued Dylan, but she didn't confront her parents. Mainly because her mother was too intimidating and her father was too sick. Instead, she photocopied the letter and the letter of adoption from the lawyers in California while her mother was out and carefully placed the original back in the files.

Her mother had scoffed on the phone about everything that had happened to Dylan since she'd met Maggie Hall.

'If it's too good to be true, it usually is,' she said in her usual pessimistic way. 'Don't fool around with the movie star dad either, that will just end up in court if he fires you because you won't sleep with him, or God forbid gets you pregnant,' she had said.

It wasn't the movie star Dylan was crushing on, though, it was Elliot. Right now he was staring at her with such hope in his eyes that she thought she might rush over and kiss him.

How could it be that she felt so close to him so quickly? She felt like she trusted him completely.

'Are you for real?' she exclaimed, looking around the space. 'This place is incredible. It's like a mini *Architectural Digest* home.'

Elliot shrugged. 'I guess. It's not used very much. I think Bradley Cooper stayed here last.'

'Bradley Cooper?' Dylan felt her mouth drop open, but then she tried to act cool.

'Yeah, he and Dad did a film together.' Elliot walked into the living area and sat on one of the white sofas.

Dylan wished there was a task she could busy herself

with, but the silent staff had taken care of everything. She sat down on a chair and crossed her legs.

'So, how is this assistant thing going to work exactly? Do you want me to read what you write? Or type stuff? Or do research?'

'I haven't actually started writing anything yet.'

'Why not?' She tried not to make her question sound accusatory. 'I thought you had, that's why you needed help.'

'Who wants to read a story about a Hollywood brat who gets a new heart?'

'People won't see it like that,' she said, shaking her head.

'I just don't want people to make assumptions about me,' Elliot said quietly. 'Besides, I talked to a writer friend of Maggie's and he made it sound so hard. I think he had been drinking before I got there also. I mean, I don't want to end up mentally fucked up.'

'So why did you hire me exactly?' asked Dylan, crossing her arms.

'I guess because you needed the job, and you seemed really nice,' Elliot said. 'I don't know, I was hoping maybe you'd inspire me. You seem so motivated, you know?'

Dylan closed her eyes briefly. Motivated by what? she wondered more and more.

What happened after she found her birth mother? What goals then? She had no idea what she wanted to do with her life, though her parents had plenty of ideas.

Pushing away the thoughts of her own future, she focused on Elliot. 'You should try to write, even if it's just for yourself. Journaling's a great way of processing what you've been through; I mean, you don't have to be Proust or anything.'

'Who's Proust?' asked Elliot, reddening a little.

Dylan smiled. 'Just a French dude who writes in a complicated way, some people love him.' Like my mother, she thought but she didn't say any more.

'I don't really read much,' he said, looking embarrassed. 'I just watch films.'

'So why don't you write it as a piece of fiction or even a film script,' she encouraged.

'But I haven't written a script before.'

'And I haven't been an assistant before. Sometimes you just have to say, Screw it, I'm trying something new.'

Elliot put his head back and closed his eyes for a few seconds and then he jerked his head up.

'Hey, do you want to go and get something to eat?'

'Sure,' said Dylan. This was her job now, he beckoned and called, and she went out for food.

'Just tell me where to go,' she said. 'What sort of food do you want?'

'No, I meant together,' laughed Elliot and Dylan knew she was reddening.

They walked out of the guesthouse and up the tropical pathway to the main house.

As Elliot opened the door for her, she heard Will MacIntyre's voice coming from another room. His Australian accent was unmistakable, as was his deep tone. She wiped the palms of her hands on her jeans.

'El, where're you off to?' she heard him ask and then he was in front of her.

He was tall, and ridiculously handsome. Dylan felt herself blushing for no reason at all.

'Dad, this is Dylan, my new assistant,' Elliot said.

Will looked Dylan up and down and then extended his hand for her to shake. 'You didn't mention she was so attractive, Elliot,' he said, looking at Dylan with what seemed like distaste.

'I didn't notice to be honest, Dad, I just focused on her skills,' Elliot said harshly.

Dylan found her nerves being replaced with something close to dislike.

Will looked Dylan up and down again. 'Well, nice to meet you,' he said, then, without another word, he turned and walked out of the room.

'My father's not really a people person,' Elliot explained as they left the house.

'I'm sure,' mumbled Dylan as Elliot opened the door of the BMW. Will MacIntyre might be gorgeous-looking, but he had none of his son's charm.

And Elliot had said he hadn't noticed her looks, probably because she had tried to look like an asexual, intellectual when she had met him. Today she was wearing a simple red skirt and pretty short-sleeved vintage blouse she had bought at a garage sale in West Hollywood. She had her hair down and a little mascara and lip gloss. Nothing too much, but enough for Elliot to be reminded she wasn't Fran Lebowitz.

'What do you feel like eating?' he asked her.

Dylan shrugged. 'I'm kind of new to the area and I haven't been able to afford to go out much. Certainly not in Beverly Hills.'

'That's okay; I know where we'll go.'

Dylan leaned back in the luxurious leather seat and adjusted her sunglasses. This was the first time ever a boy had driven her in a car. No one she knew drove in New York.

She watched Elliot's hands on the steering wheel for a moment, then glanced out the window at the mansions and their enormous gates keeping out the riff-raff.

'Do you like living in Beverly Hills, Elliot?'

'I don't know. I've never lived anywhere else,' he said, without a trace of self-consciousness.

Dylan nodded as they passed an architectural copy of the Palace of Versailles with towering golden gates. She couldn't judge him. She had never lived anywhere but New York.

'Have you ever thought about living in New York?' she asked.

'I never thought about living anywhere but where I was. Having a use-by date on your heart will do that to you.'

'God, Elliot, I'm so sorry.' Dylan cringed at her thoughtlessness.

'It's okay,' Elliot said, in a way that made her believe him. There was a simplicity and innocence about him that she really liked.

'Where are we going?' she asked, changing the subject.

'Here,' said Elliot, pulling up in front of a restaurant. Dylan looked out the window at the impressive sign and a few stray paparazzi. Even she knew what this place was.

'Nobu?' asked Dylan, laughing. 'Seriously?'

'Why not?' asked Elliot, looking confused. 'Don't you like Japanese food?'

'I like Japanese food fine, I just don't need to go to the world's most expensive restaurant to experience it.'

'If you don't like Nobu, then let's go somewhere else,' he said tersely. He pulled out into traffic and a driver behind them honked his horn loudly.

And then Dylan realized Elliot didn't know where else to go for lunch. He was a stranger in his own city, imprisoned by illness and the gates of his father's home.

She put her hand on his arm. 'I'm sorry if I sounded rude

about Nobu, I just don't need that sort of fanciness for lunch. I'm more of a low-maintenance type of girl, you know?'

Elliot glanced at her hand and then he smiled and she saw he was blushing a little and there was an odd tension in the car. Something more than just deciding on a place to eat.

'I get it,' he said. 'I just don't know anywhere else besides where Dad goes. It's not like I've been out tearing up the town in the last two years.'

She nodded. 'Do you like Korean food?'

'I don't know,' he said. 'I've never eaten it before.'

'Oh my God. You are in for a treat.'

Twenty minutes later they were inside the restaurant, where Dylan used to go for a treat if she had an extra ten dollars.

Dylan beamed at Elliot as he looked around at the plastic tablecloths and cheap-looking chairs.

'Are you for real?' he asked.

'Just wait till you try the food,' she said. 'Is there anything you can't eat?'

'Just anything high fat, high salt or high taste,' he said with a sigh. 'Wow, it smells amazing in here.'

Dylan ran her finger down the plastic-covered menu and then looked up at him. 'Can I order for you?'

'Go ahead, I have no idea what to get.'

The waiter came over and Dylan gave him the order and he returned with a two bottles of water and two soup spoons.

'Soup?' Elliot turned up his nose like a child.

'Just wait. God, I love this place, it reminds me of New York.'

Elliot glanced about the room. 'It reminds me of Korea,' he said. 'If I had ever been there,' he added, laughing at his own joke.

'Don't you want to travel?'

'Not really, I have everything I need here in LA.'

'But don't you get sick of seeing perfection everywhere you go? Even the dogs are groomed to an inch of their lives in Beverly Hills. I wouldn't be surprised if there was Botox for dogs,' Dylan said passionately.

'There is,' said Elliot, his face serious. 'So far the Shar Peis are the only ones using it with any success.'

Dylan started to speak and then saw the glint in his eye. 'Ha! You got me there,' she said good-naturedly.

Two bowls of soup were placed in front of them and Dylan leaned over and inhaled the fragrant steam.

'This is mandu guk, or dumpling soup.' She picked up her spoon, stirring the liquid around and watching the little dumplings bobbing up and down. She sprinkled some nori on top and Elliot, watching her, followed suit.

They ate in silence, Dylan savouring the delicious flavours, occasionally glancing up to see if Elliot was enjoying his meal.

He grinned at her, a little soup glistening on his chin, and she smiled.

'Did you know I've never been on a date?' he said, as though he was thinking aloud.

'Neither have I,' Dylan said. 'Not a real one anyway.'

'You? Bullshit.' He laughed.

Dylan raised an eyebrow. 'Oh, yeah. I went to an all-girls school. My parents are intensely smart, ambitious and over-protective, and they made me go to prom with my geeky cousin. Have a guess how awesome that makes you feel.'

Elliot was staring at her intently over the table and Dylan leaned back in her chair, suddenly uneasy.

Was this what Maggie had been hoping for? That Dylan

would magically become his girlfriend and lead him back into life and then they would all live happily ever after?

'Where are your friends? Why haven't *you* been on a date?' she asked him, putting down her spoon. 'I mean, you're good-looking, you seem really nice—where is everyone?'

Elliot blushed and laughed. 'Jesus, you get straight to the point, don't you?'

'I don't like to waste time,' said Dylan with a smile.

'Neither do I,' Elliot countered.

She was silent, waiting for him to answer her question. This was a tactic her father had taught her. Wait until they do the work in their own heads.

'You find that people don't usually stick around when you get sick, at least not in LA. It's hard for them, you know? My friends just kind of...dropped away.'

'Really?' Dylan thought about Addie. There was no way Addie wouldn't have come to see her every day if she was sick. She'd probably even have stayed in the hospital if she had been allowed.

'Then they're not your real friends,' she said simply and picked up her spoon again.

Elliot was quiet for a moment. 'I didn't make it easy for them to stay,' he said quietly.

Dylan looked him in the eye. 'Ah, so you pushed them away so they wouldn't be sad if you died? Or was it that you were angry at them for being well when you weren't?'

'Both,' Elliot said.

His eyes were glistening and Dylan realized she had never seen such deep sadness in anyone before. She could read on his face a heartbreaking combination of regret, vulnerability and shame and she reached across the table and took his hand in hers.

'I'm your friend,' she said softly.

'Yeah,' he said. 'Because Maggie pays you.'

But Dylan shook her head. 'If we'd met back in New York and you had asked me to go on a date with you, I totally would have said yes.'

'You're just saying that to make me feel like less of a loser.' He couldn't meet her eyes.

'Trust me, Elliot, I never say things I don't mean.'

And it was true, she *would* have dated someone like Elliot. He was cute, funny, nice and taller than her.

It was just a shame she was now working for him.

Chapter 16

Zoe lay in the world's most comfortable bed in the Maui guest room. She could hear the sound of the waves through the open window, lulling her to sleep, but her mind was too busy.

She was supposed to fly out tomorrow morning, but Jeff had insisted she stay for lunch and fly home with him on his private jet.

She really didn't have a choice in the end. Jeff was unyielding in his insistence and besides, what was she rushing back to LA *for*?

It wasn't like the husband and kids were waiting for her. Most Sundays she spent working, and watching old movies on Netflix. The older the better, and nothing too fancy either. She liked the films of Doris Day and Rock Hudson, some Sandra Dee films. Even musicals made her heart sing.

She turned over and thumped her pillow, willing sleep to come. But after fighting insomnia for another ten minutes, she gave in. She got out of bed, opened the glass doors and stepped out onto the balcony.

The moon was full over the water, and Zoe stared at it, mesmerized.

She had almost forgotten what clear, dark skies and the moon looked like, after living in Los Angeles for so long. When was the last time she had stared at night skies in LA? She couldn't remember, but she remembered the moon back in West Virginia.

The last time she had stared at the moon like this was when she was sleeping outside in the cold with the chickens.

Sleeping with the chickens wasn't so bad, but the rats coming in to steal the eggs made her feel sick and the constant clucking of the hens broke her sleep.

Some nights she would sit outside and stare at the moon, wondering what the men had felt like when they first stepped out of their rocket ship.

What did reaching your dreams feel like?

How did you even make dreams?

One day at school she had been asked what she wanted to be when she grew up, and she had said a movie star, because that's what her momma had wanted to be, before the meth replaced her dreams with a desire for the drug.

They were the best memories, curling up with her momma on the sofa, the warm rug over their knees, watching a sailor dance with a little mouse.

A chill came over Zoe and she shuddered, and turned back into her room.

Did making more money ever dispel the fear? Did all the shoes and bags in the world make up for the chicken coop, or the rough hands of her foster brothers or the insults of her schoolmates, who spent two months clucking at her whenever she walked past them, smelling of straw and chicken shit?

For the first time, Zoe seriously questioned her own personal trip to the moon.

She might have left West Virginia, but a part of her was stuck there, no matter how much money she made. That little girl was still a hostage to that butthole of a place and she had no idea how to set her free.

'Pineapple juice, Ms Greene?' asked a staff member with a wide smile.

Zoe nodded. 'Thank you, that's lovely.'

Jeff was flicking through his iPad.

'Rachel Fein's an idiot,' he announced.

'She was the one who told me you were in financial shit,' said Zoe, as she dug into half a melon.

'Then she's a snooping idiot,' Jeff said without looking up.

'That's her job.' Zoe sighed. 'What's she said now?'

Jeff adjusted his glasses. '"Rumours have it that the new deal between über-manager Zoe Greene and head of troubled studio Palladium Pictures Jeff Beerman is not strictly business. While both parties are remaining silent on matters of the heart, Zoe is spending the weekend with Jeff at his palatial estate in Maui. Stay tuned for a wipeout. Bedmates don't make good business mates, people."'

Zoe laughed. 'Okay, she was right about the financial rumours, but someone is feeding her the wrong story about everything else. I haven't heard anything so laughable since she reported that Jen and Brad were getting back together.'

Jeff looked at her over his glasses. 'Why is that so laughable?'

'Because I'm too old, remember?'

'True, but if I were pursuing you, you'd be very grateful.'

'Oh, come *on*,' Zoe spluttered. 'Are you serious? Can you possibly even *mean* that?'

Jeff frowned. 'I'm rich, powerful and great in bed, what's not to want?'

Zoe couldn't help giggling as she finished the melon.

'I'm going to get packing. Thank you for the offer of your plane, but I'll be taking that flight today as planned.' She pushed her chair back and stood up.

'Sit down, Greene,' he said tiredly. 'Please. Stay. I was looking forward to your company.'

Zoe sighed and put her hands on her hips. 'Just stop with the bullshit then, okay?'

'What bullshit?' he asked, looking offended.

'The ridiculous, chest-beating bullshit,' she said, shaking her head. 'Yes, as you said, you're and rich and powerful, but you're also alone in this incredible house that's meant for a family, so don't tell me you're happy. If you were you wouldn't have tried marriage three times so far with no success.'

Jeff stared at her, his face unreadable. 'You forgot great in bed.'

'No, I didn't forget, I can't comment on that fact, and you shouldn't take those women's words for it either. Some girls will say anything to get a man to take care of her.'

'And you're not one of those girls?' he asked, his eyes flickering over her face.

'Do I look like I've ever needed a man to take care of me?' she challenged.

Jeff stood and pushed back his own chair.

'Come on then, let's go for a walk on the beach, hold hands and tell each other our secrets,' he said with a smile.

But Zoe shook her head. 'I've got no skeletons in my closet,' she said brightly.

'Oh, really?' said Jeff, laughing. 'I've got more skeletons in my closet than the Addams Family; they're the things that make us who we are.'

If that was right, thought Zoe as they walked towards the water, then she didn't like who she had turned into at all.

Chapter 17

'Hello?' Maggie was driving towards Beverly Hills for her fortnightly hair appointment. She had already trained for two hours that morning, first an hour-long Pilates class and then her weight and cardio session with her trainer at a private gym, and then a pedicure and manicure.

Now she was in a Victoria Beckham dress and a good mood, ready for the day and new highlights.

'Maggie? It's Hugh.' His British accent cut through the speakers of her car, like a splash of cold water.

'Hey,' she said carefully.

They hadn't spoken since he had told her to leave his home and hearing him now made her both happy and cross at the same time.

'I need your help, Maggie,' he said.

'I can try,' she said, as she pulled up at the front of the hair salon.

'I need help with what I've written,' he said brusquely.

'Ok-ay,' she said, not quite understanding. 'But I'm an actress, not a writer.'

'But you understand how a script works, don't you? What makes a good one and what doesn't?'

'I guess so,' she said, thinking of all the scripts she had read over the years. Nowadays Zoe and her other staff vetted the scripts that were submitted for Maggie, but she still knew the difference between something that sung on the page and a dog.

'Will you read what I've written and give me some notes?'

Maggie paused, shocked. No one had ever asked her opinion on anything, she thought, other than what she was wearing on the red carpet and her secrets to staying young.

'Please? I'd ask Zoe, but I'm afraid she'll think it was a mistake to let me do this in the first place. I fought hard to be allowed to write the script, and I don't want to let her down.'

Did Hugh have a little crush on Zoe? she wondered. It wouldn't be the first time. Zoe always claimed she had no time for love, but Maggie believed her friend would never love anyone until she found the one love she had given up so long ago.

'Come on, Maggie. Come over and I'll make you tea and you can read it,' he wheedled.

'Why don't you just email it to me?'

'Because I want to watch your face when you read it.' He laughed. 'Then I'll know how bad it really is.'

'But I'm an actor,' Maggie teased. 'I could fake it.'

'True, but I'm learning your tells through your face.'

'Oh, really? Like what?' Maggie was laughing. Only Zoe could read her face, and even then she didn't always get what Maggie was really thinking.

'When you think someone is an idiot your eyes narrow,

and you cross your arms. When you're excited by an idea or by someone, you wave your left hand, but when you think an idea isn't so interesting, you present your argument while gesticulating with your right hand.'

'Do I? I've never been aware of what my hands do when I talk off set. What else can you tell by my face?'

Hugh was silent for a moment. 'Hmmm, let's see. Well, I can tell that you're smarter than you want people to know, and that you'd do anything to give Elliot what he needs, but know it won't be enough and that he has to do it himself. But mostly what I see in you when you speak is a bone weariness, as though you've been battling to survive from the day you were born.'

Maggie stood in the reception area of the salon, the phone pressed to her ear and felt her eyes fill with tears. It was as though he had just exposed her naked soul.

'How come you get to tell me about me and when I mention your book and Simone, I get my head torn off?' she snapped.

Hugh was quiet for a moment. 'I need to apologize for that,' he said finally.

'Yes, you do.'

'I was wrong to speak to you in that way and I am so deeply sorry,' he said and Maggie had to admit he sounded sincere, but what he didn't say was whether she was right or not.

'I'm getting my hair done now,' she said, deciding to drop the subject of Simone. 'But I could come over later?'

'Of course you are. Isn't that what all Hollywood ladies do? Forget about your hair, it looked fine last time I saw it, you always look fine.'

'Ha,' said Maggie. 'And you think you know me? I'll be

over at three.' She hung up and went through to the private room at the back of the salon.

How did he see all of that when she had only met him three times? Will had never seen it and she'd been married to him for years.

She stared at herself in the mirror, she could spend three hours in the hair salon or she could spend it with Hugh, who made her laugh and think, often simultaneously.

She stood up and pulled off the cape the hairdresser had placed carefully on her shoulders.

'I'm not going to do this today,' she announced.

The girl who was starting to prepare the colour looked worried. 'Oh, but you never miss an appointment. Is everything all right?'

Maggie smiled. 'It's fine. I just have other things I need to do. My hair can wait.'

And she walked out of the salon and got into her car, and turned it back in the direction of Malibu.

Hugh wasn't home when she arrived, but his gates and front door were unlocked, as usual.

Maggie stood in his living room looking out over the beach and then she saw him.

He was crouching on the sand, his hand outstretched to something. Squinting, she saw what looked to be the world's mangiest dog, lying as though it was about to be beaten or was about to pounce on Hugh.

Christ, he was a sucker for something broken, she thought as she slipped off her Rossi pumps and took the stairs down to the beach. She hated the feel of the sand between her newly pedicured toes, and she made a face as she tiptoed towards Hugh.

'Don't move,' he said in low voice as she neared him.

He was holding out an apple to the dog on the palm of his hand.

'An apple? It's not a horse,' she mocked.

'He's been on the beach since I moved in,' Hugh said quietly. 'I asked a neighbour about it. He said the dog has been around for about six months, but he's evaded the rangers so far.'

'Just leave it,' said Maggie. 'Forget about it, you can't fix it.'

Hugh looked up at her, his face serious. 'I would never say that about anything. Imagine if we took that attitude about people, children, the world would be worse than it already is.'

Maggie wanted to yell at him that people said that about children all the time, that they had said it about her. No one had wanted to fix her, no one handed her an apple or anything else for that matter and she was okay, wasn't she?

'You need cheese,' she said finally, after watching him trying to coax the scared-looking dog to no avail.

Hugh smiled at her. 'I still have half a Camembert in my refrigerator. It's from my welcome to LA gift basket from the studio. It came with wine, but I drank all that.'

'Of course you did,' she said.

Maggie walked back to the house, glancing over her shoulder to see Hugh maintaining his stealth position on the sand.

When she got back to the beach with the cheese, which she'd cut into small cubes, neither Hugh nor the dog had changed positions.

'Here, boy.' She clucked her tongue three times and threw

some cheese in the direction of the dog. It moved swiftly across the sand, and gobbled it up.

She threw some more and the dog responded again, until it was inches away from her and she put out her hand with the cheese.

'Hey, puppy, you lost?' she cooed and held out another piece of cheese. The dog reached up and gently took it from her hand.

From the corner of her eye, she saw Hugh standing up, watching them.

The dog took the last piece of cheese from her hand and then sat on her foot.

'It looks like you've made a friend, Maggie Hall.'

'I don't need a friend,' said Maggie, easing the dog off her foot.

Hugh smiled. 'Everyone needs a friend, even movie stars.'

Maggie turned and walked towards the house, the dog following her.

'He likes you,' Hugh called.

'He likes me because he thinks I have more cheese!'

Hugh came up the stairs behind the dog and they all went into the kitchen.

'Gosh, he's thin, isn't he? I think he's starving.'

'Who isn't starving in this town?' Maggie stared at the dog. 'He's the worst-looking dog I've ever seen.'

'I'm going to take care of him,' pronounced Hugh. 'He's going to be my new friend.'

'You're a sucker for a lost cause is what you are.'

Maggie filled a bowl of water and placed it down for the dog, who lapped it up eagerly.

'Didn't you know that about me already?' Hugh laughed as he watched the dog. 'Tell me a sad story and I'll be yours for ever, Maggie Hall. This is the face of what you Americans would call a chump.'

Maggie shrugged. 'Not me, I'm the living embodiment of how to make it in America, kiddo. When people look at me they see something to aspire to, so you're safe. No sad stories in this package.'

Hugh's brow furrowed and he gave her what might have been a quizzical look, Maggie couldn't be sure. Then he seemed to shake the mood away.

'How did you know that trick about the cheese?'

Maggie watched the dog. 'I once lived with someone who had show dogs and they used cheese for training. It's not very good for them, though. Kind of like French fries for animals.'

'I've never had a dog,' said Hugh, looking down at the animal. 'I always wanted one, but Simone hated them.'

Maggie didn't know what to say about Simone, so she focused on the dog instead.

'He needs a bath, a defleaing treatment, a collar and a leash,' she said. 'Plus a check-up at the vet for shots, and to see if he's microchipped.'

Hugh nodded. 'I can do all of that,' he said eagerly and he picked up his phone and dialled. 'Directory? Yes, I need a veterinarian clinic in Malibu.'

Maggie refilled the bowl of water for the dog, who had almost drained it dry. 'You're a sad little fucker, aren't you?' she said, and the dog wagged its thin tail at her.

'I'm not so bad, today is a good day,' Hugh said, walking back in from the balcony where he'd been speaking to the vet.

'I meant the dog, not you,' Maggie said, laughing.

'Oh? Well then, we're meant for each other.'

'Who?' she asked perplexed.

'Me and this dog, just two sad fuckers,' he said firmly. 'All right, let's go.'

'What?' Maggie put her hands on her hips. 'I'm here to read a script, aren't I?'

'That can wait. But I can't drive and you have a car, so we're going to the vet.' He bent and picked up the dog.

'Are you serious? You really expect me to put that sad-looking creature in my car?'

'Yes, and if you wouldn't mind taking the dog also, we'd appreciate it,' said Hugh with a wink and a smile, and he walked out the front door towards her car, leaving Maggie with no choice but to take care of the two saddest males in Malibu.

West Virginia
November 1995

'You home, Grammy?' Shay asked as she pushed open the door to the trailer.

The radio was on, and a cigarette was burned down to the butt in the ashtray from Florida that Grammy had bought on her honeymoon. That was the only time she had ever been out of the state, which made her think she was better than most other people around them.

Silence filled the space and Shay felt a chill that didn't have anything to do with the cold air she had brought with her from outside.

She walked down the narrow hallway to Grammy's bed-room. 'Gram?'

Opening the door, she saw her grandmother blue and cold on the bed. She knew she was dead as soon as she looked at her, and she stood, wondering if she should feel sad. Wasn't that what was supposed to happen when your only living relative died?

She dialled 911 and waited for the paramedics who then took the woman to hospital.

'It was only a matter of time before her heart gave out,' said the doctor.

Shay had nodded dumbly.

'Do you have other family?' asked the doctor.

Shay shook her head.

'And you're sixteen?' Shay nodded. 'Wait here,' the doctor told her.

Where else was she going to wait?

Not long after, she heard her name being called and looked up to see a woman in jeans and a purple knitted sweater.

'Hi, I'm Leslie, a social worker,' she said.

Shay felt panic rising inside her. 'I don't need a social worker,' she said quickly.

'Well, but you're only sixteen, you can't live alone just yet,' Leslie said kindly.

'I looked after my gram more than she looked after me, I don't need you.' Shay stood up, and that's when Leslie saw her bump.

'You're pregnant, Shay?'

Shay covered her stomach with her hands. 'What of it?'

'You really need to be somewhere safe and warm,' Leslie insisted. 'There are some lovely foster families willing to take in emergency cases like you.'

Shay paused and looked around at the hospital. The trailer was so cold, she thought. 'Okay, can I go back home first to get some things?'

Leslie nodded. 'Of course. Do you want me to drive you?'

Shay shook her head. 'No, it's fine,' she said. 'Can I have your number so I can call you when I get back here?'

Leslie handed Shay a stiff card with her name and number on it and Shay tucked it into the pocket of her Great American Cookies shirt.

'I'll call you,' she said.

Back at the trailer, Shay looked around her. There was nothing she wanted to take.

Pulling a small suitcase from under the bed, she threw in her few clothes and odds and ends of make-up. With one last look around the trailer, she picked up the leather bag Krista had given her. It was by far and away the nicest thing she owned.

God, she missed her friend, she thought. Impulsively, she dialled Krista's number.

'Krista's babysitting for the preacher,' the foster mother said.

Shay hung up and made her decision. She would go and say goodbye to Krista. She owed her at least that much.

Just before she left, she found a kitchen knife and undid the tight sewing along the split in the mattress.

God knows how many times her gram had cut it and then sewed it back up again, but this time there would be no fixing the split. Shay put her hand inside the stiff nylon fabric and pulled out handfuls of cash.

There was no time to count it. Instead she shoved it into her leather bag and closed the clasp shut. She didn't feel like it was stealing.

That money was rightfully hers, the government gave it to Gram to look after Shay, yet the old bitch had barely spent a dime on her.

Shay picked up her suitcase. There was no way she was going to another foster home.

No, she would say goodbye to Krista and then be on her way to California, where she could take care of her baby in the warm sunshine, never knowing the bite of the cold.

As she left the trailer, she walked down towards the road, when a car pulled up beside her.

'Shay,' she heard and looked up to see the social worker from the hospital in the car.

Damn, she thought, wondering if she should run but the woman was out of the car now.

'I thought I'd make it easier and take you to the foster home. I have a nice one lined up,' said the woman kindly.

The air was chilly and the sky was darkening. One night would be okay, she thought, and then she could get to Krista and tell her the plan and they could leave together.

'Okay,' she finally said to the woman.

One night wouldn't be so bad, she thought.

Chapter 18

In her two weeks as the assistant to Elliot MacIntyre, Dylan felt like she was accomplishing nothing, except for confirming her crush on him. He was so funny and sweet and kind and thoughtful, like when he said she could borrow his computer when hers needed to go to the computer store to be fixed or when he asked her about her family and her best friend Addie. She had even had a Skype session with Addie, when Elliot had come to ask her a question about his script and then Addie and Elliot had talked on Skype and it was amazing, thought Dylan.

They spent almost every hour together during the day, and even the weekends.

'You know you have the weekends off,' said Elliot, when Dylan came and knocked on his door on a Saturday.

'I don't have anything else to do,' said Dylan. 'I might as well hang with you, if you don't mind?'

They spent the weekend watching movies and reruns

of *Thirty Rock* and laughing hysterically, as much at each other as the TV show.

'Are you going to write today?' she asked him on the third Monday of working together, as she sat at his desk using his spare laptop and reviewing his calendar.

Elliot shrugged. 'I'm going to try.'

'Don't forget, you have to see that writer guy again next week and show him what you've written, Maggie emailed me about it. And your dad emailed me your hospital appointments.'

Elliot made a face and Dylan laughed as she turned to him. 'This is my job now, let me do it.'

'It's not about you, it's just so lame,' he said, shaking his head. 'I mean, I can get myself to hospital appointments.'

'What about your medications? Are you up to date on all of those?' she asked. 'Do you need me to go to the drugstore for some more?'

'No,' he said sharply.

'I should read more on your transplant, what I need to know and be aware of,' she said.

'If you want to know anything, just ask me,' Elliot half snapped and Dylan looked down at the keyboard.

Sometimes the tension between them came from her doing her job, other times she thought it was something more, but she wasn't so sure. Maybe she was just projecting her feelings onto him, she thought, thinking of her father's psychiatry lingo.

Asking Addie had been no help. 'All the boys at college are idiots,' Addie had said. 'I mean, like legit idiots. So I have nothing to compare your dude's behaviour to, sorry but he seems really nice, if that helps.'

Dylan had pondered the energy between her and Elliot,

but hadn't come up with any conclusions, other than when she was with him, he glanced at her sometimes in a way that made her dizzy and when he ran his hands through his hair when he was talking, she wanted to kiss his lovely mouth and hear him whisper her name.

'What are you doing today?' he asked casually, leaning back in his chair.

He looked good, she thought. They'd spent a fair bit of time outside over the past few days, sitting in the sun, reading, talking, laughing. They laughed a lot, she thought, almost as much as she and Addie did when they were together. Elliot now had the beginnings of a golden California tan, enhanced today by his white T-shirt.

But Elliot was distracting her from her real reason for being in LA, and though he was a pleasant distraction, there was a gnawing at her psyche that perhaps she was supposed to be doing more to find her mother, and even that she was supposed to do more with her life that cater to Elliot's wishes.

'I'm still on the hunt for any record of my adoption, but it's not really going anywhere,' she said, tearing her eyes away from him, knowing she was blushing. She opened a plastic folder with her few scant papers and information inside.

He read the letter from her birth mother, and frowned. 'Do you even know her name?'

Dylan shook her head. 'Nope, nothing; that's why I wanted to come here and try to find out what I could. I mean, I was born here and she said she was going to be an actress but that's all I know.'

'What about your birth certificate?' he asked.

'It says my parents' names, Paula Klein and Jonathon

Mercer,' she said and handed it to him as he leaned forward and took it from her.

He smelled of something delicious, she thought, finding it hard to focus because of his closeness and his scent.

'So you have a letter from the woman who gave you up and a birth certificate and what else?'

'A letter from a lawyer, saying that the adoption is valid,' she said and handed him the paper.

'Jefferson Perry, Woodland, California,' he read the name at the top of the yellowing paper aloud.

'I've searched everywhere for Jefferson Perry—online, in the legal journals, in the newspapers. Nothing comes up at all.' Dylan sighed.

'Why don't you just ask your parents? You said they always told you that you were adopted, what's the problem?'

'My parents don't know I'm looking,' said Dylan. 'I can't tell them, I want to find out myself and then speak to my birth mother. She said she was going to come back and she never did, I want to know why. If I could just find the lawyer, I'd have a lead.'

Elliot stared at the paper for a while, as though trying to see something that Dylan had missed. He looked like his dad when he concentrated, she thought, but less handsome, more approachable somehow.

Elliot looked up and caught her staring again. She looked away.

'What's your porn name?'

'What?' Her eyes shot back to his face.

'The name of your first pet and the first street you lived on,' he said, laughing. 'Come on, everyone knows that game.'

Dylan frowned. 'We didn't have a pet,' she said, thinking

about how much she had wanted a rabbit, but her mother had told her that rabbits were for hillbillies.

And then it hit her. 'Oh my God,' she said. 'I get it.'

'What?' Elliot sat forward, his eyes wide.

'Jefferson is my grandmother's maiden name, and Dad's old practice was on Perry Street,' she said, breathing heavily as shock washed over her. 'Jesus Christ, *my mom* is Jefferson Perry.'

'Christ, and I thought my parents were weird.'

But Dylan wasn't listening to him, as she sat down and opened up the search engine. She typed her mother's name and thousands of entries came up.

'I don't even know what I'm looking for,' she said, aware that her hand was shaking.

'No, search like this,' said Elliot, and he leaned over her, his arm curved around her shoulders, his longish hair tickling her cheek.

'What year were you born?' he asked.

For a moment she nearly forgot. 'Ninety-six,' she told him and he typed, his arms around each side of her.

Now she knew exactly what he smelled of: CK One and fresh laundry. She glanced up at him, seeing the light stubble on his chin, and his exposed throat just waiting to be kissed.

Do not do it, Dylan, she warned herself. *This is a job, nothing more. You just want to be held, this is ridiculous, if you need comfort, get a teddy bear.*

'There you go,' he said as he put her mother's name into quotation marks, then did the same with 'Jefferson Perry', 'California', 'adoption' and 'child', and pressed search.

Dylan peered at the screen, and there was an office registered to Paula Klein, in Woodland, California, from 1996.

'Move your butt,' Elliot said bossily, but Dylan did as he said, sitting down on the chair next to him.

He typed into the computer and soon the address came up on a map site and Elliot enlarged the picture.

'It's just some crappy office, now leased to a candy importer, nothing interesting,' he said, and Dylan picked up the paper again and stared at it, willing it to reveal more information.

'This isn't a legal adoption,' she said. 'Mom tricked my birth mother into handing me over with some fake legal crap! The poor thing's probably been looking for me all this time, but she couldn't find me because my parents are *liars*.'

Elliot leaned forward, his elbows on his knees, his hands clasped together.

'You don't know that's the truth,' he said gently.

But she shook her head, as the tears started to fall. 'I do, I know it,' she cried and in a moment he was by her side and she cried into his shoulder, inhaling his scent.

'God, this is so unprofessional,' she said, pulling away as she finally got herself together.

'Who gives a shit about professional?' asked Elliot, so close to her yet his expression unreadable, his lips slightly parted.

He's only being nice, she reminded herself. *You are feeling needy, which is why you're projecting your emotions onto him*, hearing her father's words in her head.

Her parents had a rational, scientifically based argument for everything. If she was upset, she must be tired or hungry. If she was angry, she was projecting against her frustration with herself. If she didn't do well in a test, she was rebelling against the curriculum.

But what of genuine emotion? Feelings she felt just…

because? She knew her parents loved her, but they invalidated her feelings, interpreting her as it suited them, as though she was their pet.

No wonder she didn't have a pet, Dylan thought, suddenly furious. She was *their* pet, existing for them, not for herself.

Without thinking it through, she reached up and kissed Elliot. Her lips met his tentatively, but then she felt him responding and soon they were making out on the sofa.

'What are you doing?' he asked between kisses, sounding both turned on and confused.

'I don't know,' she said, but she couldn't stop herself. 'But it's making me stop crying.'

'Then we should continue,' he said.

Kissing Elliot made her stop thinking about her mother and the lies she must have told to have Dylan in her life. His hands stopped her from wanting to call her mother and scream abuse at her, the ache between her legs distracted her from the ache in her heart.

'Do you want to stop?' he asked breathlessly.

'No,' she said, feeling his weight on hers.

He leaned away so he could gaze at her. 'You are so beautiful,' he said, his expression completely open and vulnerable.

'So are you.' She pulled his head down to hers and their mouths met again.

She wanted him, but was this love? It felt so simple and although it scared her, it also thrilled her.

She wanted him to be happy, to live a long and wonderful life, and she wanted to be with him every single day.

'Elliot?' Will's voice from the other side of door broke the fever. Elliot rolled off the sofa and onto the floor in shock, and Dylan almost burst out laughing.

Straightening up, she pulled down her T-shirt and hastily picked up a book on scriptwriting.

Elliot opened the door. 'Hey, Dad,' he said, as though he didn't have the raging erection Dylan could see when he turned sideways.

'Don't forget I'm off to Arizona today,' Will said.

Elliot nodded. 'I didn't forget. Have a good shoot.'

'You'll call me if you need anything?' he asked them both.

Dylan nodded professionally and Elliot rolled his eyes.

'Relax, Dad, we'll be fine.' Elliot reached out and hugged his father, who glared at Dylan over Elliot's shoulder.

Gee, it was like Will hated her, she thought, wondering what he'd make of what had just happened between her and Elliot if he knew.

Elliot stood awkwardly in the doorway after Will left. 'So, um, yeah,' he said.

Dylan knew she was blushing.

This should stop, she thought, as she put the book down. It wasn't good to kiss the guy you were working for; she had seen enough episodes of *Mad Men* to know it never worked in the girl's favour.

But then she looked up at Elliot, his face flushed, his hair tousled from her fingers and the ache between her legs came back and she walked over and stood in front of him.

'Stop or don't stop?' she said, her eyes searching his. 'Your choice.'

'Don't stop,' he said, pulling her into his arms, making her forget everything else but him.

Chapter 19

'I disagree,' said Maggie as she put two tea bags into two mugs and splashed hot water over them.

'That's because you're contrary,' said Hugh, looking at her over his glasses.

'Well, contrary is better than pretentious. You just said you needed a silver teapot, who are you, Prince Charles?'

'Even Smike agrees with me about the teapot,' Hugh glanced under the table at the sleeping dog.

'It's a pretentious name for a dog,' Maggie repeated. 'Naming anything from Dickens is pretentious.'

'Have you even read any Dickens?' asked Hugh, laughing.

'No,' admitted Maggie as she opened his refrigerator and took out the cupcakes she had brought with her from a bakery in Malibu.

She placed them on the table and Hugh picked one up and stared at the pretty pink icing.

'Why is everything in LA so pretty?' he asked. 'Why is there never any ugliness?'

'Oh, there's plenty of that, just not in Malibu,' she said as she took off her navy cotton cardigan as the warm air come through the open glass doors.

Maggie kicked off her black ballet slippers and put her feet up on the chair next to her, her legs a little too warm in her most comfortable jeans.

'God it's hot,' she said aloud, and turned to see Hugh staring at her.

'What?' she asked, looking down at her white silk singlet.

'Nothing,' said Hugh as Smike moved from under the table and went to drink from his water bowl. Maggie smiled at the dog, who was all washed, de-fleaed and wearing a new red collar. He was kind of cute, in a mange-ridden, sad way. He had some potential, she thought, but only some.

'I still think Smike is a stupid name,' she said, wondering why Hugh had been staring at her.

'Smike is a character from *Nicholas Nickleby*, and the saddest creature in literature in my opinion. Since he is such a sad dog, it seemed only fitting.' Hugh's voice was a little strained as spoke.

Maggie changed the subject, hoping to change the feeling in the room. Hugh ran so hot and cold, she never knew where she was with him, she thought, but at least he seemed to have stopped drinking.

'So where are the pages you wanted me to read?' she asked.

Hugh tilted his head in the direction of the coffee table.

She moved her feet from the chair, and taking her tea with her, she walked to where the pages were.

She looked up at Hugh. 'You want me to read them now?'

'Yes, please,' he said politely.

Maggie laughed. 'Yes, please,' she repeated, imitating his accent.

Sitting down, she turned over the first page and then looked up at him. 'You can't just sit there and stare at me while I read.'

'But I want to,' said Hugh with a frown. 'That's all part of the process.'

Maggie rolled her eyes and shook her head.

'If it's no good, just say so,' he said nervously.

'Shut up,' she replied. 'And give me something to write with.'

Hugh threw a pen at her from the table. She placed it to her mouth as she read the pages, occasionally stopping to write in the margins.

It was only two short scenes.

'How bad is it?' he asked her.

'It's not bad at all,' she said honestly. 'It's just a little undercooked.'

'How so?' Hugh leaned forward.

Maggie thought about the best scripts she had read and what made them so good. She looked up at Hugh.

'I think it's missing desire.'

'Desire?' Hugh made a face. 'It's not that sort of story. There's nothing sexy about cancer.'

'Not that sort of desire. I mean, these scenes are *okay*, but your characters need to want something. Fiercely. Like in this moment, when she finds out the cancer is back, what did you want? What did she want?'

Hugh thought for a moment. 'Hope?'

Maggie nodded. 'Yes, great.' She stood up, still holding the pen and the papers. 'Everyone has to want something in every scene,' she said. 'And then there must be obstacles to them getting what they want. How your characters deal with those obstacles is what drives the story forward. That's *action*. You can't just have them crapping on, like we are now, for instance.'

Hugh laughed and nodded. 'I understand. And what about the other scene?'

'Where she leaves the doctor's office and goes to buy him a new suit to wear to her funeral? I mean, that's one of the most powerful, heart-wrenching scenes in the book. But here, it's sort of matter-of-fact.'

Hugh swallowed and then put his head in his hands. 'I don't think I can do it.'

Maggie walked over and sat on the other side of the table. 'Of course you can. Writing a script isn't so hard.'

But Hugh shook his head and looked up at her, his eyes filled with tears.

'I just don't think I can relive it again,' he said. 'I did it once for the book, and look what I've become. I'm a mess.'

'So why did you say insist on writing the script?'

'Because I needed to get out of London. Zoe offered me a chance to escape.'

'You could have left anyway,' said Maggie, thinking of her own escape years before.

'No, there were too many people invested in me staying. Her family, mine, our friends—everyone wanted me to stay so they could keep bringing me shepherd's pie and doing my washing and we could all be sad together. I know I sound ungrateful, but it's impossible to move on when people want you to stay put.'

Maggie nodded, trying to understand.

She had never had that sort of pressure, mainly because she didn't have family besides Zoe. But if she told Zoe she was moving to Bora-Bora tomorrow, Zoe would insist Maggie have a spare room so she could visit.

'But I've signed a contract, I've been paid money, I'm here, so I have to do it.'

Maggie watched as he wiped his eyes with the back of his hands. And then she did something she never imagined doing for anyone besides Elliot.

'What if I help you?'

'How?'

'We could write it together,' she said, thinking aloud.

'What will Zoe say?' he asked, his eyes hopeful.

'She doesn't need to know. You'll write the whole thing, but I'll…well, I'll get you organized, and work with you to get the scenes right.'

Hugh stared at her for what felt like a long time. 'Is this just so you can play Simone?' he asked.

'No,' she said truthfully.

'Then why?' asked Hugh, his eyes searching hers.

'Because, for some bizarre reason, since I barely know you, and I think your dog's name is pretentious as hell, I want you to be happy,' she said, and she felt as surprised as Hugh looked to find that it was the truth.

Hugh smiled at her across the table and she felt herself smile back.

'You know you're really quite lovely when you're not being contrary.'

Maggie shrugged. 'It's a rare occurrence, like the transit of Venus,' she said, and Hugh laughed loudly.

'And you said you didn't need a friend,' he said. 'Look at you now, with your two new friends.'

'Two?' asked Maggie, feeling pleased in a way she hadn't experienced before and not understanding why.

'Me and Smike, of course.'

Maggie shook her head slowly.

'It's still the dumbest name for a dog I've ever heard.'

But as the dog settled on her feet and she met Hugh's eyes across the table she felt a completely unfamiliar sense of belonging, and it was both scary and wonderful as hell.

Chapter 20

Jeff arrived back in Los Angeles after his week in Maui and felt an all too familiar malaise as he pulled up to his home in Beverly Hills.

He hated this house; it reminded him of his last wife, who was like a modern-day Marie Antoinette, hence her desire to own a mini Versailles-style mansion.

He had fought for the house in the divorce court, even though he hated it, because it was the principle of the matter. He had paid for it, he should keep it.

But with the only occupants being him and his staff of six and silver frames dotted about the home of his three children who wanted nothing to do with him unless it was for more money, the house was making him more and more depressed.

It was a Monday night and the only thing he had to do to occupy his mind was work, so he pulled out the DVD of potentials for Simone, which Zoe's office had sent him.

Slipping it into the computer, he sat at his mahogany desk, lit a cigar and started to watch.

None of them were right, he thought in frustration. How hard could it be to find a star?

Zoe Greene had the knack for spotting talent before anyone else. She was the Simon Cowell of the film world, only she wasn't a complete asshole. He made a mental note to remind his assistant to book a lunch with Simon, all the same.

So given Zoe was brilliant at plucking genuine talent from the wannabes who arrived in Hollywood every day, why was she sending him such crap?

He dialled her number. 'They're all terrible,' he barked into her message service. 'Do better, send me better, stop fucking wasting my time. And call me back.'

He slumped in his leather armchair and the silence of the house smothered him. He had to get out, he thought as he stubbed out the cigar in the crystal ashtray.

The sound of his phone ringing interrupted his thoughts and he grabbed it when he saw Zoe's name on the screen.

'What are you doing to me, Greene? These women are all disasters!'

There was a pause. Then a calm, 'Hello, Jeff.'

'Hello, Zoe,' he said impatiently.

'I gather you didn't like my options?'

He could hear laughter in her voice.

'You gathered correctly. Don't tell me that's all there is out there?'

'No, but it's a start. These are the actresses in our budget.'

'They're too old.'

'They're in their early thirties.' There was an edge in her voice now.

'That's too old for this role. I want her to age through the film. This is the story of a whole relationship, not just a death.'

'So you've read the book?' Zoe sounded surprised.

'Of course I've read the book. What, did you think I wouldn't?'

There was a pause on the other end of the phone. 'No, it's just that not many executives bother to read the material that they're optioning.'

'I'm not other executives,' he said.

'Did you like the book?'

'I bought the rights, didn't I?' Jeff wasn't sure how the conversation moved off course but found he didn't mind chatting with Zoe. He never chatted with anyone any more, everything was usually orders and demands. When had he lost the ability to converse?

'That's not answering my question,' Zoe said. 'I know it's not for most men; I mean, it's pretty emotional.'

Jeff looked at his copy of the book on the shelf in his study. He had read it three times, and each time he'd found something different in the text and each time he'd wished he had known back then, what he knew now. Maybe then he would have saved himself three marriages and a ton of money.

'Yeah, it was okay, as far as books like that go,' he said carefully.

There was a pause and then Zoe spoke.

'You want someone in their mid-twenties?' she asked, her voice laced with something between professionalism and disdain.

'I want someone who is *right*. She needs to be perfect.'

'There's no such thing as perfect,' said Zoe quietly.

'Bullshit. There is, and *you* have to find her.'

Zoe was silent.

'And what about directors, where are we at?'

'I put all this in the email I sent you,' Zoe said.

'I don't read emails, my assistants do. Just tell me,' he said. 'Better still, why don't we meet for dinner and you can fill me in?'

Silence. Not a good sign, he thought.

'Because I've been working since five a.m. Now I'm home, I'm in comfortable clothes, I'm about to order take-out and I'm going to watch *Game of Thrones*.'

It was Jeff's turn to be quiet for a moment. 'That sounds nice,' he said.

Beat one, beat two, beat three.

'Would you like to come over so I can read my email out to you?' asked Zoe, the humour back in her voice.

Jeff wasn't sure if she was joking or not, but he seized on her offer. Anything had to be better than wandering about a huge house with only staff to talk to.

'What's your address? I'll bring something decent from my cellar.'

'I'll text you,' said Zoe, sounding shocked, and then she hung up.

He stared eagerly at his phone, waiting for her message.

Zoe Greene was an interesting person, he decided. She was attractive but too old for him, but she didn't pander to him like others around him, which, given her lack of experience in producing, was surprising.

Her reputation as a manager was flawless but beyond that he knew nothing of her personal life and for the first time in a long time, he was intrigued by someone other than himself.

The sound of the text with Zoe's address came through and he pounced on his phone like he was a teenager.

Now what the hell was he going to wear?

Chapter 21

Zoe stared at her phone and then texted Maggie.

Z: Jeff Beerman just invited himself over.

M: Ha. Careful you don't end up as wife no.4. I think he beheaded the others.

Z: No way. He's too weird. What are you doing?

M: Hanging with Hugh.

Z: ?? Is something happening with you two?

M: No! For a nun, you have a smutty mind.

Z: Do I have to put on real clothes? I'm currently in something stretchy.

M: Nope, he's there for biz, not pleasure. Although if he is into you he's finally showing some taste.

Z: Nope, he already told me I'm too old for him. He hates women over thirty.

M: Ugh. What a creep. Does that mean I don't have a hope in hell at Simone as far as Jeff's concerned?

Zoe paused and looked at the screen. Should she tell Maggie now that Jeff had already shot down the idea of her in *The Art of Love*?

She typed back quickly, holding her breath.

I don't know, maybe not, he's got it in his head he needs someone less expensive.

She waited for Maggie's reply, but it didn't come. Should she be worried? She didn't want to hurt Maggie, but she already knew she wasn't going to play Simone if she and Jeff had their way. Hugh was a different story.

Zoe lay back on the sofa and closed her eyes, struck by an awful thought. Was Maggie spending time with Hugh just so that he would fight for her at casting time?

Maggie had always shown integrity in her career, so why should Zoe doubt her now? And she loved *The Art of Love* more than anyone else Zoe knew.

Christ, this producing thing wasn't fun and as for last year's *Variety*'s Most Powerful Man in Hollywood coming for dinner that wasn't going to be fun either.

Zoe stayed away from men like Jeff in the small social circles of Los Angeles. Most of the successful and wealthy tended to stay together, and though Zoe could have mixed with a few of the top-tier power-players, she had yet to feel comfortable in their presence when she had a glass of wine in her hand. All her insecurities rose to the surface, like secrets in a lake after a rainstorm, and there wasn't a man in the world who she had ever liked enough to let them into her heart.

But when she had her phone and a pen in her hand and was on the other side of a boardroom table, then she was in control. Then men bowed to her whims, no treating her like she had nothing but a body to offer. She made things happen in Hollywood, and no one would ever have control of her heart and soul.

Half an hour later, the sound of a car in her driveway made her jump and she realized Jeff had arrived and she felt like she had been holding her breath since the phone call.

She thought about straightening up the living room, brushing her hair, putting on lipstick. But no. Jeff was coming into her world and he would have to take her as she was.

She had the door open before he reached the front step. He smiled at her as he approached.

'You have good hearing.'

'For an old person,' said Zoe with a wry smile. *Years of being hyper aware as a child will do that to you*, she thought.

Jeff bounded up the stairs, two shopping bags in his hand.

'You have to let that go now. I mean, it's getting boring.'

'Well, I'm not quite ready to do that yet,' she said as he handed her a shopping bag and followed her inside.

'This is nice,' he said, looking around her warmly lit house filled with artwork, rugs and comfortable sofas.

'Yes, it's all I need,' she said, thinking of his enormous estate in Hawaii.

'I was about to order food, what do you feel like?' she said, putting a selection of menus in front of him.

'Actually, I bought food to cook,' Jeff said. 'I really felt like a steak. Then we can discuss those shitty options you sent me.'

Zoe felt fury bubble up and she didn't know whether to laugh or scream.

'You have some nerve,' she said, trying not to let her voice shake. 'You invite yourself over to tell me how bad I am at my job and expect me to cook for you as well? You are kidding yourself, Jeff!'

Jeff started to laugh.

'Oh, don't be so self-righteous, Greene. I wasn't suggesting *you* cook. I thought I'd make us dinner.'

He was taking items from the shopping bags: baby potatoes, broccoli, goat's cheese, steak, mushrooms and a bottle of wine.

Zoe stood, hands on hips, and pursed her lips because she didn't know what else to do. Men like Jeff seemed so easy to read, and now he was telling her about the best cuts of prime rib?

'You want to cook me a steak?'

'Actually, I wanted to cook myself a steak but since you're here, I'll cook one for you too.'

'You really cook?' she asked, incredulous.

'It relaxes me,' he said with a smile. 'So, how do you like your steak?'

Wearing a plain white T-shirt, faded chinos and sneakers, he could have been any middle-aged man, about to cook dinner at home—expect he wasn't, Zoe reminded herself.

'Ah, medium rare, thanks,' she answered, sitting down for a moment on the sofa, and then picked up her phone and texted quickly, her back turned towards him.

Jeff Beerman is making me a steak in my house. Can my life get any weirder?

Within seconds a reply from Maggie came back.

Every time I ask that question, life generally gets weirder. Get ready cos crazy is coming. Did you mention me to Jeff as Simone?

Zoe stared at the text and then put the phone down. She would deal with Maggie later, she thought, right now she had to focus on Jeff.

Setting up her cable channel, she started to play an episode of *Game of Thrones*, as Jeff bustled about in the kitchen.

'Do you want me to be an assistant chef? I'm very talented with a knife,' she offered half-heartedly.

But Jeff just shook his head. 'As much as I would love to see your knife skills, tonight I'm the chef.' And he handed her a glass of wine. 'I found the glasses in the cupboard, hope they're okay.'

Zoe glanced at Jeff and nodded dumbly as she took the wine and Jeff held his glass out to her.

'To *The Art of Love*,' he said.

'To the art of cooking a good steak,' she said and tilted her head towards him.

'Baby, you have no idea how good my steaks are, you just wait,' Jeff said as he bounded back to the kitchen.

Zoe tried to concentrate on the TV show but she was aware of every time Jeff moved in the kitchen. The sound of chopping and frying, and water running, and Jeff singing some tuneless song to himself was almost comforting.

This is what it's like to be looked after, she thought.

Well, don't get used to it, Greene, she told herself. *Remember nothing lasts for ever, especially not the good times.*

West Virginia
November 1995

Krista was sure the preacher was out, so she snuck into his office.

The children were lined up in front of the TV again, their mother asleep in her bedroom, passed out on whatever she had taken that evening.

It was becoming too easy to steal money from the snake enclosure. As long as the snakes had eaten, they seemed to leave her alone.

A twenty here, a ten there, never anything more, a fifty-dollar note would be too obvious from the tightly rolled notes in the plastic treasure chest.

Moving towards the snakes, she saw they were still and so pushed up the sleeve of her fake Adidas windcheater and gently put her hand into the pit.

'Krista?'

She turned to see the preacher in the doorway; her hand was halfway down the glass tank.

'Hi, I thought one of the snakes was sick,' she said quickly.

'You weren't trying to steal my money now, were you?'

Preacher Garrett wasn't an attractive man, but he was a large man, and Krista had felt every pound of him, the two times he had lain on her.

'No, there's no money in here, is there?' She peered through the glass, as though looking for the hidden treasure.

'Now, now, Krista. Don't make any sudden movements, else these snakes will spring up and bite you. They know a heathen when they see one. You have to stay right there until I give them the Lord's command to let you be.'

Krista left her hand dangling in the cabinet. The two rattlesnakes lay curled unmoving in the warm light.

The preacher came up behind her, and she felt his hard penis pushing into her buttocks.

God no, please no, she prayed.

She felt his hands reach around, undo her jeans and pull them down in a single gentle movement, so as to not startle the snakes.

She started to cry. 'Please don't.'

'Girl, you're a common thief and a whore. This is just teaching you a lesson from God, who comes through the snakes,' he whispered. 'If God thinks you're worthy of saving, the snakes won't bite.'

She heard him unzip his pants.

'Please,' she cried again and then she saw one of the snakes start to uncurl, slowly, like poetry.

It hissed as the preacher rubbed himself against her and he laughed quietly. 'Someone's awake.'

She didn't know whether he meant him or the snake.

The snake wasn't hissing now, and Krista stared at it, mesmerized, as she felt the preacher's hands on her breasts under her sweatshirt.

Krista always stayed at the back of the church when the preacher raised the snakes to the altar and called on God to heal and forgive them all.

But this snake rose up and she held her breath and then it seemed almost to caress her, winding around her hand, its skin cold and soft yet hard at the same time. She stayed very still, even as the preacher kicked her legs open and reached down between them.

As the snake reared up she grabbed it by its neck and, turning, she threw it at the preacher's face.

He fell back, the snake landing on top of him.

'You useless jezebel, whore, no wonder nobody wants you, you ain't got nothing that's any good to anyone,' he yelled, as he flung the snake at the wall.

Go, go, go, her mind yelled as she ran from the house, leaving the children on the sofa, still watching TV.

Her mouth was dry as she tried to scream as she ran along the path down to the road, her heart beating so fast, she thought it might jump from her chest.

Shay, she thought, she needed Shay.

She had a note stuck in her locker at school from Shay saying her gram had died and she was at a new foster home, but she hadn't seen her at school or around town.

Running down the road, she didn't stop until she reached town and stood wondering where the hell Shay was. She didn't have her address, and no phone number to call.

Sweat ran down her back as she saw the mall ahead.

Hope and relief filled her as she walked through the automatic doors and towards the cookie counter.

But looking around, Shay wasn't there, and her heart sank. She had no one else to help her. She was going to go to jail for murder, she thought, her mind spiralling out of control.

'You looking for Shay, honey?' asked the woman in the apron behind the counter.

'Yes,' said Krista, holding back tears.

'She's staying over in at Dorothy Meers's house on Bald Eagle Road,' she said. 'Did you hear her gram died?'

Krista nodded. 'What number is the house?'

The woman walked to the pile of papers by the register and ran an acrylic nail along the paper.

'Forty-four,' she said, as Krista turned to leave.

'Tell her she's on tomorrow,' called the woman after her.

Krista ran from the mall and stood outside, looking for any sign the authorities were coming after her, but the parking lot was filled with people shopping on a Thursday night.

Getting her bearings, she wondered if she should take the bus, but then thought she couldn't chance it and instead took the back roads to Bald Eagle Road.

Half an hour later, she was outside the house.

The sound of dogs barking heralded her arrival and the door opened a sliver, and a man of about twenty stared at her up and down.

'What?' he asked.

'Is Shay home?' she asked breathlessly.

'She ain't allowed to come out of her room,' he said in a slow drawl. 'On account of her running away,' he went on, his eyes narrowing at Krista suspiciously.

'Can I see her inside then?' she asked and then she licked her lips and smiled sweetly.

The man's eyes swept over her heaving chest in her T-shirt, then he stepped back and opened the door a little more.

'I'll let you have ten minutes, if you give me ten minutes with you first,' he said.

Krista felt her skin crawl and then thought about the preacher. Nothing could be worse than the preacher, she thought.

'After I see her,' she said with more confidence than she felt.

They faced each other and Krista took in his dungarees and sweatshirt, with damp patches under his arms.

'Okay,' he agreed and he walked down the dark hallway and unlocked a padlock outside a door.

He opened and it and Krista stepped inside a dark room, closing the door behind her.

'Shay baby?' she asked and then put her hand out to find the light.

Turning on the light, a figure lay huddled in the bed and she walked to the side.

'Baby, it's me, Krista,' she said. Why wasn't Shay moving?

The lump under the bedclothes in the saggy single bed moved, and Krista took in the boards on the window and the room scant of anything else besides her backpack.

'What are you doing here?' asked Shay, sitting up. She had two black eyes and was paler than snow.

Krista felt her hands fly up to her mouth.

'I'm getting you out,' she said, forgetting her own problems.

'You can't. Judd won't let me go, his mother is never here, he keeps me as his slave,' she cried.

Krista walked to the door. 'I'm gonna leave this unpadlocked, you have ten minutes to get out and meet me in the woods where we made that fire that one time.'

'Ten minutes?' asked Shay, confused.

'Ten minutes,' repeated Krista and went in search of Judd.

She didn't believe in a God that would allow people to treat others the way she and Shay had been treated, so she didn't bother asking for his forgiveness before she entered the bedroom where the disgusting guy was waiting for her.

But afterwards, when she looked back on what she had done, she knew it was right, and just in case there was a God who happened to be watching Krista and him at that moment in the bedroom, he would know she had done the right thing also. Even if it made her a conniving bitch, because she would rather be a bitch than a victim for the rest of her life.

Chapter 22

Dylan checked through the paperwork for Elliot's visit to the doctor. She had spent most of the evening before reading up on his condition and the transplant.

'You ready, Elliot?'

Dylan looked up from the kitchen bench to see Will with his car keys in hand.

'You're back?' said Dylan surprised. 'I thought you were in Arizona.'

'I came back to take Elliot to his specialist,' Will said with narrowed eyes staring at Dylan, making her feel cold and scared simultaneously.

'I'm taking him to the doctor's,' said Dylan politely.

Will scared her with his physical presence and agitated, impatient attitude.

'I'm taking him,' he said now.

'But he asked me to.' Dylan tried to stop her voice from shaking.

'I always take him to the doctor's,' said Will. 'You might

be good at typing or whatever else he has you doing but this isn't a task for you.'

Dylan looked away as tears smarted in her eyes. How could Elliot have come from such a man?

'Hey, Dad, we're going,' said Elliot as he walked up the stairs into the kitchen.

'I told Dylan I will be taking you for your check-up,' he said.

Elliot glanced at Dylan and then back to his father.

'No, I'm taking myself,' he said firmly. 'And Dylan is coming with me.'

Dylan smiled to herself, her head still turned from Will.

'But I always take you,' Will said.

'I know, but today Dylan is coming with me,' he said.

'I came back from Arizona for you,' Will yelled.

'I didn't ask you to, Dad,' said Elliot calmly.

The men stared at each other. A father and son at war, Dylan knew, but she wasn't the prize: Elliot's independence was at stake.

'This is bullshit, she can't do anything for you. I'm the one you need.' Will's voice was raised in anger and Dylan stepped back from the scene, edging towards the door.

'Where are you going?' asked Elliot as he caught sight of her.

'I'm just going back to my room, maybe your dad should take you,' she said quietly.

'No, come on, we're leaving,' said Elliot and he grabbed the file of papers from the bench and took Dylan's hand.

'Dad, I'm fine,' he said. 'Just let me be.'

They walked out of the house into the sunlight but Dylan felt the dark cloud of Will's stare as Elliot opened the car door for her.

'Your dad hates me,' she said.

'My dad hates everyone except me and Maggie,' said Elliot as he shut the door and got into the car himself.

'Why did she marry him?' Dylan asked, trying to think of a reason why someone as bright as Maggie would end up with a bully like Will.

Elliot shrugged. 'Who knows?'

He reached over and took her hand. 'Don't worry about Dad, he's just protective, he'll come around to you soon and then he will see how amazing you are.'

Dylan said nothing as they drove out onto the street but she knew Will had no such plans and, deep down, she felt that perhaps his motivation was not so much to protect Elliot but to smother him.

Will's level of overprotection made her own mother look like a free spirit, she decided, as Elliot drove them, the engine of the Porsche humming smoothly.

She watched his hands move on the steering wheel and she breathed out with a sigh.

'You okay, baby?' he asked.

'Yep, I just like your hands,' she said and she saw the fine hair's on Elliot's arms stand on end.

'My hands? Yeah?' he asked with a laugh. 'What else do you like?'

Dylan swallowed, and ran a finger along his thigh. 'I like your thighs.'

Elliot's hand left the steering wheel and put his hand on her knee.

'I like your thighs also,' he said, his hand then drifting upwards and to the soft skin of her inside leg.

Dylan caught her breath as her body moved instinctively towards his hands.

The silence in the car was as loud as her breathing.

'What else do you like?' she asked, hearing her own voice crack a little.

They only ever made out for hours, hands fumbling and promises and whispers, and then as soon as Dylan tried to take it further, Elliot would stop her.

She didn't know why and she didn't dare ask, in case he no longer wanted her or, worse, his heart was unwell.

Elliot's hand ran gently over her skin and up to her underwear, and without thinking twice, she took it and pressed it between her legs and moaned.

She heard Elliot groan and saw him shifting in his seat, his desire evident, and his fingers pressed against the heat between her legs.

'Pull over,' she heard herself moan.

'I can't,' he answered.

'Please?'

Elliot put his hand back onto the steering wheel, leaving Dylan, aching, next to him.

She stared out the window, ashamed by her desperation and embarrassed by him not pulling over to finish what they had started.

Elliot turned up the stereo, the sound of Frank Ocean soothing the tension and she felt tears prick her eyes.

What was she doing? She was working as an assistant to a guy who didn't really do anything worthy of an assistant, who didn't want to go all the way with her, supposedly searching for her mother, and yet she hadn't done anything properly about it in weeks.

Elliot was a lovely distraction, she decided, but as soon as this doctor's appointment was over, she would resign and make the effort to do what she had come to Los Angles for.

They turned into an underground parking lot and Elliot

guided the car into a space and turned off the engine, leaving the stereo playing.

Dylan unclipped her seat belt, about to open the car, when she felt Elliot's hand on her thigh and she turned just as he kissed her.

His tongue explored her mouth, as his hand went up her thigh and rested on the ache and she felt herself pull him closer, as his hands slipped under the fabric and ran along the wetness.

'Jesus,' she whispered, as Elliot slipped a finger inside her.

He flipped her seat back, so she was almost lying next to him, and she felt one hand inside her, the other exploring under her top, along her stomach, and her breasts.

Dylan didn't care about shame now with her feet on the dash of the car, as she reached over and massaged Elliot's erection through his pants.

'Dylan, babe,' he groaned, as another finger slipped inside her and then she felt herself explode, his hands bringing her to an almost perfect place.

Finally she got her breath back, and she looked up at him shyly.

'I need to help you now,' she said.

'Later,' he said with a gentle smile. 'Besides, this is something I've always wanted to do and never have.'

'What?' she asked confused.

'Make out with a beautiful girl in a car,' he answered with a laugh. 'Granted, I thought it would be at night, looking out over the lights of the city, not in a dark parking lot on the way to the heart surgeon, but hey, whatever works, right?'

Dylan sat up and kissed him. Maybe she would just wait a week on her decision to leave. Elliot was right, whatever works, and right now, the hum in her body told her that everything was working just fine.

Chapter 23

'Everything looks fine,' said the doctor as he pulled down Elliot's T-shirt and put away his stethoscope. 'All your tests are normal, you're doing very well. It was a healthy heart you received.'

Elliot wondered if he should ask about the donor again but remembered the doctor was careful to say nothing other than it was a young person's organ.

How young? Elliot had wanted to know. How did they die? Who were they?

'Do you have any questions?' asked the doctor, and Elliot paused. Yes he did, and he cleared his throat before speaking, hoping his voice didn't tremble.

'What about sex?' he asked.

The doctor frowned. 'Yes? What about it? Are you having sex or planning on it?'

Elliot felt himself blushing. 'Planning on it,' he said.

'Any erectile issues?'

Elliot shook his head. 'No, all fine.'

'Well then, you can assume your normal routine as soon as you're ready, and get back to having sex again.'

The doctor was sitting at his desk and Elliot moved from the table to the chair.

'I hadn't had sex before the operation,' he said quietly. God, this was embarrassing.

The doctor looked up at Elliot and his brusqueness was replaced with a smile.

'You'll be fine, just make sure your partner has the all-clear of infections, like yeast, bacterial, herpes and so on, those types of things can get into your heart.'

Elliot thought about Dylan waiting outside the doctor's office. How on earth could he ask her to have a screening for infections? It was like accusing her of being a slut.

Elliot rubbed his forehead and nodded. Maybe he wouldn't have sex with her then, he thought, but since their kiss the week before, things had only been getting more intense between them. If he could have, he would never stop making love to her...if only he knew how, and if only he knew he could.

He knew Dylan wanted him and he wanted her more than anything else in his life, but he had been worried he wouldn't be able to have sex, and now he had to ask her to have tests done?

God, it was so embarrassing.

Elliot stood up and thanked the doctor and went into the hallway, where Dylan was reading a booklet on 'Everything you need to know about your new heart'.

'How did it go?' she asked, smiling at him, still glowing from their dalliance in the car.

'Fine,' he snapped, trying to stop himself.

Dylan stuffed the booklet into her bag and walked with him from the office and into the lift.

'You okay?' she asked. 'You're all weird and quiet.'

'No, I'm fine,' he said, not looking at her.

Dylan reached over and took his hand, but he felt himself pull away.

He couldn't ask her, he thought. He wouldn't. This was it. He would rather die a virgin than ask her to get tests done, just so he could have sex with her.

'What's wrong?' she asked, her beautiful face worried, and her eyes glistening with tears. 'Is there something wrong with your heart? Is it being rejected?'

'No,' he snapped.

'Then why are you rejecting me?' she asked, putting her hand on his forearm.

Just the slightest touch from her made him crazy but he shrank back, so he was against the steel wall of the lift.

'What is wrong with you?' asked Dylan as the lift stopped and a woman got in.

They stood in silence as the lift came to the bottom floor and Dylan stormed out into the car park.

Elliot walked slowly behind her and followed her to his car, where they drove in silence to the house.

He wished he was better equipped to deal with this issue, he thought; he wished he could talk to his dad but Will had barely been civil to Dylan since she had started.

God, his dad was such a bully sometimes. He wished he could stand up to him and tell him control wasn't the same as love, then tell his hippie, hoax of a mother that she was a selfish bitch for not bothering to see him when he had his transplant, and most of all he wished he could tell Dylan the truth about two things.

The first was the tests and the second was that he loved her.

He knew he loved her because he wanted her to be happy

more than himself. He wanted success for her, and for her to find her mother. He would do anything for her, so why couldn't he ask her to do anything for him?

He would have asked Maggie but she was paying Dylan's salary and there were so many lines being crossed, he wondered if he could be sued for sexual harassment. God, he felt so out of his league, he thought, as he pulled up to the house and pressed the remote control to the gates.

The gates opened and Elliot drove up a little too fast, then stopped in front of the house with a slight screech to the brakes.

Dylan swept out of the car and slammed the door and started to walk around the side of the house.

'Where are you going?' he called after her.

She turned, her eyes boring holes in him, even in the blinding sunlight.

'To the guesthouse. If you need assisting with anything writing wise then let me know, and if you plan on telling me why you're being such a prick after seeing the doctor, then let me know. Meanwhile, I would like to be left alone.'

Elliot watched helplessly as she disappeared and with a sigh, he walked inside the house.

For two days he wrote, only because Dylan wasn't accepting his calls, only emails, and would only answer if it were related to writing. He rang Hugh, and told him the whole story.

'If you really like her, then tell her the truth,' he said.

'It's too hard.'

'Then go and pack her bags for her, because this girl, whoever she is, sounds like she isn't a pushover and you sound like you're desperate for her to stay.'

The idea that Dylan might up and leave hadn't occurred to him but it was cemented when he saw her leaving the house without explanation.

Panic had set in that she was looking for a new job and a new place to live.

Just tell her, his mind said, but he didn't know how to bring it up, and least of all, ask her to do that for him.

One hundred times he composed an email, but each time he got to the vital part, he lost his nerve. When he did see her, she was entirely pleasant and polite but no more kisses, it was as though nothing had happened between them.

'Stop punishing me,' he said to her on the fourth day.

'Then tell me what happened at the doctor's,' she said. She had taken to wearing her glasses again, as though they were a set of armor of some sort, but he noticed she looked pale and sad.

'Nothing, the heart is fine, I'm fine,' he answered, not looking her in the eye.

'Bullshit,' she said and went back to her quarters again.

Christ, Elliot, he thought, *just man up and tell her.*

He tried to write for another hour but spent most of it thinking about Dylan and finally found the nerve. He was just getting up when the door opened and Dylan stood in the doorway, papers in her hands.

This was it, she was resigning, he thought, closing his eyes for a moment.

She was leaving because he couldn't be honest with her because of his stupid pride and now it was too late.

'This is for you,' she said. She was wearing a pink short skirt with a pale blue T-shirt with clouds all over it, and he thought she looked dreamy, except now it was a nightmare because he had been so stupid.

'I don't want you to go,' he said, feeling like he might cry. *Jesus, I'm pathetic*, he thought. *Why would she want to be with me anyway?*

'Just read the paper,' she said sternly and he glanced at her. Was that a twinkle in her eyes?

He pulled a piece of paper out of an envelope and read the top, *Dylan Mercer*, and his eyes ran over the rest and he looked up and Dylan had shut the door and was leaning against it, a sly smile on her gorgeous mouth.

'I had the tests, I'm as clean as a whistle,' she said with one raised eyebrow.

Elliot felt himself both turned on and overwhelmed as she walked towards him.

'How did you know?' he asked, as he pulled her to him.

'I read that booklet from the doctor's office and I realized— I mean, I guessed—but I think I knew,' she said and she leaned down and kissed him.

'I'm sorry I was a bitch,' she said gently. 'I should have been more understanding. I just thought you didn't want me any more.'

'I'm sorry I was a coward,' he said as he looked up at her. 'And it was the opposite, I want you so much, I just didn't want to ask you to do anything more than what you were giving me.'

'Please always be honest with me,' she said, a frown covering her face.

'You too,' he said. 'No games.'

'No dramas.'

Dylan pulled him to his feet and held his hands.

'Elliot, come to bed with me,' she half whispered.

Elliot smiled and leaned down and kissed her. 'I thought you'd never ask.'

Chapter 24

'We have come to your place every day for two weeks. Why can't we ever go to my place to write?' Maggie complained

'We can go to your house,' Hugh said, sounding surprised. 'I thought you didn't want me in your abode because you never offered. I'm just a lowly writer, after all. I might steal your silverware and precious jewels so I can live for another year.'

Maggie laughed. 'You are so full of shit sometimes.' She was still in bed, and she rolled over onto her stomach so her head hung off the end of the bed, her hair veil-like, creating a waterfall. A suspiciously brassy waterfall, she thought, knowing it was beyond the time when she should be getting the colour corrected.

'Well, are you coming over or not, writer boy?' For a moment she wondered at what point teasing rolled into flirting. Had she just crossed the line?

'I'll be over soon,' Hugh said firmly.

'But how are you going to get here? Don't I have to come and get you?'

'Oh no, Smike and I will walk. I have your address from Zoe,' he said, and before Maggie could answer, he had hung up.

Walk? Was he crazy? No one in Malibu walked, unless it was on the beach.

She got out of bed, and pulled on a pair of yoga pants and white T-shirt.

She had always slept naked, which used to worry Will. 'What if Elliot comes in?' he'd ask back when they were married.

But Elliot never did come into their room, he never asked for any comfort, not even when they thought he wasn't going to live. Just thinking of him made Maggie feel happy, as she put on the kettle to boil and glanced at the clock and texted him.

Hey, El, how're things going with Dylan? Hope you're get-ting lots of writing done. M x

Humming a little, she made a cup of tea. Once a com-mitted coffee drinker, now she drank as much tea through-out the day as Hugh. She opened her blinds to see dazzling sunshine hitting the water. Stepping out onto the balcony, she inhaled the morning air and sat on one of her rarely used outside chairs, ready to watch the beach wake up.

Hugh made her feel smart and clever and her dry sense of humour seemed to work for him.

Their routine was becoming comfortably familiar: a cup of tea on her arrival, a walk on the beach with Smike, and open, free-ranging conversations unlike any she'd had with other men in her life.

Hugh was genuinely curious about her life. Sometimes she gave him deliberately vague answers to his questions— only Zoe knew the whole truth of her past. She felt herself almost spilling some of the things that had happened, about how she came to Hollywood, about the struggle and the victories over her life, but she couldn't quite get there. She wanted to trust him, but could she?

Hugh asked her opinion on world matters, as if she might have something useful to say so she had started to read the news headlines and non-American news websites as a matter of course.

But what they didn't talk about was Simone's death, unless it was in relation to the script.

She knew some days were harder for him than others, and twice she had turned up to find him so hungover he couldn't function. But she had just put him to bed, and when he woke, they went back to work, which seemed to involve a lot of arguing.

'You can't tell me what happened, *you* weren't bloody there,' he'd said at one point during their last session.

'Neither were you, you were pissed all the time,' Maggie shot back.

'How do you know that?'

'I guessed,' she said, and then she was quiet. 'Did Simone know?'

'That I was a drunk? I suppose so, but she didn't care. She was dying, so what did it matter?'

Maggie looked him straight in the eyes. 'I'm damn sure she *did* care, Hugh. Maybe she just didn't have the strength to take on your battle as well as her own.'

Hugh was silent as he stood up and she worried he was about to tell her to get out but instead he kissed the top of her head as he walked past her to make more tea.

The kiss felt like nothing and everything. As though she was his friend, confidante, partner, but not his lover.

Hugh hadn't suggested anything more than a working friendship, and Maggie wasn't sure she wanted more than what they had anyway. Time with Hugh went so fast, she sometimes just wanted to hold onto it and put it under a glass dome like a butterfly. She knew nothing good lasted for ever.

Before she knew it, Hugh was on the intercom's security camera, wearing a bike helmet and peering into the lens like he was looking into a fish tank. She burst out laughing as she pressed the button to speak.

'God, that was quick. Did you fly over?'

'I rode my new bike,' he said proudly.

'A bicycle? That's cute.'

Hugh wheeled in a shiny red bicycle and propped it against the wall. As soon as he unclipped Smike's lead, the dog ran over and jumped up on Maggie.

'Hello, friend,' she said, gently pushing him down.

Hugh kissed her on the cheek, something he hadn't down before, and walked inside.

First a kiss on the head and now one on the cheek. He was getting warmer, she thought, amused at herself.

'We live very close, actually, and Smike enjoyed the walk, he did a healthy bowel movement on someone's fake lawn, which amused me greatly,' he said in his clipped accent. Maggie laughed as she followed him in, Smike trailing after them.

Hugh looked around the house and nodded. 'Very nice,' he said, 'although it isn't at all what I thought it would be.'

Maggie crossed her arms. 'Oh, yes? And what did you think it would look like?'

Hugh glanced about the room. 'It's all very modern; I thought it would be more cosy.'

Maggie laughed. 'Cosy? Nothing about me says cosy, I hope.'

'What's wrong with cosy?' asked Hugh with a frown. 'I happen to like cosy. My dream house will be cosy, but with a view.'

Maggie went into the kitchen to make Hugh's tea. 'And where is this dream home? Not in LA, I assume?' Even as she asked she felt disappointment flood her at the thought of not seeing him every day.

'France. I want to live in a stone cottage where I can read and write and eat cheese and roll my eyes at tourists.'

Maggie laughed. 'You're such a cliché of a writer.'

The sound of Hugh's phone stopped her continuing to tease him.

'Oh, hello, Zoe,' he said, turning away from Maggie and then he laughed. She wished she could hear what Zoe was saying on the other end of the line as Hugh said 'Uh-huh' repeatedly.

Then he laughed again, and said goodbye, shaking his head as he hung up.

'That woman is relentless, I can see why you're friends,' he said.

'What did she say?' asked Maggie, smiling at him but going through the potential conversation Zoe and Hugh had just shared.

'Oh, something about pushing the head of the studio for

more budget. She's very good at keeping me in the loop about the whole thing. Without her I would never have sold the rights.'

'Oh, why is that?' asked Maggie.

'Because she didn't promise me the world, she just told me that sometimes a change of city, sunshine and palm trees can take the bad memories away. The next thing you know I'm in a rehab centre and now I'm here with you. She really is a miracle worker.'

A flush ran up Maggie's neck, and she felt her jaw stiffen.

'Do you have a crush on her?' she asked.

Hugh started to laugh. 'Not at all. Why, are you jealous?'

She didn't know if it was his turn to tease her or if he was serious.

'We should go out for coffee,' she said, walking towards the door.

'In that?' said Hugh unapologetically, and then he looked her up and down and gave her a wink. 'You're usually more formal?'

Maggie realized she was still in her old yoga outfit. 'I'll just go and change,' she said quickly.

'No, why? You look great.'

Maggie didn't know whether to be disturbed that he thought she looked fine like she was or happy that he didn't care, but vanity took over and she crossed her arms.

'I'll just change,' she insisted.

She rushed to her bedroom and pulled on underwear, jeans and a striped T-shirt, and brushed her hair.

When she came back Hugh was wandering around the huge living room, inspecting the art on the walls.

'You like modernism, I see,' he said, standing in front of a large neorealism painting of clouds.

'I suppose,' she said, looking at the painting for the first time since she had approved its purchase by the interior designer.

'You don't like modernism?' he asked, his face confused.

'I don't really care about art. I just bought it because they said I should have something on the walls.'

Hugh laughed loudly. 'Oh, you're priceless, Maggie Hall.'

'Are you making fun of me?' she asked, crossly.

'No, I just think it's so refreshing that you're not a complete tosser; good for you.' He glanced around the room. 'Gosh, being a movie star has it perks, though, doesn't it?'

Maggie looked at the elegantly sparse room, with the white Minotti sofas and chairs, contemporary rugs on polished concrete floors, white walls and custom-designed lighting to show off the artwork. None of it meant anything to her.

'I guess, but it's only stuff, isn't it?'

'I think this one room is bigger than our whole apartment in Pimlico,' he said, shaking his head.

Maggie felt a prickle at the back of her neck. Hugh never spoke of Simone and their life together unless it was about the script, and even then it was confined to what was in the book.

'How long were you there for?' she asked casually as she put down a bowl of water for Smike, who was out on the balcony basking in the morning sun.

'About ten years,' he said. 'Have you got something I can dunk into my tea?'

Maggie thought for a moment. 'Wait there,' she told him. When she returned she brought with her an unopened packet of shortbread.

'What is this—contraband?'

'A Scottish actor I worked with sent them to me. Of course I'd never eat them,' she said. 'You might want to check the use-by date.'

Hugh already had one in his mouth.

'Did you eat breakfast?' she asked with a frown.

'No, did you?'

Maggie made a face at him. 'I never eat breakfast. Then again, I'm not a recovering alcoholic.'

'So what are you recovering from?'

'Nothing, I'm as pure as the driven snow,' she said with a small curtsey and Hugh snorted.

'Come on. Surely you have something you find hard to tame or manage? You can't be that perfect. What's your greatest fear? Sharks? Spiders? Snakes? Come on, tell all.'

Maggie turned away.

'Aha, it's snakes, isn't it? I saw the way you shivered.' Hugh was behind her now, and made a hissing sound, just joking around, but Maggie wasn't laughing. She felt sick, her body hot and cold at the same time.

'I need a cardigan, I'll be right back,' she said, quickly walking away.

In her bedroom she put her head against the wall and closed her eyes. *Don't even think about it*, she told herself, but she couldn't stop. She took a deep breath and stood perfectly still, trying to stay calm, but the memories came flooding in—the snake's scales brushing against her skin, the flicker of its tongue, the preacher's breath hot in her ear—

'Maggie?'

She turned, almost unseeing. Hugh was in the doorway.

'Are you all right?' He came to her side and looked at her closely. 'No, you're not all right at all, are you? God, I was just having a joke. I'm so sorry, Maggie. Come on.' He put his arms around her shoulders and gently led her to the bed and sat her down.

'I'm such a smart-arse sometimes, I didn't even think, please forgive me,' he was saying, but Maggie couldn't answer so he went to her walk-in wardrobe and came out with a pale cashmere cardigan and draped it around her shoulders.

Maggie couldn't stop shaking. Hugh held her hands and rubbed them, as though he was warming them up.

'Of course everyone has a fear,' he was saying. 'I mean, yours does seem a little extreme, but then who am I to talk, with my drinking and all that rubbish. Whatever it is, it's over now.'

Maggie was silent as she tried to push the memories back into the rarely visited place in her mind.

'Can we talk about your favourite things now? Flowers? The ocean? The scent of French perfume? Let's talk about lovely things, all the things you love the most.'

The sound of Hugh's voice was calming and Maggie felt her body starting to relax. She blinked a few times, as though coming back into the room after being hypnotized.

'The smell of a newborn baby,' she said slowly, not looking at him.

Hugh was quiet for a moment, but he still held her hand.

'That's quite a lovely scent, I'm sure,' he said eventually, his eyes searching hers, and he slowly leaned forward.

She closed her eyes, tilting her face towards his.

Then she felt a soft kiss on her forehead and disappointment replaced fear and she didn't know which one felt worse until she opened her eyes and looked at him and burst out laughing.

'What?' he asked, looking worried.

'You're still wearing your helmet,' she said, looking up at his earnest face, topped with the safety device.

Hugh nodded solemnly, but she saw the smile in his eyes. 'This is why I'm here, Maggie Hall, always at the ready to protect and defend you.'

Maggie tried to smile and squeezed his hand. 'Thank you,' she answered.

'You know, one day you might even trust me enough to tell me your secrets,' he said gently.

'Maybe,' she said.

But she doubted she would ever trust anyone with her secrets, not even Hugh.

Chapter 25

It was pleasant days like this in LA that Zoe loved. Not too warm, but never cold. She hated the cold and with her new yet-to-be-released Mulberry bag on her arm, and a gorgeous new black suit from Donna Karan, Zoe was feeling on top of the world when she walked into her glass-fronted office.

The reception area was elegant and tasteful, white Barcelona lounges and the latest issue of *Variety* on the glass table. The Orrefors bowl of complimentary mints was filled and her Prada pumps made a pleasant sound when she walked across the polished walnut floors.

Zoe stepped into her office, dropped her bag on her desk and accepted the coffee that her new assistant Paul handed her.

'Arden Walker wants you to call her urgently,' he said with an appropriate eye-roll and Zoe felt her good mood evaporate.

'Tell her I'm in meetings all morning, but I'll call her at noon,' she said and started surfing through her emails.

Arden Walker was a needy and neurotic actress, and if her action franchise didn't make so much money, Zoe would probably have dumped her a year ago.

Paul put his head around the door. 'We have a Code Crazy on line one. She won't take no for an answer.'

Zoe threw up her hands in resignation. 'Okay, put her through. Hi, Arden, what's up?'

'Oh, Zoe, he won't return my calls,' Arden sobbed.

'Well, I've told you before, he isn't right for you.'

'But I love him!'

'Maybe.' Zoe's voice was cool. 'But if it was true love, if it was meant to be, he'd love you back.'

'You hate me,' cried Arden, and Zoe softened.

'Of course I don't hate you, Arden. But you knew he was married, and you knew he would never leave her for you.'

'But they're separated now, so why doesn't he want me?'

Because he's come to his senses. 'Because he knows he's too old for you, and he knows you need to grow as a person,' she soothed. 'He's doing the right thing for you, Arden.'

'And there's something else,' she said now, sounding calmer. 'Zoe, I want to do *The Art of Love.*'

Zoe almost burst out laughing. Arden was so transparent, she thought. This was the real reason for her call.

'Your old assistant Josh told me you have the writer in town. I want to meet him.'

No way would she allow Arden near Hugh, she thought. Arden would turn up with some vodka and maybe a little cocaine and Hugh would be like every other man, unable to resist her siren call.

'Josh shouldn't have spoken to you about that,' said Zoe firmly.

'Is Maggie Hall going to play the role? She's way too old.'

'We haven't cast it yet,' she said, trying to keep the sigh out of her voice.

'Good, because I can stand to lose to just about anyone but her,' said Arden, and she slammed down the phone.

Zoe sat with her head in her hands as Paul knocked and walked back into her office.

'All finished with crazy?' he asked and sat opposite her desk, his iPad at the ready for her to-do list.

'Are you kidding?' said Zoe. 'It's not even nine. I expect crazy will run right through to noon at least.'

Paul went through the list of outstanding matters while Zoe listened and scanned emails at the same time. 'And one important piece of information about today,' he said.

'It's April Food's Day?' she asked with a smile, one eye on the computer.

'No, it's Jeff Beerman's birthday,' Paul said professionally.

'How do you know?' Zoe asked, her eyes off the computer screen now.

Paul leaned forward. 'His assistant Sandra is in my yoga class. She asked me what she should get him, although apparently Jeff doesn't want anyone to know it's his birthday.'

'His birthday,' Zoe repeated, thinking aloud. 'Why doesn't he want anyone to know?'

'I don't know,' said Paul. 'Should I send over a gift basket?'

'No,' said Zoe quickly. 'Leave it with me.' She turned back to her computer.

Jeff hadn't mentioned his birthday when she's seen him yesterday for lunch, or the day before that, or for the last month. At some point they had become friends, she realized. When had this happened? Was it a real friendship? Did

Jeff even have any friends? Some days she felt fine with his friendship and other times she was scared witless. What did he want from her? Didn't all men want something?

First he just happened to be coming by her house with Thai takeout and then they watched *American Idol* and argued over who deserved to win and soon it morphed into easy lunches and even Sunday brunches.

To her amazement, Jeff hadn't said anything particularly insulting or offensive in her presence for a while now. When he chose to be pleasant, he was actually great company, and filled her with an unusual affection. She dialled his number on impulse.

'Zoe,' he said, sounding pleased to hear from her. 'How's the script going?'

Zoe paused, she hadn't heard from Hugh despite her emails and calls and when she drove down the day before, he hadn't been at home.

'Good,' she lied, 'we should have something to read soon.'

She typed another frantic email to Hugh while holding the phone with her shoulder.

She could hear Jeff puffing on the other end of the line.

'Have I caught you at a bad time?' she asked.

'Nope, I was just walking the stairs at Brentwood,' he said. 'What's up?'

Zoe paused. Maybe this wasn't such a good idea after all.

'Zoe?' he asked, his voice softer this time, and she yielded to his tone.

She wished she could play it all cooler. They were merely friends, she reminded herself. So why did she wake up thinking about him most mornings, or see things and make a mental note that Jeff might like that tie, or the Jensen cufflinks she just picked up for him one day because she thought they would look good with his crisp white shirts.

'I was wondering if you'd let me take you out for a birthday dinner tonight,' she said, trying to calm her sudden nerves. 'Unless of course you have a date or plans with your family or whatever...no biggie.'

Did she just say no biggie? Was she eleven?

Jeff was silent for what seemed like too long and she cleared her throat. 'Yeah, no, it's cool, of course you're busy, it was just a thought. Anyway, I have to go call Hugh and see how the script is coming,' she babbled. 'Have a great birthday, Jeff.'

She rang off before he could say anything and groaned out loud. *God, what a loser.* Her phone rang and she saw it was Jeff calling her.

'Hey,' she said in a businesslike fashion. 'You didn't need to call me back.'

'When you ask someone out, it's usually a good idea to give them time to accept,' he said, and she could hear laughter in his voice.

This was entirely new territory for Zoe. She felt slightly faint and happy at the same time.

'So, you do want to have dinner with me tonight?'

'Sure, why not? It's not like I'm doing anything else.'

Zoe felt her thrill fall to the floor and she remembered what a prick Jeff could be sometimes.

'Yeah, well, why aren't you? Don't you have kids who should be hanging out with you? Making you shitty cards and asking for money?' she asked.

'My kids are grown up,' said Jeff, 'and they don't talk to me unless they have to.' He laughed but Zoe could hear something like pain in his voice.

There was a long silence. Zoe gestured impatiently at the phone, willing him to speak. But somehow she knew Jeff wasn't going to make the first move to resolve the uncomfortable moment.

'So, dinner?' she asked again.

'Sure,' he said easily.

'We can just, you know, talk about the film and stuff.'

'Zoe, listen to me.' His voice had changed. Now it was deeper, slower, more thoughtful. 'Frankly, I can think of nothing better than spending my birthday with you.'

Zoe felt her heart skip in either joy or panic, she wasn't sure, as she stuttered, 'Okay, great, I'll pick you up at eight.'

Then she hung up and found herself grinning stupidly for the rest of the day.

Zoe has a crush on Jeff, she heard a sing-song voice say in her head. Was it the man or his power, though? she wondered.

It wasn't like she hadn't had crushes before, but not like this, she thought, wondering if she should call Maggie to discuss. But Maggie seemed to be busy elsewhere lately. Not returning calls and being cryptic about her whereabouts. Did she have a new lover? she wondered.

Anyway, Jeff had already stated she was as old as time itself. Also he was too short for her, not to mention that he could be a real asshole without even trying. But something about the way they were when they were together got under Zoe's skin.

She had dated on and off over the years, but had never invited anyone to be fully part of her life. How could she, when she lay in bed at night, listening for the past to come back and haunt her? She had never wanted to share a house, let alone be married or have children. For Zoe, her work was her life.

It was in the ordinariness that she found herself lonely, and since Maggie had been MIA, Jeff had infiltrated her world more than she would have thought possible.

As she pulled up to the gates, she pressed the intercom, and hoped she didn't have lipstick on her teeth.

Sitting in the car, she wondered if it was too late to leave when she heard Jeff's voice.

'Come on in,' he said and she drove up the long driveway to his mansion and parked at the front of a set of steps that probably rivalled the ones Jeff had run that morning.

How did Jeff live in such a huge house alone? she wondered, imagining the noises that she would hear in the night.

There was no way she would sleep in a place like this, she thought.

Jeff was at the top of the stairs, in pants and shirt. He looked good, she thought and waved.

'Get in,' she called out the car window.

'You don't want to come in for the grand tour?' he asked, looking surprised.

'Meh, you seen one mansion, you seen them all,' said Zoe cheekily and Jeff laughed as he ran down the stairs, a jacket over his arm and a smile on his face.

When he got in the car Zoe noticed he was wearing the cufflinks she had bought him last week.

'Nice bling,' she said.

'These? They're just out of a Christmas cracker,' he said and Zoe slapped his arm playfully.

Was this flirting? Was she flirting with Jeff Beerman? Somebody stop her!

She reached into the back seat and handed him a long

package gift-wrapped in silver paper and tied with a big red bow. 'Happy birthday,' she said.

'You didn't need to do that,' he said gruffly, but Zoe could tell he was touched.

He pulled off the wrapping and stared nonplussed at the ironwork end and the long wooden handle.

Zoe laughed. 'It's just a bit of fun, really. It's a steak brand of your initials. I know you like to put your name on everything, so now you can put it on your steaks,' she rushed on, feeling silly.

'I love it,' he said slowly and then he took her hand and pressed the cold iron brand onto her palm.

'And now you're mine,' he said, his eyes unreadable in the dusk light.

And Zoe had absolutely no idea if he was joking or not.

Los Angeles
January 1996

Shay watched her reflection in the bus window. Krista was in the picture too, leaning heavily on Shay's shoulder and fast asleep.

The two-day bus trip had cost them two hundred dollars each.

Krista hadn't said what she had done to Judd to keep him occupied and Shay hadn't asked. She needed to be able to accept what had happened to herself first before she could understand the sacrifice that Krista had made for her.

They had shared a plate of fries at a road stop and Krista had bought Shay a small bottle of milk.

'Your baby needs milk so it can grow good strong teeth, otherwise it will look like Juney Watling,' she said of the woman who chewed her own gums while playing the church organ.

Shay had shared the milk with Krista, who only took two small sips, and now she lay, rocking to the rhythm of the bus, warmed by Krista and the distance growing between her and her past.

She didn't feel bad about missing her grammy's funeral, that's if she even had one.

Resting her hand lightly on her stomach, she imagined her baby's teeth and fingernails forming. Krista talked about how they would raise the baby and give her—they were both sure the baby was a girl—everything they'd never had.

But it isn't a doll, Shay wanted to say to her friend. How were they going to look after a baby when they could barely look after themselves, with no education, no family and no jobs?

When the bus pulled into to Los Angeles, Shay and Krista were sitting upright, silent, prepared for the worst. This was how life worked for them. They didn't hope for the best because it had never happened.

Krista stood up and stretched.

'Let's go,' she said, but Shay sat still in the seat, her hands clasped tightly around her backpack.

'But *where* will we go?' she asked, looking up at her friend, her eyes filled with tears. 'We don't know anyone, we've got hardly any money—we haven't even finished high school. What place in the world will want girls like us?'

Krista laughed, took Shay's hands in hers and pulled her to her feet.

'Hollywood, babe, where else?'

Shay blinked a few times, trying to remember she was free and safe, for the time being.

'What did you do to Judd?' she finally asked. Krista had seemed so businesslike when she had left the house, Shay hiding in the woods across the road.

It was a side of Krista she had never seen before. Colder, almost matter-of-fact about the situation.

'Judd can't hurt you now,' was all she'd said, and Shay had been afraid to ask but needed to know.

Krista laughed, with none of the trauma Shay had expected.

'Did you kill him?' She half whispered the question.

'Kill him?' Krista laughed. 'No, I just took off my shirt, let him see and feel someone else's titties, other than his mother's, and then I tied him up, told him I was into bondage. Dumb idiot was so turned on, he let me—he's probably still tied to the bed, pissing in his own dungarees.'

Shay smiled a little at the thought and they walked down the aisle of the bus and then out onto the road.

Los Angeles was busier than anything she had seen. People were everywhere at the bus terminal, some with cases, some with bags, people of different colours walked past her, different languages sang in her ears.

Krista walked to a news stand and picked up a newspaper and paid the man a quarter.

'What do you want with that?' asked Shay. Krista never looked at newspapers back home, as far as she knew.

'I'm looking for two things,' said Krista, 'a report of a man dying from a snakebite and a place to live.'

'What?' Shay wondered if she was dreaming.

Krista looked up from the paper, her face serious. 'The preacher tried to rape me, I threw a snake at him,' she said. 'I think it bit him; that's why I came running for you.'

'Jesus Christ,' said Shay in shock.

'Yup,' said Krista, her beautiful face hardening, 'that's who he called for when it bit him,' she said. 'But I don't think there's such a thing as Jesus or God or a saviour, because if there were then why the hell are we the ones being punished?'

Shay couldn't answer her, so instead she reached down and kissed her friend on the top of the head.

'You're my saviour, babe,' she said and Krista looked up at her and smiled.

'Come on, let's go get famous and screw everyone who ever messed with us.'

Chapter 26

The sound of an email pinged into Hugh's inbox as he set up for another morning of writing.

He scanned it and then ignored it. Zoe would get the script when it was ready, and it wasn't ready yet, he thought defiantly.

Working with Maggie was just the panacea he needed and he was feeling better than he had in a long time. The walks on the beach with Maggie and Smike had given him some muscle tone, he had a light tan, and Maggie had insisted he accept the excellent fresh meals she had sent over each day, made 'by one of the most sought-after chefs in Malibu'.

'Who seeks him?' Hugh had asked when Maggie gave him the lecture about how much better he would feel if he ate well.

'What?'

'You said this chef is sought after and I'm asking you, who seeks him?'

'Oh, you know, movie stars, rich people, models,' she had said, more than a little crossly.

'Well, if the chef is good enough for them, he will certainly be good enough for me,' he'd teased.

Maggie had frowned, in that way she did when she wasn't sure if the joke was on her, but then she laughed.

'God, I sound like a wanker, as you would say,' she'd admitted.

'A little bit. But thank you for caring.'

He'd wanted to say so much more, but what could a woman like Maggie Hall possibly see in him?

She was rich, famous and gorgeous. Her home resembled something between the Guggenheim and a high-end fashion store. Everything was perfectly put together, just like Maggie herself.

He had the sought-after chef prepare some small low-fat muffins last time Maggie came, and she had eaten two of them, which for some reason had made him insanely happy.

Hugh looked at the pages of dialogue on the screen and deleted a line and then reinserted it again.

Why was the script taking so long? he wondered. He worked on it every day, he and Maggie talked about it all the time, so why wasn't it ready?

He rubbed his eyes as the doorbell rang and walked over to the sliding door to let Smike out for a run, yelling 'Come in' over his shoulder. Maggie usually just knocked and then barged straight into his space in a cloud of blond hair and perfume, bringing with her a side of acerbic humour.

And then it hit him: he didn't want to finish the script because he didn't want to stop seeing Maggie. He didn't want to drink again and he didn't want to feel terrible any more. Maggie made him happy—happier than he had ever been before—and he was, without a doubt, falling in love with her.

The door opened, and he felt his stomach flip as he looked up, but it wasn't Maggie who stood there, it was a young woman with red lipstick and jet-black hair cut with a severe fringe

'Can I help you?' he asked mildly.

'Hi, I'm Arden Walker.'

He shook his head and shrugged, made an apologetic face.

'I'm an actress,' she explained. 'I'm with Zoe Greene's management also.'

'Oh,' said Hugh. The girl couldn't have been more than twenty-two, he thought. She was beautiful, in a lacquered way, but there was no warmth to her.

'Oh, yes,' he said, remembering her face from a movie poster he had seen on the side of bus.

'*I* am your Simone,' she said dramatically.

Hugh felt his eyes widen. She was so far away from *his* Simone, he felt like laughing.

'Oh, yes? And why is that?' he asked as he checked his phone, willing Maggie to come through the door to witness this extraordinary display of ego.

'Because this will be a great chance to show my range,' said Arden, walking into the space and sitting on his sofa. 'And because I can bring something unique. I know Will MacIntyre is slated to play you. And of course—' she gave him a sultry look '—Will and I are close. Very, *very* close.'

Hugh frowned. Her heavily buckled shoes reminded him of bear traps, worn with leather leggings, she was a huntress on the prowl. God, those legs were thin, he thought, perhaps he should offer her the number of the sought-after chef?

Before Hugh could speak, a sandy Smike came running back inside, soaking wet from his swim. He bounced up to Arden and smiled at her, his red tongue hanging from his mouth like a happy flag.

'Eww,' said Arden and Hugh felt his blood boil.

'Yes, eww, exactly. Outside.' He walked to the front door and opened it, standing with his hand on the handle.

'Outside!' Arden repeated to Smike, who just walked to his bed and lay down. Then she noticed some script pages on the coffee table and forgot about the dog. She dropped into a chair and started to read them.

Hugh sighed. Arden clearly wasn't leaving in a hurry.

'This is an excellent start,' she said. 'I will have notes, though. I assume you're okay with me adding my special touch to Simone.'

Hugh texted Maggie.

Help, I'm being held hostage by an actress who won't leave, come at once.

After ten minutes of listening to Arden talking about herself and her vision for the role, Hugh realized Maggie either hadn't got the text or didn't care, and that he would have to deal with Arden himself.

'Ah, Arden, it's been super meeting you, but I really think you need to go now,' he said finally.

'Why?' asked Arden, not looking up from the pages.

Before Hugh could answer, he heard the gate open and there was Maggie, dressed in white, her sunglasses firmly in place, her mouth set in a straight line, her hands on her slender hips.

He rushed out to meet her.

'Was that text a dig at me?' she demanded. 'If you think we're spending too much time together, just say so!'

'No,' said Hugh, grabbing her by her shoulders, 'I love seeing you every day. But there's an actress in my house claiming she is Simone and she's scary, I think she might turn me into a winged monkey or something.'

Maggie's eyes narrowed and she looked at Hugh. 'Okay, you have to go with me on this.'

'Should I be worried?' he said, feeling nervous.

'Just go back inside.'

He hesitated.

'Just do it,' she said crossly.

Hugh did as she said. Arden was now standing at his open laptop, flicking through the script.

God, this girl has some nerve, he thought, his temper rising.

'Sweetie?'

He turned to see Maggie in the doorway.

'What's going on?' she asked, looking confused at seeing Arden.

Arden stared at Maggie with pure dislike and Hugh smiled at Maggie gratefully.

'Honestly, I don't know,' he said.

Maggie walked down the stairs and put her hand in his. 'Arden, what on earth are you doing here?'

Arden's eyes took in Maggie's hand in Hugh's and she raised her chin. 'I'm here to speak to Hugh about playing Simone.'

Maggie turned to Hugh. 'Oh, that's odd; you didn't mention it to me.'

'I didn't know,' he said honestly.

Smike jumped out of his bed and ran over to lick Maggie's hand. She patted him on the head. 'Morning, buddy, have you been for a swim?' she asked the dog and then looked at Arden again. 'I think there's been a mistake, dear. I'm working with Hugh on this script and the role.' Maggie spoke as though she was talking to a toddler and Hugh tried not to laugh.

Arden gave an ugly little snort and rolled her eyes. 'I can see that,' she said, looking at their entwined hands. 'Not your usual style, Maggie, but I guess as you get older, you get more desperate, huh?'

Hugh stepped forward. 'If you must know, I wanted Maggie for the role long before we started our relationship, so you need to apologize to her for what you've just said.'

Arden squared her shoulders and laughed. 'Do you honestly believe Maggie Hall wants to be with *you*? God, you poor sap. You're kidding yourself.'

'Arden, I don't give a damn whether I play the role or not,' Maggie was now saying, her hand tightly holding Hugh's. 'That isn't what this is about. I am *so* lucky to have Hugh in my life. One day you might also discover that there are things in life worth more than any role, like love, for example.'

Arden scoffed and walked up the stairs. 'You're so full of shit, Maggie, you don't love anyone, you never have. Will's told me all about your redneck upbringing and your fucked-up childhood. You can't love, you're incapable of it.'

'What do you mean? When did Will ever talk to you about me?'

She had told Will a few scant details, but only Zoe knew the real truth. She felt betrayed by Will in every way. He knew her life hadn't been easy, and even though he didn't know the whole truth, he had seemed concerned and kind. Instead, he had gossiped about with Arden.

Maggie's hand was clinging tightly to Hugh's. He turned to her and saw her face drain of colour, her eyes wide and scared. For an instant she reminded him of how Smike had been when he first came to the house. Scared of shadows, worried by every sound.

'Oh, didn't Will tell you?' Arden's head tilted to the side and she was obviously pausing for effect. 'Will and I were involved for a while there towards the end of your marriage. He told me you'd already mentally left by then, so we figured it was okay that we were fucking. Actually, he's the one who told me I have to play Simone.' She looked at Hugh. 'If you want me, just call Zoe and tell her I'm your Simone,' she said, and then turned and walked out, leaving the door open.

Maggie was still holding his hand.

'Will and Arden?' she was saying. 'I can't believe it.'

Hugh led her over to the sofa and sat down next to her, their hands still entwined.

'I have to call Zoe,' she said. She dropped his hand and walked to her bag for her phone.

'What can I do?' he asked, feeling helpless and stupid. For a moment he thought she had meant everything she said, and then he remembered she was an actress.

'Nothing.' She turned to him, her eyes filled with tears. 'I don't even know why I'm upset. I mean, *I* left *him*.'

'Infidelity can hurt more than death, I think.'

Maggie frowned. 'What do you mean?'

'Just that it happened to a friend of mine. His wife cheated on him and it was impossible for them to repair the relationship. Her betrayal killed it. I always felt sorry for him.'

'God, that's awful. I couldn't cheat, I'm too honest,' she said with a rueful smile.

'I know.' Hugh laughed. 'That's one of the reasons I love you,' he said without thinking.

There, it was out in the world, he couldn't take it back, she would have to do with it what she wanted, he had no control over that, but he did love her, every kind, compassionate, funny, self-deprecating, vain inch of her.

Maggie blinked a few times and put down her phone.

'You love me? You mean…as a friend?'

'I will love you however you want me to love you,' he said slowly. 'If as a friend, then yes. If as something more, I would be honoured. But you choose.'

Maggie stared at him and he swallowed nervously and then she leaned forward and kissed him on the forehead.

'That's because I love you as my friend.'

Hugh felt his stomach lurch in disappointment.

She held his face in her hands and moved closer and he gazed at her, revelling in how truly beautiful she was, inside and out.

'I know you,' he whispered just before their mouths met.

'Who am I?' she asked as her lips hit his.

His arms moved around her slender frame and he pulled her on top of him and felt her body respond.

'Who am I?' she repeated, her eyes open and wide, fear and intrigue on her face.

'You're perfect,' he said.

'There's no such thing as perfect,' she said, pulling away a little.

He smiled. 'Perfectly flawed and yet perfect for me. You're too bossy, too skinny, too smart—too everything! But I love you, Maggie, with all my heart.'

'I thought I loved you before I met you. And then I was so disappointed to find out what a mess you were. But now that makes me love you in a different way, a real way, if that makes sense?'

He nodded. 'I understand.' She fell back on top of him and he felt her undoing his shirt. 'What about the stuff with Will, did you want to deal with that?'

She shook her head. 'Will can wait.'

He felt her hand on his chest and then her lips.

'And for the record, I don't care about the role, I don't even want to do it any more,' she said. 'I just want to be with you. Do you believe me?'

He searched her face, her tear-stained cheeks, the smudges of make-up under her eyes, the tiny lines showing at the corners of her mouth, the darker roots of her hair, and he thought she had never looked more beautiful.

'I do,' he said softly. In fact, he had never been more sure of anything in his life.

Chapter 27

At some point between their main course and the dessert, things became weird between Zoe and Jeff at his birthday dinner.

Just thinking about it now made her wish she had been hit by a meteor before she had had that final glass of wine that pushed her over the edge.

They had drunk a lot, more than Zoe usually drank—she always was 'a cheap date', as Maggie used to say.

And Jeff had flirted with her, hadn't he?

She ran through the evening for what felt like the one-hundredth time in her mind.

She had taken him to dinner.

He had told her how smart she was, how insightful about actors and the industry, how she didn't look her age.

All the things that appealed to her ego.

She had then told him how sexy he was. *Sexy? Jesus, that's unprofessional*, she thought now.

'I'm sexy?' Jeff had smiled and looked pleased.

'Yup,' Zoe had said, careful to not hiccup her wine.

'And I know you think I'm too old for you, but I'm not, I'm in my prime, in fact, I should be the one who has a younger man, cos I'm all about sex now,' she had said.

Jeff had laughed, which only infuriated her.

'You couldn't handle a woman like me. That's why you like younger women, because they let you boss them around.' She had pointed a finger at him from across the table.

'Is that right?' he had said, laughing.

'Yup,' Zoe had said again.

He had ordered his car and driver to come and pick them up, since she was too drunk to drive and in the back of his Bentley, she had laid her head on his shoulder.

'You okay, Greene?' he'd asked.

'I'm lonely,' she had said. Even now, to her own ears, it sounded pathetic.

Since when had she ever been lonely? She questioned herself now.

But drunk words were sober thoughts, her grammy used to say and she wondered if it were true.

Before Jeff, she hadn't ever question her aloneness, because she always had Maggie, but Maggie wasn't as available now and Jeff stepping in made her see how alone she was.

She had fallen asleep by the time they pulled up at her house, and he had helped take her inside and opened the front door with the keys from her bag.

'You wanna come in and watch the *American Idol* I recorded?' she had gestured for him to come in.

Jeff had stared at her for a while, his hands in his pockets. 'No, Greene, I think I better go.'

Zoe remembered the feeling of disappointment as he leaned forward and kissed her on the cheek and then turned and walked up the path to his waiting car.

'I'm in my prime,' she had called, 'I'm amazing.'

'Already aware, Greene,' he had called back as he opened his car door and with a brief smile he got in and was driven away.

That was two days ago and Zoe hadn't heard from him, yet she was too embarrassed to call and apologize. She had been an idiot, she thought.

The only way to handle her shame was by impressing him with business.

She picked up her phone and dialled Hugh's number as she walked to the window and stared out over the street below.

He answered on the first ring. 'Hello?' he said cheerfully.

'Hi,' said Zoe chirpily as Paul walked in with a coffee and put it on her desk. 'How's it all going?'

'The script? Finished.'

Zoe stood up straight. 'When did you finish it?'

'Two days ago.'

'Why didn't you send it to me?'

'I've been busy,' he said vaguely, 'and I wanted to make sure it was okay.'

Zoe could hear a dog barking in the background and then Hugh calling out a name.

'Have you got a dog?' she asked, confused.

'Yes, he's a new addition, but settling in wonderfully.' Hugh laughed.

'And his name is Mike?' Zoe asked, shaking her head.

'Smike,' Hugh corrected her. 'It's a character from *Nicholas Nickleby*. Have you read Dickens? You really must—'

'Hugh,' Zoe broke in impatiently. 'The script?'

'Yes, of course, I'll email it to you now.'

Zoe hung up and went back to her desk and stared at her computer screen, chewing her thumbnail as a new email from Hugh popped into her inbox.

She opened the file and sent it straight to print. She didn't want to read it on screen, she wanted to hold the words in her hands and be able to savour them.

When the printer spat out the final page of the script, she carried it to her sofa, lay down and stared at the front page.

Please let it be good, she prayed to the gods of screen-writing, and then she started to read.

Two hours later, she wiped her eyes, and sat for a moment. There was only one actor who could play this role, she thought, and picking up her bag she walked out of her office.

When she pressed the intercom, she heard Stella's accented voice, or was it the housekeeper? Zoe kept it vague.

'Hey, it's Zoe, is Will home?'

'Zoe? It's Stella,' said the voice and Zoe smiled and waved into the camera.

The gates swung open and Zoe drove up the familiar driveway and parked the car in her old spot. She had spent many hours at this house during the years Will and Maggie were married.

Stella opened the door. 'Will is with his trainer, but he will be back soon. Do you want to wait?'

Zoe felt the weight of the script in her bag and nodded. She didn't want to leave this with Stella.

'Thanks, that would be good,' she said as she walked inside. She and Stella stood awkwardly in the foyer for a moment. 'Is Elliot downstairs? I might say hi.'

Stella shrugged. 'Yes, he is always down there.'

Zoe could hear laughter as she went downstairs. So Elliot had a friend over? Maggie would be delighted, she thought, making a mental note to tell her later.

'Hey, El,' she said as she got to the door.

Elliot was sitting on the sofa, and there was a spectacularly beautiful girl on his lap.

Zoe stared at her and knew her jaw was open.

It was a visceral response to the girl's looks, but also to her energy.

She had launched herself off Elliot's lap and was now picking up some papers from the table and shuffling them as though she had a purpose.

'Oh, hi, Zo,' Elliot said, his face reddening.

Wow, Elliot had a girlfriend? Oh, Maggie was gonna flip at this, she thought happily. Could the day get any better?

The girl looked at Zoe and blushed. She was long-limbed, with the usual Cali-girl golden tan, but there was something about her Zoe couldn't place.

After working with actors for nearly twenty years, she thought she could pigeonhole any woman in seconds—there was the starlet, the slut, the girl-next-door, the geek girl, the art-house star, the movie star—but this girl was something else.

Elliot awkwardly introduced them. 'Zoe, this is Dylan. She's been helping me out with some stuff.'

'Nice to meet you, Zoe,' said Dylan with a smile that made Zoe almost forget about everything that had ever troubled her. Great charisma was like that, and she never tired of finding someone with the X factor.

Zoe leaned forward to soak in the girl's voice. Husky, yet smooth and rich, like toffee. Jesus, if this girl could act, she might be the greatest thing to hit the screens since Emma Stone.

'How's things, El?' She sat down uninvited on the nearest chair. 'What have you been up to?'

Once Elliot had told her she was his second best friend in the world, Maggie being the first, but now they felt like strangers.

Elliot paused and Zoe saw Dylan spin on the desk chair.

'He's writing a script,' she said proudly.

'Really, El? That's fantastic,' she said genuinely. 'What's the elevator pitch?' Zoe asked Dylan, trying to include her in the conversation.

Dylan frowned. 'I'm sorry but I don't know what that is.'

Zoe felt her skin tingle in the way it did when she was faced with someone exceptional.

'It's too early to say,' said Elliot sharply.

Zoe felt Dylan's eyes shift between them.

She took the hint and stood up. 'Sure, but when you're ready for someone to read it, let me know, I'd be happy to help.'

Dylan stood up also, and held out her hand. It was a polite, old-fashioned gesture, something Zoe didn't see very often in her world.

'It was a pleasure to meet you,' she said.

'You too,' said Zoe. Their hands touched briefly and she smiled at Elliot and walked slowly back up the stairs. The girl both intrigued and unnerved her, and Elliot was being really odd. Maybe she wouldn't tell Maggie about the girl after all, she thought as she heard Will's voice booming as he walked through the door.

'Zoe, what are you doing here?' Will asked with a smile.

Even with sweat stains on his T-shirt and a reddened face, he was still so handsome. He would be perfect, she thought.

Will threw a training bag on the floor and the housekeeper came from nowhere to pick it up and take it away.

'I need you to read this script,' she said, clutching her bag. 'It's the best thing I've read in years. Jeff thinks you'd be perfect for the role and, frankly, so do I.'

'Okay,' said Will, looking puzzled, 'leave it with me.'

'I can't,' said Zoe. 'I have to get Jeff to read it and sign off on it, but I want you to consider this film, you would be the only big name in it, it could be Oscar material for you.'

Will shook his head. 'If it's that *Art of Love* film, I can't do it, Zoe. You know why.'

'Oh, come on, Will, this is going to be a brilliant picture and you're perfect for Hugh. That book was *not* the reason your marriage broke up; we both know why it didn't work.' She proffered the script again. 'You've always trusted me, Will. Have I ever spilled your secrets? Given you bad career advice? Trust me on this,' she said quietly.

Will sighed and took the script. 'Every time I don't listen to you, things don't work out,' he admitted.

'Lose your ego for a moment and just read the script, I'll wait in the other room,' she cajoled.

'Why don't you go say hi to Elliot, he's trying to write a script too,' said Will, as he took the pages from her and walked towards the living room, where the light was perfect for reading.

'Oh no, I just saw him, and I met his girlfriend too, they looked pretty busy,' she said with a laugh.

Will stopped in his tracks. 'Dylan's not his girlfriend.'

'Okay, his friend with benefits then,' she said, smiling. 'They were all over each other when I walked in. Is she an actress? She's absolutely gorgeous. I'd love to test her for this,' she went on, nodding at the script in Will's hands.

Will said nothing, but Zoe saw his jaw tighten as he left the room, leaving her alone in the foyer.

Would it be weird to go downstairs again and ask Dylan for her number?

Even Jeff would have to admit that she'd found the face of the decade, she thought, almost hugging herself with happiness.

As far as looks went, Dylan was *perfect* for Simone. But if Will said yes to the role, and if Dylan was right for Simone, she wondered how Elliot and Maggie would react to them playing lovers on screen.

Zoe pushed the thought out of her head. She would cross that bridge when she came to it, she thought. First she needed to find out whether or not Dylan could act.

Chapter 28

Dylan put her finger over the camera on her laptop and made a face of frustration at her parents on the screen.

Getting her parents to understand Skype was a task in itself, let alone trying to get them to understand she was staying in LA for the time being.

'So you're working for Will MacIntyre?' her father kept repeating. 'Is he nice? He seems nice,' he said again, as though he didn't want to hear anything but that famous Will MacIntyre was pleasant.

'Yeah, he's fine, Dad,' she lied.

The truth was that Will *wasn't* very nice and made Dylan feel like she was up to no good, even though she wasn't. He was sceptical, rude and brusque to her, which she could handle, but she hated the way he was condescending to his own son and made constant jokes about his writing.

As much as Dylan was angry at her parents for not telling the truth about her birth mother, at least they weren't total arseholes 24/7 like Will.

'So he wants you to stay there and do exactly what for him?' Her mother was less scathing about Hollywood and Will MacIntyre.

'I'm just helping out, doing assistant-y stuff,' Dylan said vaguely. 'This is just a temporary thing until I get into the acting thing.'

'You want to be an actor?' The question sounded painful for her mother to ask, as though Dylan was running away to join a mysterious cult.

'Is this because of Will MacIntyre? Are you having an affair with him?' asked her mother sternly, crossing her arms. 'Is he influencing you? Promising you things?'

Dylan burst out laughing. 'Oh my God, Mom, are you serious? He's so *old*.'

'What about college, Dylan?' her mother asked. 'If you want to be an actor,' she said the words distastefully, 'you can study theatre at college, you know?'

'I know,' said Dylan flatly.

'If you come back now, you can start in the next semester,' coaxed her mother.

'No, Mom, I told you, I'm giving this a year to see if I can make it work. If it doesn't I'll come back then.' Dylan sighed. How many times did she have to explain?

'As an actress or as an assistant?' Her mother shook her head. 'I still don't understand this, Dylan, you never told us you wanted this. Now it feels like you've run away to pursue some crazy dream, which we were never included in. Do you know how low the odds are of you succeeding?'

Dylan saw her father's eyes drop as her mother spoke. 'How are you, Dad?' she asked, desperate to change the subject.

'I'm okay,' said her father with a smile, but she could see a new tremor in his jaw.

Before she left New York, the tremor was only in his hands, but she had researched Parkinson's enough to know it wouldn't end there.

'Have you been going to your specialist appointments?'

'Of course he has,' her mother interjected, leaning forward, and Dylan felt herself instinctively lean back. 'Life does go on without you, Dylan, believe it or not.'

God, her mother was a piece of work sometimes, she thought. All she wanted to do was scream at her, to demand to know why she had kept her birth mother from her, but she was silent. Not yet, she thought, wait until you have all the facts.

'Have you had any auditions yet?' asked her father. 'Now you're in Will MacIntyre's world, you'll probably meet people who can help you.'

Dylan thought about the call she'd received from Zoe Greene the day before.

'Actually, I have been offered an audition,' she blurted out.

'That's great, baby, what for?'

Her father had always believed in her, whereas it felt like her mother just pushed her to meet her own expectations.

'A feature film,' said Dylan, thinking about Zoe's insistence that she audition.

'But I'm not an actor,' she had said.

'I think you can be. And I'm never wrong about this. Will wouldn't have a career without me,' Zoe had said firmly. 'I'm going to send you some pages of a script. Learn them, and I'll set up a time for you to be filmed at the studio.'

The pages had been delivered to Dylan by a messenger

and she had signed for them, hiding them from Elliot's curiosity by telling him they were papers from her parents for college, which only caused more questions.

The truth was she was kind of excited that Zoe had seen in her something her mother told her wasn't possible. Why *couldn't* she be an actress? It wasn't like she knew what the hell else she wanted to do, and if she got the role she'd be able to stay with Elliot.

'What's the name of the film?' asked her mother suspiciously.

'*The Art of Love*; it's based on the book,' said Dylan, clutching the seat, waiting for her mother's response.

'I don't know it,' she said.

But Dylan knew the fact that the film was based on a book would raise the project slightly in her mother's eyes.

How hard could it be? she had thought when she read through the pages, and had impulsively rung Zoe back and told her she'd do the audition.

That was yesterday and her audition was tomorrow. What she needed was someone to tell her it was going to be okay.

'Well, let us know how it goes,' said her mother, pursing her lips.

Dylan knew this was neither approval nor disapproval, simply her mother deciding Dylan was of sane enough mind to make her own decisions.

'Have you made any friends out there?' her mother went on.

This was her chance to edge Elliot into the conversation, so that when she told them she and Elliot were in love and planning to spend the rest of their lives together, no one would be surprised.

'There's a guy called Elliot,' Dylan began.

'A boy? You're not there for romance, Dylan,' her mother snapped.

Dylan saw her father put his hand on her mother's arm, the shaking more pronounced. 'Elliot and I are together, Mom, and he's great, the best thing that's ever happened to me, so please stop telling me every single thing I do is wrong, just because it's not what you would do,' she said defiantly, wondering if it was the distance or mode of communication making her braver than she had ever been.

Or was it Elliot? He was so supportive. He thought everything she did was amazing, even the way she made them milkshakes. 'You totally could be an actress, you know,' he had said to her, his head on her lap.

She'd run her fingers through his thick dark hair. 'And you could be a manager, the way you smooth talk me.'

Yes, Elliot definitely empowered her, and she knew she did the same for him.

He had opened a Facebook page at her insistence and friend requests were flooding in.

'See, you're not a loser.'

He'd scoffed. 'Why? Because people want to be my virtual friend on Facebook?'

But she had noticed him spending more time on it, and even having a few chats with old friends.

Dylan heard a knock at the door and she leaned forward. 'I have to go, guys, I'll call you,' she said quickly, closing the laptop before her parents could answer.

Getting up she walked to the door, expecting to see Elliot, but it was Will on the other side.

How much had he heard?

'Hi,' she said, trying to be casual. Will intimidated her

in a way she thought only her mother could. He was hand-some, but his eyes were cold as he stared at her.

'Hello,' he said, looking her up and down as though she was wearing something inappropriate, instead of jeans and pink T-shirt.

Did she invite him in? It was his guesthouse after all.

'Can I help you?' she asked, deciding on her tone.

'I wanted to know how Elliot's writing was going?'

Dylan hesitated. 'Okay, great—why don't you ask him yourself? I am sure he'd love to talk to you about it.'

'Come on, Dylan, don't be coy,' Will said. 'You're his assistant, surely you can tell me?'

'Well, yes, I'm his assistant, not yours, so I think client-assistant privileges have to be adhered to,' she said, putting her best legal talk to work.

'You're an assistant, not a lawyer,' he said with a smirk. 'I wonder what other *privileges* my son is getting from you as his assistant?'

'Excuse me?' Dylan grasped the door frame with her hands.

'I mean, what exactly do you two do down there in his room all day? Do you really expect me to believe you're helping him with his *writing*?'

Dylan felt so cheap and disrespected, but before she could defend herself, she saw Elliot walking down the path to-wards them.

'Hey, Dad,' he said as he saw Will and then looked at Dylan's expression and frowned. 'What's up? Is everything okay?'

'Yep, all good,' said Will and he looked Dylan in the eye. 'Let me know if there's anything else you need, won't you?'

Dylan watched as he walked away and wondered what

exactly would have happened if Elliot hadn't turned up when he did. She had no idea if Will was going to hit on her or fire her. God, this Hollywood world was crazy, she thought, thinking of her parents in their New York brownstone, the newspapers on the kitchen table, the sounds of life going on outside their door and Dylan's cosy bedroom with its big windows looking out over the West 83rd Street. A swell of homesickness hit her so hard, she felt like she had been winded.

'What did Dad want?' Elliot asked as he came inside.

'He just wanted to see if I was doing my job properly.' Dylan turned away so he couldn't see her glistening eyes.

Elliot pulled her into a hug. 'And did you tell him that you're amazing in every way and that I am completely in love with you?'

Dylan stood perfectly still in the circle of his arms.

'I need to resign, El,' she said. 'We can't do this with me still taking money from Maggie. It's not right.'

'Soon,' Elliot soothed. 'When the script is finished. I promise.'

But Dylan had a strong feeling it couldn't wait that long.

Los Angeles
January 1996

The hotel pool hadn't been filled in years, and at some point had become the central area for all the hotel guests to throw what didn't fit into the bins.

'It's a fucking Petri dish of disease,' Shay said each time she walked upstairs to the room she and Krista shared.

Lately she had taken to holding her breath when she passed the pool, just like when she was a kid and passed a graveyard.

'Don't breathe in the ghosts,' her mother would say.

Shay lay on the bed, the baby kicking her whenever she lay on her back. Krista was out looking for work, which wasn't proving easy to find, since they were essentially on the run from Family Services.

'One more year,' Krista kept saying to her. 'Then we'll be eighteen and they can't tell us what to do any more and we'll have our baby and you can go be an actress.'

But Shay knew it wasn't that simple. Life in and out of foster homes and then her mother and grandmother's neglect had shown her what a baby needed—and that was everything she never had.

Krista had four shifts a week bagging groceries at a local supermarket, but it was barely enough to cover the room, let alone food.

Shay hadn't had any luck finding work, her bulging belly not exactly helping her employment prospects.

She rolled onto her side and stared at the flock wallpaper.

How could she give her child a good life? Had her own mother felt like this when she was pregnant with her? she wondered.

Shay thought about everything she wanted for her baby and how little she had to give, and felt the tears fall.

It wasn't going to work, she knew it. And she knew that, deep down, Krista knew it also.

The only thing to do was to find her baby a new home, a place where the child could have everything it needed and wanted, somewhere that Shay could visit, even get the baby back once she landed on her feet.

Back in West Virginia, every day had been about survival. This feeling of planning ahead was an entirely new experience.

Maybe getting pregnant wasn't the worst thing in the world, thought Shay, as she wiped her eyes. If she could become successful and get enough money to buy all the things she and Krista and the baby would ever need, they would be all right. She just needed someone to care for the baby while she made it all happen.

But no foster parents. No way.

She needed someone who wanted a baby real bad, someone who would bend the rules enough for her and the baby, maybe even help them out with money for food while they waited for the baby to be born.

Buoyed by her plan, Shay sat up on the edge of the bed and slipped her feet into Krista's fake Reebok sneakers. She left the hotel room, holding her breath as she passed the pool and letting it out in a huge rush as she got to the street.

If there was one thing her grandmother had taught her, besides how not to be a parent, it was that everything in the world had someone looking for it, someone who wanted it.

At the nearest drugstore she immediately found what she wanted and she treated herself to a small raspberry Gulp to celebrate.

Taking her items, she sat on a bench outside in the sunshine, took a large sip of her frozen drink, so her brain hurt a little, and opened the pages of *The Pennysaver.*

Adoptions: Babies wanted, she read, and started to scan the ads placed by couples looking for a baby.

Chapter 29

Maggie's phone was ringing as Hugh kissed her neck and then ran his hands down her shoulders and lightly over her breasts. She shivered with pleasure, the butterflies churning in her stomach. She hadn't felt butterflies before, not even with Will.

All her life, Maggie had leveraged her looks to gain power, yet in Hugh's arms she felt powerless. None of her games or usual moves felt right, it was as though they were another character's costumes.

Her phone stopped ringing and then started again, as Hugh slipped the strap of her tank top down and kissed her collarbone.

Maggie sighed. 'I should see who it is,' she whispered. 'We've been in my bed for the past three days. People will think I've been kidnapped.'

'You have,' said Hugh.

She felt the weight of him on her as he began to move

down her body, kissing her breasts and belly, moving all the way down between her legs.

'I need you inside me,' she said greedily.

'Say please,' he murmured.

'Please,' she gasped.

'Tell me what you want,' he said, holding himself up on his arms above her, his eyes looking into hers intently.

'I want you inside me,' she said shyly. Everything felt like the first time with Hugh and she tried to pull him down to her, but he was stronger than she expected.

'Maggie, tell me exactly what you want me to do to you,' he said, his eyes burning into hers.

Maggie felt like she was falling backwards as desire flooded through her and her breath came short and fast.

'I want you inside me, Hugh, so much,' she whispered.

'And then what?' he said, as he slowly pushed inside her.

She closed her eyes. 'I want to ride you.'

He rolled her over so she was on top of him and she started to move, finding her own rhythm.

'And what else do you want, Maggie? Tell me,' he said, his voice husky with desire.

She didn't care what she looked like, she didn't think about what faces she was making or how her body looked, all she wanted was to pleasure herself with Hugh's hard cock.

'Fuck me, Maggie, you made me hard, now do something about it.'

She felt herself close, so close, as she moved.

'What do you want, Maggie?' he demanded. 'Tell me what you want.'

And then she cried out with the most exquisite pleasure

she had ever felt. 'You, I want you,' she said through the throes of orgasm.

She fell on top of Hugh, embarrassed and happy, and her phone started to ring again.

'Oh, for God's sake, answer it, so that I can fuck you again,' said Hugh, sitting up and running his hand through his hair.

Maggie giggled as she clambered over him and picked up her phone and looked at the screen. 'It's Will,' she told Hugh.

She didn't want to talk to him. In fact, after Arden's revelation, Maggie thought she would be happy never to see Will again. But then she thought of Elliot and steeled herself in case Will had bad news.

'What do you want, Will?' she asked tersely.

'Hello to you too,' he said, his voice cold. 'Did you know Elliot and that assistant you hired are fucking? Is that why you hired her? As some sort of whore to entertain him?'

'Really?' asked Maggie and then she smiled at Hugh. 'Well, good for them.'

'I don't like it,' said Will firmly.

'Why not? They're kids, of course they going to have sex, that's what kids do, isn't it? God knows he's stunted in every way, no doubt she's giving him quite the education.'

'Is that why you hired her?' Will asked again, his voice caustic, and Maggie felt anger surge through her.

'Don't be such an asshole, Will, she's not like that at all and neither is Elliot. God, you can be a nasty piece of work.'

Will laughed meanly. 'She's a gold digger. Did you know Zoe wants to audition her for *The Art of Love*?'

Maggie took a sharp breath. Had she been played by the girl?

'What do you mean Zoe wants to audition her?' she asked.

'Zoe saw them making out, told me she's enthralled by her and now wants to test her. Maggie, you were an idiot for our entire marriage, but this time you've outdone yourself!' he yelled.

'I'm on my way over,' she said and hung up the phone.

'I have to go,' she said to Hugh as she stood up and picked her clothes up from the floor and pulled them on haphazardly.

'What's happened?'

'It's about Elliot,' she said. 'Just let me go and sort something out. I need to talk to Will in person.'

'I can come with you, if you like?'

Maggie thought for a moment and then shook her head. 'Honestly, I don't think that'd be a great idea.'

Hugh nodded. 'Okay, but let me know if I can help at all.'

Maggie picked up her handbag and walked to the front door and paused and turned to him. This was her chance to be honest, she thought, to start a real relationship based on truth.

'My life is messy, Hugh. My relationship with Will is complicated and if it weren't for Elliot I'd never see him. He blames you for the break-up of our marriage.'

'*Me?*'

'Well, because of the book. When I read it I realized I wanted nothing less than what you had with Simone,' she admitted. 'That's why I left him. Well, part of the reason,' she said with a wry smile.

Hugh shook his head. 'You shouldn't put relationships up on a pedestal,' he said with a frown. 'Things are never as perfect as they seem.'

'I know, but what you had with Simone was exceptional, even you can admit that,' she said as she opened the door.

'Exceptional is one word for it,' Hugh muttered.

'I don't think I can ever be to you what she was to you,' she finally admitted.

Hugh gave her a gentle smile. 'Why don't you stick around and find out?'

But Maggie shook her head and stepped outside into the sunshine. 'I have to go; Will needs me. Elliot needs me.'

'What if I need you?' he asked and Maggie couldn't tell if he was joking or not.

'You'll survive—' deciding it was a joke '—you've managed this long without me, a few hours more won't harm you.'

And she turned and rushed from the house, running towards the other men in her life.

The gates were open when she arrived at Will's house and she could hear him yelling even as she parked up.

Christ, she thought, as she walked inside and followed his voice to the open living area. She stood in the doorway, taking in the scene.

Dylan and Elliot were sitting on either end of the sofa, their hands in their laps, eyes downcast. Will was looming over them both, red in the face from yelling.

It was like a classic moment from a family sitcom, except there was no mother wringing her hands helplessly in the background. Was that her role now?

'You can't fire her, Dad, she's already resigned,' Elliot was saying.

'Then she needs to leave,' roared Will.

'But I don't want her to leave, we can live together in the guesthouse,' said Elliot and Maggie saw Dylan glance at him gratefully.

Will shook his head. 'That's not going to happen.'

'We're in love,' said Elliot and he reached out and took Dylan's hand.

'You're just kids. You don't even know what love is yet,' said Will, turning his back on them.

'Yes, we do! We know more than you do about it.'

Will turned back to his son. 'What's that supposed to mean?'

Elliot stood up and Dylan followed suit. 'I know about you and Arden Walker. She used to ring here all the time and send you letters—I stole them all, and I wiped her messages too, because I thought if you didn't know, you and Maggie would be okay.'

Dylan looked embarrassed, but Elliot was calm.

'You pushed Mom away, you pushed Maggie away, Stella's about to leave you, and now you're trying to push Dylan away too. But we're together and we love each other and there's nothing you can do to change that,' he said.

He had never seemed more grown-up and Maggie felt fiercely proud of him.

'Oh, you *love* each other, do you?' Will shook his head in disbelief. 'You're such an innocent, Elliot. This girl's a user. She used Maggie to find her way into this house, and she's used you to get to Zoe and then to get a shot at being in that fucking film.'

Dylan looked horrified. 'What are you even saying?' She turned to Elliot. 'Don't listen to him, El! None of that is true.'

'She had the book of *The Art of Love* in her room, I saw it,' Will said triumphantly. 'And I saw emails from her father asking how her acting career was going. And when was she going to become a star?'

'Is that true?' Elliot asked Dylan, his face falling.

'Oh my God, I borrowed the book from the library, yes,' said Dylan, dropping his hand. 'It means nothing. And the emails from my father are because he thinks I'm here to act, but you know why I'm really here, Elliot,' she pleaded.

Elliot stood, torn between his father and Dylan, and Maggie realized she needed to step in.

'All right, everyone cool their jets,' she said, holding up her hands.

'This is all your fault, Maggie!' yelled Will, turning to her with fury in his eyes.

'No, it's not, and I'm sick of you blaming me for everything that goes wrong in your life,' she said, and then turned to Dylan. 'So, Dylan, do you want to audition for *The Art of Love* or not?'

Dylan made a face and shook her head. 'Yes, no, I don't know! I didn't even think about acting until Zoe asked me.'

Maggie studied Dylan's face, but she couldn't read her expression.

'So why did you tell Zoe you'd audition for the role then?' Will sneered.

Dylan was crying now. 'I said yes to Zoe because she offered me a chance to stay in LA. I *need* to stay here. I knew I'd have to resign from this job as soon as Elliot and I told you about our relationship.'

'You said you'd audition?' Elliot had backed away from her and stood next to his father now. 'So you lied to me?'

Dylan was trying to speak when Will laughed meanly. 'You chose the wrong MacIntyre, Dylan. You should have worked on me, not the kid. I've decided to take the role, so now you'll have to be in love with me instead.'

Dylan gasped and ran from the room.

Elliot moved, lightning quick, and punched his father in the jaw. It wasn't a perfect punch, but it was enough to send Will stumbling backwards into a large table, knocking off several photos that fell and smashed on the slate floor.

'Fuck you, Dad,' Elliot said as he ran out of the house.

Maggie was torn between running after Elliot and punching Will herself. She took a deep breath.

'Jesus, you're a cruel bastard, Will. Why is there so much hate in you?'

Will stared at her from his place on the floor. 'Maybe it was having my hopes and dreams smashed by you, ever think about that?'

'I am not taking responsibility for you being a prick. You're in charge of your own behaviour, and you should know better!' She was yelling too now, the house reverberating with the sound of their marriage.

Will stood up and touched his jaw.

'I'm sorry, Maggie,' he said, hanging his head. 'That was out of line, I know it.'

'Well, it's not okay,' she said. 'You're out of control. What the hell is going on?'

Will looked at her, his face filled with pain. 'She's taking him away from me.'

'Who? Dylan?' Maggie asked in shock.

'Yes,' said Will, walking over to a chair and slumping in it. 'It's always been me, I've done everything for that kid and now he's replaced me with her. He feels so far away from me.'

Maggie sighed. 'They're kids, it's intense, they're in love,' she said gently.

'Love,' Will scoffed. 'They don't know what that is.'

'Do you?' she asked. 'Because this sure is a funny way of expressing it.'

He looked at her intently. 'I love you,' he said.

'So why did you sleep with Arden when we were still married?' And then she raised her hand to stop him answering. 'Actually, I don't care any more, I've moved on. I'm in love for the first time and I know that's a cruel thing to say, Will, but it's true.'

'Who with?' he asked, leaning forward.

'Hugh Cavell,' she said proudly.

Will snorted. 'Are you kidding me?'

'No, I'm not. And please don't try to insult me or him with your poisoned opinions.'

Will threw his head back and laughed. 'Oh, my darling Maggie, ageing doesn't suit you at all, does it? You're fucking *the writer* to get the role? Starting a bit lower on the ladder than usual, aren't you?'

'I'm not going to listen to your crap any more.'

'Anyway, you couldn't do that role if you tried, the script's far too complex.'

'Are you suggesting I couldn't understand the script?' she asked, seeing white flashes before her eyes and feeling her jaw tense.

'It's true,' said Will, picking up a few frames and putting them back on the table. 'I might have hated the book, but the script's a fucking work of art. I haven't read anything this good in years.'

Maggie stepped forward so she was centimetres from his face, the broken glass crunching underneath her feet. 'You listen to me, you egotistical piece of shit. I wrote that fucking script with Hugh, so don't tell *me* what's too complex and what isn't. And if you think I'm going to let *you* play the role of the most wonderful person I know, you are even crazier than I thought you were.'

And then Maggie did what she wished she had done earlier. She punched Will as hard as she could, on the other side of his jaw.

Chapter 30

Dylan ran down the manicured street, wishing there was someplace she could hide, but the houses—were like fortresses, some even with security guards and nasty-looking Rottweiler dogs behind their ornate gates. She would find no salvation amongst the rich and famous.

'Dylan!'

She turned to see Elliot trying to run after her.

'Don't run,' she yelled over her shoulder. 'It's not good for your heart.' And then she turned and started to run again.

'Then fucking stop for me, Dylan,' he yelled back.

Dylan stopped and put her hands on her hips, trying to catch her breath.

Elliot caught up with her, breathing twice as heavily as she was. 'Where are you going?' he puffed.

'I don't know,' Dylan admitted. 'I just can't be in that house any more with your father.' She started to shake and Elliot put his hands on her shoulders. 'He's horrible.'

'I know,' said Elliot. 'But why didn't you tell me about the audition?'

'Because I wanted to surprise you, to show you I was good at something. I wanted to make you proud of me,' she said, feeling tears coming fast.

He looked bewildered. 'But I *am* proud of you. You make me proud every day I'm with you. You don't have to be a movie star for me to be proud of you.'

His beautiful face was so trusting.

'But what if I *wanted* to be a movie star?'

'Well, do you?'

'I don't know!' she yelled. 'I don't know anything about what I want. All I know is that I want you. But the whole time I've been here, I haven't *done* anything, El. I haven't found my mother, I haven't helped you with your search for your donor, I've just lazed about and told you to write occasionally. I'm wasting my life.'

Elliot looked hurt. 'Well, I'm sorry I'm such a waste of your time.'

'No, that's not what I meant,' cried Dylan in frustration. 'I meant I don't know what I'm doing.'

'I do.'

'What then?' she demanded.

'Falling in love. It's hard to do anything else when that's happening, I've recently found out.' He spoke so gently that Dylan started to sob harder than before.

'But your dad thinks I'm using you or him or whatever,' she cried.

'Who cares what my dad thinks?'

'You do, at least you will one day, even if you don't now. I care about what my mother thinks of every decision I make.'

'Which mother?' He smiled.

'Both,' she said seriously. 'But I don't think it's going to happen, I can't find my birth mother, so I'm going home to New York and I'm going to forget this happened.'

The desire to see her mother was overwhelming and she started to sob. She had spent all this time searching for something that she already owned, and guilt spread through her body, causing her to shake.

What had her mother thought when she left? Had she broken her heart? Why did she hurt the woman who loved her more than the one who gave her up?

Her mother wasn't perfect but she loved her and she needed to her hug her and hear her say that everything would be okay.

Elliot took his hands off her shoulders.

'Will you forget me?'

'If I have to,' she answered bravely and then looked at the ground.

'But I love you,' he said, his voice breaking.

'Your dad is right, you haven't lived enough, and neither have I. How do we know what love is? You've never been with anyone else.'

Elliot sighed. 'That's bullshit and you know it. I don't have to have lived for years to know that you're the best person in the world for me and I am the best person for you.'

He put his hand on his chest. 'You think I don't know a good thing when I see it?' he asked and then he took her hand. 'I have never felt really alive until I met you, Dylan Mercer. And now I know you are the reason I was given a new healthy heart, so I could love you completely.'

Dylan sobbed and closed her eyes. 'Stop making it so hard for me. Everyone wants something from me, and I don't have anything to give.'

Elliot pulled his phone from his pocket and dialled a number.

'Zoe? It's Elliot, I need your help.'

Just as he spoke, a car came flying down the road and screeched to a halt beside them.

'Get in the car, Elliot, I'm taking you to my place.' Maggie had wound down the window, her face stony as she glanced at Dylan.

'Not without Dylan,' Elliot said, putting his hand over the receiver of the phone.

Dylan looked away, but then heard her mother's voice in her head: *Don't ever let anyone think they are better than you. Do you understand me, Dylan?*

Lifting her head high, she walked to Elliot's side and put her hand in his. She looked Maggie squarely in the eye.

'I know how this looks to you, but it isn't what you think. I'm in love with Elliot. I didn't plan it, and I didn't plan to be asked to audition for the film either. I'm not here to be an actress, but the truth is I'm not here for college either.'

'Then why are you here?' Maggie asked.

'With respect, that's none of your business. But please know I'm not any of the things Will said I was.' Dylan felt Elliot squeeze her hand.

Maggie looked at Elliot and shrugged. 'Listen, kid, love is hard, and painful. Love isn't easy, I don't want you two to get hurt, and neither does your dad, Elliot.'

But Elliot shook his head. 'No, love isn't hard, Maggie. You were the closest thing I ever had to a mother and you left me, and I survived. And I still love you.'

Maggie was silent and her eyes filled with tears.

'My heart was broken, and Dylan healed it, and I know, I absolutely know, we are meant to be together. So I know you're angry and I know you think she had some ulterior motive, but she didn't and neither did I. It just happened.'

Maggie was speechless.

Elliot smiled at Dylan and held her gaze as he went on. 'I think love comes when it's not invited, Maggie, and you have to choose if you're going to answer the door or not.'

Dylan stared at Elliot and wondered if she could ever love anyone more that she loved him right now.

'I won't audition for the film,' she said quickly.

'Yes, you will,' he said.

'No, I won't.'

'You will,' he repeated, his voice a little louder.

She frowned. 'Don't boss me around. You're not my husband, this isn't the last century.'

'Dylan, don't be so ridiculous,' he said crossly.

'I'm going back to New York,' she yelled at him.

'Then I'm coming with you,' he yelled back.

'You can't,' she said.

'I can too,' he said in the same childish tone she had used.

Maggie watched them and burst out laughing.

'Jesus, you two *are* in love,' she said, and pressed the button that unlocked the car doors. 'Get in,' she ordered.

'But Zoe's coming to get us,' said Elliot. 'I just called her before you came.'

'We'll call her from the car,' said Maggie. 'Now get in.'

Dylan and Elliot glanced at each other and got into the back seat as Maggie called Zoe.

'I've left all my things there, my papers and everything,' Dylan said to Elliot. 'I can't go back and get them.'

'I'll go,' said Maggie. 'I'm not afraid of Will.'

'Thank you,' said Dylan in a small voice. 'Because I am.'

'Where are we going?' asked Elliot, leaning over to the front seat.

'My house,' said Maggie.

'Really?' asked Elliot. 'You want us to stay with you?'

'I'm not there much these days,' said Maggie, glancing at Elliot in the rear-view mirror.

'Okay,' said Elliot, sitting back in the seat. 'Where are you then?' he asked eventually.

'That's none of your business,' Maggie said, repeating Dylan's words and catching Dylan's eye in the rear-view mirror. The women shared a smile and Maggie was sure her original instinct about the girl had been right. After all, Maggie had never been wrong before, had she?

Los Angeles
February 1996

Krista ripped the page out of the copy of *Variety* sitting on the café table.

'Hey, you can't do that, other people want to read it,' said a man's voice from behind the counter.

You're lucky I didn't just steal it like I usually do, Krista thought, as she walked out and headed for the nearest pay-phone.

The advertisement seemed too good to be true.

Actress required for lead role in new independent adult comedy. Must be between 18–24 years old. Slender body type, bring a bathing suit to audition. You will receive a full credit on the film and $200 cash.

Taking a quarter from her purse, she dialled the number.

'Hi, this is Krista Calkins,' she said, trying to blunt the edges of her Appalachian accent. 'I'm ringing about the ad-vertisement in *Variety.*'

'How old are you?' asked the man on the other end of the line.

Krista paused. 'Eighteen,' she lied.

'When can you come in?'

'Any time,' said Krista. Two hundred dollars would really help them right now.

'Be here this afternoon at two,' he said, and gave her the address, which she wrote down on her hand.

She stepped out into the street, feeling proud of herself for making the audition happen. Now all she had to do was steal a bikini. Finding the nearest mall, she walked into a JC Penney and went straight to women's swimwear.

She found a red striped bikini in a size four. Taking a size six, she tucked the smaller size inside the bigger one and walked to the change room.

'Just the one,' she said to the girl, who handed her a plastic number one.

In the change room, Krista slipped the smaller bikini over her underwear and pulled her clothes back on.

When she came out, she handed the larger size back to the girl with the plastic one and shrugged. 'Not right,' she said and left the mall.

Back at the apartment, Shay was lying on the bed watching *Jeopardy* when Krista walked in.

'Hey,' she said to Krista, who was stripping off her clothes. 'Why are you wearing a bikini over your underwear?'

'Because I have an audition and they want me to wear a bikini, so I had to nick one,' said Krista, taking off her bra and readjusting the halter-neck top of the swimsuit.

Shay frowned. 'What sort of an audition?'

Krista handed her the piece of paper from *Variety*. 'I have to be down there at two.'

Shay read the ad and then shook her head. 'You're not going to this audition.'

'What? Why not? It's worth two hundred bucks.'

'Yeah, because it's for a porn film, Krista. You're not doing it.'

Krista snatched the ad from Shay's hands. 'A porn film? How do you know?'

'I've been reading those *Variety* papers you bring in sometimes and I read all the ads. Trust me, these ones are for porno.' She reached down and took a paper from under the bed and turned to the auditions pages. 'See, these here are porn ones, but there are others, like these, that are for extras at good studios,' she said. 'I read about the studios and who's who in the articles at the front of the paper.'

Krista nodded, impressed. 'Okay. So can you tell me which auditions I should go for then?'

Shay shrugged and smiled at her friend. 'Sure, it's not like I have anything else to do right now.'

Krista went into the bathroom and admired herself in the mirror. 'At least I got a new bikini,' she called.

'Yeah, now you just need a pool that's not filled with shit to swim in and you're on your way, Miss Hollywood.'

Krista came out, her hands on her hips. 'You sure you don't mind managing my career for a while?'

Shay nodded. 'It's fine. I mean, as soon as I have the baby and get the weight off, I'll be right there auditioning with you. Maybe we'll even get our own TV show one day. We could be like Rachael and Monica from *Friends*.'

Krista clapped her hands. 'Oh, I see it, you have to be Monica, though, cos she was once fat.'

Shay frowned down at her belly. 'I'm not fat, I'm *pregnant.*'

'I know, I'm just teasing,' said Krista as she pulled on a pair of shorts over her bikini. 'But I'm totally Rachel.'

She ducked as Shay threw a pillow at her. 'I won't be pregnant for ever. One day I'm going to be star, just you wait and see.'

Krista smiled at her. 'I know, babe, I do. No one believes in you more than me, and you're gonna have it all, I promise, the career, a hot guy and your own little baby girl to love for ever.'

Chapter 31

Zoe pulled up to Maggie's house, her heart beating faster than normal, and her palms sweating. Why was she so nervous?

Ever since she had met Dylan at Will's house, she hadn't been able to get the girl from her mind. Yes, she was beautiful and that voice needed to be recorded for posterity, but there was a quiet grace in her that Zoe hadn't seen in anyone her age before.

She felt protective, and worried. Anxiety shot through her, as though something bad was about to happen, and it reminded her of being a child.

Explosive events were regular in her childhood and she had worked her whole adult life to ensure she was on a safe ship, with herself firmly at the helm.

Not that there hadn't been drama with her clients. Scandals, drug overdoses, emotional and physical breakdowns—all these she could cope with, but with this girl something felt different.

She pressed the intercom to Maggie's fortress and waited till she heard the click of the gate, allowing her to step inside.

Maggie was waiting for her at the front door.

'What an absolute clusterfuck this is,' was her greeting.

Zoe hugged her friend hello. 'What's happened?'

'Will's kicked Dylan out for supposedly "using" Elliot; Elliot has now run away with Dylan, and I found out Will had an affair with Arden before we broke up, so I punched him in the face,' Maggie said breathlessly.

'Jesus. I'm kind of sorry I missed it.'

'It's *The Bold and the Beautiful* for real,' Maggie said with an eye-roll. 'Did *you* know about Arden and Will?' she asked, watching Zoe's face carefully.

Zoe swallowed. Of course she'd known, she knew everything about her clients, but now was not the time. Maggie had enough to deal with.

'No, I didn't,' she lied.

Maggie sighed in relief. 'I hate her. She's a conniving little bitch. Did you know she turned up to Hugh's to try to get him to cast her as Simone?'

'And what did Hugh say?'

'He told her she wasn't right. I mean, when we wrote that script, we weren't thinking of *her*, for God's sake.'

'*You* wrote the script with Hugh?' Zoe's heart sank.

Maggie smiled. 'Of course, didn't Hugh tell you?'

Zoe pushed her sunglasses up on top of her head. 'No, he didn't,' she said slowly.

This was turning from a clusterfuck into a clusterdrama. Maggie would want a credit, and she would demand the role of Simone. If she didn't get it, she could refuse to release the script, and it was the best script Zoe had read in a very long time. Jeff would fire her for this, for sure, she thought.

'What's wrong?' asked Maggie, frowning.

'Nothing, we can talk about it later. How are Dylan and Elliot?' she asked, trying to process the whirl of revelations.

Maggie sighed dramatically. 'Upset, buoyed only by their love.'

'And you believe she loves him?'

'I do,' said Maggie with a shrug. 'As much as two kids can be in love.'

Zoe nodded, trying to understand. Love had remained a stranger to her all these years, not that she'd tried too hard to find it. She'd been busy looking after everyone else, how could she focus on a relationship as well? This was her excuse and she was sticking to it and so far, it had worked well for her.

Maggie pushed opened the door. 'They're downstairs,' she said and Zoe followed her through the house to the magnificent living area, the doors opened onto the deck that overlooked the ocean.

Dylan was curled up on a sofa, scrolling through her phone. Elliot was beside her, his hand on Dylan's knee. She looked up and smiled at Zoe.

Zoe felt herself smiling back.

'Hi,' said Dylan shyly.

'Dad's being a complete prick, Zo,' said Elliot.

Zoe said nothing, but she secretly agreed. Will had changed since Maggie had left him and Elliot had been sick, and none of the changes had been for the better.

'Are you all right?' she asked Dylan.

'I'm okay, I was just a bit shocked,' she said in her gorgeous husky voice.

Zoe sat down opposite them.

'I'm not going to audition for the film now,' Dylan said.

Zoe saw Elliot's hand tighten on her knee as he looked at her.

Maggie cleared her throat. 'Honestly, I don't think you would be right anyway,' she stated. 'I mean, I did write the script with Hugh, we really know what we're looking for.'

'You mean, you wrote the script for you, and you're what you're looking for?' Elliot said, failing to keep disdain from his voice.

Maggie bristled. 'I don't think that's fair, Elliot.'

'So you don't want to play the role?' he asked, with one raised eyebrow.

Zoe noticed how much he resembled Will with this facial gesture and glanced at Dylan, who was reddening.

'El, it's fine. I couldn't do it anyway; I've never even been in a play before.'

'You never know what you're capable of until you try,' he told her in a soft voice.

Zoe felt her eyes prickle with unexpected tears. When did Elliot grow up? she wondered.

'I need to go back to New York,' said Dylan to the room. 'I came here for a specific reason and it didn't pan out.' She looked pointedly at Maggie. 'And no, it wasn't to be an actress. I have to go home and start my real life now.'

'What about me?' Elliot's hand was no longer on Dylan's leg and his face was hurt.

'I don't know, Elliot. What do you want to do?' she asked.

'I want to be with you. So if that means New York, then I'll move to New York,' he said passionately.

'And what the hell will you do in New York?' asked Maggie, throwing her hands up in the air as she paced the room.

'I don't know, but I'll work it out.'

'I'd never ask you to give up anything for me, Elliot, least of all your family,' Dylan said and Zoe saw a tear fall down one cheek.

God, she was beautiful. The camera would adore her.

'My family?' scoffed Elliot. 'You mean my controlling father who thinks I'm wasting my time writing, being with you, breathing?'

Dylan reached out and took his hand and then looked at Maggie. 'No, I meant Maggie,' she said.

Maggie burst into tears. 'Jesus Christ, can you stop being so fucking perfect?' she yelled.

Dylan leaned back in shock.

Maggie sat down next to Zoe, opposite Dylan and Elliot. 'I mean, you're so great, I want to be in love with you too,' she said crossly to Dylan, and Zoe started to laugh.

Dylan was laughing and crying at the same time.

'Whoever your mother is, tell her from me she's raised one hell of a kid,' said Maggie.

But Zoe saw a shadow cross Dylan's face, her eyes lowered, avoiding Maggie's gaze, and she wondered if there was more to her than met the eye.

Chapter 32

'Dylan, hi, it's Zoe Greene.' Zoe was pacing her office, her stomach churning. 'Can you talk?'

'Sure. Maggie's at Will's getting my things, and Elliot is writing. Why, what's wrong?' asked Dylan, sounding genuinely concerned. 'Are you okay, Zoe?'

'Nothing's wrong.' Zoe smiled. Her clients never asked how *she* was, always concerned only with themselves. Such was the role of the babysitter of narcissists, she thought wryly.

'I was wondering if you'd be able to come in and do that screen-test?' she asked, her heart in her throat.

Dylan was silent for a moment. 'I really don't think I should. Maggie doesn't want me to and she's done a lot for me, I don't want to go behind her back.'

Zoe shook her head in frustration. 'I know what Maggie said, but I really think you should try. I mean, if not for this film then for something else that might come up. I just want to see how you look on camera.'

'I don't even know if I can act,' Dylan said, unconvinced.

'You can learn,' said Zoe. 'You have the looks, the voice, the presence—you owe it to yourself to try. I don't know why you haven't modelled, at least.'

Dylan laughed. 'You're nice,' she said. 'But my parents didn't put any stock on that sort of stuff.'

'That sort of stuff can be very lucrative.'

'I'm sure,' said Dylan. 'I just never thought about it before.'

'Well, you're young, you should try everything once,' said Zoe, grasping at straws.

Dylan was quiet again. 'I really don't want to go behind Maggie's back, though. She's been so good to me and Elliot.'

'I understand.' Zoe's mind was whirring. 'Look, Dylan, how about we get you to read for the film, but we won't put you up for it, just use the test to see if you have something or not. I mean, what is there to lose?'

The silence while Dylan made her decision was excruciating. Any other girl would have jumped at the chance to audition for the best manager in LA and the biggest romantic lead in a film since *Titanic*, but then Dylan wasn't just any girl.

'Okay,' she said slowly. 'But please don't let Maggie or Elliot know, they have enough to think about right now. I mean, it sure won't come to anything.'

Zoe did a little fist pump in the air.

'Of course it will be just between us, I promise,' said Zoe. 'When can you come in?'

'It has to be soon because we're leaving for New York in two days.'

'Wow, that soon?'

'Yeah, I have to speak to my parents about some stuff

and I need to see my best friend, I miss her like crazy.'
Dylan laughed.

At the mention of her best friend, Zoe felt a surge of guilt
about going behind Maggie's back, but then she reminded
herself, this was show business, not show friends. Jeff was
relying on her to bring in someone amazing for the role,
and more than anything she wanted to impress him. Maggie would understand, wouldn't she?

'What about this afternoon?' asked Zoe, walking to the
computer and looking at her calendar.

'Today? Really? I don't know; I mean, I'm in Malibu.'

'Oh, don't worry about that, my assistant can pick you
up and have you back there in no time. Just come in, do a
little test and then you can go back to your life and forget
about it,' said Zoe breezily, holding her breath at the end
of the sentence.

'Okay,' said Dylan finally. 'Thanks, Zoe. I'll just tell
Elliot I have to go to library and do some research. What
should I wear?'

'Just come as yourself, you're perfect as you are,' said
Zoe as she messaged Paul to come into her office. 'See
you soon.'

Two hours later, Zoe was in the conference room, the
video camera set up, and some pages of the script printed
out on the table.

Please let this work, she prayed to the God of movies
stars as the door opened and Dylan walked into the room.

Wearing a white sundress dress with spaghetti straps,
with her hair out and the most almost no make-up, Dylan
was a picture of everything every teenage girl wished they
could be and every boy wanted to date.

'Hi,' Zoe said excitedly, and then she impulsively hugged Dylan. It had been a long time since she'd been so excited by a potential new client.

Dylan hugged her back. 'Elliot says so many nice things about you. He said you're his favourite aunt.'

Zoe turned away for a moment so Dylan couldn't see her emotion. 'Are we ready, Paul?' She poured some water into a glass and handed it to Dylan and they sat down at the table. 'Now remember, this is just for fun, so don't be nervous, okay?'

Dylan smiled. 'No, I'm not too nervous, actually.' She shrugged. 'I guess I have zero expectations anything will come of this.'

Zoe laughed. 'I didn't take you for a pessimist, Dylan.'

'Oh, I'm not! It's more that…well, whatever happens, whatever the outcome, it'll be okay, you know? It usually is, I've found.'

Zoe shook her head. How did a kid get to be so smart? 'I thought we'd just read through the scenes I sent you,' she said casually as she slid some pages to Dylan. 'You know the basic plotline of the book, don't you?'

'I read the back,' said Dylan. 'She dies at the end, right?'

'Yep, she dies, but before that happens we go through their entire relationship. So it's much more about life than death. It's a love story, really.'

Dylan nodded and then read the scenes through a few times. 'Okay, I think I'm good to go.'

Zoe was amazed at her confidence, but there wasn't a shred of arrogance either.

'We'll just get you to stand over there. Paul will read the other parts and you can say the lines, no big deal,' she said, knowing if it paid off it would be a very, very big deal.

Once Dylan was standing in the right spot Zoe nodded to Paul to turn on the camera. 'Action,' she said in a businesslike manner. 'Dylan, can you please just say your name to the camera and where you're from.'

Dylan turned towards the camera. 'I'm Dylan Mercer, and I'm from New York,' she said, her voice sounding natural and relaxed.

Zoe took a deep breath. 'Okay, let's start on a scene,' she said.

Paul read the first line.

Dylan paused and then started to laugh, the sound filling the room. 'Sorry, can we start again?'

Zoe wiped her sweating palms on her black silk pants and nodded.

'From the top?' Dylan asked.

'Sure,' Zoe said, as if nothing depended on this moment.

Paul started again and then Dylan spoke the lines. It was the scene where Hugh and Simone first meet, filled with humour and sexual tension. As Dylan read, Zoe almost forgot she was watching an audition. She utterly believed that Dylan was Simone from the way she used her one free hand to gesture her words, to her subtle reactions to the dialogue from Paul.

When the scene was over, Zoe and Paul were quiet for a moment.

'Was it okay?' asked Dylan, looking worried.

'It was great, let's try another scene,' said Zoe casually, not looking at her, as she shuffled through the pages and found the moment where Simone discovers she has inoperable cancer.

Zoe handed the pages to Paul and then walked over to Dylan.

'This is a tough scene. Simone's whole world is ending, she knows there's nothing more the doctors can do, it's desperation and denial at its best. I don't know how anyone who hasn't been there can understand that, but just do what you can.'

Dylan looked at the pages. 'I get that,' she said softly. 'My dad has Parkinson's disease. I felt like this when he was diagnosed.'

Zoe nodded and went back to her seat. Hoping for the best, she nodded to Paul again, who started to speak as the doctor and Zoe watched Dylan.

Her eyes filled with tears, and she bit her lip. When she spoke the lines, her voice cracked slightly, but not too much. She seemed so incredibly brave that Zoe felt her own eyes pricking with tears.

When the scene was finished, there was a silence. Paul glanced at Zoe, and raised his eyebrows. Zoe struggled to get a grip on what she had just witnessed. But she needed to see Dylan through the camera lens to be absolutely sure.

'Thanks, Dylan, that was terrific. If you can wait outside for a moment, Paul can get you coffee or a tea?'

Dylan picked up her bag. 'No, I'm fine, thanks.' She smiled and walked outside.

Zoe looked at Paul, and they watched it at once.

'Play it again,' said Zoe.

He did.

'Again,' Zoe said, and they watched it a third time.

Zoe slumped back in her seat.

'Oh my God, that's her,' she said to Paul. 'That's our Simone.'

'She's dynamite,' he agreed. 'Where did you find her?'

'She found me,' said Zoe softly.

Chapter 33

'Go away,' said Will through the intercom. 'You said you didn't want to see me again, remember?'

'No,' Maggie replied calmly, lowering her sunglasses and looking over the top of them into the security camera. 'And if you don't let me in, I'm going to call TMZ and have your butt all over the web after I tell them what a complete dick you are.'

The gates swung open.

'What do you want?' Will called from the front door as Maggie pulled up in front of the house. He looked more than a little wary of her.

'How's your jaw?' she asked as she got out of the car.

'Fine, thank you, takes more than a punch from a kid and a woman to flatten me.'

'You looked pretty flattened to me,' she said as she walked past him into the house. 'Where's Stella?' she asked, looking around. Usually Stella was hovering close by, but the house was stilled by her absence.

'Didn't you hear? She's left me,' said Will with a sigh. 'She said I was a terrible boyfriend, which I suppose I am.' He sat heavily on the sofa, put his feet up on the coffee table and looked at her, his eyebrows raised. 'Well, come on, it's your turn. Tell me what a shitty husband I was and we can make it the trifecta.'

Maggie laughed. 'You weren't a shitty husband, you just expected too much. Don't hate yourself, I don't,' she said kindly.

'Even though I cheated on you with Arden?' he asked, shaking his head.

Maggie paused. 'Regardless of me, Arden was a kid and you should have known better.'

'She was twenty,' said Will aghast. 'That's not a kid.'

'Might I remind you, you must have been twice her age when you slept with her. That's too old, dude.'

'You're too old to use the word *dude*,' he replied sulkily.

Maggie laughed. 'Maybe, but I don't care any more, I'm sick of being perfect.'

Will was silent for a moment. 'Arden calls me all the time; she says she's in love with me.'

Maggie frowned. 'Don't mess with her, she's crazy,' she warned.

'I'm not leading her on or anything, but she's unrelenting.' Will sighed. 'All I want is to get Stella back. I know you think she's a bimbo, but she loves me and I've treated her like shit.'

'Then just tell them both the truth,' said Maggie impatiently.

'I have! But Arden won't listen and Stella won't return my calls. Zoe said she'd speak to Arden but nothing has changed.'

'*Zoe* knows about this?' Maggie asked, a cold chill running through her body.

'Yeah, of course, she's my manager. Didn't she tell you?' Will looked at her confused.

'No,' said Maggie, tasting bile in her mouth. 'Listen, I'm not here to solve your problems,' she went on sharply. 'I've come to get Dylan's things before she and Elliot head to New York.'

'New York? What the hell is Elliot going to do in New York? Besides, none of his doctors are there; he needs to stay here to be with his specialists.'

'They have doctors in New York, Will,' Maggie said with a smile.

'She's a conniving little piece,' said Will. 'You watch out for her.'

'No, she's not, she's actually incredibly sweet and she's mad about Elliot, so maybe don't rush to so many conclusions next time.'

'Why are you really here, Maggie?' he asked tiredly.

'Like I said, I'm here to get some of the kid's things, but you have to let go of the bad stuff you're still stewing over. Our marriage didn't work because of a combination of factors, and that's sad. But we shouldn't be nasty to each other any more. I'm tired of it, and I know you are too.'

Will was silent for a moment. 'I didn't hate you for leaving me; I get my role in that. I think I hated you because you left Elliot.'

Maggie felt her eyes fill with tears. 'But I never left him. Just because I wasn't with you doesn't mean I didn't think of El every single day, and you know how often I came to see him. But you helped him in ways that I couldn't when he was sick,' she said as she took Will's hand. 'I know how much you love him.'

'I feel like I screw everything up, Mags. I know I can be a vindictive prick sometimes and I hate myself for it. I've driven Stella away and now my own son is running away from me.'

Maggie breathed out heavily and patted Will's hand. 'You're being an idiot. If you love Stella, go and win her back. If you want a relationship with your son, stop being a controlling ass and support his dreams. And if you want to be more liked in this town, stop offending everyone you come into contact with. I guarantee you'll be much happier and so will everyone else.'

Will smiled wanly. 'I'll try. Do you think Elliot will talk to me?'

Maggie paused and smiled. 'Give him time,' she said as she stood up. 'I'll grab that stuff from the guesthouse.'

'Sure, Maria's packed it all up.'

'I'll see you later then,' Maggie said, ruffling Will's hair as she walked past.

'Bye, Mags, thanks,' he said.

Maggie walked down to the guesthouse. Dylan's suitcase was packed, as Will had said, and a pile of papers and an old laptop computer sat on the desk in a shopping bag. Dylan had been adamant that she needed these papers back, yet she still hadn't explained to Maggie or Zoe why she was in Los Angeles.

Maggie pulled the papers from the bag and sat down on the bed to examine them.

She wasn't ashamed about her snooping habit; a childhood of moving houses gave you a certain disregard for other people's things. So many social workers had packed up her stuff without any thought for her privacy, and she had survived.

She'd already been through Hugh's house when he wasn't home. She'd found nothing of interest whatsoever, not even porn on his computer history.

Dylan's papers were in a plastic sleeve and Maggie slipped them out and looked at the top document. It was a birth certificate.

Name: Dylan Mercer
Sex: Female
Mother: Paula Klein—Attorney
Father: Jonathon Mercer—Doctor of Medicine

Some kids were just born to the right parents, she thought as she flipped over to the next page, and then she felt her stomach drop. Unclipping the documents, she spread them out on the bed and looked through them, checking the dates on the birth certificate and then going back through the documents again until she was sure.

'Jesus Christ,' she said aloud, and looked around the room hoping for someone to whom she could confess the unbelievable: 'I've found her!'

Los Angeles
March 1996

'Hello? Paula Klein speaking.'

Shay took a deep breath.

'Hi, I'm ringing about your ad in *The Pennysaver*,' she said nervously.

The woman was silent for a moment. 'Go on,' she said.

Shay heard her apprehension and decided to get straight to the point.

'I'm having a baby and I can't afford to keep it right now

and you said you would help young mothers and I just need someone to help look after her until I can raise her myself,' she said, the words spewing out in a rush.

'You're having a girl?' asked the woman.

'I think so,' said Shay. 'I mean, I don't know, but I feel like I know, do you know what I mean?'

'No,' said the woman sharply.

'I'm sorry,' Shay said. 'I didn't think.'

'That's okay. When are you due?'

Shay counted back the months from her last period. 'Sometime in May. I don't have an exact date.'

'Have you seen a doctor yet?' asked the woman, her voice concerned.

'Not yet,' answered Shay. 'I haven't really had the money. But I am trying to eat right, and I have orange juice whenever I can. And milk,' she added quickly.

'Where exactly are you?'

'On the corner, in the drug store,' Shay said, wiping her clammy hand on the side of her skirt that didn't do up any more.

Krista had stolen two maternity dresses from Target for her, but they were drying in the bathroom at the hotel.

'I mean, what state?' laughed the woman kindly.

'Oh gosh, sorry, I'm in Los Angeles, California,' she said, knowing she was turning red. She wanted this woman to think well of her. The couple's ad in *The Pennysaver* had been different to the others.

We are a wealthy married couple, but sadly we are unable to have children of our own. We want to adopt a child and are willing to help the birth parents stay in the child's life. If you want to have the best for your child and still be in their life, then we are the best couple for you and your baby.

The phone beeped and Shay fed another quarter into the phone.

'You need to see a doctor,' said the woman.

'I can't afford it,' said Shay, swallowing her pride.

The woman paused and then spoke. 'Let me take your name and number and organize you an appointment. My husband and I will pay for it. What's your home phone number?'

Shay paused. 'I'm living in a hotel,' she said quietly.

But this fact didn't seem to bother the woman. 'Okay, so just give me the name of the hotel and I'll call you there,' she said calmly.

There was something about the way she spoke that soothed Shay, and she felt her breathing slow down.

'Okay,' she said, trying not to cry. 'It's just…I don't know what else to do. I love my baby, I just can't look after her for a while and I don't want her in a foster home, I was in one and they aren't the right place to raise a dog, let alone a baby.'

'I understand,' said the woman. 'Let's just start with the first thing, which is making sure you and the baby are healthy, and then we can sort out everything else. What's your name, sweetie?'

'It's Shay. Shay Harman.'

'That's a pretty name. I'm Paula, and my husband's name is Jonathon. I think I know exactly what you need, Shay, and we can help you if you'll let us. Do you and your family or the baby's father have a lawyer you're dealing with?'

Shay felt the dam of tears break and she started to sob. 'I don't have any family, no lawyer, and no, the father isn't in my life.'

'Shhh,' said the woman soothingly, 'it's going to be okay.

You can use our lawyer, his name is Jefferson Perry, he'll get all the papers together so you don't have to worry about a single thing, except looking after yourself and your baby, okay?'

'Okay,' said Shay, crying harder now, but also feeling a great weight lifting from her shoulders as someone else took charge. 'Thank you, Paula.'

'It's my pleasure, Shay,' Paula said excitedly. 'It's my absolute pleasure. You have no idea how much of a pleasure it is.'

Chapter 34

Hugh watched Smike run along the foreshore as though sniffing for a trail that led only to the ocean. It was his morning routine and one Hugh found perplexing.

What was the little dog waiting for, Hugh wondered, as he watched him sitting panting at a certain spot on the water's edge, the same place every time, and staring out over the ocean.

He whistled. Smike turned his head to Hugh, then back to the ocean and then reluctantly he trotted to Hugh's side and lay down with his head on his paws.

'What are you looking for, my four-legged friend?' Hugh asked as he laid his hand on Smike's back. 'Waiting for your ship to come in?'

The sound of his phone ringing in his pocket set his pulse racing, hoping it would be Maggie. He couldn't get enough of her.

But it was Zoe's number that flashed on the screen.

Since Maggie had come into his life, Hugh had hardly seen Zoe, but he supposed making a film was hard work.

'Greetings, Ms Greene, how are you on this splendid morning?' he said in a deliberately pompous tone.

'You don't actually talk to people like that, do you?' laughed Zoe.

'No, I just do it to stir up you Americans. How was the script?'

'The script is *amazing*. You did such a great job.'

'*We* did,' he corrected. 'Maggie and I wrote it together.'

'Yes.' Zoe was silent for a moment. 'I just wish you'd told me you were writing it with her.'

Hugh watched Smike run back to the edge of the water and sit patiently. Hugh understood how that felt. He knew what sitting and waiting was like. He had done it when he sat by Simone's bed, waiting for her death, when he had waited for Maggie to see how he felt about her, it felt like his whole life was spent waiting.

'Why? What does it matter? She said she didn't care if she got a credit. She says she doesn't want to play Simone now but I think she could.'

'That's the thing, Hugh,' said Zoe, her voice strained. 'She's too expensive—the film's budget wouldn't cover Maggie playing Simone. Plus, Jeff thinks she's too old.'

'Jesus, that's a bit rough!' Hugh was outraged on Maggie's behalf.

'Well, it is what it is. That's how Hollywood works, I'm afraid. I can talk to Jeff about getting Maggie a co-authored credit on the script, which means you'll have to split your fee with her.'

'Oh, I don't care about money,' said Hugh, laughing. 'And I don't think Maggie will either.'

Zoe was quiet for a moment. 'Has something happened between you two?'

Hugh thought about Maggie's words to him earlier that morning when he mentioned them heading away to Europe for a bit once the script was finished. 'I can't go anywhere right now, I have to be here for Elliot and Will, they can't function without me and right now, they're functioning badly.'

Hugh hadn't said anything but he wondered about Will. She spent so much time talking about Elliot and Will, he wondered if he was just a placeholder.

'No, nothing's happened, we're just friends,' he answered. 'She is, as you said, a very smart person.'

'Good, because, and I know this sounds callous, and it is, but we're going to have to sell you as the sad widower during the publicity campaign,' she said. 'And if you had a thing with Maggie and she played your dead wife, that would be weird, right?'

Hugh watched Smike, his heart feeling heavier than it had in a long time. He was tired of being the widower, he wanted to start a new life with Maggie and Smike and live happily ever after. Simone was dead and he was ready to live again and deep down, he knew Zoe was right.

But what did Maggie want? He realized he didn't know the answer to the question and fear filled him.

Maggie felt like his lifeline but what was he to her?

Was he trying to replace Simone with Maggie?

Zoe was talking and he brought his mind back to what she was saying. 'I've found someone who I think is worth seeing as Simone,' she said. 'I'm also sending the tape over to Jeff this afternoon.'

Hugh trudged back to the house, Smike following him up the beach.

'Shouldn't the director be a part of this decision?' he asked.

'We don't have one yet,' Zoe said. 'I'm still trying to find someone who understands our vision and who can work within the budget.'

'Okay, I'll email you after I've watched the tape,' he said tiredly.

'Thanks, Hugh,' she said. 'I know this whole business is frustrating but it'll be worth it when we find the right girl.'

Hugh said goodbye and thought about Zoe's words. Was Maggie the right girl for him?

He opened his computer and the screen flickered to life. He opened his email while Smike settled comfortably on his feet, and two emails came through.

One from Zoe, as promised, and the other was from Arden Walker. How the hell did she get his address?

Hi Hugh,

I just came from Will MacIntyre's house, where I learned he and Maggie are getting back together. Apparently this is something she has wanted for a while, and something that will be right for her, Elliot and Will.

I know she won't tell you herself until after the casting's been formalized, but I thought you had the right to know now.

I'm very sorry to be the one telling you this, but I don't want you to have your heart broken the way Will has broken mine.

Welcome to Hollywood!

Ardently,

Arden x

Hugh looked around the light-filled rented house with its incredible view over the perfect white beach and glittering water. He thought about his cosy house back in London, full of all his familiar things, and the yearning for change overwhelmed him.

Maggie had been secretive and snappy over the past few days. She'd told him she had been to see Will last week, but she hadn't said why. She no longer seemed to want him coming to her house and they hadn't slept together again since the first time.

Who was he kidding that Maggie wanted *him*? What she had always wanted was to inhabit the ghost of his wife on screen. He was a deluded old fool, he thought, as he opened the file that Zoe had sent him. The very worst kind of fool, one who assumed that he could measure up to Maggie's fantasies of who he was in the book. He wasn't that man he wrote about, he wasn't anyone.

He realized in that instant that he didn't even care about his story any more. He was tired of himself, and of Simone— tired of the whole damn mess. Zoe could cast whatever actress she wanted in the role, he just wanted to get away from it all.

Without even watching the girl on screen, he emailed Zoe.

I know you said to call, but I don't have time. I agree, the girl seems perfect. Exactly what Simone was when she was young. Cast away, Zoe. I'm heading back to London. Send me anything else you need signing.

Thank you for everything. I will be always grateful.
Hugh

PS: I want Maggie to get full credit for the script, it's the least I can do since she won't get the role now.

Within minutes he was in the bedroom, pulling his suit-case down from the wardrobe and throwing his few items into it and zipping it closed.

Filling Smike's bowl with food and making sure he had plenty of water, he patted the dog on the head.

'Maggie will be here in a bit, my friend, and it's time I went on my way. I don't think you'd like it where I'm going, there's no ocean,' he said sadly.

Scribbling a note, he left it on the table and picking up his passport and wallet, he walked out of the house, slamming the door behind him.

It was time to go home and start a new life, free of Simone, Maggie, Smike and anyone or anything that required something of him. The desire to drink was overwhelming, and he shook his head, as though trying to shake the thoughts from his mind.

He wanted to drink to spite Maggie for leaving him, just like he drank to spite Simone for leaving him. God, he was hopeless, he thought. No wonder no one wanted to be with him.

No, he wouldn't drink, he decided as he dialled for a cab and waited at the front of the house.

He would just disappear, which was all he ever wanted when he drank, but he was never brave enough until now. Maggie Hall had pushed him over the edge, and he doubted he would ever quite recover from her.

Chapter 35

'Hugh?' Maggie opened the door with the key Hugh had given her and Smike came running to her.

'Hello, mutt,' she said affectionately as she patted his head. 'Where's your dad?'

Then, on the coffee table, she saw the note.

Maggie,

I'm heading back to London. I'll leave Smike with you because I don't think he would like London. No beaches, you see. Anyway, you were always better at training him than me. I leave the laptop, which has the final draft of the script on it, please make any changes and send it to Zoe. I have asked for you to receive full credit. And return the laptop to Zoe after you've used it, please.

I don't know if you will play Simone, it's out of my hands now. I'm sorry if your time with me was wasted. I understand things became complicated and confused.

To be honest with you, I believed you for a second, but I understand now: you did what you had to do to survive and get what you want. Just like I did when I chose to stay with Simone.

The truth is, I can't have Simone in my life any more. Even us, whatever it was, was about her. I thought coming to America would solve that, but grief has a passport and Simone came along for the ride. I need to let her go now. I need to let The Art of Love *go, and anything else that comes with that territory.*

I'll be in London until I work out my next move and what I'm going to do with the rest of my life.

You're an amazing woman, Maggie Hall, and I meant what I said and I said what I meant—I just forgot for a moment that you were acting.

I hope you and Will become happy again as a family and that Elliot writes his story one day.
Always,
Hugh

'What?' Maggie yelled aloud. Grabbing Smike, the laptop and the note, she headed straight back to her house.

Walking inside, she screamed for Elliot.

'Hey, a dog!' he said as he ambled out of the study.

Smike ran to Elliot's side and jumped up at him.

'Hey, buddy,' said Elliot, laughing as he crouched down and the dog licked his face, his tail wagging ferociously.

'This is Smike,' she said and opened the laptop.

What the hell had been said to Hugh that had made him leave her? She felt sick at the thought of him thinking she was going to be with Will again. Who would have told him that? Then she found Arden's email.

As she read it, she screamed.

Elliot looked scared. 'What's wrong?'

'Nothing, just leave me alone,' she snapped. Elliot looked scared of her but she didn't care about his reaction, as she picked up her phone and dialled Will's number.

'What the hell did you say to Arden Walker about us?' she started as soon as he picked up.

'Nothing,' he said, too quickly.

'Bullshit! Tell me now or I promise you'll live to regret it.'

Will sighed. 'I told her I couldn't be with her because you and I were getting back together.'

Maggie slumped in her chair as though winded.

'She didn't care if I was with Stella, but she's scared of you,' Will went on.

'So she should be,' she hissed. 'You have just screwed up my whole future, you weak, stupid asshole.'

Slamming down the phone, she saw an email from Zoe and clicked on it to open the attached file, feeling like she was in a scene from a movie, except this one was real.

She saw Dylan speaking to camera and then she heard Zoe's voice. She watched Dylan say her lines in the two scenes and felt pure rage as it finished.

Then she read the response Hugh had sent to Zoe.

I agree, the girl seems perfect. Exactly what Simone was when she was young.

Maggie stood up and slammed the laptop closed and walked into the study, where Smike sat at Elliot's feet.

'Where's Dylan?'

'Downstairs, reading,' he said. 'Is everything okay?'

Maggie didn't answer him. She found Dylan lying on a sofa, reading *The Art of Love*.

'Get out of my house,' said Maggie in a low voice.

'What?' Dylan jumped up and put the book behind her back.

'I said, get the fuck out of my house!'

She heard Elliot yelling at her from the top of the stairs but she didn't care.

'I saw your audition, Dylan, and I saw your papers when I picked them up. You look so young and innocent, but you're a designing little piece of work, aren't you? Tell me, were you planning on blackmailing Zoe into giving you this role?'

Dylan shook her head. She looked utterly shocked. 'I don't know what you're talking about. Yes, I auditioned, but I only did it as a favour to Zoe, I told her I didn't want to do the film,' she said, her voice cracking.

She was a good actress, Maggie thought wryly.

'You're a liar, Dylan Mercer. I know exactly why you're here. And if you think I'm going to let you break Zoe's heart, then you're kidding yourself. Just get on that plane and never come back to this town, do you hear me?'

'Break Zoe's heart? How could I? It's just a film,' Dylan cried.

'Maggie, what are you *doing*?' Elliot yelled from behind her. 'Stop it!'

Maggie turned to him. 'You're a fool, Elliot. She's here to find her mother, did you know that?'

'Yes, I knew that,' he said, frowning. 'What's that got to do with you?'

Maggie laughed meanly. 'Oh, so she didn't tell you the rest of it?'

Elliot looked at Dylan, who shook her head, tears streaming down her face.

'I auditioned for the film after all, because Zoe asked

me to and because I didn't know how to say no,' she cried. 'She seems so nice.'

'You deliberately worked on me at the Oscars party, you used me just like you've used Elliot, and it was all so you can get to Zoe, wasn't it, Dylan? Admit it.' Maggie was still yelling and Smike started to bark.

'Shut up, Smike,' Maggie yelled at the dog.

Elliot looked at Maggie and then to Dylan. 'What the hell are you talking about, Maggie?'

Maggie laughed again, it sounded hysterical to her own ears but she didn't care, it was time Dylan admitted the truth to Elliot, and if she wouldn't then Maggie would do it for her.

'Zoe is Dylan's birth mother,' she said. 'We gave her to Dylan's parents for thirty thousand dollars two days after she was born. Isn't that right, Dylan? Isn't that why you're here? This is your way of getting closure *and* a career.'

She had won, she thought. She had beaten the girl at her own game and shown Elliot who Dylan really was.

But Dylan fell to the floor in a sobbing huddle.

Elliot's face was ashen. 'Dylan, is this true?'

'No,' cried Dylan, her body heaving. 'I didn't know Zoe was my mother, I promise I didn't.' She started to retch, as she sat on the floor.

'Oh, please, cut out the dramatics,' Maggie said coldly.

'Jesus, Dylan,' Elliot breathed out as he spoke, his voice shaking.

'I didn't know!' she cried again.

'You expect me to believe in a coincidence like this?'

Dylan looked him, and Maggie saw the heartbreak on her face and for a moment she felt sorry for her. Then she remembered the audition and she steeled her heart.

'The fact that you could doubt me makes me realize you're just like everyone else,' she gulped tearfully to Elliot, and then she turned to Maggie.

'You're a sad person, but I am really glad for one thing.'

'What's that?' sneered Maggie. 'That now you think you can walk into the role of a lifetime?'

'I'm just glad *you're* not my mother,' Dylan said. And with that, she walked up the stairs and ten minutes later Maggie heard the front door slam.

'Good, she's gone,' she said to Elliot who was sitting on the sofa, his head in his hands. 'Aren't you glad you know now?' she crowed triumphantly.

He looked up at her with an expression she'd never seen before, and it scared her.

'No, I'm not glad. In fact, right now I hate you, Maggie, and you know what else? I'm glad you're not my mother either.'

He stormed from the house, the slam of the door like a full stop, and she started to cry. She cried until she was on her knees, her head on the floor, screaming into the carpet.

She was unlovable and she drove everyone away, she told herself. Why did she jump to conclusions so quickly?

Years ago Will had told her to get therapy, that she assumed the worst of people all the time and didn't give them time to respond or explain.

She had told him it was because she had seen the worst in people, and had yet to be proved otherwise.

But Elliot had showed her otherwise, and then Hugh, and always Zoe, and look at what she had done to them.

When had she become such a terrible person? she wondered. Was it back in the mountains, singing in church and giving sexual favours to Preacher Garrett for abortion money?

Or was it when she rifled through people's lives, looking for something for her benefit?

She didn't know the answer but she did know that she could not live with herself any longer like she was. Something had to change, she thought, and then she realized: it wasn't something else, it was her. She had to change but the question was, how?

Chapter 36

Maggie had sent the dog over to Will's house the next day, claiming he'd been crying continuously since Elliot had left.

Elliot doubted that Smike had been crying for him—it was more likely that Maggie couldn't be bothered looking after him herself, he thought—but he was grateful for the company.

His father had been happy to see him, but distracted, as usual. There was no mention of the punch Elliot had delivered to his father's jaw and no mention of Dylan.

It was as though nothing had happened, yet everything had changed.

Stella was back, which at least made his father slightly happier, but to Elliot, the house seemed colder and more silent than before. His computer waited for him to sit down and start writing, but whenever he tried, the words wouldn't come.

Nothing made sense without Dylan, yet her story didn't

make sense either. How could she not know Zoe was her birth mother?

Smike rolled over and Elliot scratched the dog's stomach as his phone rang.

He snatched it up, hoping it would be Dylan even though he knew it wouldn't be. She hadn't returned his calls or responded to his texts or emails since she had walked out, and he hadn't returned any of Maggie's calls either. It was a huge circle of non-communication.

'Hello?'

'Hello, this is Paula Klein, Dylan's mother. I'm sorry to disturb you, but Dylan gave me this number in case of emergencies and I haven't been able to get hold of her for days.'

'Hi, this is Elliot,' he said. 'Um, she said she was going back to New York,' Elliot went on, going to check his emails again. But the inbox was empty.

'When did she say this?' asked Paula impatiently.

'Three days ago, the last time I saw her,' Elliot said slowly.

Then he remembered, Dylan hadn't actually said she was going home, she had just walked out of Maggie's house.

'How was she when she left?' asked Paula, worry in her voice.

Elliot was quiet for a moment. 'She was upset,' he admitted.

'Why?' Paula's voice was now accusatory.

As well it should be, Elliot thought, guilt running through him. 'There was a…a misunderstanding at work,' he said.

'I see,' snapped Paula. 'Well, will you please contact me the moment you here from her?' And she rang off before Elliot could say another word.

Elliot sat stunned. Then he heard the ping of an email arriving and, jumping up to check, he saw it was from Dylan. Relief flooded through him.

She was okay, he thought gratefully, as he started to read.

Elliot,

I got your emails and your messages. You keep asking me to explain how this happened, but I can't. I didn't know about Zoe, I swear on my life, but no one will ever believe me now, especially if I become an actress and Zoe helps me.

I've been working on something for you these past weeks. I know you wanted to find your donor and I'm almost certain I have. I've attached the newspaper articles about him and his family. His parents say they would love to meet the person who received their son's heart, but they know it is a long shot.

So I think they'd be happy to meet with you, if you reached out to them. I thought this would be something we'd do together, but everything is different now. I know it won't be easy, but I'm sure you will be fine on your own.

I'm staying with a friend for a while, until I work out what to do next. I don't want to speak to my own parents, knowing how they bought me for money and I don't want Zoe to know who I am in case she thinks like you and Maggie do about me.

Look after yourself and that heart. You're amazing, Elliot, and I will love you always.

Dylan

X

Elliot reread the email and then dialled the number on his phone that had flashed up minutes before.

'Dylan's just emailed me, she's okay,' he said when Paula answered.

'Where is she?' demanded Paula.

'She said she's staying with a friend,' he said carefully.

'Which friend?'

'She didn't say.'

'This is ridiculous,' said Paula. 'What the hell happened to make her run away?'

Elliot reread Dylan's words. If she was truly the person Maggie said she was, then why was she prepared to sacrifice both Zoe and her adopted mother?

The realization made Elliot feel sick and he paused. Maggie had created this mess, so she could sort it out.

'I think you need to speak to my ex-stepmother,' he said. 'She knows what's happened.'

As he gave Paula Maggie's number, he knew it was time the whole truth came out, not just about Dylan, but also about himself. He went to find his father.

'Dad, I need to talk to you.'

Will narrowed his eyes at Elliot. 'Is everything okay?'

Elliot shook his head. 'No, it's not actually. Come downstairs, I want to show you something.'

'Are you sick?' Will's voice was panicked.

'No, Dad, just come with me,' Elliot answered.

Will followed him and Smike down to Elliot's space and sat on the sofa.

'Okay, I'm about to tell you something that is crazy, but don't say anything or ask any questions until I've finished, you understand?'

Will nodded, as though shocked by Elliot's composure, and Elliot felt more in control than he had ever been before. Will clasped his hands in his lap, his brow furrowed, listening intently to his son for the first time in twenty-three years.

An hour later, Will was leaning forward, his jaw dropped and shaking his head.

'And she sent you the articles on the person whose heart you received? Who is he?'

'I don't know; I haven't looked at them yet.'

'Why not? If this is what you've been desperate to know since the operation?'

'Because I wanted someone with me when I did,' Elliot said quietly.

Will stood up, pulled Elliot to his feet and held him in a long hug.

'I'm always here. I know I fuck things up, but I do try my best not to.'

Elliot smiled, feeling his eyes fill with tears and he pulled away.

'Thanks, Dad,' he said and he sat down at the computer and started to read the files Dylan had sent.

A teenager was found floating off the popular surf spot of Hermosa Beach, Los Angeles County. He was brought into shore by fellow surfers and CPR was administered until paramedics arrived. He was taken to hospital where he is in a critical condition.

He opened the next article.

Tyler Mathers, beloved son of Penny and Bill Mathers and loved brother of Jenna.
Our beautiful boy will be riding the waves in the

skies for ever. Every time we see a rainbow we know
you caught the big one.

And finally a small interview with Tyler's parents on
organ donation in their local newspaper:

'We miss him every day, every minute of every day,
but we are proud to know he saved another life and
we hope that person is making the best of their time
here with a part of Tyler inside them. It's an amaz-
ing gift. Knowing that Tyler helped another person
to live is what gets us through each day,' says Tyler's
mother, Penny.

Will read the article over Elliot's shoulder and Elliot
turned to his father, not caring that he was sobbing in front
of his father.

'Will you help me, Dad?'

'Of course, kiddo, I'd do anything for you,' Will answered, his voice choked up.

Elliot wondered how he would ever be able to thank the
girl who had given him his heart and whose heart he had
broken in return.

Los Angeles
March 1996

'Hey, hey,' Krista called excitedly as she walked into
the shabby hotel room she and Shay shared. 'I have news!'

Shay waddled out of the bathroom and looked at her ex-
pectantly.

'I got the speaking part on *Days of our Lives*!' Krista

jumped on the bed and did a victory dance. 'I get my SAG card and the job pays five hundred dollars,' she cried.

Shay clapped her hands. 'I'm so proud of you.'

'I wouldn't have been able to do it without your help,' said Krista seriously. 'You telling me about it in the first place. And then how you rang up and pretended to be my manager.'

Shay smiled. 'I have news also,' she said slowly.

Krista fell to her knees on the bed. 'What's up?'

'I've decided to give the baby up,' she said. 'Just for a while—until we get our lives together.'

Krista gasped. 'You're not sending her to a foster home?'

'No way. No, I've been talking to a woman in New York who says she can look after the baby until I'm able to get her back, and she says she can give me some starting-out money too, to help us. I mean, you and me.'

'But I thought we were going to raise the baby ourselves,' Krista said, her voice breaking.

'Here?' Shay gestured around them at the hotel room. 'How can we raise a baby here?'

Krista looked at the small, dingy room. 'It's okay. Better than where I was living back home.'

'Well, I want more for my baby. She *deserves* more,' Shay said emphatically.

'But we could take it in turns while we go out to auditions, and you're much better than me so you'll get great jobs. We can do this, we can be famous and rich and give the baby a great life!' Krista cried.

Shay shook her head. 'I can't, I won't,' she said. 'I'm going to the doctor's tomorrow and if everything's okay, I'm going to sign a deal with this woman for her to look after the baby until I can.'

Krista stood up and smoothed out her denim miniskirt, a newly acquired steal from Macy's.

'I hate you doing this! You know I want this baby as much as you do and you haven't even asked me what *I* think,' she said, tears falling down her cheeks.

Shay was resolved, her voice calm. 'I'm sorry, Kris, but you don't get a say.'

'Why not?' Krista implored. Ever since they'd arrived in LA she had imagined her and Shay and their baby being like two sisters with their doll. She wanted to love this child as she herself had never been loved and to give her everything she never had.

She pulled open a drawer and took out a yellow jumpsuit with tiny white ducks printed on the fabric. 'Look what I got for the baby yesterday. Won't she look beautiful in this when we take her out for walks?' she coaxed.

Shay took the jumpsuit and laid it across her swollen stomach. 'It's perfect,' she said and then she took Krista's hand and squeezed it tightly.

'We *will* get her back,' she said. 'It's just for a while, just until we get ahead. We won't let her go like our mothers did. We'll always be there for her, no matter what, isn't that right?'

Krista nodded fiercely through her tears. 'No matter what,' she echoed.

Chapter 37

'She is something else, I agree. She's fucking perfect,' said Jeff, as he paused on Dylan smiling on the screen.

Zoe tried not to get too excited. After all, she still had to convince Dylan to do the film and deal with Maggie when she found out, but she did have Hugh's approval, albeit via email.

She had wondered for a moment about his return to London, but then let the concern go. This was work, not friendship. She didn't have time to worry about Hugh. He had delivered the script and that was all she needed for now.

'Is she single?'

Zoe started to laugh. 'Come on, are you serious? She's nineteen, for God's sake.'

'I was just asking, I'm not interested in dating her.'

'Why? Is she too old?' Zoe snapped.

'I'm insulted,' said Jeff indignantly.

'No you're not,' said Zoe with an unapologetic shrug. 'Hands off, she's dating Will's son, Elliot.'

'Didn't that kid have a kidney transplant or something?'

'Heart,' corrected Zoe.

'Ah yes, I remember. I let the hospital use my private plane to bring in his surgeon from New York.' Jeff said it as though he had just loaned a lawnmower.

'That was very nice of you,' said Zoe sincerely, looking at him closely. Why did he always surprise her? She needed to be more prepared for his moments of humanity.

'Well, as long as it helped,' he said irritably.

'You don't like being reminded you can be a decent person, do you?' she laughed.

Jeff went a little red, and he fiddled with the cufflink that Zoe had gifted him. 'Decency is bullshit. How I can be decent when I have three divorces under my belt and three kids who hate me?'

Zoe looked him in the eye. 'You let your cock choose your wives, so more fool you. As for your kids, you can work on those relationships. You just have to let them know you want to be in their lives.'

'Oh, how would you know, Greene? You don't have kids, do you?'

'No, I don't,' she said abruptly.

Any intimacy was lost, replaced by a tension Zoe hadn't felt before. She wondered if Jeff felt it too but he just narrowed his eyes at her and then shuffled some papers in front of him. 'Will it be a problem having Will in the lead?' asked Jeff. 'I can afford him, if you do a decent deal on the girl.'

'I'm sure it won't be,' Zoe said confidently. But already her mind was racing ahead. How on earth could she get Dylan and Will to star opposite each other?

She stood up and slipped her black silk jacket over her white dress.

Jeff smiled and looked her up and down approvingly. 'I'm liking you in that dress,' he said. 'Fits like a glove.'

Zoe laughed again and shook her head. 'Thanks, but I didn't wear it for you, I wore it for me.' And she walked out of the office, still smiling to herself. As soon as she had stopped seeing Jeff as some sort of God, her life had eased considerably.

Driving along the Pacific Coast Highway, heading for Maggie's house, Zoe felt the pleasure of driving her car on the road, with the water on one side and the magnificent hillside homes on the other. Life was good, she thought, and in a moment of rare contentment, she turned up *The Best of Mariah Carey*, one of her guilty pleasure CDs, and sang along.

Maggie would be fine once she settled down, Zoe told herself. Christ, she had a sole writing credit on an Oscar-worthy script, she might get nominated, might even win Best Screenplay, Zoe dreamed happily. That would have to salve her wounds somewhat.

Pulling up at the front of Maggie's house, she gathered her nerves and tried to distil them into reason. Giving Dylan the role of Simone was the best thing for the film, surely even Maggie would see that eventually. She pressed the intercom and smoothed down her hair.

'It's me, let me in,' she said as she peered into the camera.

'No, go away!' said Maggie. 'I don't want to talk to you!'

'What?' Zoe faltered. Had Maggie found out about Dylan already? 'Why?'

'I saw the email you sent Hugh.'

Maggie's voice was icy cold.

'What email?' Zoe was confused and then she remembered.

'Don't insult me. I saw her audition.'

Zoe was silent for a moment. 'I'm sorry, Mags, I was going to tell you. There was just some stuff I needed to check first.'

'Bullshit,' said Maggie through the speaker. 'You have no idea what she was about. She's a lying little bitch who is after everything and you have absolutely no idea.'

Zoe felt her temper rising and her voice as well. 'Oh my God, Maggie, stop being so paranoid. What's wrong with you?'

'Nothing's wrong with me,' Maggie cried. 'And why did you lie to me about Will and Arden? He said you'd always known, why didn't you tell me?'

Maggie's voice was hoarse with tears and Zoe felt her own tears coming.

'Open the door. Let me in so we can talk about it,' she pleaded. 'Please, Maggie.'

Zoe pressed the button again, but Maggie didn't answer, so she pressed it over and over again.

Maggie's lost the plot, she thought despairingly, after what seemed like hours of pressing the button. She was just about to admit defeat and leave, when the gate clicked open.

Maggie was standing by the front door in her dressing gown, with swollen red eyes and greasy hair.

'What the hell, Mags? You look like shit,' Zoe exclaimed.

'Thanks, bitch,' said Maggie as she turned and walked inside.

Zoe followed her into her bedroom, where Maggie got back into bed and pulled the covers up to her chin.

Zoe sat on the end of the bed. 'What's going on?'

Maggie started to sob. 'You lied to me!'

'I know,' said Zoe. She couldn't deny it and she wouldn't deny it, Maggie deserved that much from her.

'Why didn't you tell me about Will?'

'You were so fragile then, and you'd already decided to go. If you knew about Arden, would you have been able to be there so much for Elliot? He used to ring me and cry because he was so worried you'd hate him as well as his dad if you found out.'

Maggie shook her head slowly.

'I didn't tell you because it wouldn't have made anything better, it would have made it worse.'

Maggie blinked a few times and then sniffed. 'Well, what about the audition with Dylan? Why didn't you tell me about that?'

'Because you would've hated her and it might have ruined your relationship with Elliot. I didn't know she'd be so good but she is wonderful, Mags, really, she reminds me of you when you were just starting out.'

At this, Maggie burst out crying again, almost hysterical. 'Everything's broken,' she cried.

Zoe had never seen Maggie like this, even in the worst of times. Maggie had a fighting quality that had saved her many times. Other people would have given up on life if they'd been dealt her hand, but Maggie had always found a way to go on, until now.

'I've lost Hugh, he's run away from me and gone back to London, and I've had a huge fight with Elliot and he said he hates me and never wants to speak to me again,' she wept.

'Oh, babe, don't cry. I'm sure it can all be sorted out, it's just misunderstandings. And until then you always have me.' She smiled.

But Maggie just cried even harder.

'No, you're going to hate me too.'

Zoe laughed. 'You could never do anything to make me hate you.'

Maggie rolled over and pulled the covers over her head.

Zoe tried not to laugh but failed. 'Seriously, you have to stop being so dramatic. Nothing can be that bad, Maggie, honestly. I mean, we've been through so much together.'

Maggie threw the covers back and looked Zoe in the eye.

'Did you ever look for her?'

Zoe frowned. 'Who?'

Maggie stared at her like a crazy woman. 'Your daughter. I want to know if you ever went looking for her.'

Zoe was still as she opened the memory drawer in her mind.

'Once,' she said slowly.

Maggie sat up in bed. 'You never told me,' she said wonderingly.

'She was seven. I found her, and she was happy. I mean like *really* happy, riding a bike with her parents in Central Park. They were such a little unit, who was I to break that up? I thought I had it together, you and I had had some success and the company had just started, but when I saw her, so cute in her little pigtails, I couldn't bear to take her away from what she knew to be family. It was selfish of me to think I could do better, just because we have the same DNA.'

Maggie was silent for a moment and then she took a deep breath.

'What if I told you she was looking for you now?'

Zoe felt as though she was spinning and she took a sharp breath inwards.

'What?' she asked, wondering if she had heard correctly.

'I've found her,' Maggie said slowly. 'She's here, she's looking for you.'

'What do you mean? Where is she? How long have you known this? Does she know who I am?'

The questions came tumbling out of her mouth, which felt dry as she spoke.

Maggie ducked under the covers again and Zoe heard her speaking from underneath.

'What? I can't hear you,' she said, pulling the covers off Maggie. 'Who is it? Where is she?' Zoe was yelling now and she couldn't control her shaking voice or hands.

'It's Dylan!' Maggie yelled back. 'It's Dylan, all right?'

'What? Dylan? Dylan Mercer?' Zoe stood up.

'Yes,' Maggie sobbed.

'How do you know?' Zoe gasped.

'Because I found her papers and the letter you wrote her and everything,' Maggie wept.

'How long have you known this?' Zoe asked.

'Only a few days,' she replied.

Zoe's mind whirled, trying to remember everything about Dylan and coming up blank. The girl who had been burned on her brain now seemed like an apparition and she needed to see her more than she had needed anything before.

'Where is she now?' Zoe asked in a calm voice. 'Does she know who I am?'

Maggie nodded. 'I screwed it all up, Zo. We had a fight, and I accused her of blackmailing you and then she and Elliot had a fight and then Elliot and I had a fight and then she left for New York,' Maggie sobbed.

'Jesus Christ, Maggie, you should have *told* me! She wasn't blackmailing me.' Zoe's eyes filled with tears.

'I know that now,' said Maggie.

'Don't hate me, I want to fix it,' Maggie pleaded.

'All right, what the hell? Start at the beginning,' said Zoe, sitting on the chair away from Maggie, who sat on the edge of the bed.

Maggie began the story, stopping occasionally for questions.

'Did she know who I was?' asked Zoe at the end.

'She swore she didn't.'

'Where is she now?' Zoe crossed to other side of the room and disappeared into Maggie's walk-in wardrobe.

'I don't know. Her mom rang me from New York saying she didn't know where she was.'

Zoe spoke from inside the wardrobe. 'Her mother rang *you*? Paula Klein?'

She hadn't spoken to her since she had handed the baby over and she remembered the look in the woman's eyes. Once she thought it was possession, now she knew it was love.

'Elliot gave her my number,' Maggie said in a small voice. 'I'm so sorry, Zoe, I should have told you, but I thought she was just using us all to get what she wanted, which was the role in the film. I understand if you never want to speak to me again.'

Zoe pulled a pair of jeans, a T-shirt and a white cashmere sweater from Maggie's wardrobe and came out and threw them at Maggie.

'Get your skinny ass into those jeans,' she said in a firm voice. 'We're going to New York. First we're going to find Dylan, then we'll sort out Hugh and Elliot.'

Maggie was crying again. 'You don't hate me?'

'No, I don't hate you, I'm pissed off with you,' said Zoe, shaking her head, 'but I get it, this stupid movie is making everyone crazy. Besides, I went behind your back and you went behind mine, it wasn't because we don't love each other, it's because we're nuts.'

Maggie jumped from her bed, ran to Zoe and hugged her.

'Let's go get your girl,' she said.

'Our girl,' corrected Zoe. 'But first, have a shower— you smell like a dead raccoon,' she said in her best Appalachian accent, and Maggie laughed and cried all the way to the shower.

Chapter 38

William and Elliot arrived in Hermosa Beach in Will's Porsche. Elliot was in the passenger seat and Smike sat on his lap, the dog with his head out of the window, tongue flapping in the breeze.

'Why can I smell bacon?' asked Will as they turned a corner and pulled into a quiet street.

'Because I fed him bacon.'

'You should've left him at home,' grumbled Will. 'I have enough to cope with, let alone your dog's farts.'

'I can't leave him, he just tries to escape,' said Elliot.

Smike needed to be with Elliot at all times, which was endearing but also annoying. But since Elliot wasn't speaking to Maggie, he couldn't return the dog.

Besides, sometimes Smike sat and gazed at him and Elliot felt more understood and accepted than he had ever since his heart transplant, but to say this out loud would have made him sound weird and his dad didn't like weird.

'God, I'm so nervous,' Elliot said, looking at the small

suburban houses lining the street. It was so different to where he had grown up.

'They really want to meet you,' Will reminded him.

Will had rung the Mathers the day Dylan had emailed Elliot the articles. Elliot had spoken to them a little on the phone, but the conversation was awkward and stilted. He felt like they wanted evidence Tyler was still in the world, and he didn't know he could give it to them.

Will stopped the car outside a modest middle-class Californian bungalow.

'Here we are,' he said and opened the car door.

Elliot and Smike followed suit and they walked up to the front door together.

Will glanced down at the dog. 'Does he have to come?'

'He'll just fart bacon in the Porsche and rip the leather otherwise,' Elliot said.

Smike was wildly excited as they rang the doorbell and Elliot looked down and touched the dog's head.

'Shh, you've gotta be on your best behaviour,' he said as the door opened.

Penny and Bill Mathers stood in the doorway. Their eyes went from Elliot to the dog and they gasped in amazement, then reached down to pat Smike, crying and laughing at the same time.

Penny looked up at Elliot. 'I'm sorry, you must be Elliot and Will, of course, and Bill and I don't mean to be rude, but—oh, I can't believe it! Where did you find Kelly?'

Elliot glanced at his father, confused. 'Who is Kelly?'

'*This* is Kelly, he's Tyler's dog, he's been missing since Tyler died, he was at the beach waiting for him to come in from his surf—' Penny couldn't go on.

'My ex-stepmother found him on the beach,' Elliot said, feeling faint at the news. 'I didn't know he was Tyler's.'

'We heard he was on the beach, running up and down waiting for Tyler, but they couldn't catch him and then he disappeared. We assumed he'd been taken to a pound or hit by a car or something,' Penny went on, wiping her eyes and composing herself. 'Please, come in, I'm Penny and this is Bill. We're so happy to meet you both.'

Elliot shook Bill's hand and then hugged Penny.

'I'm so sorry about Tyler,' he whispered.

'Thank you,' she whispered back and Elliot felt a sense of peace, though he didn't know why.

Bill led them into a sunroom with pictures of Tyler on one wall, yellow sofas and chairs and a huge vase of sunflowers on a piano. They all sat, and Smike lay on the floor at Elliot's feet.

'Kelly, Kelly,' Bill called. The dog walked over and licked his hand, but turned and went to sit at Elliot's feet again.

Penny looked at Bill. 'He doesn't know us any more.'

'Nonsense,' said Bill, and Will saw that the pain of the loss of his only son was deeply etched into his tired face. 'He knows you, but he also knows Tyler is here and he doesn't want to leave him.'

Elliot realized he was right. The dog knew he had some of Tyler in him and refused to let it go.

Had the dog known Maggie? Could he sense Tyler's heart in Elliot *through Maggie*?

The thoughts spun around his head until he felt dizzy.

Elliot's eyes stung with tears, but he felt strongly that this wasn't his loss to grieve. He had gained everything and this couple had lost everything.

Penny went over to the bookshelf, took out a copy of the Bible and opened a piece of folded paper.

'This is the letter we got from the transplant organization. They can't give many personal details. They just said a young person of twenty-three received Tyler's heart and that he was doing well and hoping to get back to his normal life soon.'

She looked at Elliot. '*Are* you living your life now? Are you happy and strong and well?'

Elliot nodded, feeling the weight of her hope. 'I am, ma'am,' he said politely.

Penny came and knelt in front of Elliot and held his hands and looked into his eyes.

Smike put his head on her lap and sighed deeply and Elliot felt the tears escape and bit his lip.

'I can see him in your eyes,' Penny said.

'I feel him in me,' Elliot said. 'I don't know if it's real or not, but I do feel calmer on the beach, when I'm at the edge of the sea.'

Penny looked at Bill, who was weeping, his head in his hands.

'He always said he liked to stand on the shore and think he was on the edge of the world,' he said to Will, who felt overwhelmed by the grief and the joy in the sunny room.

'And the dog, the dog makes me happy—he loves me and I love him,' said Elliot.

Penny smiled, and knelt up to kiss Elliot's forehead.

'A dog must be with his owner,' she said brusquely. 'Isn't that right, Bill?'

Bill nodded, and his face crumpled into tears once more, as he stood and pulled Elliot off the sofa and into a hug.

'Don't be a stranger to us, Elliot. You go ahead and live

the life Tyler couldn't and take care of that crazy dog for us all.'

'I promise to look after Tyler's heart and to do my best to live the life he couldn't,' he said solemnly.

Penny smiled. 'Okay, now we can have some lemonade and I'll show you Tyler's photo albums,' she said and she laughed as she looked down at the dog. 'What are the odds of you finding Kelly on the beach? Or did he find you, I wonder? It's funny how life pushes us in the direction we need to be, even if it feels wrong at the time. Sometimes things work out how they're supposed to.'

On the trip home, Elliot was quiet, thinking about Smike or Kelly, as Tyler had called him. He rubbed the dog's head. 'Hey, Kelly,' he said and the dog licked his face.

Will glanced over, eyebrow raised. 'He's back to being Kelly now?'

'Yeah. Kelly is what Tyler named him, so I should at least honour that. Dad, I was thinking about what Penny said about me and Kelly finding each other,' he said slowly. 'What do you think the odds are?'

'A million to one,' said Will. 'If it was in a movie, no one would believe it.'

Elliot turned away and thought about Dylan.

Sometimes things happened in life that couldn't be explained, but were simply perfect, like him and Dylan meeting and falling in love.

He couldn't hold the pain of losing her inside any more. He cried and cried as Will drove him home. He cried for Tyler, for Dylan, for Zoe and for himself.

'It's okay, mate, just let it out,' Will kept saying, his voice breaking with his own emotions 'A good bawl session is long overdue; cry until you're out of tears and then get up tomorrow and start to live your life. Go and get everything you want, don't be afraid. Go and get what you need. I look at those poor people and their enormous loss and I know how close I can to losing you, mate. I want you to be happy and go for whatever makes you happy.'

Elliot nodded through his tears. He knew exactly what he needed and he was going to get it, even if it meant flying with a farting dog all the way to New York.

Chapter 39

'Where's my poster of Will MacIntyre?' asked Addie as she dumped her books on the table next to her bed.

'I burned it,' said Dylan without looking up from the college course guide she was leafing through.

Addie sat on the bed next to Dylan. 'Are you serious?'

'Yep.'

Addie was silent for a minute. 'Have you heard from Elliot since you emailed him?'

'Nope,' said Dylan, putting the course guide down on her stomach. She was wearing Addie's onesie with yellow ducks all over it and a pair of pink fluffy bed socks.

She had stayed in Addie's room for the past week, alternately crying or hatching plans to become independent of her parents, Zoe and her feelings for Elliot.

'You know you can stay here as long as you like—Celia's always at her boyfriend's dorm,' Addie said, gesturing to the bed next to them.

'Thanks,' said Dylan as she sat up and hugged her friend.

'But I have to make some sort of decision soon. I can't stay here for ever.'

'Why don't you talk to your mom? You know she's ringing me every day and I have to lie to her, and she's a fucking lawyer—bitch *knows* I'm lying,' said Addie in silly voice.

Dylan smiled ruefully. 'I know, and I'm sorry, but I can't deal with her now. I still can't believe she paid Zoe thirty thousand dollars for me.'

Addie sighed. 'It's all so shit.' Then she looked at Dylan and smiled. 'Wanna get drunk?'

'And that's your solution to this shitty situation?' Dylan laughed. 'To drink?'

'Hell yeah, it's worked for my parents for years,' said Addie with a wink.

Three hours later, Dylan was dancing to Rihanna in her onesie, a half-empty bottle of vodka in her hand.

Addie was lying on the bed, legs in the air, as though riding an invisible bicycle upside down.

A knock at the door made Dylan stand still.

'Shhh,' she said to the stereo.

'Quick, hide the bottle,' hissed Addie.

She jumped off the bed and Dylan dived under the covers on Celia's bed and turned to the wall as Addie opened the door slightly.

'Oh, hi, Mrs Mercer,' Dylan heard her say.

'Hello, Adeline, forgive us for disturbing you, but is Dylan here, please?'

'No, as I said on the phone, I haven't heard from her.' Addie was slurring a little and Dylan repressed the desire to giggle.

'Bullshit, I know she's in there,' came another familiar voice. *Maggie?*

Dylan sat straight up in bed.

There in the doorway were Maggie, Zoe and her mother.

'Oh, mother*fuckers*,' she said, and threw up all over the bed.

'Dylan Mercer, have you been drinking?' asked Paula as she pushed past Addie into the room.

Dylan raised her chin and stared at her mother. 'Yeah, and what of it? You're a big fat liar and you have no say over me.'

'Why don't we come back when she's sober?' Zoe suggested quietly to Paula.

'Better still, why don't you fuck off and go spend your thirty thousand dollars,' said Dylan, stumbling out of bed and trying to stuff the bedcover into the rubbish bin. 'Oh, wait, no, you would've done that nineteen years ago, when you *sold* your baby.'

She heard Zoe gasp but she didn't care, she just needed to leave. She pulled her case down from the top of Addie's wardrobe, but in her anger she misjudged her strength and the case came down on her head. She burst into tears.

She felt a pair of arms around her and she tried to pull away, but the arms stayed firm until she finally relaxed and started sobbing as though her heart was going to break.

When she finally pulled away, aware she had left vomit, snot and tears on someone's shoulder, she looked up to see it was Maggie who held her and her eyes were also filled with tears.

'I'm sorry,' she said as she touched Dylan's face. 'I should have done everything differently.'

Dylan blinked and looked at Maggie's blue eyes. 'I didn't know,' she whispered.

'I know,' said Maggie, and they held each other's gaze for a long time.

'Can we please explain?' asked Paula, her face pained. She looked tired, Dylan noticed, even in her blurred vision, thinner, perhaps older.

'Can I shower first?' asked Dylan. 'I smell like a dead possum.'

At which point Maggie and Zoe burst out laughing.

After Dylan's shower, she sat on Addie's bed, with Addie and Maggie, while Zoe and Paula sat on the other side of the room, on Celia's bed.

Dylan was in clean pyjamas and had Addie's quilt over her knees, while Addie held her hand.

'So start,' said Dylan with an edge to her voice.

'I was seventeen when I had you,' said Zoe. 'I'd been in and out of foster homes, I had a grandmother who didn't care a dot about me and then she died, leaving me with nothing. I couldn't have raised you by myself, although Maggie and I wanted to. We knew it wasn't going to work. Think about it. We were years younger than you two are now.'

Paula cleared her throat and Dylan thought she had never seen her mother so nervous. 'And I couldn't have a baby and I was too old to adopt,' she said. 'So I put an ad in *The Pennysaver*; I didn't think it would work, but I was desperate. I knew I shouldn't pay for a baby but I didn't know how else to become a mother.'

Zoe glanced at Paula and then spoke again.

'I thought I'd come and get you when I was able to look after you myself, but it took so much longer than I thought to get ahead and by the time I was able to find you, you were happy,' Zoe said.

'What do you mean?' asked Paula, frowning. 'I never knew you came back.'

Zoe smiled at Dylan. 'I went to find you when you were

seven. I don't know why I thought it would be okay to take you back then, but I did. Stupidity, I guess. Your mother never tried to hide you from me, she had given me the right address, and there you were, riding your bike through the park.'

Zoe turned to Paula. 'You were so proud of her when she was able to ride,' she said, crying. 'I couldn't split that up.'

Paula was smiling and crying. 'I remember that, do you?' She looked at Dylan, who nodded numbly.

She did remember it, and the sounds of her parents cheering her on as she rode unsteadily into being a big kid without training wheels.

'So why did you sell me?' Dylan spat at Zoe but with a little less venom.

'I didn't, I just took the money to help Maggie and I get started in LA,' Zoe tried to explain. 'I planned on paying it back when I came to get you.'

'Except you didn't,' said Dylan.

Zoe looked down at her hands.

'Does Dad know about this?' Dylan challenged her mother. 'The fake adoption contract was in your name, Jefferson Perry isn't a real lawyer,' she said, proud of her detective skills, but Maggie and Zoe didn't baulk.

'He doesn't know anything,' said Paula. 'I just told him I adopted you and he was so enthralled with you, he didn't ask anything more than that. I don't think I could have seen a man happier to have a child.'

Dylan felt tears falling down her face at the mention of her father.

'You lied to him as well as me. I don't know how you can live with yourself.'

Paula stared at her daughter and her face hardened.

'Why? Was life with us so bad?' she asked. 'Did we fail you in some way? Tell me how we could have loved you more? I did what I did because I wanted to raise you.'

'And if Zoe had come back for me? Would you have let me go?'

'But she didn't,' said Paula.

'But if she did,' asked Dylan.

'But she didn't,' said Paula.

'But if she fucking did?' screamed Dylan.

'But I didn't,' said Zoe in a quiet voice.

The room fell into silence.

'If you can remember the day you rode your bike with no training wheels, then I imagine you would have remembered being taken at seven to live with a woman you didn't know,' said Zoe finally. 'That sort of memory changes who you are and how you respond to the world. I never wanted that for you.

'That's what happened to me when I was taken from my own momma and I was in and out of foster homes and then with my awful grammy until I was sixteen,' she went on, her eyes meeting Dylan's. 'I never wanted that to happen to you, I wanted you to have constant love and shelter. Everything I never had. Don't hate your mom for doing the right thing. She never kept you from me, I kept myself from you.'

'What do you mean?' Dylan asked, her voice sharp with bitter tears.

'Your mum sent me photos and invited me to come to things, like your birthdays and things but I didn't, I chose not to.'

'Why?' Dylan cried plaintively. 'You said you loved me.'

'I did love you, so much that I couldn't bear the pain of missing out on you, so I asked your mum to stop asking me to things, to stop sending me photos. I guess after I saw you on the bicycle, I knew that whatever fantasies I had about taking you back were over.'

Dylan looked down at her hands while she processed the information and then she finally looked up at her mother and narrowed her eyes. 'You should have adopted them both, Mom, she was a baby having a baby, you should have known better.'

'It wasn't that simple,' cried Paula.

'It wasn't, honestly, Dylan,' said Maggie with a gentle smile.

'It was; you could have helped them.'

Paula was shaking her head. 'Do you think two young girls with hick accents and wary eyes were going to trust me and your father that way? That I could put them up and that was going to all work out and you could have two mothers? Come on, Dylan, don't be so naïve.' Paula was almost yelling. 'I did what I thought was best and yes, I made mistakes, but so did you. You ran to Los Angeles, and you lied to us this whole time. Why didn't you just ask me the truth?'

'Would you have given it to me?' asked Dylan steadily, holding Paula's eyes.

Paula paused and then shrugged. 'I think I would have,' she said, and she looked over at Zoe.

'I never wanted you to be hurt by me, that's why I gave you to your parents,' said Zoe, tears falling. 'And now I've hurt you more than I could have imagined.'

There was silence in the room, as each of them tried to make sense of the confessions and accusations.

Addie burst out crying and all the women turned to her.

'This is, like, sadder than *The Notebook*,' she sobbed.

Dylan started to laugh through her tears and Maggie, Zoe and Paula joined in.

'I just need some time,' said Dylan, raising her chin and looking at the women.

This wasn't how she'd imagined her reunion with her birth mother. But then one thing she'd learned in Hollywood was that life wasn't like it was in the movies, even when the main players were movie stars.

'Of course,' said Zoe.

Maggie nodded and then the women got off the bed.

'You have my number,' said Zoe, as she stood by the door.

Paula was twisting her hands as she sat.

'What about me, Dylan?' she asked.

Dylan swallowed and looked at her mother.

'I will come into the city for brunch tomorrow,' she said, and Paula nodded carefully, as though not to scare the baby creature away.

'Your father will be so happy to see you,' was all she said as she walked to the door.

'Mom?' she asked and Paula turned quickly, her face hopeful. 'Can you make pancakes?'

Dylan saw the look of delight on her mother's face, knowing she had never made her happier than in that moment, and it felt good.

It would take some time to heal—there were so many secrets and lies—but pancakes were a really, really good start.

Los Angeles
April 1996

'Shay?'

She heard her name and looked up to see a woman with a short brown bob and a slash of red lipstick.

'Hi,' said Shay shyly.

They had arranged to meet at the coffee shop next to the doctor's office where Shay had had a scan a few days before and been told everything was in order.

'I'm Paula Klein. I'm so happy you're well,' said the woman.

'I like your shoes,' said Shay, because she didn't know what else to say and she did think Paula's shiny leather heels were nice.

Paula stuck out a foot. 'Sergio Rossi,' she said. 'Always buy the best if you can, Shay, the best you can afford, anyway.'

Shay nodded and tucked the titbit of information away in her mind. *When I get you back, I will only buy you the best*, she promised the baby now kicking inside her.

'Feel this.' She took Paula's hand and placed it on her stomach. The baby paused and then gave an almighty kick.

'She's always busy in the mornings, then she sleeps in the afternoon.'

Paula's eyes gleamed and she smiled at Shay. 'She sounds like me.'

Shay felt herself tense up. *She isn't your baby*, she wanted to remind Paula. 'How will this work? I mean, I really just need someone to mind her for a few years until I get on my feet. Do you think you can do that?'

'Of course.'

Shay swallowed. 'And you can help me get sorted financially?'

'Of course,' Paula repeated, this time taking Shay's hand and patting it. 'You take as long as you need, we'll be waiting when you're ready.'

Shay allowed her hand to be held for a moment. It felt

nice. She wondered if the people in the coffee shop thought Paula was her mother and that she was helping her to make all the right decisions.

'All you have to do is sign the adoption papers and hand her over to us. I'll give you the money and you come back when you're ready to raise her yourself.'

Shay nodded. It sounded smart, a plan that worked for everyone, but most of all for the baby. All she had to do was get a great job and an apartment and she and Krista could raise her daughter in a stable home.

They had already talked about the future with more hope than either of them had ever dared dream of before.

'I'm going to live by the beach,' Krista had said.

'And I'm going to have one of those fancy walk-in wardrobes filled with brand-new clothes and bags and shoes, just like you see on TV,' Shay had enthused. 'I'm never going to wear someone else's clothes ever again.'

'It will probably only be for a year at the most,' said Shay. 'And I'll pay you back the money.'

'Take as long as you need, Shay,' said Paula with a smile.

Shay felt the baby kicking again. It was a good omen, she thought, as she sipped the chocolate milkshake Paula had bought her.

'Okay,' she said finally. 'Let's do it.'

Chapter 40

'I've texted you his address in London,' said Zoe. 'Don't be too hard on him, I don't think he's as strong as you,' she added.

'Who is?' asked Maggie with a wink.

Zoe smiled and held her hand. 'Not many,' she said and impulsively hugged her friend. 'I'm sorry I turned into such an asshole,' she whispered.

Maggie held her close. 'You just kind of lost your mind for a while, but I'm giving you a leave pass, since you were hanging out with Jeff Beerman—the man could charm snakes for a living.'

Maggie pulled away and held Zoe's hands. 'What about you? Are you going to stay in New York with Dylan for a while?'

'I'll stay for a bit and see if she wants to hang out. I don't want to rush her, though.'

'Of course not,' said Maggie, turning as she heard her flight being called. 'Does Jeff know about her and you?'

asked Maggie as she picked up her bag and walked through the VIP lounge towards the gates.

'I haven't told him yet. I stood him up for dinner the other night and now he's not returning my calls.'

'Christ,' said Maggie. 'He knows this isn't high school, doesn't he?'

'It's not like that,' said Zoe, laughing. 'We're just friends.'

'Again, I ask: does *he* know that?'

'He's not so bad, Maggie; he kind of grows on you, especially when he's being himself,' Zoe said, knowing she was blushing.

Maggie snorted through her nose. 'I will trust you because you do have good taste in people, particularly best friends, but he better not hurt you.'

'He won't, he doesn't think of me as anything other than a friend and a producer on the film. I'm too old and too smart for him.'

Maggie touched her friend's face. 'Then he doesn't know what he's missing.'

Zoe pulled her into a hug. 'Call me when you get there.'

Maggie hugged her back and kissed her on the cheek. 'Thanks for forgiving me,' she said. 'I've been such a crazy bitch.'

'Hey, me too.' Zoe shrugged. 'But I couldn't live without you, Krista,' she said and Maggie felt her eyes prick with tears.

'You neither, Shay baby,' she said as she gave her a wink and a final wave before handing over her ticket, leaving Zoe standing alone in the nearly empty lounge.

Zoe dialled Jeff's cell phone, but he didn't answer.

Goddammit, Jeff, stop being so immature, she thought as she headed out of the airport. When her phone rang she answered it immediately, hoping it was him. She wanted to explain to him about Dylan, about how she was her mother, about how much she missed him as her friend and about how much she regretted.

'Zoe, it's Rachel Fein, *Hollywood Reporter.*'

'Hello, Rachel,' said Zoe with a sigh as she waited for the driver of the town car to pull up to the kerb.

'We thought you might like to make a statement on the Jeff Beerman situation, since you're working so closely with him on *The Art of Love?*'

The car pulled up and the driver stepped out to open the door for her.

What had Jeff done now? *Please don't have gone and got married to some twenty-year-old*, she silently prayed, *please don't have sold me out of the deal for the film.*

So many ideas for what constituted 'the Jeff Beerman situation' ran through her head as she pressed the phone to her ear.

'I don't know what you're talking about, Rachel,' she admitted, too emotionally spent from the events of the last few days to play games.

'You don't know about his heart attack? You didn't hear?' crowed Rachel. 'He's in Cedars having surgery, but it's not looking so good, according to inside sources.'

'When did this happen?' asked Zoe, gesturing to the driver to not pull away from the kerb.

'Two nights ago,' said Rachel, her voice softening a little. 'You didn't know?' she asked again.

'No,' said Zoe. 'I've been in New York. Who was he with?'

She closed her eyes as she waited for the answer.

'No one, that's why he's so sick, his housekeeper found him, but it was hours later.'

Without saying goodbye, Zoe ended the call and looked at the driver.

'Sorry, I have to go back to LA,' she said. She stepped out of the car and ran to the domestic terminal, dialling as she ran.

'Dylan? It's Zoe. Something's come up in LA and I have to fly home. It's life-and-death stuff, a friend of mine's had a heart attack and he might not make it. Please call me when you get this message. Think about coming back to LA when you can and spending some time with me. I'd really, really like that. I love you, Dylan, and I hope you understand me leaving. Don't see this as anything other than me having to be with a friend who might not make it through the night.'

She closed her eyes as the plane started down the runway.

Please let Jeff live, please let him be okay, I don't want anything now. I have Dylan in my life, I have a job, I have Maggie, I have my health. I don't want anything else but for him to be well. I don't even want him to love me back, just make sure he's okay.

She repeated the prayer for the entire seven-hour flight and when the plane landed she went straight to the hospital.

'Hi, I'm here to see Jeff Beerman,' she said to the nurse in reception.

'He's in ICU,' she said, looking up at Zoe after checking on her computer. 'You can go up, but they might not let you in if other family members are with him.'

Zoe nodded and took the lift up to ICU. She was tired and felt dirty from the flight, but she knew she wouldn't be able to focus on anything else until she'd seen him for herself.

The doors to ICU were closed and she pressed the intercom button.

'I'm here to see Jeff Beerman,' she said into the speaker.

'What's your relationship to the patient?'

She paused. What *was* her relationship to Jeff? She couldn't really answer.

'He's my friend,' she said, worried this wouldn't be enough to gain entrance, but the doors clicked open and Zoe stepped inside.

A nurse sat at a round desk and pointed at a corner. 'He's in there,' she said. 'The doctor will be around soon, you can have a chat with him once he's done his rounds. I know he would like to talk to someone who knows Jeff, no one has been in so far.'

'No one?' asked Zoe incredulously.

'No,' said the nurse with raised eyebrows. 'No one.'

Zoe walked to the corner of the ward, past other people in beds surrounded by noisy machines and drips, and grim-faced relatives beside them.

And there was Jeff.

He looked so old. He had a breathing tube in and clear surgical tape on his eyes. There were specks of foam in the corners of his mouth, and his hair, usually perfect, was tousled, like a small child's.

Zoe took his lifeless hand and was surprised by its warmth.

'Hey, Beerman, so you do have a heart after all,' she said as she sat down on the chair and then bowed her head and cried.

'Please God, look after Jeff,' she mumbled into his hand and then she heard a voice.

She looked up to see a kindly faced man.

'Hi, I'm Dr Hughes,' he said.

'Sorry, just saying a prayer to a God I didn't know I believed in.' Zoe smiled ruefully.

The doctor smiled back at her. 'I think these walls have heard more prayers than any church,' he said as he picked up the chart hanging from the end of the bed.

'How is he?' she asked.

'He's not great,' said the doctor, pulling up a chair and sitting next to her. 'His heart was fairly damaged. I mean, we've done what we can, but the rest is up to him and his body. Sometimes you just have to wait.'

Zoe nodded and stroked Jeff's hand.

'I must ask you if you're able to let the family know his situation? He hasn't had any visitors or calls since he came in.' Dr Hughes flicked through the medical notes. 'We need to know his wishes if things don't improve.'

'I'll call them,' she said and she felt a light squeeze on her hand. 'Can he hear me?'

'He might be able to, yes. He's in an induced coma so his body can heal without the stress of trying to heal. It doesn't hurt.' The doctor stood and nodded to Zoe. 'Call me if you have any other questions.'

Zoe sat on in silence for a while, still holding Jeff's hand. Eventually she stood and leaned over to kiss Jeff on the forehead.

'Get better, you old bastard,' she said. 'I'm coming back. I just have to sort some stuff out.'

She took a cab to her place, picked up her car and drove straight to Jeff's mansion. Pressing the intercom, she heard the housekeeper answer.

'Hi, it's Zoe Greene, I'm here to pick up some things for Jeff.'

The gate clicked open and Zoe drove down to the house and parked, rushing inside.

The housekeeper stood by the front door. 'How is he?' she asked in her heavy Spanish accent.

'He's okay,' said Zoe with more optimism than she felt. 'Can you perhaps put together some toiletries and pyjamas for him?'

The woman nodded, obviously grateful to be able to do something for her boss.

'He has been very kind to me,' she said, her eyes filling with tears. 'He gives me time off, pays me more than my friends get, helped me get my son into college in San Francisco.'

Zoe nodded. Somehow she wasn't surprised.

'You go and get the items,' she said. 'Oh, and he also needs his phone.'

The woman walked to a hall table and took out Jeff's phone and wallet.

Zoe looked at the framed photographs of a small girl in fairy wings and two boys in matching sweaters.

'What are his kids' names?'

The truth was, he never mentioned his family to her, besides the odd joke about his poor choice in choosing wives.

'That is Taylor and Greg, and this is Ashley,' said the woman affectionately.

When she went upstairs Zoe snapped opened Jeff's phone and scrolled through the contacts until she found Greg's number.

She had a feeling that if Jeff's sons saw their father's name come up on their phone, they wouldn't answer.

She walked into Jeff's study and sat on a leather chair

and looked around the room as the phone rang. Everything was so sterile, as though it were a movie set, she thought.

'Hello?'

'Hi, this is Zoe Greene, I'm a friend of your father's. I think you need to know that he's had a heart attack and he's in hospital in a critical condition,' she said, getting straight to the point.

There was a long pause.

'And why do I need to know that? I haven't spoken to my father in over three years.'

'You need to know because he's your father and one day, if he dies, you're going to be sorry that he died and you weren't there, and the fact that you weren't there will haunt you every day and then you'll end up in therapy, and then if you have kids of your own you'll probably have a fucked-up relationship with them and the whole cycle will just perpetuate itself.'

She stopped to catch her breath.

'Wow,' said Greg. 'Okay. You obviously feel pretty strongly about this. Who did you say you were again?'

'I'm a friend of your dad's, but it doesn't really matter. The point is, he might be *dying*.'

She heard him swallow.

'Which hospital?' he asked.

'Cedars, and call your brother, too. I'll call Ashley,' she said in her most businesslike manner. Then she hung up and dialled Ashley's number.

'Hello?'

Zoe thought of Dylan.

'Hi, this is Zoe Greene, I'm a friend of your dad's,' she said.

'Okay,' said the girl warily.

'Your dad's had a heart attack,' Zoe said, waiting for Ashley to process the information.

'Is he going to be all right?' Her voice trembled.

'Well, the doctors certainly hope so, but it's too early to know for sure, he's only just had surgery.'

'Oh my God, surgery? Which hospital? I'll come now,' Ashley cried.

Zoe gave her the details as the housekeeper came into the room with an overnight bag.

Zoe impulsively reached out and hugged her.

'I will pray for him,' the housekeeper said.

Zoe smiled at her. 'That's lovely,' she said.

He's going to need all the prayers he can get, she thought, as she sped back towards the hospital, bracing herself to face Jeff's children and the fact that he might not make it through the night.

Chapter 41

'What the hell are you doing here?'

Hugh stood in the doorway of his house, looking none too friendly. He had grown a beard, which was patchy at best.

'You've got ginger whiskers,' said Maggie as she peered closely at his face.

'Is that what you came here to tell me?' he asked, his hand on the doorjamb, the other one holding the door.

Maggie looked past him and saw moving boxes lining the hallway. 'Where are you going?'

'None of your business,' he said crossly.

'Can I please come in?'

'Did you bring Will?' He tried to push the door closed, but Maggie put her foot in the way.

'Stop being such a dick,' she said, exasperated. 'I didn't understand your dramatic exit from LA until I spoke to Will, who admitted he lied to Arden to get rid of her.'

Hugh was silent but she couldn't tell what he was feeling. His face was guarded and hard.

'Why didn't you just ask me, Hugh?'

'Because I thought you would lie,' he said, looking her in the eye, as though trying to read the truth.

'Why would you think that? I've never lied to you!'

He sighed, the hard mask on his face cracking a little. 'I know. You better come in.' He stepped back and opened the door wide.

Maggie stepped into the hallway, trying not to feel the ghost of Simone in the space. She knew the house so well from Hugh's descriptions in the book. Two bedrooms and a study upstairs. A sunroom next to the kitchen, a small living area and toilet with a water hammer every time it was flushed.

She slipped off her black Rick Owens trench coat and hung it over the stair balustrade.

'You always did look good in black,' he said, his eyes sweeping over her and the coat.

'What the hell is going on? You said you loved me,' she said, her arms crossed in her black blazer.

Hugh sat on a packing box marked 'books'. 'I do love you.'

'So why did you run away?'

'I have a tendency to do that since Simone died.'

The sound of Simone's name rang off the walls and into Maggie's heart and she felt the tears fall.

'I can't compete with her! She was perfect, I'm not,' she cried. 'I'm selfish and impulsive and I've never truly loved anyone, except Zoe, who is my soul sister, and Elliot, who's like my own kid, but I have never loved a man. I thought I did, but I realize now I was acting the way I thought I should be.'

Hugh said nothing.

'I've never trusted a man,' she rushed on. 'When I was a child, grown men assumed things about me because of my looks, they used me, and I didn't think that would ever change. Then I met you. You! You didn't seem to care what I looked like, and you told me how smart I am—I mean, no one has ever said I was smart—and you listened to me, no one listens to me, not even Zoe. And you're such a dork, I mean like the dorkiest of the dorks with your stupid Charles Dickens dog names, and yet I love you. I love you!'

She paused for breath.

'And now you think I'm cheating on you, that I'm a user? I don't know. I don't even *want* the role any more, I just want you, but you still want her.'

She was sobbing now and she saw Hugh blink a few times, tears in his eyes.

'Simone wasn't perfect, Maggie,' he said in a very calm and low voice.

'She must have been!' Maggie cried. 'The way you wrote about her was poetry, there will never be anyone as wonderful as her, you've said that in every goddamned interview. You nearly drank yourself to death over her. Come on, Hugh, what the hell? In your heart, she's irreplaceable.'

Hugh crossed his arms.

'It doesn't matter now, she's dead.'

'Of course it matters,' she said. 'I told you the truth, now it's your turn.'

Hugh bit his lip and Maggie had never wanted to kiss him so badly but she stayed still, silently willing him to have courage and to trust her enough with the truth.

He cleared his throat, and then he spoke.

'She was cheating on me with my best friend,' he said slowly.

'What?' Maggie's knees went weak and she sat down abruptly on the box next to him, then promptly fell inside, her feet sticking up in the air.

Hugh started to laugh as he helped her out. 'That one's not packed yet.'

'No shit,' said Maggie as she tried to recover her dignity and made a safe choice by sitting on the stairs.

'If we wrote that scene, it would be considered farcical,' he said.

Maggie laughed a little as she rubbed her back where she had scraped it on the cardboard.

'I suppose it's good to have an intense moment broken up by some slapstick,' she said tartly. 'Now what the hell did you just say about Simone and your friend?'

Hugh shrugged and clasped his hands in his lap.

'It had been going on for two years, but I only found out after she became sick. He left her when she got the diagnosis, apparently.'

Maggie was still. 'And what did you say?'

'What could I say? She was dying, and the man she loved had dumped her because she was broken in his eyes. I did what anyone would do. I stayed, I was kind, I forgave her and I looked after her, and I have hated her every day since she died.'

'So why did you write about her like that?'

'Because I didn't want my friend—my ex-friend—to think he had the best of her and I only got the sick bit. Does that make any sense?'

Maggie nodded. 'I think so.'

They sat in silence for a while and Maggie reached out and took his hand.

'Thanks for telling me,' she said and turned to look at him.

Hugh looked back at her. 'You're the only person I've told. I didn't even say anything in rehab, or to Zoe, I didn't trust anyone until you.'

'Well thank you, I am sad that that happened to you and to her, but I am glad you trust me,' she said, grasping his hand in hers. 'I do love you, Hugh, so much.' Her voice almost broke when she said it and she felt Hugh drop her hand, stand up and pull her up into his arms.

'You know I'm a brooding, angry, introverted writer, don't you?'

'Yep,' she said, putting her arms around his neck. 'And you know I'm a vain, age-denying, narcissistic actress, don't you?'

'Yep,' he said and he kissed her like he would never stop. Maggie sighed as they moved apart.

'So where are we going?' she asked, looking at the boxes.

'You assume you're invited?' He laughed, his hands sliding into the back pockets of her jeans.

'I don't need an invitation,' said Maggie with a smile. 'I'm officially your stalker now.'

'I've always wanted a stalker,' he said as they kissed again.

'You really don't want the role in the film?' he asked, looking into her eyes.

'Nope, I don't, I don't care if I never act again, I just want to be with you. We could write more scripts, though. I have an idea,' she said shyly.

'Oh, yes? What's your idea?'

'Two friends, one has a baby, puts it up for adoption. The child comes back and becomes intertwined with the women without even knowing who they are.'

'Too coincidental. No one would believe it.'

Maggie laughed. 'You want to hear about coincidences? Let me tell you about your dog Smike.'

As she told him, Hugh stood perfectly still, his jaw dropped open.

'Are you serious?'

'As a heart attack,' she said, and Hugh sat down on the stairs.

They were silent for while, holding hands, and then Hugh looked at the boxes and then to Maggie.

'I don't want anything else from this life, I only want you. Will you come to France with me, Maggie Hall? Walk barefoot amongst lavender fields, make me laugh, let me make you laugh, hold my hand until we're both old and misanthropes?'

'Sure,' said Maggie with a shrug. 'It's not like I've got anything else going on.' Then she laughed at the worried expression on Hugh's face. 'Yes, you goose, I'll go to France with you. Hell, I'll even go to the moon if you asked. I love you! I can't say things the fancy way you do, but it's as though I was waiting for you my whole life. Let's not waste any more time. Let's get old together.'

Hugh kissed her nose. 'You did okay for a girl who thinks she doesn't have any fancy writer talk.'

He stood and pulled her to her feet and picked up his wallet and phone from the hall table.

'Let's go to France,' he said.

'But…what about all this?' Maggie gestured to the boxes.

'I don't care,' he said. 'I'll get my sister to donate it all. Let's start again. I don't need anything except you, Maggie.'

'Really?' She looked around at all the stuff and realized it was true. They didn't need the books or the clothes or the china or anything she had once thought was so important.

Love isn't something you can buy, she thought, as they walked out the door, *it's like finding a lucky penny on the pavement. You stumble across it when you least expect it, and God knows you have to hold on to it for all it's worth.*

Chapter 42

'I've decided I'm going to go to college,' Dylan announced over breakfast.

After the night with Maggie, Zoe and her mother in Addie's dorm room, Dylan had returned home to her parents' apartment.

'That's great, darling,' her mother said a little too excitedly. 'Which one?'

'I'm going to audition for acting school,' she said, waiting for the barrage of protestations from her mother.

'That sounds like a good plan,' Paula said, as she turned the pages of the *New York Times*.

Her father nodded his agreement.

'You don't think it's a stupid idea?' she asked, wondering if this was some reverse psychology trick they were using on her to bring her round to sensible thinking.

'Not at all, Zoe said you're very talented,' Paula said, still reading. 'If you're talented, you have an obligation to try to hone those skills, whatever they might be.'

'Who are you and what have you done with my mother?' asked Dylan suspiciously.

Paula looked up from the paper now.

'Honestly, Dylan, it's like you think I'm Joan Crawford sometimes. I just want you to be happy and safe. You heading off to Los Angeles with nothing in order to pursue an acting career seemed very rash at the time, not understanding your true intention.'

Dylan looked down at the table. Her mother had handled Dylan having Zoe in her world so much better than Dylan had thought she would. And although Zoe had rushed back to LA, Dylan didn't feel abandoned by her, in fact quite the opposite.

'But first I'd like to go back to LA and hang out with Zoe for a little while,' she said, clasping her napkin under the table.

Her father nodded at her mother. 'We think that's an excellent idea.'

'What is going on?' said Dylan, throwing her napkin on the table. 'Why are you being so reasonable?'

Paula looked at her with love. 'We've had you for nineteen years, darling, and you were the best thing in our lives, but we're older and you're so young. You need to have someone else in your life besides us, and Zoe is your mother, after all.'

Dylan started to cry. 'No, *you're* my mom,' she said, feeling about ten years old.

Paula got up from the table and walked around to sit next to Dylan, taking her hands.

'Darling, I am your mom and so is Zoe, you're kind of blessed. Don't think I'm not slightly envious of her biological connection to you, I'm so jealous of the legs you inherited from her but I think she's wonderful and I think you're right to try to forge a relationship with her. I'll always be your mother and that means being honest and pulling you up and reminding you to be safe while you follow your heart.'

Dylan nodded through her tears.

'And your father is about to go in for surgery next month, so it will be a busy time here. So take your break in LA and—'

'Surgery?' Dylan almost screamed. 'For what?'

'I've decided to have deep brain stimulation for my Parkinson's,' said her father. 'I miss work, I want to be useful. I want to be the husband and father I used to be, and DBS offers me a chance to do that. It's time to come back to my life.'

Dylan grabbed her father's hand and looked at her parents. They were ageing, but still so together. She realized that through her whole life as their daughter, she had never doubted their marriage, they were a true partnership. She thought about Elliot.

'When did you know you were meant for each other? That it wasn't going to get any better than each other?'

Her mother laughed and looked at her father, who smiled back at his wife.

'When she told me she had to break up with me because she couldn't have children and I wanted them. I realized I wanted her more than children.'

Dylan looked at her mother, who was crying now.

'Mom?' she asked.

'When he said to me he didn't care if we didn't have children and when he didn't stop me from adopting you, even though he knew it wasn't kosher, he just wanted me to be happy.'

Dylan was quiet for a moment.

'If Zoe had come back into my life, would you have let me see her?'

Paula nodded. 'Of course.'

'And if she'd wanted me back? Would you have let me go?'

Her mother was quiet and then she shrugged. 'I'd like to tell you yes, sweetie, and I *hope* I would've said yes, but I honestly don't know. I think it would have been impossible to let you go.'

Dylan reached out and hugged her mother. 'I like it when you're honest, Mom, it makes you more real to me. Less perfect.'

Her mother held Dylan tight. 'A wise person told me a long time ago there's no such thing as perfect, least of all perfect people.'

'Oh, yeah, who was that?'

'Your mom, when she gave you to me. Seventeen years of age and she already knew more about life than I did. It took me a long time to learn that what she said was true, but I think I understand it now.'

Dylan arrived at LAX and looked around for Zoe.

She had called to say she was on her way and ask if she could stay for a while, but making it clear she didn't need babysitting, she had things to sort out. They both knew she was talking about Elliot.

Thankfully, Zoe didn't ask any questions. She was spending a lot of time at the hospital with the guy she'd described as her 'friend', though Dylan assumed he was her boyfriend.

Dylan saw her name written on a whiteboard. Disappointment flooded her as she realized Zoe had sent a driver to pick her up.

But when she looked at the driver she saw Elliot's smiling face.

'Elliot!' she yelled and ran at him full pelt, causing him to drop the whiteboard as he lifted her up.

She kissed him over and over again.

'I'm sorry I was an idiot,' he said in between kisses.

'Yes, you were a massive idiot, but I still love you.'

Finally he set her on her feet and they stood facing each other.

'Why?' she asked. 'Why did you believe I lied to you about Zoe? I know I should've told you about the audition, but I honestly thought it was such a long shot.'

Elliot blinked and she saw tears in his eyes and his lip trembled.

'What? What is it, Elliot? Talk to me!'

'Why are you with me? You know I might die early, why do you want to be with me?' he said, not looking at her.

'Jesus, Elliot, we're all going to die,' she said, shaking her head. 'I mean, I might get hit by a flying refrigerator tomorrow, who knows?'

'What?' he asked with a frown.

'That actually happened, but it's another story, totally worth Googling,' she said, with a wave of her hand. 'My point is, weird shit happens, things you can't plan for, and crazy things bring people together and tear them apart. I'm with you because I love you. I know we're meant to be together and you know it too, so let's not waste time listening to other people telling us how we're not old enough to know about love. I don't care what anyone else thinks, just you.'

Elliot pulled her into a hug. 'I love you, Dylan.'

As they walked out to the car park towards a black SUV, Dylan heard a dog barking.

'Oh, do you still have Smike?'

'Actually, his name is Kelly,' said Elliot as they got to the car.

'Kelly?' She patted the dog through the open window.

'Get in and I'll tell you a story that's going to blow your mind,' he said with a laugh.

Dylan got into the front seat of the car and the little dog jumped into her lap.

'Try me,' she said with a smile. 'Although I have to tell you, nothing really fazes me now.'

Elliot started the engine. 'Just you wait till you hear this one, beautiful girl.'

Dylan reached over and kissed him. 'I want to spend the rest of my life hearing your stories,' she said, looking into his eyes.

'Good,' he said. 'Because you're going to be my leading lady in every single one.'

Los Angeles
May 1996

'Paula's not going to make it,' said Krista as she came back into the delivery suite at UCLA Hospital. 'But she's on her way.'

'Push, Shay, push,' said the nurse.

A guttural moan came from Shay's lips and then the sound of a baby crying filled the room.

Paula had arranged for Shay to deliver at UCLA because it was the best. She had planned to arrive in LA the following week, when Shay was due, but the baby had different ideas and had made a swift early entrance into the world.

'It's a girl,' the doctor said.

Krista looked at Shay, who smiled weakly.

'You did it,' said Krista excitedly.

Shay fell back onto the pillows as her tiny, pink-splotched baby girl was put on her chest.

'Do you want to cut the cord?' asked the doctor and Krista smiled her consent.

She held the scissors up to Shay and waved them in the air. 'I could be a doctor,' she crowed to the amusement of the room.

Shay smiled a little as the baby bleated and snuggled into her chest. She looked down at her daughter. The love she felt for her was instant, and overwhelming, as though her heart had been empty before and now it had a purpose.

How could she give her up?

'We have to take her now,' said the nurse, lifting the baby from her chest.

'Take her where?' asked Shay in a panic. Surely she didn't have to give her up yet?

'We're just going to clean her up, honey,' said the nurse.

Krista sat down next to her, her pretty face shining with pride. 'You did so good,' she said.

'It *hurt*,' said Shay, making a face at Krista.

Krista laughed. 'There was no time for the drugs, you were so speedy.'

'When you have your next baby, you might want to come in the minute you feel the contractions starting,' said the doctor.

Her next baby? She couldn't even look after this one. Shay wondered how she would have survived without Paula's help over the last few weeks. She and Krista finally had enough food to eat and had moved from the world's worst hotel to a small two-bedroom apartment in West Hollywood.

Without Paula, they would be destitute, but was the final price too much to pay?

Back in her room, with the baby swaddled in a plastic crib on wheels next to her, Shay gazed at her daughter and picked her up.

'I want you to have the best of everything, baby girl,' she said softly to the sleeping bundle. 'That's why I have to do this.'

Krista watched her from the doorway, Shay unaware of her presence.

'You know I love you, don't you, little angel face?'

But the deal was done.

Krista stepped into the hospital room and sat quietly on the chair next to Shay's bed. Shay, exhausted, lay sleeping, the baby tucked in next to her in the bed.

Shay's baby. Krista's baby. Paula's baby. The child had more mothers than she knew what to do with, thought Krista, as she watched them sleep, but only one of them really knew what true loss was.

Chapter 43

'I'm sorry I haven't called you since last week, but I'm in France,' Maggie said when Zoe answered the phone.

'What? Why?' Zoe's voice rose an octave and Maggie giggled.

'Because I've moved here with Hugh,' said Maggie, as she lay on sofa in the villa they were renting, raising a leg to admire her new Isabel Marant sandals. Just because she was now living the life of the French countrywoman, didn't mean she had to go barefoot, she had told Hugh after she ordered them online.

'Bullshit,' Zoe cried.

'*C'est des conneries,*' said Maggie.

'What?'

'That's how you say "this is bullshit" in French,' explained Maggie. 'Hugh and I are learning French, but it seems only the swear words stay with me.' She laughed.

'I don't know what to say,' said Zoe. 'I mean, if you're

happy I'm happy but Jesus, France? How long will you be there for?'

'I don't know, but as soon as I do, you'll be the first to know,' said Maggie, as she saw Hugh walking in the door, carrying a strong bag of shopping with a breadstick poking out of the top.

'How are you? How's Jeff?'

Zoe paused. 'He's okay,' she said finally. 'He's improving slowly.'

'He just has to follow the doctors orders,' said Maggie. 'Tell him to do everything those heart doctors tell him, I know Elliot found it annoying to do those slow walks on the treadmill and the exercises but it's vital he does what they say.'

'Yeah, well, Jeff doesn't like taking orders,' said Zoe with a sigh.

'Then tell him to choose a casket,' said Maggie.

'Jesus, you're brutal,' Zoe half laughed.

Maggie sat up. 'What's going on?' she asked. 'You're being weird.'

'Am I?'

'Yes, I know you and you're being weird,' Maggie stated.

'You're the one who moved to France,' said Zoe.

Maggie frowned at the phone and then she paused. 'Zo?'

'I don't know what to say,' she said. 'I haven't said it aloud yet.'

'Just tell him,' said Maggie.

'What?' Zoe said.

'That you love him,' said Maggie.

There was silence.

'Zoe?'

'I have to go,' she said. 'I'll call you later about work stuff.'

Zoe was in love, Maggie was sure of it, but she knew she wouldn't do anything about it.

Zoe made amazing things happen for other people, but not for herself, it was as though she had spent her life punishing herself for giving up Dylan, she thought sadly.

'I bought lunch,' Hugh said as he lifted her feet so he could sit down on the sofa with her.

Maggie lay looking at the ceiling.

'What's on your mind?' asked Hugh.

Maggie glanced at him and decided to keep Zoe's secret to herself.

'I'm thinking about my career options,' she said brightly.

'You could work at the store in town,' offered Hugh with a smile.

'Or I could give acting lessons to the tourists.'

'Or you could open a zoo for rare and wild animals.'

Maggie laughed.

'Why do you have to do anything?' he asked.

'Because I've always done something,' she said, sitting up and curling her legs beneath her. 'It feels weird to not work, I've done back-to-back movies since I was twenty-two, I don't know how *not* to work.'

Hugh nodded. 'I understand, but maybe it's time to just relax for a while and explore other things? I mean, if you find you still want to act, then act, but is there something else you've never had time for?'

Maggie paused. 'I did want to be a game show hostess, like Vanna White,' she said with a giggle.

'Hey, never say never,' said Hugh, as he played with her hair and stroked her neck.

Maggie felt tingles run through her body and she leaned in to kiss him. No man had ever thrilled her like Hugh could, she thought, as he pulled her towards him and slipped the straps of her sundress off her shoulders.

'You know you're a very good lover,' she whispered.

'And you are an extraordinarily beautiful woman, Maggie Hall, but the thing I love the most about you is not your shoulders,' he said, kissing each shoulder in turn and tracing her collarbones with his fingers.

He lowered the zip of her dress until it fell open at the back and she wriggled out of it, exposing her breasts to him.

Sex with Will was okay, the lovers before were okay, but with Hugh it was ridiculously good, better than good, she thought. She wanted him all the time, and it seemed he wanted her just as much. They were like teenagers, she thought, as he sucked gently on a nipple.

'And your breasts are absolutely spectacular, but they're not what I love the most about you either,' he said as he pushed her back on the sofa and kissed her stomach.

Maggie felt her hips rise involuntarily to his mouth, and he opened her legs.

'Nor do I love the velvet-smooth skin on the inside of your thighs the most.' He pulled aside her underwear and gently teased her with his tongue. 'Nor your sweet taste,' he said as he drifted back up her body, to her mouth and kissed her, so she could taste herself on him. She felt for his erection, rubbing it through his pants.

And then he kissed her forehead. '*This* is what I love the most about you, Maggie Hall,' he said gently.

'What? My botox?' she said in shock, her hand reaching up to touch her face. 'I did it once, once, it should have worn off now, it's been years!'

Hugh laughed until he fell off the sofa, crying, as he sat on the floor and Maggie pulled her dress off the ground and covered her body.

'What?' she cried as she moved her brow up and down.

'Not your forehead,' Hugh said as he turned to face her, kneeling down. 'Your brain, I love your brain.' And he burst into fresh peals of laughter.

Maggie started to laugh with him.

'I'm always so cool and put together, that's my reputation—and yet around you, I fall into boxes, make stupid comments, don't worry about what I look like, I'm bossy and silly and I've never been happier,' she admitted. 'I feel like my real self, except I didn't even know I existed until I met you.'

Hugh took her hand and held it tight. 'Will you marry me, Maggie? Crazy, silly, smart, beautiful Maggie?'

Maggie felt her eyes widen. She had sworn off marriage after Will.

'If I say no, will you think I don't love you?' she asked, her heart beating fast in her chest.

Hugh smiled. 'Not at all, it's an idea, not an ultimatum.' He stood and pulled her to her feet. 'Let's spend the afternoon in bed, shall we?'

Maggie slid her arms around him and held him tight, sighing into his neck.

He didn't want anything from her, just her presence. No demands, no order or instructions, just acceptance of who she was, the real Maggie. She pulled back, her arms still around his neck, their eyes meeting.

'My real name is Krista,' she said quietly. 'I changed it when I was eighteen.'

Hugh looked surprised and then he nodded slowly, as

though processing the information. 'Okay then. Would you like me to call you Krista?'

Maggie thought about that girl who had been through so much and had survived.

'No, I don't feel like she's me any more,' she said. 'But I just wanted you to know. And there are other things, stories I need to tell you, things that happened to me, not that I want to share them now, but there are things that shaped me and not all in the best way.'

Hugh kissed her nose. 'Whenever you're ready to talk, I'll be here to listen.'

And that was when Maggie knew Hugh was her lucky penny, and she pulled him to her and kissed him in the greatest love scene of her life.

'Yes, I'll marry you,' she said.

Chapter 44

Zoe paced the hallway outside ICU thinking about her phone call with Maggie. Damn her for guessing, she thought. It was as if she kept it to herself, then it wasn't real but Maggie calling her out unnerved her. Now it was real. For the first time in her life she wished she were a smoker, just because it would give her something to do with her hands.

While Jeff was still in his induced coma she had come to know his children a little, to hear their stories about their father, his failings but also his acts of great love and other qualities of his that they had chosen to forget in their bitterness.

Zoe had listened, cautiously counselled and laughed as they told her of Jeff's indiscretions and his generosity to his ex-wives after he had done them wrong. They had been surprisingly accepting of her.

The more she heard about Jeff from the people who knew him best, the more she realized what a complicated man he was, definitely not the sort of guy you should fall for.

Taylor and Greg were like their father in their assertive natures, but were scathing of Jeff's failure to make a relationship work.

'He tends to choose women who are beautiful, but stupid as fuck,' said Greg candidly.

'Hey,' said Ashley, 'that's my mom you're talking about!'

And they all laughed a little, because it was funny, but also sad that Ashley knew her mother wasn't the brightest star in the sky.

Ashley was sweet, although incredibly naïve, Zoe thought, thinking of herself at that age and then thinking of Dylan. Somewhere in between would be good.

She had barely seen Dylan since she had arrived in LA, but that was okay. Dylan had been with Elliot, who was now staying at Maggie's place with the dog, every day.

Finally, when Jeff was brought out of his coma, they had all stood around his bed as the drugs were lightened and the breathing tube removed.

When he opened his eyes, he groaned as he saw them. 'I'm dying, aren't I?' he croaked.

'No, Daddy, you're not, you're getting better,' Ashley said, starting to cry, and Greg put his arm around her.

Zoe smiled and stepped back from the scene, moving towards the door. This wasn't the time for her, she thought, this was for family.

Jeff closed his eyes again.

'Greene, get back here,' she heard him bark in a dry, hoarse voice.

Zoe turned back to look at him. 'I should go now. I just wanted to know you're okay.'

'She's the reason we're here, Dad,' said Greg and he

smiled with such warmth at Zoe, she thought she might start crying.

Biting her lip, she nodded. 'Just making sure you were all together, that's all. That's how family works.'

She left them alone and went home, showered and slept for fourteen hours. When she woke, she found Dylan had let herself in with the key Zoe had given her and had cooked her pancakes.

'Shouldn't I be doing this for you?' she asked as they sat outside with their breakfasts.

Dylan laughed. 'No biggie, I like making pancakes. Although they're really all I can cook,' she admitted.

'How's Elliot?'

'He's amazing,' said Dylan with such a dreamy expression that Zoe laughed. 'What? That's pretty much what you sound like when I ask about your friend in hospital, except you don't say he's amazing, you just get that look.'

Zoe said nothing as she mopped up maple syrup with the last of her pancake.

She had to get over her feelings for Jeff. God knows it would never work, even if he did feel that way. There would always be another girl, more beautiful, younger and ambitious, who would turn his head.

Dylan sat nursing a mug of coffee. 'I've decided not to do the film,' she said. 'I'm going to audition for acting schools, do the college thing for a while.'

'Which colleges?' asked Zoe casually, as though it didn't matter.

'Oh, you know. Cali Institute of the Arts, UCLA, Cali Uni, San Diego,' Dylan said nonchalantly.

Zoe paused, wondering if she was right to give advice to Dylan, she didn't want to act like she had a newfound right to tell her daughter what to do, but then, she thought, she was still her manager.

'You could do both, you know,' she said.

'Really?' asked Dylan.

'Of course,' said Zoe. 'We wouldn't film till later next year and we still have to find a leading man and director. Don't shut it out completely, let's see what happens.'

'Okay,' said Dylan, seeming happier. 'I didn't know I could do both. I mean, I want to do everything but I want to do them properly, you know? College, Elliot, and the movie and two moms, it's intense. But I don't know about the film, especially if Will is in it. Besides him being a total dick, it would be weird since he's Elliot's dad.'

Zoe smiled. 'Will's not doing it, he feels the same way and he wants you to have your shot at this,' she said. 'In fact, Bradley Cooper is interested.'

'Oh my God,' squealed Dylan, 'I love him.'

'Does Elliot know this?' laughed Zoe.

'Oh, Elliot knows I'm totally into him and him alone,' she said confidently. 'I mean, we're going to be together for ever, I just know it.'

Dylan had never sounded younger, thought Zoe, filled with love for the girl, and she reached out and grabbed her hands. 'I'm so glad you chose to come to the West Coast. I mean, I'm sure it's about being with Elliot, but I'm happy I'll be able to see you more too.'

Dylan smiled. 'Elliot was a big part of my decision, but so were you,' she said shyly. 'I want to get to know you.'

Zoe felt her eyes prick with tears. 'I feel like I've known you all my life,' she said as she looked at her daughter.

Dylan blinked back tears of her own. 'Maybe we have

some sort of soul connection, more than our biology or something, because I feel the same way.'

Zoe drove back to the hospital feeling different, lighter. She felt as though she was whole again.

Now she paced the hallway while Jeff was having further tests on his heart. His children had left to return to their own lives for a while but since Zoe didn't really feel like she had a life outside of the hallways of the hospital until Jeff was well again, she stayed.

She felt the pressure to support Jeff if the results of the tests weren't positive. She ran through several scenarios in her mind as she paced and at the end of each one, no matter how dire, she was by his side.

'Damn you, Jeff,' she muttered to herself. 'Goddamn you, Jeff Beerman.'

'Why, what did I do?'

She turned to see Jeff walking towards her, a physiotherapist supporting him on either side. He looked frail and older, in his navy silk pyjamas, but he was beaming with pride.

'What are you doing?' she cried as she rushed up to him.

'The tests were great, the docs are amazed. Then again, they didn't know what I was capable of. I said to the doc, I'll be back to my old self soon.'

Zoe nodded, clutching her bag to her side, wishing she could run away from everything she was feeling. She just wanted to go back to her old life, when she could sit in her walk-in closet and the smell of a Hermès leather bag would be enough to comfort her.

'I'm so glad you're feeling better,' she said quickly, interrupting his boastful tirade. 'Listen, Jeff, I'll see you soon, but I have to go now.'

'Go where? I've moving to the ward today, I have a private room.'

'That's great,' said Zoe, not meeting his gaze.

They were by the door to the ICU.

'Give me second,' he said to the physiotherapists, who glanced at Zoe and walked over to the nurses' station, out of earshot.

'Why are you leaving, Greene?' he asked, his face confused.

'Because I have to,' she said, hearing her voice break.

'But I don't want you to,' he said, looking affronted. 'You're my best friend.'

'I can't be your friend any more, Jeff.'

'Why not?' he asked, sounding genuinely hurt. 'You're the greatest fucking thing in my life. I mean, you brought my kids back to me. Taylor brought his wife and baby in yesterday, can you believe that? I'm a grandfather now, I'm so fucking old!' He laughed and Zoe nodded in agreement, avoiding his eyes.

'Come on, Greene,' he said gently and he lifted her chin up with his hand.

'What?' She looked at him, her eyes burning with tears.

'I can think of nothing better than spending the rest of my life on your sofa, eating steak—except I'm not allowed steak any more—and watching your shitty TV shows and laughing and arguing with you. I love you, Zoe Greene.'

Zoe blinked a few times, trying to take in what he was saying, 'I'm too old for you, remember?'

Jeff laughed loudly. 'No, baby, I'm too fucking old for you. But that's just too bad.'

They stood staring at each other.

'I would kiss you, but that'd give me a boner and apparently I'm not allowed to have sex for at least six weeks.'

'Jesus Christ, you're unbelievable,' said Zoe, shocked and pleased at the same time.

'Save that phrase for about six weeks' time,' he said as the nurse opened the door for Jeff to go back to bed while Zoe was laughing.

'Time for bed,' said the nurse. 'I have to do some obs before we move you to the ward.'

Jeff turned and winked at Zoe.

'Come on, Greene, you heard her, time for bed.'

Zoe laughed again.

Jeff settled into bed and Zoe sat down next to him and he reached out her hand, which she handed to him.

'I like hearing you laugh,' he said.

'I like that you make me laugh,' she said as they stared at each other again, like teenagers.

Jeff squeezed her hand. 'I don't know when I'm going to be able to go back to work.'

'I don't care about that, I only care that you're okay right now,' she said, wiping her eyes.

'You're gonna have to manage *The Art of Love* yourself for a while ' he said.

'That's okay,' said Zoe. 'I'm sure I'll cope.'

Jeff stared at her for a while. 'Have you told your kid she got the role yet?'

'My kid?' Zoe looked at him closely. 'You mean Dylan Mercer?'

'Yeah, she's your kid, isn't she?'

'How did you know that?' she asked him in shock.

'The way she looked, the way she spoke, she's like a

younger version of you,' he said. 'Why didn't you tell me
you wanted me to see her act? You could have just told me.'

Zoe started to laugh, incredulous. 'I wish you'd told me,'
she said with a smile.

Jeff listened while she told her story and at the end, she
sighed. 'So it's a crazy tale. I mean, if it hadn't happened
to me, I wouldn't believe it could be true.'

But Jeff just smiled and shook his head.

'After thirty years in this town, the one thing I know is
that *anything* is possible. This is Hollywood, after all.'

Two weeks later Jeff was at home with a private nurse
and annoying Zoe through the day.

'When are you coming over?' he would ask her over the
phone.

'Later, when I'm finished with work,' she'd laugh. 'You're
so needy.'

Three weeks later, he was staying at her house, claiming
his had too many stairs and he didn't like the nurse.

'It's not as glamorous as your house,' Zoe had said, feeling slightly embarrassed by the lack of Jeff Beerman lux-
uries.

They lay together like teenagers in bed, making out, Jeff
desperate to move to next base and Zoe insisting he had to
wait the six weeks.

By week four, she was counting down the days until she
could have Jeff. He awakened in her a desire she never knew
existed. The way he worshipped her, praised every part of
her body, the way his hands worked their ways around her,
bringing her to orgasm with his mouth and fingers. She
felt selfish, while Jeff lay next to her, his hardness strain-
ing to be released.

'Don't be silly,' he said, kissing her head. 'I can't get enough of your noises and the way you cry my name. Even if I never get to finish myself, I will never be tired of making you come.'

On the sixth week, Zoe felt nervous when she came home and saw Jeff had lit candles, set the table, and he was cooking her dinner.

She sipped wine while Jeff drank mineral water, and they ate their Moroccan chicken salad, while chatting about inconsequential nonsense.

The air was thick with sexual tension but Zoe didn't want to rush. She wanted to savour the moments with Jeff. She never thought she would find love like this and it wasn't about the sex, it was friendship and love, a perfect blend.

'When did you know about me?' she asked, leaning back in her chair, her tongue loosened by the wine and her desire fuelled by the way he looked at her from across the table.

'Know?' he asked, his face amused by her question and her confidence.

'Yes, when did you know I was the one you wanted?'

'Honestly?'

She nodded, almost afraid to hear the answer. She didn't know what to expect but she felt nervous.

He paused, enjoying the moment.

'When you...' He raised his eyebrows a few times at Zoe.

'Come on.' She threw her napkin at him.

'I admired you at the Oscars when you played such hardball, I liked your honesty in Maui when you refused to let me get away with being such a sour prick. I became friends with you when we spent our nights here watching TV and eating takeout, but when did I love you?'

She nodded, her heart beating fast, and her breath shallow.

'I knew I loved you when you were drunk after my birthday dinner when you asked me in to watch *American Idol* and you told me that you were amazing.'

Zoe laughed in embarrassment.

'But you didn't come in, which was a bit shattering.'

'Because you told me you were lonely, not that you wanted me. I never wanted to be a place-filler in your life, it was all or nothing with you. You're not the sort of woman who deserves anything less and I'm not the sort of man who settles for anything less.'

Zoe put down her wine glass and stood up and walked over to Jeff and leaned down and kissed him.

'Come to bed,' she said softly and he smiled.

'I thought you'd never ask,' he said and he allowed her to lead him into her bedroom.

'Get your clothes off, Beerman.' She tugged at his shirt, as she kissed him.

'God, so aggressive, so pushy, so demeaning,' he said as he kissed her back. 'I like it, keep going.'

Zoe screamed with laughter as she pushed him onto the bed and straddled him.

'You're an idiot,' she said.

'Yeah, but I'm your idiot,' he said and he pulled her down and kissed her.

His hands moved up under her top, and they made out leisurely, her hands on the waistband of his jeans, him jumping at the touch of her fingers on his skin.

'We don't have to do anything,' she said, worrying for a moment, but Jeff was pulling at the zipper on her skirt, sliding it down, kissing her stomach, then between her legs.

His shirt was open, and she ran her hands over his scar on his chest.

'I'm so glad you made it,' she whispered, her eyes filling with tears.

Jeff kissed her. 'Shhh, I did make it and you're the reason why, you're my reason for everything.'

And then their bodies moved as though they had always known each other. Clothes falling to the floor, no words as they found each other and they moved slowly, until Zoe felt herself on the edge of an orgasm.

'Come for me, Zoe,' he said, his voice thick with desire.

'I don't want to, I want this feeling to last for ever,' she said, her fingernails digging into his back.

'This isn't a one-time thing, Greene, I plan on fucking you well and often,' he said, and then he moved faster and Zoe let go, feeling the surge of power come from her core and she cried out his name, and then felt him join her until he collapsed on her for a moment.

'Jeff? Jeff?' She poked him in the ribs.

'Jesus, I'm not dead,' he said as he raised his head and she laughed. 'But I couldn't think of a better way to go.'

He rolled off her and she laid her head on his chest.

'You're amazing,' he said and she looked up at him and smiled.

'Already aware, babe, already aware.'

Epilogue

September 2015

Dylan walked into her new apartment and Paula followed. She was holding a large box, which she set down on the table

'This is the last of it,' said Paula, as she peered inside the box and picked up a worn pair of pink Converse sneakers. 'Are you really going to need these old shoes?'

'Yes, Mom.' Dylan sighed as Zoe and Ashley walked in. Trailing behind them was Jeff, carrying two giant pink teddy bears.

'Really, Jeff, teddy bears?' asked Dylan with an eye-roll, but Zoe noticed Dylan took one and hugged it just a little longer than normal.

'I couldn't stop him,' said Zoe as she set down a bag of groceries.

'Hello, Paula,' said Jeff, as he leaned over and kissed Dylan's mother on the cheek.

Paula blushed, which was normal whenever she was around Jeff.

If there was any discomfort springing from Zoe and Dylan's newly formed connection, Jeff smoothed it over with his flattery, stories and determined inclusion of Paula and Jonathon in Dylan's West Coast life.

Ashley and Dylan were laughing in another room. Zoe walked through the apartment and found Dylan opening a suitcase and pulling out a froth of hot pink tulle.

'I love it!' she said to Ashley, as she twirled around the room. She stopped when she saw Zoe. 'Ashley has the best clothes,' she said as Paula bustled into the room with a bag and put it down.

'Here are those shoes you wanted,' she said and Dylan pounced on them and slipped them on.

'OMG. I love them,' cried Ashley.

'They're Givenchy,' said Dylan proudly.

'Where did you get Givenchy shoes?' asked Paula.

'Maggie gave them to me the night I first met her,' Dylan said, stretching out her foot and twirling a slim ankle. 'These were the shoes that started me on the path to where I am now,' she added sagely.

Zoe smiled at the serious look on her daughter's face.

'What? It's true,' cried Dylan as she almost tripped.

'Stop prancing and start unpacking,' said Paula and Dylan quickly took off the shoes at her mother's command.

Zoe walked back into the living area, where she saw Jeff fixing the cable to the television.

'You don't have to do that, I'm sure they want to do some things for themselves,' said Zoe as she leaned over and kissed his cheek.

'Our girls are living together, we need to make sure they have everything they need,' he said firmly.

Dylan had been accepted into the UCLA theatre pro-

gramme, where Ashley was studying production. The minute the girls had met they'd got along beautifully.

Screams of laughter came from the bedroom as Paula
walked out and threw her hands up in surrender.

'I have to get back to New York. I need to keep an eye on
Jonathon post his surgery,' she said, picking up her handbag. 'Dylan, I'm going now,' she called.

Dylan came skidding out of the bedroom and into her
mother's arms.

Zoe turned away. No matter what their DNA said, Paula
was Dylan's real mother and Zoe was, at best, like an older
sister to her.

Jeff glanced up at her from his spot in front of the television. 'Hey, Greene, hold this for me, would you?' he said,
handing her a cable.

She was grateful for something to do and sat down on
the floor beside him, holding the cable.

Jeff was more intuitive than she'd expected, but then
the man did have an amazing eye for making hit films and
finding new talent, so perhaps it wasn't so surprising that
he seemed to understand the conflicting emotions running
through her as Dylan and Paula embraced.

'Zoe?'

She heard her name and turned to see Paula at the front
door.

'Look after our girl, won't you?'

Zoe nodded, afraid that, if she spoke, the tears of being
acknowledged would fall and she would become a snotty
mess on what was Dylan and Ashley's day.

'We've got them covered, Paula. You get yourself home
and look after that husband of yours,' Jeff said jovially and
again Zoe felt a rush of gratitude towards him.

It wasn't as though it had been a smooth road for them. Jeff had struggled with his new lifestyle regime post heart attack, and it wasn't until Zoe threatened to break up with him, telling him if he wasn't serious about his health then he wasn't serious about their future, that he began to make the necessary changes.

Now he was making plans to scale down his role as head of the studio.

'We're going,' said Jeff, flicking through the channels on the television and seeing everything was in working order.

'Really?' whispered Zoe. 'Will they be okay?'

'Of course they will. Anyway, I have a meeting.'

'Now?' Zoe frowned. 'Who with?'

'The person I want to take over the studio,' said Jeff, checking his phone.

Zoe scowled as Dylan came out, dressed in Ashley's pink tulle concoction, with Ashley close behind wearing one of Dylan's tops.

'We're swapping clothes,' said Ashley joyfully.

Zoe laughed. 'I guess you're never too old for dress-ups,' she said, thinking about how much she missed Maggie.

She hugged Dylan and kissed her forehead. 'Call me if you need anything, you promise?'

'I promise,' Dylan said and they held each other tight.

'Thanks, Mom,' she said in Zoe's ear.

Zoe pulled back a little, and looked at Dylan's beautiful face. 'Are you sure you want to call me that? I don't want you to feel you're beholden and I don't want you to upset Paula.'

Dylan shook her head. 'It was Paula's idea. She said it'd be good to have a mom on each coast.' She laughed. 'I guess I have bicoastal moms.'

'Not that there's anything wrong with that,' said Zoe, laughing.

'Come on,' said Jeff impatiently as Zoe kissed Ashley goodbye.

'I have to go, your dad has a meeting,' she sighed to Ashley.

'That's okay, I'll see you guys at the weekend anyway,' said Ashley, reminding Zoe of the once-a-month Sunday-night dinner that was becoming a ritual for Jeff's children.

'Can you at least drop me home first?' Zoe asked as they drove towards West Hollywood.

'Sorry, no time.'

'So what am I supposed to do while you're in your lunch meeting? Go shopping?' snapped Zoe. 'I am not one of your Beverly Hills wives, Jeff.'

Jeff was unperturbed. 'Come and eat, you might find it interesting,' he said.

Zoe crossed her arms and sulked as Jeff drove to Soho House and handed the valet his keys.

'You need to find time that isn't taken up with work, that's why you had a heart attack,' she admonished him as she closed the car door a little harder than necessary.

'Say you, you're a workaholic,' he laughed.

'I'm learning not to be,' she said piously, as she followed him into the exclusive club.

Zoe wasn't a member, although she had dined there with clients before. It was the ultimate Hollywood club, and even though she pretended she didn't need to belong, part of her desperately wished she did, the way only a kid who was born on the outside could wish.

They were greeted at the door of the roof garden and led

to the best table in the centre of the space, where Jeff could show off to the heir of Palladium Pictures.

Zoe sat down and tried to not notice Jack Nicholson laughing with Diane Sawyer in the corner and she waved to a few clients who were dining and drinking at other tables.

'I wish you'd told me, I would have worn something better than this,' she hissed, glancing down at her navy linen trousers and plain white T-shirt.

'You look great,' said Jeff, not looking up as he perused the menu. 'You look like the next head of Palladium Pictures.'

Zoe stared at him, unsure that she'd heard him correctly. 'What did you say?'

Jeff put down his menu. 'I want you to take over Palladium for a few months, Zoe,' he said. 'I want to spend time with my kids and my grandkid. I want to be able to just make movies again and not have to think about everything else.'

'Really?' she asked, trying to understand his thinking.

'I have this great girlfriend,' he said, his eyes meeting hers. 'I love her more than any woman I have ever known, she's smart as hell and keeps me on my toes. I think she'd be a brilliant studio head.'

Zoe looked down at the menu, trying not to cry and laugh at the same time. Then she shot him a suspicious look. 'You're not going to boss me around from your cell phone on the golf course, are you? I will be able to make my own decisions, not just be your puppet?'

'I don't play golf,' said Jeff. 'And I hate puppets.'

Zoe put down the menu. 'But…people will say I only got the job because we're together.'

'No, people will know you're smart, competent and more

than capable to handle this. But if you're gonna worry about what people think of you and how you got where you are, then go back to managing other people's careers for the rest of your life.'

Zoe frowned. 'Hey, that's not fair; I have a right to ask.'

'I never give people anything they don't deserve,' said Jeff in a serious tone. 'I always thought you were one to watch, even when Maggie Hall was your only client and you were hustling on Sunset to get the up-and-coming new actors. I've watched you all this time, Greene, you're my woman for the job—and for me.'

Zoe nodded, and then waved to a waiter. 'Can I get a pen and paper, please?'

'What are you going to do? Make me sign a contract on Soho House letterhead?' laughed Jeff. 'You will have a proper contract, I promise.'

The waiter bustled back and placed a new pad and pen next to her. Zoe picked up the pen and chewed on the end for a moment.

'What are you doing?' asked Jeff, leaning across the table.

'Starting work,' said Zoe. 'Now what productions are on the slate, and where the hell are we up to with *The Art of Love*?'

Jeff laughed so loudly that people stared.

'Jesus Christ, I've hired a monster,' he said proudly.

Zoe laughed and looked him in the eyes. 'I think I've been waiting all my life for this, Jeff. I just needed someone to give me the chance.'

Jeff smiled and reached for her hand.

'You just had to give yourself a chance; you always had it in you. You just had to wait until you were ready to be the woman you were destined to become.'

'The woman I was destined to become,' she repeated. 'I like that. I like me.'

'Good, cos I love ya, Greene,' he said as he picked up the menu and she saw a glint of tears in his eyes, which made her smile.

'I love you too, Beerman,' she answered. 'But don't even think about ordering the steak.'

On the other side of the world, Maggie woke up next to Hugh in the French farmhouse they had bought and stared at the uneven ceiling. Something didn't feel right, she thought, and she sat up.

The unease spread through her, from her toes to her throat, and she clutched the bed sheets and then ran from the bedroom as Hugh rolled over, the sound of her feet on the floorboards waking him up.

'What's wrong?' he asked as she pushed open the bathroom door.

But she couldn't answer as she fell to her knees and was violently sick. Hugh walked in behind her and rubbed her back as she retched into the bowl.

'I must have eaten something off last night,' she said, as the nausea subsided.

She flushed the toilet and slowly stood up to brush her teeth and splash her face with cold water.

Hugh frowned. 'But I ate everything you did, and I'm not sick.'

Maggie shrugged. She lay back down on the bed, her hands on her stomach, and then put them on her breasts for a moment.

'I can do that for you if you like,' said Hugh cheekily.

'Oh, shit,' said Maggie, ignoring him. She sat up and

reached for her phone, clicking through the calendar before turning to Hugh. 'Do you think you could go into the village for me? Will the shops be open yet?'

He checked his watch, looking puzzled. 'Sure, what do you need?'

'A pregnancy test,' said Maggie, one eyebrow raised while she held his shocked gaze.

Hugh was out of bed before she had even finished speaking, pulling on his jeans and a T-shirt.

'That's my T-shirt,' said Maggie, looking at his exposed stomach.

'I don't care!'

And then he was out the door, keys for the Citroën in hand.

Maggie laughed until he came back. Not just at the absurd image of Hugh in her T-shirt, but at the absurd possibility of them being pregnant.

Hugh ran in and put down a white paper bag on the bed.

'Une teste de grossesse,' he said, breathing heavily.

Maggie glared at him. 'What? I'm not gross.'

'It's how you say pregnancy test in French,' he gasped.

'Great, I'm going to get *grosse*,' she said as she took the pack from the bag and read the instructions.

'Okay,' she said, looking at him. 'A baby, yes or no?'

Hugh's eyes widened. 'What do you mean?'

'Do you want to be a father or not?' Maggie kept her face still and her voice calm. If she was pregnant, could she do it by herself?

Would she do it by herself?

Hugh's face crumpled. 'I've always wanted to be a father,' he said. 'Simone never wanted children, though.'

Maggie reached out and touched his face. 'I never thought

I wanted kids either, but with you, anything I thought I knew has gone by the wayside. Let me go and pee and we'll make plans once we know for sure.'

Hugh laughed. 'What a romantic notion,' he said as Maggie took the test and went to the small bathroom.

A baby? She'd thought she was too old to have a child now, not just hormonally but mentally, but the idea that she had created something with Hugh made her tingle all over.

She lay the test down on the basin and opened the door. Hugh was pacing outside, still wearing her tiny T-shirt.

'You look ridiculous,' she said as he walked into the bathroom and peered at the test.

'How long does it take?'

'Three minutes,' she answered and they sat on the edge of the bath, staring at nothing.

She glanced at Hugh, who was mouthing something. 'What are you doing? Praying?'

'Counting,' he said. 'We've got one more minute.'

Maggie reached out and took his hand. 'I love you,' she said softly.

'Baby or no baby, I love you too, Maggie.'

Maggie looked at the test and gave a deep sigh, her shoulders slumping, her back turned towards Hugh.

'It's okay,' he said, standing up and hugging her. 'I want to be with you for you, not for children, don't think of it, but if you really want to try in earnest, then let's get cracking,' he said, stroking her hair.

Maggie held him tight and kissed his cheek. 'And that, my friend, is why I am a movie star, cos we are pregnant,' she said, waving the test at him.

'What?' He snatched it from her and stared at it. 'But you seemed so despondent.'

'Yes, which is why I get fifteen million a film,' she said with an evil laugh and she ran past him and into bed.

Hugh chased after her, but her phone rang and she picked it up. 'Saved by the bell,' she said as he tried to kiss her. 'Wait, it's Zo.'

Hugh lay back on the bed, laughing. 'Hurry up then,' he said good-naturedly.

'Oh my God, I was going to ring you,' Maggie told Zoe excitedly.

'Hey,' said Zoe. 'I'm in work mode, and I'm about to go into a meeting, but I have to ask you about *The Art of Love*, are you still interested?'

Maggie laughed. 'Um, I don't think I'm right for the role any more,' she said, making a face at Hugh.

'No, no, not to play Simone. But I was wondering how you'd feel about directing the film?'

Maggie sat still, knowing her mouth was open in shock. *'Me?'*

'Why not? You know the script back to front, you know the book, you get the style, you're great with text and you know the medium—all you need is a great DOP and the rest is easy. It's not a huge film and Jeff's already approved it, all you have to do is get Hugh's approval and you get to cast it as you wish.'

Maggie was silent for a moment while she thought. Could she have both?

'Hang on.' She put the phone on mute and looked at Hugh. 'Zoe wants me to direct *The Art of Love*,' she said.

Hugh blinked a few times. 'What do you want to do?'

'I want to do it, but I don't know if I can,' she said. 'And I don't want to upset *you*. And I want to have the baby.'

Hugh stroked her arms. 'You can direct it, you're the

bossiest person I know, you won't upset me. In fact, I'd feel safe with the story in your hands. And as for having the baby, take a chair on-set and you can sit down between takes. Plenty of women have babies and work, you can do it.'

'Why does everything seem so simple when you say it?' she said, kissing his mouth.

'Because it is simple,' he said with a smile. 'Not everything has to be complicated.'

'I'm used to complicated.' She laughed as she took Zoe's call off mute. 'Okay, Zo, I'll do it.'

'You will? Oh my God!'

'But I have one request,' said Maggie, looking at Hugh.

'What's that?' asked Zoe carefully.

'I'm going to need a chair on-set and can you ask your kid if she's available for babysitting for my kid, who is due in about eight months?'

Maggie heard shrieks and the sound of the phone being dropped. 'Zoe? Zoe?' she said and then turned to Hugh and shrugged. 'She's lost it, but she'll call back in five seconds.' She hung up and rolled into his arms.

'How can you be so sure?' whispered Hugh into her ear as she counted aloud and right on cue the phone rang.

'Because I know her so well,' said Maggie as she lifted the phone to her ear.

* * * * *

Marianne Baker is happy.
Sort of.

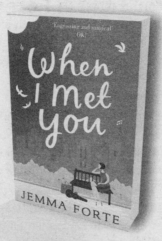

She's worked at the same job for years, lives at home
with her mum and her love life is officially stalled.
Playing the violin is her only real passion—but
nobody like her does that for a living.

But when the father who abandoned Marianne as a
child turns up on her doorstep with a shocking secret,
suddenly her safe, comfortable world is shattered.

If her father isn't the man she thought he was, then
who is he? And, more to the point, who is *she*?

It's time to find out who the real Marianne Baker is.

HARLEQUIN®MIRA®
www.mirabooks.co.uk

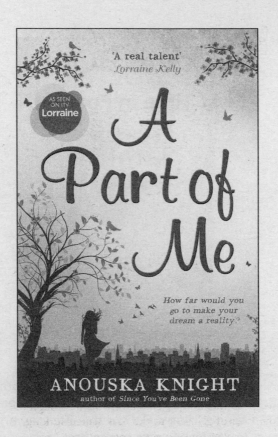

*Seven scandalous celebrities
Seven deadly sins...*

SEVEN INFAMOUS CELEBRITIES

The supermodel, the thief, the senator, the heiress, the paparazzo, the pop prince and the playboy

SEVEN DEADLY SINNERS

Someone is watching. Someone has seen through the shimmer of glamour to the dark secrets lurking beneath. Someone sees sinners.

ONE PUNISHMENT FITS THEM ALL

The island does not welcome visitors. There is no safe way to arrive on these shores. Once here you cannot leave. This is a forbidden paradise. No one escapes.

Join

Victoria Fox

on some other mini-adventures in her

Short tales of Temptation

Available as eBooks

Is there such a thing as the *perfect* size?

Vivian Ward is in total control of her life. Actually, scrap that—she's thirty-five, estranged from her family, a failed actress and working in a London members' club to pay the bills. Truth is, the only thing she's in control of is what's on her plate…

But then she meets movie star Maximilian Fry, who's just as screwed up, and journeys into a world of celebrity even faker than the one she was already living in. Will image triumph, or will she realise that some of her answers lie within?

www.mirabooks.co.uk

There was a moment when
Ivy Heartley could have told the truth.
But she didn't.

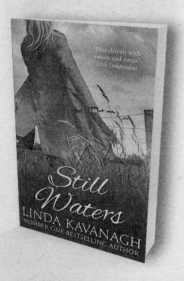

Now she's burdened with a terrible secret—
something so awful that she must constantly live
in fear, since its disclosure could destroy her
marriage, her career as a popular soap-star, and
turn her own son against her.

Will she ever be able to forget what happened?
Or will her past destroy her future?

www.mirabooks.co.uk